FAT

Also by Rob Grant

Incompetence

Rob Grant

The right of Rob Grant to be identified as the author of this
work has been asserted by him in accordance with
Copyright, Designs and Patents Act 1988.

First published in Great Britain in 2006 by
Gollancz
An imprint of the Orion Publishing Group
Orion House, 5 Upper St Martin's Lane,
London, WC2H 9EA

This edition published in 2007 by Gollancz

1 3 5 7 9 10 8 6 4 2

A CIP catalogue record for this book
is available from the British Library

ISBN-13 978 0 57507 820 8
ISBN-10 0 57507 820 0

Typeset at The Spartan Press Ltd,
Lymington, Hants

Printed in Great Britain at Mackays of Chatham plc,
Chatham, Kent

The Orion Publishing Group's policy is to use papers that
are natural, renewable and recyclable products and made
from wood grown in sustainable forests. The logging and
manufacturing processes are expected to conform to the
environmental regulations of the country of origin.

www.orionbooks.co.uk

For my sweet Lily Rose

It's unclear precisely when it became illegal to be fat.

Of course, technically it's not, even in this day and age. Even with the blatant persecution of all tubbies, there's no official legislation on any statute book that comes right out and says fatness is against the law.

But it is.

It started slow, as these things do. It just gradually became increasingly uncomfortable to be overweight. Just inch by blubbery inch, less and less acceptable. It probably truly reached a critical mass with the airlines. They began charging by body weight. And how could you argue? It costs more money to lift a fat person off the runway than a thin one, no question. Fuel-to-weight ratio. Simple arithmetic. Oil crises. Fuel prices through the stratosphere. Somebody had to pay. Why not the fat?

Of course, there were protests. But nobody took them seriously. Fat people are fat because they're lazy, weak-willed or stupid, or all of the above. They could stop being fat if they really wanted to. Who's going to listen to that kind of pressure group? Let them eat lard.

So there it was: your airline ticket was priced according to your body mass index, and that was that.

But it was never going to stop there, now, was it?

Because now it was tangible. The slow and swirling loathing that had long been churning in the undercurrents and eddies of public prejudice had been given form. Fat people were subnormal. Fat people were less than acceptable. Fat people were second class.

And so they started paying extra on all transport. On Tube

trains. On buses. An extra little fuel duty when they filled their cars, because, hey – fuel is precious, and they use more of it than the rest of us to get their cellulite-pocked backsides from A to B.

And then some Health Authorities who were facing swingeing budget cuts had to make some harsh decisions. And they decided they would not carry out certain operations on the obese, such as hip and knee replacements. If fat people wanted to punish their joints by forcing them to bear excessive loads, why should the rest of us pay for the repair work? And why should they take up valuable operating room time with heart bypasses when they were only going to clog up their new arteries with all kinds of saturated fats anyway?

And because one Authority got away with it, it spread. It spread to the whole of the National Health Service. If you're fat, and sick, don't even think of calling an ambulance. Don't waste your time sitting in a doctor's waiting room. Here's the prescription, you dummy: Lose Weight.

And you couldn't call it persecution, in truth. Not even when fat suits became commonplace props for comedians. Not even after the odd street-kicking, or the wave of fat attacks videoed on mobile phones. Not even when the Government brought in the fat tax, nor when they set up the euphemistically named 'Well Farms', optional at first, but soon, of course, not so optional.

Because all of this, all of it, really, was for the fat person's own good. The ridicule, the humiliation: it just might help fat people to buck their ideas up and become more desirable people. Which is to say: thin people.

It was in their own best interests.

Well, here's a little tip. When somebody does something you don't like, and then tells you they did it in your own best interest: run. Run, my friend, till you drop. And don't look back.

PART ONE:

March 1st

BREAKFAST
Menu

Carrot Juice
Some Sort of Shitty Muesli Pot with Yoghurt
and Honey

$\backsim$

A Double Sausage & Egg McMuffin™
Another Double Sausage & Egg McMuffin™
(Both with Hash Browns)

$\backsim$

Absolutely Nothing At All

'I had to fast. I can't do anything else,' said the hunger artist. 'Just look at you,' said the supervisor, 'why can't you do anything else?' 'Because,' said the hunger artist, lifting his head a little and, with his lips pursed as if for a kiss, speaking right into the supervisor's ear so that he wouldn't miss anything, 'because I couldn't find a food which I enjoyed.'

(Franz Kafka: *A Hunger Artist*, 1924)

ONE

Grenville Roberts got out of bed. That was no mean achievement, by any means. The effort left him breathless and slightly dizzy, and he had to sit down again for fear he'd faint. Then he'd have to lift himself up off the floor, which would be a substantially more gruelling enterprise, even assuming he sustained no major damage from the fall.

Of course, now he was sitting on his bed once more, and sooner or later he'd have to stand up again. What if that left him equally breathless and dizzy? Would he be condemned forever to stand up and sit down on his bed, like a victim of some mythological Greek torture? That would be a fine thing, to spend eternity helpless as a gigantic jack-in-the-box. He supposed it was only a matter of time before things would get that bad. Before he could no longer leave his bedroom without the aid of an elephant-rescue winch and the coordinated efforts of the Air-Sea Rescue Team.

But his dizziness passed, his breathing eased and he stood, this time successfully, and made his way to the bathroom.

He performed his ablutions efficiently and without relish. He took a shower, of course. He couldn't remember the last time he'd taken a bath. He did, however, remember that he'd barely got out of it alive.

He dried himself, again, no meagre challenge. There was a lot of him to dry, and vast expanses of it were harder to reach than the hidden jungles of Papua New Guinea. For all he knew there were nomad tribes concealed in inaccessible creases in his back.

Now came the really hard part: getting dressed.

He selected his clothes. Not too difficult. He had very few

7

that still fit him. And today the choice was dictated for him anyway.

He paused at the dresser drawers where he was sifting through the vast expanses of black cotton that constituted his underpants these days, and caught his reflection in the mirror. It always shocked him to see his face, even though he'd seen it not fifteen minutes earlier, when he'd shaved. It was nothing like the image of himself he still carried around in his head.

How had this happened to him? How did he get here? It wasn't as if he'd entered cow-pie-eating competitions on a daily basis. It wasn't as if he chewed through his own weight in beef dripping every morning, or sat down to lavish banquets every dinner time, the table creaking and groaning under the weight of suckling pigs and roasted swans.

Some are born fat. Some achieve fatness.

Others have fatness thrust upon 'em.

And so it had been for Grenville.

He wasn't born fat. He had been, for most of his life, actually quite slender. In fact, when he'd suddenly noticed he'd acquired a slight belly in his late twenties, he'd been quite shocked. Horrified, even. He'd assumed it was a consequence of his happy love affair with beer, a beautiful relationship he'd regretfully abandoned. It had become clear he could no longer indulge himself with whatever comestibles took his fancy and remain trim. Furthermore, it seemed inevitable he would have to start consciously taking, God help him, some kind of *exercise*.

Exercise.

Dear oh dear.

But he did it. He sucked it up, and he did it. He endured the mindless boredom of lifting up weights and putting them down again in expensive gymnasia for a while. He tolerated the moronic repetitiveness of Healthclubland, with its vile liniment smells mingled with brutally over-applied aftershaves, and the casual fashion display of depressing male genitalia in the changing rooms, and the eye-gouging chlorine in the swimming pool, and the six-hour wait for a cup of coffee in the cafeteria. He put up with it all until the very prospect of dropping a coin into the slot of a gym locker filled him with such dread, he could no longer face it.

But by then, the rebellious belly had been pounded into submission.

Or so he thought.

It crept up on him slowly, with all the relentless patience and irresistible brutality of tectonic plates. His trousers started getting tighter, cutting a bright pink band of pain around his midriff, which he didn't even notice until he unbuttoned them at night.

He finally, with some reluctance, gave up the morning wrestling match, lying flat on the bed, trying to tug two-and-a-half-feet width of material over three feet of waistline, and moved up a size.

Thirty-two inches. Thirty-four. Thirty-six.

After that, things started to get harder. He spent many a Saturday on his hands and knees in obscure corners of department stores and tailors' shops, desperately seeking out a stray pair of Wranglers in the inexplicably, unfairly and unforgivably rare size of thirty-eight inches.

He still remembered the glorious day he had chanced across a pair of branded khaki slacks that measured an insanely generous forty-two inches. Forty-two inches! How had they come into being? Were they discarded props from *Land of the Giants*? Had they been part of a clothing consignment bound for Texas that had been caught by the wind and somehow wafted all the way across the Atlantic to land in this very store? Whatever mysterious magic brought them there, they were Grenville's now. True, they were *slacks*, but Gren had long ago given up even dreaming of making a stab at dressing fashionably. Simply being able to dress at all was ambition enough.

They were slacks, but they *fitted* him. They fitted him

9

easily. And for a while, Grenville enjoyed the bliss of sartorial comfort again. Experienced the indescribable delight of owning a pair of trousers that zipped up without a struggle. A pair of trousers that didn't force his testicles to grind together like Tibetan worry balls with every step. He wanted to seek out the magnificent seamstress who had constructed those ingenious pantaloons, smother her with kisses, shower her with gifts and propose marriage.

And then, one day, and all too soon, even the forty-two-inchers could no longer accommodate him. True, he'd worn them virtually non-stop for the best part of two years, and they were all but falling to pieces, but his drifting girth had outgrown them anyway.

He went hunting again, but after five consecutive Saturdays of crawling through obscure piles of stock to no avail, he had to face up to the terrible truth.

It could no longer be blamed on the moronity and short-sightedness of all clothing manufacturers, their suppliers, their buyers and the bastard parents who spawned them all.

Grenville Roberts was no longer Off The Peg.

Somehow, he had fallen outside the accepted limits of human dimensions. He was no longer a member of the category labelled 'normal'.

In a curiously insane twist of logic, the only sort of apparel he could reasonably expect to buy in a regular clothing store that might actually fit him was sportswear. Drawstring jogging bottoms, jogging tops and offensively coloured plastic shell suits.

Now, just exactly who, along the clothing supply and demand chain, took the imprisonably lunatic decision that the only clothing that overweight people might ever be allowed to purchase should be ugly exercise gear? That all fat people really yearned for was unsightly neon-orange and lime-green jogging suits. Did this madman look out of his window one day and say: 'You know what: all you ever see these fat people doing is running and exercising. If we could only cater to that market, we'll make a mint.' Whoever he was, the man was a fucking business genius. You have to take your hat off to him. Though, let's face it, it will probably be a pink and purple baseball cap.

But you mustn't get the impression that Grenville stood idly by and allowed all this to happen to him. That he just let the weight pile on and on without trying to get on top of it, to wrest back control of his body from his mad metabolism. He did not go quietly into that dark night.

He dieted. Of course he dieted. He dieted to Olympic standards.

He gave up fats. He gave up sugars. He gave up dairy. Red meat? Forget about it. He even, Lord have mercy, gave up *alcohol*. He gave up any food that was in any way remotely pleasant. He ate bread the same texture and flavour as sandpaper-encrusted cardboard smeared with the merest hint of fly duty posing as tasty yeast spread. Then he gave up wheat altogether. He found himself eating tiny garam-flour pancakes smudged with a tiny suggestion of Fuck Me If That's Not Butter. And then he read a terrifying article about the carcinogenic properties of chickpeas and had to relinquish even this pathetic balm to the appetite. He became sitophobic: from being a sensual delight to anti-cipate with pleasure, food now seemed to belong in the same category as weapons of mass destruction. The fat content of nuts made them as deadly as bullets. An avocado pear started looking as lethal as an anti-personnel fragmentation grenade.

He joined clubs. He had red days and green days. He lived only on Speedslim shakes. He followed Rosemary Conley's advice for his hips and his tum. Then he stopped combining proteins and carbohydrates. Then he gave up carbohydrates altogether. Then he gave up proteins *and* carbohydrates. He never snacked. He would sooner have shot his own mother than have eaten a chocolate bar. He stopped eating altogether after one o'clock in the afternoon. He tried living on raw fish and rice. Then he even gave up the rice. He ate *kelp*. Kelp and only kelp, Lord have mercy.

And each new effort, each new push, would produce the same results. For the first few weeks, he would lose weight. Then he would stop losing weight and tighten up his regimen. He would lose a little more weight, and plateau out again. Then he would be starving, eating only nonsense, and still not losing weight, and he would give up. Then, in a few short weeks, he would be back at his original size, and then some.

And one day, he found himself standing in front of a salad bar and realised there was nothing in there he was allowed to eat, that he'd ingeniously managed to negotiate himself into a position where pretty much all he thought about was food, and yet he could not eat any of it.

So he gave up giving up.

He decided that if he'd never started any of this diet nonsense, he'd probably be about four stone lighter than he was right now. Enough was enough. Or rather not enough was enough. He would eat what he wanted, within reason.

And that worked, in a way, for a while. His girth stopped growing. It wasn't going away, but it wasn't getting any bigger.

Result: happiness. After a fashion.

And then he met The Girl.

He'd imagined all that was behind him, that he'd never have to go through all that dating palaver again, and he'd settled into his fairly comfortable and happily successful routine, was almost cruising through his slightly lonely existence, when *Blam!* she'd walked through the door of his life, and he was, to all intents and purposes, sixteen again.

And he'd gone back to the diet drawing board.

It was hard to find one that hadn't already failed him at least once. He managed to boil it down to the GI diet and the Paul McKenna 'I Can Make You Thinner' regime. Paul McKenna sounded quite interesting, but Gren had serious doubts about employing mesmerism as a dietary aid, so he plumped for the GI, which seemed like an almost sane version of Atkins. Once again, he'd stripped out his kitchen cupboards and stocked them only with acceptable fare. Once again, he'd studied the diet guides, not that they were called diets any more. All new diets nowadays started off with 'This is *not* a diet', for some reason. And, once again, he had to face up to the advice that exercise was an essential prerequisite to success.

Which meant but one thing.

It meant he had to swallow his pride, having first assessed its calorific value and Glycemic Index, of course, and go back to the gym.

Gren laid out the hideously coloured jogging suit on the bed and sighed a long, weary sigh of acceptance.

TWO

Jeremy Slank woke with an erection so towering, it would have required all four of the valiant marines from the Iwo Jima monument to prop it upright. He enjoyed that rare and blissful pleasure of waking from a wonderful dream to an even more wonderful reality. This had every chance of being the very best day of his life. The Groundhog Day he would choose, if ever the option arose, to live over and over again for the rest of eternity.

His eyes and his memory still being a little sleep-fogged, he blindly patted the bed beside him in case there was anyone there with whom to share his random engorgement. The chances, these days, were about 70-30 in his favour. But there was no flesh within his reach. Oh, well. Not too much of a disappointment. He often found a dream-induced stiffy had very little to do with sexual desire, and had oftentimes had a good deal of trouble coaxing it into something more purposeful once he'd initiated a grappling session. Besides, morning sex was not his favourite pursuit. All that avoiding each other's bad breath and bad hair and stale perfume tended to put a dampener on desire.

He rose and slipped on his dressing gown. His penis protruded from it comically, like a pink Dalek's eye. He swaggered around the bedroom for a few moments, exclaiming 'Exterminate! Exterminate!' till his erection began to wilt and it was possible to contemplate peeing.

For Jeremy, hygiene, both personal and domestic, was a necessary evil, to be performed in the shortest possible time, and preferably whilst simultaneously doing something else more useful. During the brief, weekly scamper over the living room carpet with the vacuum cleaner, for instance, he would be listening to a podcast or an audio book on his iPod. He would wash the pots – again, once a week – whilst making his obligatory parental phone call with his Bluetooth headset on.

In this spirit, his morning ablutions had become fine-tuned to an almost ritualistic routine. He would lay out his clothes for the day on the bed, stacked in reverse order, so his suit jacket would be on the bottom and his socks and underpants on the top. He would click on the shower room light and enter. He would then load up his toothbrush, which lay on top of his cistern, in precise order next to his toothpaste, his can of shaving foam, his razor, mouthwash, deodorant, aftershave and cologne. He would turn on the hot tap in the sink, then sit on the loo, simultaneously evacuating his bodily waste whilst cleaning his teeth. By the time he'd performed both of these functions, the water would be warm enough for his shave. He would turn on the shower and then shave, swiftly, if not comprehensively, then rinse off the razor, the toothbrush and the sink, before pouring himself a capful of mouthwash and moving the bath towel from the back of the door to the radiator by the shower cubicle, where it would be convenient for the wetly blind post-shower grab. The shower would now be warm enough to use, and he would shower and gargle at the same time. The shower routine was rigidly observed: wash hair, then armpits, then crack, sac and penis, and let the rest of the body take care of itself. Rinse off, step out. Dry hair, back and armpits, wrap towel around waist, apply roll-on deodorant, then aftershave, then cologne. He would sit on the bed and drag his socks on his clammy feet, which very act would dry his bottom sufficiently for the application of underpants.

He would be fresh and dressed, if still a little damp, within seven and a half minutes from rising. He had striven to improve this time, but any attempts at short cuts had led to minor disasters, including unsightly shaving cuts, dried soap stains around the neck or the omission of one or more odour inhibitors and a subsequent perceptible drop in office popularity.

All of which meant he now had a small window (thirteen minutes) before he thrust himself into commuter bedlam. Time for a coffee, of the instant kind, and a phone call, of the subtly bragging kind.

But to which friend might he best flaunt his latest success? Why, obviously the one who was currently failing most. As Gore Vidal said: it is not enough to succeed: others must fail. Derrian, then. Derrian did something naff in the City, and, rumour was, had been doing it rather badly of late.

Derrian didn't quite qualify onto Jeremy's cellphone speed-dial. He was, in fact, Jeremy noted, the thirty-fifth entry in the handset's phone book. As the call connected, Jeremy wondered where he ranked in Derrian's contact list. Probably in the top twenty, if not in the speed-dial list itself. He was, after all, in Government now. More or less.

'Yeah, mate. All right?' There seemed to be a lot of shouting where Derrian was. The Exchange? Christ. Did he start work before eight o'clock? Barbaric.

'I'm good, my friend.' Jeremy adjusted his tie in the mirror and wondered if a blob of hair gel might be called for. 'Long time no powwow.'

'Yeah, mate. What's happenin'?' 'Mate', again? He'd been spending too much time with those barrow-boy traders, had old Derrian.

'Wondered if you'd like to hook up for lunch some time?'

'Sounds good. When?'

'Well, let's see. Can't make it today, I've—'

'Not today, mate.'

Damn! *Boastus interuptus*. Maybe he could still squeeze it in. 'Well, obviously not today. I've got a—'

'Not this week, mate. I'm in Brussels.'

'Brussels?' Bloody hell. Jeremy struggled not to sound interested.

'Yeah, mate. Then next week, bloody Amsterdam.'

Brussels? Amsterdam? Jeremy was buggered if he was going to ask why. 'Cool. Just call me when you get back.'

'No problemo, mate. Catch you later.' And Derrian disconnected him.

Disconnected *him*. The pikey bastard. No opportunity, no gap at all, to drop his proud little bombshell.

Can't make it today. Got a big yawn of a meeting with the bloody Prime Minister. Mate.

Jeremy grabbed his breakfast from the *Prêt À Manger* by the Tube. A carrot juice and some sort of shitty muesli pot with yoghurt and honey. Given a choice, he'd rather have tucked into a full greasy spoon café fry-up. In fact, given a choice between the shitty pot of yoghurty muesli and a blender full of used French letters, he'd have opted for the condom smoothie, but he was briefing on health; he was, to all intents and purposes, a health expert, and he really had to show willing.

In the Tube, he was crammed between a disgustingly fat woman and the rest of the disgustingly fat woman. She really was enormous. Herman Melville could have written a book about her. When the train lurched off, he was seriously worried he might trip and fall into her voluminous bosom and suffocate before a rescue team could winch him out again. How did they live with themselves, people that gross? How did she find time to travel on the Tube? Surely you had to spend every waking minute eating pure hydrogenized saturated fat to maintain those dimensions. He noticed with revulsion that there was something glistening greasily on the woman's chin, no doubt a remnant of the pint of melted lard she'd quaffed that morning, doubtless to wash down the whole suckling pig she'd consumed for breakfast, and her breathing was laboured and unpleasant. He began to feel nauseous. Then he was suddenly struck by a terrible vision of him puking up all over the seated commuters, and the woman falling on them greedily to lap up his vomit, and he had to get out.

He fought his way out of the carriage at the next stop and crammed himself into the adjacent one. As the train moved off again, he caught a glimpse of the blimp woman in the next carriage through the intersecting windows. She'd spotted him. She'd realised why he'd moved carriages, and a look of deep, resonant sadness filled her eyes before she cast them down at the floor.

A brief, a very brief, pang of guilt stabbed him, but he dismissed it easily. Yeah, well. She should do something about it, the weak-willed cow. Nobody was forcing her to eat whole herds of animals on a daily basis. No one put a gun to her head and made her devour the entire Irish potato harvest at every sitting. She needed educating. And educating fat people was what Jeremy was about to get famous for.

He joined the flow out of the Tube station and paused for a few minutes at the Emporio Armani window, his second-favourite shop, suppliers of the very nice suit for which he'd stretched the plastic especially for today's meeting. Of course, he'd like to have a full-blown regular Armani suit, but that was out of his reach, just for the moment. Soon, very soon, he would be able to crank up his spending a gear or two, restock his wardrobe with full-on Armani, and his treasured Emporio suits would be gracing the racks in his local Mencap shop.

He moved on. Now here was his favourite shop. A high-quality lingerie store. La Perla knickers. Wolford stockings and tights. The stuff that drool is made of. He was amazed how thoroughly aroused he could become looking at these items adorning lifeless mannequins. Christ, they didn't need to have arms or legs to turn him on. They didn't even need *heads*. What did that say about the male libido? What did it say about him?

He bounded up the steps to the office, thinking he'd definitely need a shag tonight and thumbed through his phone's contact list in the lift, looking for his most likely prospect.

THREE

Hayleigh knew the alarm was coming. Her hand was hovering over the stop button for several minutes before the first hint of a buzz, and she managed to snap down on it before it had a chance to disturb anyone else in the house. Wednesday. Crap. Wednesday was just about the cruddiest day imaginable. Possibly, it was worse, even, than Monday. Because here you were, adrift and becalmed, slap bang in the middle of the week, the last Saturday morning long gone, and next Saturday so far off in the distance, you could hardly make it out on the horizon.

She swung out of bed and tucked her feet into her novelty kitten slippers. It was cold, of course. The heating wouldn't go on for another half an hour, and Mum refused to leave it on all night because it was unhealthy. They could be stuck in a snowdrift in the middle of the Ice Age and Mum would not keep the heating on overnight.

She shivered into her oversized dressing gown and padded into her bathroom. She felt around for the string dangling from the ceiling and tugged on it. The sudden shock of light stabbed into her eyes and she winced and squinted. It hurt a lot. Tears were actually forming. Her eyes seemed to be getting more and more sensitive to intense light. Photophobia, it was called. She'd looked it up on Wikipedia.

When her eyes adjusted she looked up. To her absolute horror, her towel had slipped from her bathroom mirror and she was face to face with her own reflection. She stood there, frozen in shock and disgust, before she managed to gather her wits, grab up the towel and tuck it back in place.

My God. What a pig she was. Hideous, hideous, hideous.

19

She looked exactly like Napoleon in *Animal Farm*. The bit at the end, where he was all bloated and drinking and smoking with the humans. *'And she looked from pig to Hayleigh, and from Hayleigh to pig, and she couldn't tell the difference.'*

Her heart was thumping from the awfulness of it all. She couldn't afford to hang around too long, though. The parents would be up in, what? Twenty-three minutes. Move it, girl. Shake that giant booty.

She scooped up her toothbrush and ran it under the tap until the water was just cold, rather than actually so far below Absolute Zero it would unquestionably snap your limbs off.

Even so, it was still a shock when the wet bristles hit her gums. Even her gums were getting more sensitive these days. She'd have to see if there was a word for that in Wikipedia.

Her mouth tasted bad, really bad, as if bugs had been queuing up all night to poo in it. She would have liked to use toothpaste, but she did not dare. How many calories were in toothpaste? A hundred? A million? Who knows? They didn't put it on the packet, which Hayleigh thought was probably illegal. Millions of people all over the world brushing their teeth every day, in complete ignorance of the calorific values they were inadvertently ingesting. She shuddered involuntarily.

She washed her hands and face in cold water. Not that she was worried about the calories in warm water, silly. No, first thing in the morning, the pipes started banging if you used the hot tap, and the heater whooshed on noisily in the main bathroom, and she couldn't risk disturbing her parents.

She did *not*, however, use soap. Definitely not. She'd seen *Fight Club* at a sleepover at Fabiola's one night, and discovered, to her gobsmackment, that *soap is made from fat.* Totally made from *fat*. In the movie, scrummy Brad Pitt made it out of human fat, but Hayleigh assumed most soap was made out of regular animal fat. Appalling or what? Here you are, madam: rub this block of beef dripping all over your body. Let it seep in through the pores. Watch the pounds pile on. I think not, girlfriend. No way.

She dressed as quickly as she could, back in the dark of her bedroom. Her clothes were all laid out in distinct, discrete piles so she could find them easily without having to turn the light on, and there was less chance of catching a glimpse of the rolls of fat that wobbled around her hips and belly. She tugged on her black woolly tights, trying not to touch the gruesome cellulite that pocked her thighs. She hated wearing tights precisely because they were exactly that: tight. She liked all her clothes to be loose. As loose as possible. But it was very cold outside, and school uniform was school uniform, there was no getting around that. She could, of course, have opted for trousers. But picture this scenario: she comes out of school and Jason Black from Big Boys Cry drives past in his limo with all his posse and sees her standing outside the gates in *boy trousers*. Nightmare! Would he stop the car and invite her in? I think not, girlfriend. Would he whisk a girl in boy trousers off to his Wembley Stadium gig, so she could sit backstage, or, better yet, just slightly in view so all her friends could see her there, with Jase looking over every few seconds in total love with her? Not going to happen. *Cela ne se produira pas.* Tights were really the only option.

The skirt, though, was absolutely voluminous, and that was good. It was pleated, which made it almost twice as bulky as a regular skirt. The shirt was loose and billowy, and the cardigan was practically a Girl Guide tent. Excellemoso!

She cracked open her bedroom door and took a large stride over the two creaky floorboards that lurked under the carpet just outside her room. She also had to avoid the third, eighth and ninth steps on the stairway. She crept down to the hall with as much stealth as her elephant frame could muster, then paused, still as a deer, and listened, wide-eyed and alert. She was rewarded with the gentle hum of a snore from her mum and dad's bedroom. Fantabuloso. She'd made it. She exhaled and the tension oozed out in her breath.

Now was a tricky bit. There were two major obstacles in the hallway.

They were mirrors.

The toughest one was in front of her on her right, just by the front door. It was huge. It was virtually impossible to walk past that mirror without catching a glimpse of your disgusting wobbly self in your peripheral vision, and *believez moi*, she had tried. She had campaigned long and hard against that mirror. It was far too big for the tiny hall. But that was the point, Mum had said. It creates the illusion of space. Uh, no, it creates the illusion you're a woolly mammoth in a school uniform. She had even, in desperation, seriously smashed it to total pieces. But it was a poorly thought through plan. It had been difficult to explain how she had managed to accidentally swing her hockey stick no less than five times at the mirror ('I was wearing ear muffs, and didn't hear it') plus, of course, her parents had simply replaced it with, if anything, a slightly larger mirror. Genius.

But that was not the problem mirror right now. She could easily avoid its accusatory glare by hugging her huge bulk tightly to the stair pole as she turned right to face the kitchen. The other mirror ran along the hall parallel to the stairs. Again, we're creating the illusion of space, here. Here's a wild, crazy thought, Mum: try creating the illusion of space by moving to a bigger house. That ought to do it for you.

This mirror was bad because it was long. Seriously long. Two metres. Maybe more. Fortunately, it was not very tall, and it was hung quite high up, so all you had to do was duck below it. Of course, that caused its own problems if anybody else was around and caught you walking down the hall as if you were scurrying through a low tunnel, as that could start Mum off on one of her Famous Lectures, so you had to check there would be no observers before you could brave the trip to and from the kitchen. Sometimes you could be trapped in the kitchen for aeons, which could be an exquisite torture all of its own when that was positively the very last place on Earth you wanted to be.

She ducked down and ran the gauntlet to the kitchen.

Another tricky bit.

Nothing was easy in this house, and that was a fact.

First off, the door handle was noisy. You had to turn it very, very gently. Second, the upper half of the door was paned with glass. In the daylight, no problemo. In the morning half-light, it was pretty much another mirror, and you had to keep your gaze just in front of your porky little feet so you could just see the door handle on the edge of your vision. Again, she'd campaigned against the glass, on the grounds that it was (a) dangerous and (b) the kitchen, nice as it was, did not constitute a sufficiently engaging view to warrant a window, and nor did the hallway, so what the heck was the window for? For light, of course. It created the illusion of light. They were creating so many illusions around this place, they must have thought David Copperfield was moving in.

She got the door open almost silently, and closed it behind her with the same intense concentration. Again, she exhaled. She looked at the digital clock on the cooker. Nineteen minutes to go.

She crossed to the kitchen window and made sure the shutters were closed as tight as they could go. The kitchen window was, technically, in view from Mum and Dad's room, though you probably had to be standing at a very strange angle with the curtains open to glimpse any light spillage. Still. Who knew what they got up to in there? It could very well involve striking strange poses for curious reasons with the curtains open.

Satisfied the shutters were as sealed as was humanly possible, Hayleigh flicked on the kitchen light. She had an easy, well-practised routine now, and she could just about do it in her sleep.

Switch on the grill, fill the kettle and put it on. Take the bacon and eggs out of the fridge. With the kitchen tongs, put the bacon on the grill pan and slide it under the heat. Get out the frying pan and put it on the hob. Turn the gas on. Put some olive oil in the pan. Get the slices of bread out of the cupboard and pop them into the toaster, ready to hit the on button just after the eggs have started frying. When the kettle boils, warm the teapot and empty it out. Put the tea bags in and fill up the teapot. Check the bacon. When it's ready to turn, turn it with the tongs and crack the eggs into the frying pan, then turn the timer on the toaster to just less than two. Put the glass lid on the frying pan, so the eggs cook without having to splash them with oil. Lay the breakfast table.

Now, check the timing. This was the crucial part. Seven twenty-seven precisely, put the bacon and eggs on the plates. One egg for Mum, one for Jonny, two for Dad, one for her. Three rashers of bacon for Dad and Jonny, two for Mum, one for her. At the ping of the toaster, remove the toast to the rack and put another load on, this time with the timer set just above one because the elements are already hot.

With the tongs, smear the single rasher of bacon around her plate, leaving as much greasy residue as possible. Then, with a knife, break the egg and smear some of the yolk around the plate, and then – great touch, this one – just dab a little of the yellow goo on yourself. Could be on your sleeve, on your shirt, wherever. Just so long as it is discreetly visible. This morning she does a daring one: she pats a tiny blob just by the corner of her mouth.

Now, with the tongs, lift up the egg and drop it into the waste disposal, then do the same with the bacon. You don't want the plate to look like it's been scraped, thank you so much. Leave the plate by the sink. Put a slice of toast on a side plate and cut it with a knife to leave a convincing number of toasty crumbs. Put the toast in the waste disposal, fish the tea bags out of the pot and pop them in the waste disposal on top of everything else. Now, with one hand on the waste disposal switch and the other on the tap, a combo that is probably potentially lethally dangerous, you wait.

You wait until, on the stroke of seven thirty, Mum and Dad's radio alarm blares into life. You turn on the tap and switch on the waste disposal and, *voilà* – your work is done, and you can finally chill. Just pour yourself a cup of hot water and kick back with your magazine, drooling over piccies of Jase, and wait for everyone to slouch into the kitchen with their silly hair and sleep-confused expressions. Same old same old, every day.

Only this time, it didn't work like that.

This time, when Maroon Five blasted down the stairs with 'This Love' from her parents' radio alarm, Hayleigh hit the tap and water cascaded into the sink, and she flicked the waste disposal switch and nothing happened.

OK. No panic. She flicked the switch off and back on again. Still nothing.

This had happened before. Not to Hayleigh but to her mum, and there was some kind of button you pressed under the sink that made it work again.

She flung open the cupboard doors and crouched down low. There were so many bottles and packets down here you could hardly see anything. She certainly couldn't see a switch.

She heard the floorboards creaking upstairs, and somewhere, a toilet flushed. She felt around under the waste disposal, but found nothing remotely button-like. Her hands darted frantically over every exposed part of the machinery. Was this dangerous? She gave up, closed the doors and straightened.

In round about thirteen seconds, a parent was going to come into the kitchen, spot the charade and Hayleigh's life, as she knew it, would effectively be over.

FOUR

Grenville pulled up in the health club car park. It was a vast car park, and there were at least sixty or seventy free spaces, but dozens of people all seemed to be cruising around it, trying desperately to find the nearest space possible to the entrance. It seemed odd to Gren that anyone would expend such effort simply to avoid a walk of, at worst, seventy yards, especially since, he had to assume, they were coming to the health club to exercise. Baffling. They would avoid walking two hundred feet in order to go upstairs and jog two miles on a running machine. That's the gym crowd for you.

He got out of his car. Again, not as easy as it sounds for a man of Grenville's bulk. Any kind of bending hurt. All kinds of activities that are normally simple and mundane for Off The Peggers are arduous for people of Grenville's bulk. Pulling on your underpants, for instance. When you are of Grenville's bulk, you cannot balance easily on one leg, as if you are a delicate, lithe flamingo. You have to do it sitting down. Pulling on your socks, harder still. You have to sit down and contort your legs into very strange angles. Very strange angles that your legs do not want to remain in. You have to strike poses that cause pains in strange parts of your body, and you have to pull the sock on quickly before you inflict permanent damage. It can take upwards of five attempts just to get one sock on, by which time the theoretical heel of the sock can be just about anywhere. Sometimes, Grenville seriously considered giving up and going sockless for the day, but it hadn't quite come to that. Not yet, anyway.

Shoes. Shoes were in their own league from hell. You could kill yourself trying to put on a pair of cowboy boots, as Gren had learned to his despair. No. Slip-ons were best, and even then you needed a three-feet-long shoehorn, bodily contortions, some steps or a stair, bones made of India rubber and a high pain threshold. But Gren had not been able to secure a pair of slip-on trainers, and so had to endure the double agony of actually getting his feet inside them and then having to do up the laces.

By the time he was dressed for the gym, Gren felt he'd already exercised sufficiently to lose a stone or two.

He walked into the club, and as soon as he passed the reception desk, the liniment aroma hit him. Who *used* that stuff? What did they use it *for*? He'd managed to live his whole life so far without ever feeling an urgent need for liniment, without encountering any injury that needed linimenting, even slightly.

Entry to the club proper involved running your pass card through a reader and squeezing through a turnstile. It looked ungenerous, the turnstile, and he had visions of himself stuck in it, and having to be cut free by firemen with oxyacetylene torches. There was a disabled entrance, but you had to ask the receptionist to operate that, and Grenville decided the rescue services option would be the less embarrassing.

He knew where he was going. He'd joined the club a few weeks earlier, and this was to be his induction assessment.

It would not be an outright lie to say that Grenville was dreading this more than anything he'd dreaded since his school days.

He thought that at least if he was already dressed for the gym, he could avoid the changing room and its depressing penis parade, though, truth be told, since he could no longer see his own penis without the aid of a mirror, unless it was very happy indeed, looking at other people's might bring something lost back to his life.

He jogged, slightly, up the stairs to the gym, or at least up three or four of them. He didn't want to arrive at his fitness assessment completely shagged out and knackered.

His appointment had been with a male gym assistant, but, of course, the lad had reported in sick and a pretty young woman was covering for him, so as to absolutely maximise Grenville's humiliation. He'd expected no less.

She made him run through the usual diseases and disorders list, none of which Grenville had, and most of which disgusted him. Grenville decided, anyway, to tick the box that said 'menstrual cramping', just to lighten up the proceedings a tad, but the girl just clucked impatiently and brought out a fresh sheet for him to start all over again. Even claiming he'd thought it had read 'minstrel camping' drew nary a smile.

She then took his blood pressure. Then she took his blood pressure again, because, Grenville assumed, she was so astonished the machine didn't out and out explode. It turned out his blood pressure was, amazingly, fine. As was his resting heart rate. She made him do five minutes on the exercise bike, which seemed excessive to Gren, but his heart rate actually went down during the exercise. The girl tapped the digital read-out quite violently, but the figures didn't change.

Apart from the discomfort the physical exertion had caused him, Grenville was actually beginning to feel good about the whole experience.

Which feeling was soon to pass.

Because next came the physical measurements.

First came his waist. He held out his arms and prayed that, first and foremost, she could actually distinguish his waist from the rest of him, and second, that the tape would actually be long enough to reach all the way around him, and she didn't have to leave a chalk mark and do him in sections or something.

She wrote the measurement down in his chart. Grenville was hoping she would write it in centimetres, which he found hard to convert, but she wrote it in inches, and he was glad the blood pressure armband wasn't still around his arm, because the figure almost gave him a heart attack.

How many inches?

Why, surely not.

That could not be.

Was that not, in fact, his *height* she'd in some way unintentionally measured? Had she somehow written down the dimensions of some plunge pool the club was thinking of having constructed? Did she accidentally wrap the tape measure around two other people who'd been standing behind him, queuing to use the body balls?

But he had no time to recover from that shock before the next ordeal confronted him.

The weighing machine.

Now, Grenville really had no idea precisely how much he weighed. His own bathroom scales had been put down humanely long ago because of the accusing way they looked at him when he emerged from the shower. He prayed there were enough counterbalancing weights to cope with his bulk.

'If you'd just like to step onto the scales now, Mr Roberts.'

'What? Just like that?' The words leapt from his throat in some bizarre kind of falsetto. Grenville was aghast. He *never* weighed himself with his shoes on. He never weighed himself with his clothes on. In fact, normally he would even remove his wristwatch and trim his nails before going anywhere *near* a set of scales. He hadn't eaten breakfast that morning, precisely in preparation for this moment, but he really needed to vacate his bladder and bowels before he was ready to—

'Just step right on.' The idiot girl beamed.

Grenville stepped right on.

The girl fiddled with the counterweights. She seemed to have underestimated, because she fiddled with them again. In all, as every spare droplet of blood in Grenville's body made an emergency detour to his face, the girl fiddled with the counterweights twenty-three times before she achieved equilibrium. Then she smiled, like you might smile at an off-duty circus freak, and invited him to step down.

Grenville didn't want to look at what she'd written in his chart, but he couldn't help himself.

How many pounds?

No.

Surely some mistake.

Could it really be so?

This was much, much worse than he had even dared dread.

Was that not, in fact, precisely the same weight as his motor car?

Gren looked over his shoulder in case he was inadvertently giving a piggyback to a human pyramid comprised of the Metropolitan Police motorcycle formation team.

There had to be some explanation. Dark matter had somehow leaked in from another dimension at the precise spot and moment he was being weighed. These were the wrong scales, the product of some comical mix-up with scales used to ensure lorries did not exceed the maximum load a bridge could bear. He suddenly started to panic because he was not on the ground floor and at any moment could bring the entire building crashing down around their ears. He was definitely thinking they had better not ask him to do any jumping or skipping.

The girl was looking at him oddly. Clearly, she'd been speaking to him, and Grenville, off in his terrible funk, had not heard her.

'I'm sorry?' The man-mountain smiled.

'What we need to do now is list your targets.'

Targets? They were giving him targets now? What were they going to do? Stuff him into a super gun, aim him at the Middle East and use him as some kind of human smart bomb? 'Targets?'

'Your personal targets. What you hope to achieve from your exercise programme.'

'My targets, right.' Well, let's see now. His primary target, right now, was to get the hell out of this place and never come anywhere near it again. Secondly, he'd like to destroy his chart, and, while he was at it, the weighing machine, the tape measure and probably this idiot girl who was a first-hand witness to his humiliation. Or, at the very least, some-how wipe her memory of the whole sorry affair. 'What do I hope to achieve from my exercise programme?'

Normalcy. That's what he'd like to achieve. He'd like to be normal. He'd like to be Off The Peg again. He'd like to be able to buy and wear decent clothes in colours that were not even vaguely psychedelic. He'd like young girls like this to look at him, if not with lust and desire, then at least without pity. He'd like to be able to trim his toenails without fear of fainting. He'd like to be able to get in a bath and then get out again, instead of floundering for hours on end like a helpless giant squid with seven broken tentacles. He'd like to get on an aeroplane and fasten the safety belt, and not have to endure the humiliation of asking for a seatbelt extension normally reserved for pregnant women. He'd like to get in and out of his car without pain. How about that for a target?

'General fitness?' The girl arched her eyebrows.

'General fitness, definitely.'

'Weight loss?' she offered helpfully.

'Weight loss would be good,' Grenville agreed. 'Weight loss would be dandy.'

'Shall we set a monthly target?'

Again with the targets. Grenville would have liked to set a target on this girl's forehead and use it for crossbow practice. 'OK, a monthly target.'

'Say, two pounds a month?'

Two pounds? Grenville could lose four pounds with a decent bowel movement. 'Two pounds doesn't seem like much.'

'We recommend a slow but steady weight-loss pro-gramme.'

'Fine.'

She took him around the machines and devised for him an exercise programme that wouldn't tax a bedridden octogena-rian with plastic bags for lungs, and a truly dismal low-fat, no-sugar diet sheet which had failed Grenville three times so far. A pound a fortnight? Brilliant. With iron will and rigid discipline, Grenville could be down to his recommended body weight by the age of three hundred and forty-seven.

FIVE

The detritus of Hayleigh's unconsumed breakfast was floating round the sink like debris from the *Titanic*. She had to
think fast. OK. A plastic carrier bag. There was a sack of them
hanging on the cellar doorknob, just outside the kitchen. She
dashed to the kitchen door and flung it open. She heard her
parents' bedroom door open. Crappy crud burgers.

She snatched a Waitrose bag out of the sack, raced back
into the kitchen and flung the door closed to buy her a
second or two of extra time. The door slammed loudly, and
she would get a ticking off for that, but so what, now? She
heard her dad's clumsy footsteps on the landing. He would
be down in seconds. *Seconds.* He didn't have to step over the
creaky floorboards outside his door, or dodge over stairs
three, eight and nine. Neither of the mirrors held any kind
of terror for him. He could practically *race* down the hall.
And to Hayleigh that sounded exactly like what he was doing.
He negotiated the stairway with all the easy grace of a herd
of hysterical hippopotamuses fleeing a jungle fire with Doc
Martens on their feet.

She fished around in the sink with her tongs and caught up
a slice of soggy toast, but when she lifted it clear of the water,
it disintegrated wetly and dropped back into the water.

Dad landed on the polished wood of the hall floor like a
Sherman tank that had been dropped from a plane and its
parachute had failed to open.

Nothing for it. She had to abandon the tongs and, grimac-
ing like a first-time vet shoving his arm up a cow's backside,
she fished the bacon and the bits of egg out of the water and
dropped them into the bag. She went in again and scooped

out as many of the soggy remnants of toast as she could manage, dumped them into the bag and tied off the top of it.

Now what? Mercifully, Dad seemed to be hesitating in the hall. Possibly he'd caught sight of himself in the mirror and was desperately failing to adjust his hair so it might look marginally less silly. The taunting mirror, ironically, had become her saviour.

She thought about the pedal bin, but it was too risky. There was a chance Mum might find the Waitrose bag and wonder what it was doing there, and . . .

With no choices left, she lifted up her skirt and stuffed the bag down the back of her tights. Ha! Her hideous tights had come to the rescue. Of course, her bum now looked even more monumentally fat than ever, and the very notion of the greasy swill in the Waitrose bag pressed so close to her skin was enough to induce a heaving fit, if she thought about it too much, so she tried not to think about it at all. She tried to think about something nice. She tried to think about Jase. Dad yawned into the kitchen, with hair so thoroughly silly, a team of highly trained barbers would have to work round the clock for weeks on end on scaffolding to rescue it even marginally.

'Hey, Hay,' he said, as he did every morning, finding new bits of himself to scratch every second or two. 'What up?'

Hayleigh leaned back against the sink with her arms outstretched so he wouldn't be able to see into it. There was still evidence floating around in there: small slivers of wet toast and streaks of congealed yolk she hadn't managed to scoop. As she leaned back, though, she heard the bag in her tights rustle, and she was pretty sure Dad heard it too, but he didn't seem to react. ''Sall good.' She forced a smile. 'Made brekkie.'

He turned his sleepy eyes towards the table. 'Lush.' He grinned.

Hayleigh rolled her eyes. Dad picked up what he thought were cool words by secretly reading her magazines, and, of course, he always used them incorrectly. He slouched towards the table. 'Good girl. I'd give you a kiss, but I'm afraid my mouth smells like a New Orleans swamp with bodies floating in it.'

Hayleigh rolled her eyes again. Dad had a fairly sick sense of humour. Hayleigh's eyes got a lot of exercise when Dad was around.

He sat at the table, took some toast from the rack and started buttering it. 'Where's yours?'

Damn. Hayleigh liked to time it so she could be pretending to finish the last mouthful when the first witness arrived in the kitchen. Then she could lean back, chewing air, pat her stomach with counterfeit satisfaction and move her plates to the sink making yum-yum sounds. This morning, of course, there had been no time for that little playlet. Worse, the plates were in the wrong place. They were by the toaster, where she'd never normally leave them. Trying to look casual, she picked them up and popped them by the sink, where any suspicious eyes could scan them in vain for forgery. 'I finished mine, you lazy boneses. I've still got some homework to do.'

Dad just grunted. He preferred them all to take their meals together whenever it was possible. Hayleigh found watching everyone else stuffing their gullets a rather arduous experience, if you want to know the truth. Thoroughly unpleasant. But unfinished homework was the Rolls Royce Silver Shadow of excuses. Not that Hayleigh ever fell behind with her homework for a millisecond. Let's face it: what else did she have to do in her sad, blubbery life? She headed for the kitchen door so she could traverse the hall before . . . darn it.

She heard Mum's footfall on the stairs. Alarmingly, Mum was an even bigger clomper than Dad. Mum coming down the stairs sounded like the ceiling was collapsing under the weight of a fully equipped abseiling SWAT team, though she was less than one point seven metres tall and weighed a steady sixty-one kilos.

Now Hayleigh was trapped in the kitchen.

Mum was a much better detective than Dad. Dad, bless, was useless. He was worse, even, than Inspector Lestrade. He was worse than Lieutenant Randy Disher, Captain Leland Stottlemeyer's useless sidekick, who in turn was utterly useless compared to Mr Monk. Dad wouldn't have made it as a traffic cop in that series. Mum, however, made even the great Adrian Monk, who could solve murders in other continents just by reading a newspaper, look like an unobservant, witless blind man. She could sniff out a fake alibi while you were still composing it in your head. She could spot a tiny inconsistency in a slightly invented version of reality you told her years ago with something you said today, and unravel the entire truth in minutes. Hayleigh had to admit, albeit grudgingly, that the lady was a genius. Quite why this genius expended so much energy trying to get a hopelessly fat girl to eat even more was a mystery that would have eluded the combined wits of Poirot, Holmes and Monk.

Mum burst through the door, smiled a good morning at Hayleigh and opened her arms and croaked: 'Morning hug.'

The plastic bag!

Hayleigh shook her head. 'I don't think so, *maman*. Your breath smells like a New Orleans swamp with bodies floating in it.'

Dad laughed. Whether that was because he'd forgotten he made the joke in the first place, or because he'd remembered, or simply because he enjoyed any joke made at Mum's expense, Hayleigh did not know.

Mum raised her eyebrows. 'Charming.' She glanced around the kitchen, her camera eyes scoping the room like it was a bloody crime scene. 'You've finished your breakfast? Again?'

'Yes. Can't hang around all the livelong morning for you bunch of sleepyheads.'

'But *again*?'

'You know, some mums would be happy their daughters

made breakfast for everybody. Some mums would be glad not to have to be the first one out of bed.'

'But Hayleigh, I asked you last night to have breakfast with us all. Just this once, at least.'

Hayleigh just shrugged. With Mum on the detection trail, it was best to say as little as possible. It wasn't even a good idea, she'd found from bitter experience, to try to change the subject. That could actually make things worse.

Mum crossed to the sink. Hayleigh's heartbeat accelerated. She thought it might be best to volunteer the information, so the sink inspection might not be quite so rigorous. 'Waste disposal's broke. I think it's the buttony thingy underneath, but I couldn't find it.'

'What have you been putting in here?'

Hayleigh shrugged again. 'Tea bags, mostly. Few crumbs of toast.'

Mum gave up in the sink, bent over, found the buttony thingy and pressed it. She flicked the switch and the waste disposal roared and gobbled down the damning evidence greedily. Hayleigh tried not to sigh.

'Please don't use this again, Hayleigh.'

'Sure.'

'I've told you before: it's dangerous.'

'Sure.' Hayleigh made a mental note of the rough position of the button. This was definitely not going to happen again. 'Sorry.'

Mum ran the hot water tap and wiped the grease from the sink. The inquisition seemed to be over, praise de Lord. At least for now. Could she go without arousing more suspicion? Yes, she thought she probably could. She grasped the kitchen door handle, called back a casual 'Love yous' and shuffled out into the hall, trying not to rustle. She took the small step up to the right and paused in the blind spot between the kitchen and the mirrors, and gathered herself. Why couldn't this family be *normal*, for crying out loud? The smallest of things, the most mundane family rituals, which were carried out daily and unremarkably millions of times in billions of households across the globe, were ordeals fraught with deadly danger in this one. Sometimes Hayleigh thought she was the only normal person she knew.

There was a loud and sudden rattling at the letterbox, and the post thumped onto the mat.

Hayleigh looked over at it. Of course, it was Wednesday, and the one bright spot in this most wretched of days was that her magazine *Chick Chat* arrived. She squinted down the hall. The mag was wrapped in cellophane and doubled over with an elastic band, but it certainly looked as if that was the bottom-left corner of Jason Black's smile on the cover. No one in the world had dimples on their cheeks that were quite so divine.

She couldn't ignore that and do the sensible thing by slipping straight back up the stairs to the safety of her room. She couldn't leave Jase lying on the mat all folded over.

She had to brave the mirrors.

She crouched low and dashed forward, doubled up, like she was Matt Damon racing down a tunnel chased by an explosion. When she hit the second mirror, she had achieved sufficient speed, she reckoned, to throw herself onto the floor and slide along the polished boards all the way to the mat. A little extreme, maybe, but fast and efficient.

She scooped up the magazine, tenderly eased off the elastic band and straightened Jason out. Now *there* was lush. Lushness incarnate. A face brimming over with lushiositude. She hugged him to her chest.

She grabbed the rest of the mail and stood up, so her back was towards the mirror. She was about to slip it onto the dresser behind her when she spotted something dangerous.

It was a blue envelope bearing the crest of Milton House. It was a letter from her school. Now, it might be something innocuous, such as a bill for fees, or notice of some dreadful event like a play or a cake sale, or some such form of ritual pupil torture. On the other hand, Mrs Mellish had had That

Little Chat with her on Monday, and there was a chance that Hayleigh's denials had not been sufficiently credible, and the damned woman was taking it a step further. She could not risk her parents seeing that kind of nonsense. Why couldn't people just get on with their own lives and stop trying to run hers?

She slipped the letter down the front of her tights. She now had more contraband stuffed down there than a Columbian drug mule. She put the rest of the post on the dresser behind her without turning and sidled sideways towards the stairs like a giant demented crab.

She reached the stairs and turned, and, horror of horrors, Jonny was sitting at the top of them in his underpants and T-shirt, watching her with an expression of delighted contempt.

SIX

Jeremy Slank was waiting to see the Prime Minister.

It wasn't quite how he'd imagined, or hoped. But Jeremy Slank was waiting to see the Prime Minister. Of Great Britain.

He'd imagined and hoped it would be at Number 10. He'd imagined and hoped some paparazzi would have flashed him as he nodded politely at the policeman at the door. Perhaps there would be foreign dignitaries milling about in the hall. The odd A-list celebrity, even. A quick smile and gentle nod in the direction of David Schwimmer and Elton John, the knowing smile of men on equal standing, and he'd be ushered through to an ornate drawing room that smelled of ancient cigars, where the Prime Minister would rise from behind an enormous Louis XIV desk, smile, shake his hand and offer him a seat on a huge, winged red leather chesterfield armchair, under a portrait of Sir Winston Churchill or Sir Robert Peel, perhaps. He'd politely decline the eighteen-year-old whisky in the cut-glass crystal decanter that President Grant had sent as a gift to Benjamin Disraeli, and, after a few pleasantries – he would laugh gracefully at the Prime Minister's witticisms, the PM would guffaw at his – they'd get down to business. Jeremy's presentation would be smooth, orderly, swift, yet incisive, sharp and polished. He would close his laptop, the Prime Minister (they might still not be on first-name terms just yet) would nod, impressed. He might even offer genteel applause, or at least a 'Bravo!'. He would rise from his desk and shake Jeremy's hand, sealing the deal. As they walked together to the door, the PM would say that he needed good men such as Jeremy, that he liked the cut of Jeremy's jib, and, once this project was successfully concluded, perhaps Jeremy might consider something more permanent and intimate in the PM's own coterie. Jeremy would agree at least to think about it, and, just as he was about to leave, the Prime Minister would casually invite him to Chequers for the weekend. There would be a few young people there – did Jeremy know Beyoncé and Lucy Pinder? No, he didn't as yet, but he was sure they'd be fun. And after one last Prime Ministerial slap on his back, Jeremy would wind his way back down the hall, brushing past Gerhard Schroeder in animated conversation with Jacques Chirac, or perhaps, even – be still his beating heart – one of the Saatchis, and he'd wink casually at Ricky Gervais and Ben Stiller, who doubtless would be joining him at Chequers that weekend, before stepping out into Downing Street, politely declining a BBC interview, which would doubtless lead to headlines in the morning paper speculating as to the identity of the intriguing hotshot 'mystery man' who was the Prime Minister's new confidant.

Well, perhaps there was slightly more imagination than hope in the fine details of that putative scenario, but he thought the meeting would run pretty much along the same tramlines.

It did not.

Instead, Jeremy was directed to a cheerless modern Government building where he was logged in, paraded through a metal detector *and* an X-ray machine, and subjected to a body search that stopped just short of his cavities. He was then escorted by a pair of armed uniformed security guards who, in turn, handed him over to a plain-clothes security guard, who ran his body over with yet another metal detector and then patted him down most thoroughly yet again. He was then ushered into a stark room with a whiteboard, a wall clock, a glass table and a couple of chairs and left alone for some considerable time.

He exhausted the entertainment value of the room's

furnishings fairly quickly. He took out his laptop and ran through his Keynote presentation at accelerated speed four or five times, but he was already fluent, and it was pretty much a waste of time. He took out his carrot juice and set it on the desk, with the label pointing towards the door to make sure nobody thought it was Sunny D or some such insalubrious nonsense. After an hour he'd started to panic. Had he been forgotten? Was he destined to remain locked in this barren room in some kind of bureaucratic Kafkaesque limbo for the rest of his life? After an hour and a half, he'd pretty much given up on hoping the meeting would still occur. After two hours, he was playing Marble Madness on his laptop.

Finally the door burst open, barely giving him time to close his laptop before a burly man in a dark suit and red tie blustered into the room.

'Slank?' he asked, bluff and Northern.

Jeremy stood. 'That's right, Jeremy Slank.' He offered his hand, but the burly man ignored it.

'Right. Let's have it.'

Jeremy was confused. Who was this man? 'Have what?'

'You've got a meeting scheduled with the PM, right?'

Jeremy nodded.

'Show me what you were going to show him.'

Jeremy's heart sank. He wasn't going to meet the PM after all. He was just meeting some bloody lackey. Brilliant. 'I'm sorry? You are?'

The burly man rolled his eyes impatiently. 'We haven't got time for this shite, lad. I need to know what you're planning to present to the Prime Minister. Quick about it.'

Jeremy shrugged. Maybe this was just a pre-meeting screening. Maybe he would get the meeting, after all. 'Fine.' He opened up his laptop.

'Whoa, whoa, whoa,' the burly man yelled. 'The fuck are you doing?'

'I'm giving you the presentation.'

'Not PowerPoint. He's not going to sit through some fucking PowerPoint presentation, you fucked-up little monkey-boy. The Prime Minister of Great Britain is not going to sit around cooing at your fucking Venetian-blind transitions and your fucking 3D cubic wipes and listening to your fucking hip-hop background music shite, now, is he?'

The man was arching over Jeremy in an extremely menacing way by the end of this diatribe. His face was bright red and the cords in his neck were strained to breaking point. On the second usage of the word 'shite', a globette of spittle had leapt from the man's blubbery lips and landed on Jeremy's cheek, but Jeremy did not flinch, or make any move to wipe it off. Nor did he succumb to the urge to leap over the table, fling open the door and race out of the building as fast as his legs would carry him, though it was a very strong urge indeed. Instead, he struck a pose of intelligent fascination, as if this violent brute were explaining the intricate mathematics of a Bach fugue in a most illuminating and scintillating way.

When the man appeared to have finished, Jeremy left a polite pause and said: 'It's not PowerPoint, it's Keynote.'

The man thumped the laptop closed with his astonishingly large and hairy fist. 'It's shite, is what it is. How long is the fucking presentation?'

'Twenty, twenty-five minutes,' Jeremy confirmed, confidently. 'More, depending how many questions—'

'Twenty-five fucking minutes!? Are you fucking out of your fucking banana tree, you fucked-up fucking fuckwit?'

Jeremy hoped that was a rhetorical question, because he certainly couldn't think of an answer.

The bruiser looked at his watch. 'You will have, you dirty little arsewipe, an absolute maximum of two minutes of the Prime Minister's precious time, and only if you can convince me right here and now that it won't be an utter waste of those two precious minutes, which I very much doubt.' He folded his arms. 'Go on, monkey-boy. Amaze me.'

No pressure, then. Jeremy's future depended on impressing this Piltdown bastard with his ability to boil down a complex thirty-minute presentation (Jeremy had lied, in fact) to a few exceptionally grabby sound bites, and to do it on the fly, and without the benefit of Venetian-blind transitions or the amusingly ironic backing of Groove Armada singing 'Shakin' That Ass'.

And he did it.

The hit man gave a tiny nod, unfolded his arms and leaned into Jeremy's face again. 'All right, you dipshit. You've got your moment in the fucking spotlight. But two minutes and no more than that. And speak up. Don't embroider, do not fucking stutter. Do not exchange pleasantries. If he speaks to you at all, listen very carefully and do exactly what he says. Do not ask for embellishment or explanation. He is, my lad, the Prime Minister of Great Britain, and he's got a fucking country to run. You will kiss his arse, without hesitation and with great relish. You will, in fact, French kiss his arse, and you will really get your tongue up there and wiggle it. If, after this meeting, your tongue is not thoroughly coated in Prime Ministerial poo, I'll want to know why. Clear?'

Jeremy nodded. He thought he was smiling attentively, but he'd pretty much lost control of his lip muscles by this point.

The Goliath shot out of the room, slamming the door. Jeremy stood for a few moments, swaying slightly on the spot. He hoped he hadn't involuntarily evacuated his bowels. When it became obvious the man wasn't going to come back into the room again and hit him, Jeremy wiped the spittle off his face.

Well, so far, so good.

He glanced at the wall clock. He'd been in this cell of a room for two hours and ten minutes. He had no idea how much longer it would be before the Prime Minister showed up. Should he sit down? Probably not.

Jeremy stood, pretty much stock still, staring at the door in anticipation for another twelve minutes. He'd decided on the precise expression he would wear for the Prime Minister's entrance – confident, yet respectful; intelligent, yet undogmatic – but his facial muscles were beginning to tire, and he was having trouble holding it. It was a complicated expression to maintain, and he was considering a less demanding alternative – just plain servile, perhaps – when the nation's leader entered the room.

There were two other people with him, and the Prime Minister was in conversation with them. None of them seemed to notice Jeremy. He waited, trying on the one hand not to listen nosily, and on the other to make sure he didn't miss his chance to launch into his presentation without wasting a precious nanosecond.

Finally, with a little joke his two cronies found intensely amusing, the PM turned to Jeremy and smiled. One of the cronies whispered in his ear. The PM nodded and smiled again at Jeremy. 'Gerald.'

Jeremy smiled and nodded. 'Prime Minister.'

'Right, we were very impressed with your work on the Met volunteer promotional, and we want to see what you can do with the Well Farm project. I'm going to be rolling it out in just over a fortnight and I want some good angles. Some great angles. Think you can accommodate?'

'Absolutely, Prime Minister.'

'Good. Don't drop the ball. I'm going to want a complete plan by Monday.'

Monday. Fuck. 'Absolutely, Prime Minister.'

'T'riffic. Debs will deal with you.'

And with that, the great man turned to one of his cronies and started a completely different conversation as they swept out of the room, leaving Debs behind to 'deal' with him.

Marvellous. Jeremy really must have impressed the big cheese with his pithy dialogue and uproarious wit. He'd said three words. Three words! Not even a verb had left his lips. Well, the PM would probably be buzzing with the memory of that meeting. He'd probably relive it tonight as he climbed into bed with his wife. 'Had a *fascinating* meeting with this total genius today. Gerald, he was called. He said "Prime Minister" three times and "absolutely" twice. He's practically Oscar fucking Wilde. You have *got* to meet him, darling. He's a fucking laugh riot.' Incredible. Still, at least he'd got the gig. He was, he supposed, at least one step closer to the weekend at Chequers.

'Right.' Debs, a sharp, power-suited woman Jeremy would definitely classify as a 'babe', handed him a thick folder stuffed with documents. 'There's all the blurb we've got so far. You can go through it en route.'

'En route to where?'

'Norfolk. We're flying you out to inspect the launch project.'

They were flying him to Norfolk? Flying? Norfolk? 'When?'

'Right now. Chopper's on the roof. I'll take you up there.'

She turned and walked briskly out of the room. In less than a minute, Jeremy realised he was supposed to follow her. She was almost at the end of the corridor by the time Jeremy caught up. She hadn't even looked round for him. She stopped and pressed the button to summon the lift.

'Got any overnight stuff?'

'Not really. A toothbrush, that's about it.'

'Always pack for overnight in your future dealings with us, if you should be so lucky.'

'Sure. Of course.' Overnight. In Norfolk. Damn, he'd have to call Susie and cancel his shag.

The lift arrived and Debs stepped in. She slid some kind of card through a reader. As the lift slid upwards, she fixed Jeremy with a piercing stare. 'This is a flagship project for the PM. Do *not* fuck it up, or I will crush you. I will personally come round to your home and crush your testicles under my heels like overripe kumquats. Am I clear?'

Jeremy looked down at the folder and pretended to sort

through the pages. He tried, very deliberately, not to notice Debs' heels. He wondered if it wouldn't be marginally less scary working with the Russian Mafiya.

SEVEN

'You're an idiot.' Jonny grinned. 'You are a mentalist. You are a total nutter.'

Hayleigh tried to ignore her brother's cruel, pathetic taunts and started climbing the stairs.

'You are a headcase,' he carried on, relentlessly. 'You are a loony. Looooony. Wayne Loony, that's your name. You are barking mad.'

She shrugged past the little shit, but the heckling didn't stop.

'You are a head-the-ball. You are a psycho. You are braindead.'

And so on, and so on. Same old same old. And even when she'd reached her sanctuary and closed the door behind her, on and on he went.

'You are batty. You are so far round the bend, you can see your own arse.'

She started up her computer, clicked on iTunes and let Jason and the boys drown the little bastard out with 'Some Kinda Lurve'.

Didn't stop him right away, of course. He pressed right up against her door and shouted even louder. 'Nutball. You are a nutball. You live in Nutball City Limits.' Great. Maybe there were some households in Birmingham or Manchester that hadn't heard him yet, but Hayleigh doubted it. Brilliant. Please God, don't let him tell Mum and Dad what he's seen.

What had he seen, in actual fact? Besides the, yes, admittedly, slightly bizarre trip down the hall and back, which must have looked inexplicably strange if you didn't know why she was doing it. Had he seen her tucking the letter away? That would be bad. If she was caught intercepting mail from the school, well, frankly, everything could come unstuck.

There was a lock on her door, but if she was ever caught using it, suspicion was inevitably aroused. Still, on this occasion, she might risk it. Jonny was, after all, laying siege to her room and shouting insults and taunts at her at volumes better suited to a thrash metal concert.

She slipped the letter and the plastic bag behind the big fluffy cushion on her little sofa, crossed to the door, twisted the key, and immediately Jonny started shouting: 'She's locked the door! Hayleigh's locked her door! She's locked the door so she can do loony things in secret!'

Damn! She'd achieved exactly the opposite of her aim. Instead of a few moments of privacy and secrecy, she could now expect the attention of both parents, and possibly Jonny, too, trying to peer past their knees. She undid the lock, cracked open the door and said, very quietly, to Jonny, 'Fuck off.'

Jonny yelped in delight. 'Yaah! Hayleigh said "fuck off"!' he chanted. 'Hayleigh said "fuck off"! Hayleigh said "fuck o-off"!'

She slammed the door shut and pressed her back against it. And the chanting continued.

'Hayleigh said "fuck off".'

She heard her dad at the foot of the stairs. 'Jonny, leave her alone!'

'She's a mentalist.'

'I'm sure she is, now leave her alone.'

'She said the fuck word.'

'I'm not going to tell you again, Jonny.'

She heard Jonny start down the stairs. 'She should be locked up in a loony bin. You should line her room with padding.'

And Dad, the saviour, led him off to the kitchen with the fading words: 'I'll be padding your bottom, laddo.'

Not for the first time, nor, doubtless, the last, Hayleigh

49

wished she'd had the good fortune to acquire a kid sister rather than the freaky kid brother from hell that fortune had blessed her with. Or just a kitten. Frankly, a giant ugly scabrous rat riddled with bubonic plague, weeping sores and rabies would have been infinitely more desirable.

What to do, now, with the plastic bag? She could try flushing the contents down the loo, but that wouldn't necessarily work, as she had discovered to her cost on other dangerous and thoroughly unpleasant occasions. For some reason, food tended to be more buoyant *before* you ate it. Your body did something to food when it turned it into poo that made it sink. She really didn't want to risk trying to flush away the breakfast debris only to have it float menacingly to the surface time and time again, and wind up having to fish it out and put it back in the bag.

She couldn't access her school-bag just yet, which would have been the easiest option. That was downstairs in the kitchen, where her mum was probably at this very moment filling it with the calorific nightmare she euphemistically called Hayleigh's 'packed lunch'. Packed death trap, more like. Mother had really put her foot down on this one. She had checked through the packed lunch Hayleigh prepared for herself one time, and all hell had broken loose. As if three short sticks of celery was a criminal offence that ranked just below matricide. So, instead of getting a lunch she could actually enjoy (you expended more calories eating celery than you did from ingesting it), Hayleigh was packed off to school with a cornucopia of inedible horrors, and so ate nothing at all. On top of which, she had to peel the bananas and oranges and kiwi fruit or whatever, dispose of the deadly flesh and put the peel back in the bag, along with the emptied-out plastic bottle of freshly squeezed orange juice, the cellophane and crumbs from the discarded sandwich and the wrapper from the (unbelievable!) chocolate bar, which, had she actually consumed it, would have rendered her of sufficient size to be launched into outer space and technically designated a new planet. Instead of having a small, pleasant lunch, she was sent off with a back-breaking sack of supplies that would have allowed Napoleon's army to take Moscow comfortably, all of which then had to be dealt with in all kinds of complicated ways, and the decaying detritus brought smellingly home. Nothing in Hayleigh's life could ever be simple. Nothing.

She could not leave the bag in her room. Mum would, without any kind of doubt, relentlessly search the room with more ruthless efficiency than Gil Grissom's entire night shift of crime scene investigators. 'Oh, here's the murder weapon, Grissom: the moron stuffed it behind a large fluffy pillow.'

She could not risk leaving the house with the bag rammed down the waistband of her tights. There would be hugs at the door from Dad, and the threat of plastic rustling getting into the car, and all through the entire journey she would have to sit perfectly immobile, and Mum would definitely think that was strange, plus another hug risk at the school gate. No. It would be far too fraught.

She could transfer it, though, to another container. Something that wouldn't rustle. But what? She scoured the room. Her eyes lit on a discarded sock. Brilliant! She could easily stuff it into a sock and tuck that down her tights, then neatly fold the plastic bag and ferret that way in her drawers. Even if it were found, it wouldn't be horrendously suspicious. It would just look as if she were being excessively neat, which, last time she'd read the statute book, was no longer a capital offence.

But, then, the stuff was quite wet, wasn't it? What if it seeped through the sock and started dribbling down her leg? That could cause considerably more problems than it solved. Add incontinence to the list of Hayleigh's Imagined Ailments.

On top of which, the sock solution wouldn't solve the problem of the letter. The letter had to be kept intact in case it was something innocent but important, like a bill. No matter what she hid that in, she ran the risk of making telltale crinkling sounds.

Why was everything so *hard*?

Her eyes fell on Jason's lovely smile, and she hit on a solution that was both terrible and perfect at the same time.

She could hide the food debris *and* the letter between the pages of *Chick Chat*!

She could open the plastic outer bag carefully and reseal it. Then it would be a simple matter of dropping it quickly into her school-bag on the mad dash from the house.

Of course, the soggy food waste would soak into the mag, rendering it unreadable and destroying any posters she might have wanted to keep. But she could easily get another copy. The worst part was, it might ruin Jason's picture. Pictures, even. There was probably more than one inside the mag, and that seemed somehow sacrilegious, even though she was going to replace them all.

She looked down at those yummy dimples. Wait a minute. What was that? Did Jase's picture actually *wink* at her? It couldn't have. Could it? Of course it could. True love is a very powerful thing. Miraculous, even. Jason was telling her he didn't mind. He was letting her know it was OK to defile his picture, in a good cause like this one. He was reaching out to her all the way from America, where Big Boys Cry were at this very moment preparing for the Shea Stadium concert in New York that would crack the US market for them, and make them the biggest band in possibly the entire history of the universe, and he'd have a million and seventy-one other more important things on his mind, but he'd taken the time out to send her some magic. Now, how thoughtful was that?

Tears came to her eyes and she clutched the magazine cover to her breast and squeezed it tight. Jason would never, ever let anyone hurt her.

Some kinda lurve, huh?

EIGHT

The whole thing seemed needlessly cruel to Grenville. He'd got himself up off his backside and tried to do something positive, he'd *carpe*d the *diem*, but he'd wound up depressed and defeated. His induction interview at the health club had been one of the most soul-destroying hours of his entire life.

He slumped down the stairs, though all he felt like doing was lying on the floor and going to sleep for a couple of decades, squeezed through the stupid turnstile and out through the automatic doors to the car park.

He crammed himself into his car, which now seemed ludicrously small, given he was such a behemoth, and started up the engine. The CD player burst into life, but the chirpy, upbeat Vivaldi he'd happily hummed along with on his way to the health club seemed vastly inappropriate now, and since he didn't have the 'March of the Russian Slaves' or 'Massa's in de Cold, Cold Ground' on CD in the car, he snapped it off.

He slipped off the handbrake and drove towards the exit barrier. He waited with a fair facsimile of patience for the arm to rise. It didn't. For some reason, the barrier required you to enter a code before it would let you leave. Grenville, of course, did not know the code. He tried punching in a few numbers at random – the obvious four-number combinations, such as one, two, three, four, and so on – but the barrier refused to budge.

He considered getting out of the car and trying to snap off the offensive red-and-white-striped arm and break it over his knee, which would have given him considerable satisfaction, but thought better of it – it might have been the source of some unpleasant publicity, and he was, after all, a bit of a minor celebrity now, and he had to mind his p's and q's – and drove in a mutteringly angry funk back to the health club.

What kind of madness was it, preventing people from leaving a health club car park? There was no barrier stopping people from entering, which would have made some kind of sense. It would probably not be very good for business, but it would keep out undesirables and stop non-customers from availing themselves of the car park facilities, if that's what you were trying to do. But why try to keep non-customers and undesirables *in*? It made no sense at all. What were they trying to achieve? Did they hope non-customers and undesirables would be forced to drive round endlessly until they dropped dead of starvation? Yes, that would show them, wouldn't it? That would teach the bastards to use car parking facilities they weren't entitled to.

He parked in a yellow crisscross box reserved, theoretically, for people with small children – he thought this was a slightly less offensive crime than taking up a disabled space, though he was still breaking car park law: he was still a car park criminal, and liable to serve car park time in the car park penitentiary if convicted – and stormed through the automatic glass doors, which barely had time to open.

He stood at the reception desk, but the blonde behind the counter was doing something so fascinating and vital with a checklist that she couldn't tear herself away, even for a split second, to acknowledge his presence, offer a smile or murmur a simple: 'Be with you in a second, sir,' for fully ten minutes. No matter that Grenville coughed. No matter that he brooded darkly with a thunderous expression on his face. No matter, even, that he actually came right out with it and said: 'Excuse me, can you tell me the barrier code?' For all she knew, there could have been an entire convoy of non-customers out there who'd been driving around the car park aimlessly in a hopeless nomadic funk since Christmas 1972 and were now at death's door, but the blonde had her vital checklist to check, and nothing was going to tear her away from it. Grenville looked down at himself, just to make sure he hadn't become invisible, or somehow drifted into an alternative dimension that rendered him undetectable to people on this physical plane, but no, he seemed to be intact.

He was about to leap over the desk and throttle the life out of the blonde floozy when he spotted a giant sign that Mr Magoo himself couldn't have missed, informing anybody who cared to look that today's barrier code was twelve ninety-nine.

To Grenville's mind, that seemed to make even less sense. Why stop people leaving the car park with a security-coded barrier and then display the code in full view, for everyone to see? Wouldn't it be better to put the sign by the barrier? Wouldn't it be better – and this is a totally whacked-out, off-the-wall, wild and crazy notion – wouldn't it be infinitely better *not to have the bloody barrier there at all*?

He strode out through the automatic plate-glass doors, once again barely allowing them time to open, and walked to his car, thinking this whole health club business had been a world-class mistake, when things suddenly got substantially worse.

His car was hemmed in by a woman in a Sport Utility Vehicle who was struggling to extract a wailing child from a stupidly complex baby seat with one hand, whilst holding a bewildering array of bags, soft toys and chewable books in the other, with a collapsed pushchair tucked awkwardly under her arm.

Grenville cranked up his expression to just below pleasant, which was the best he could muster right then, and said, in a voice that was hardly pissed off at all: 'Excuse me?'

The woman rounded on him like a rampant Gorgon, wide-eyed with hate and venom and screamed: 'What!!??'

Grenville fully expected her hair to unfurl into a twisting

nest of hissing snakes. But he stayed almost calm. He pointed to his car. 'I need to—'

'Where's your *child*?' the woman spat. 'Where's your bloody child?'

Grenville's child was at university, as a matter of fact, sucking what little life hadn't already been leeched out of his bank account by his darling ex, thank you very much. Quite what that had to do with this hag was beyond him. 'I just need to get out, and then you can—'

'That space is for people with small children, you selfish bastard.'

'Well, I was only popping in for a couple of—'

'Well, you can bloody well wait.'

Grenville looked around, as if he might find some arbiter of sanity who could make a quick ruling on this matter, but there was none. Interestingly enough, though, there was a perfectly accessible car parking space not ten feet away.

'But there's a space there.' He smiled with a decent approximation of agreeability. 'You could have used that.'

'*You* could have used that,' the Medusa spat. She'd finally liberated the banshee child from its protective webbing and was struggling to erect the pushchair, an endeavour which looked like it might very well be impossible, given she now had no free hands at all.

'It wasn't there when I—'

'You can bloody well wait,' she spat again, and snapped the pushchair open.

Grenville looked at the parking sign again. He was starting to lose it now. 'Look, lady: that sign is a *suggestion*. It's not like it's the law of the *land*. It's not an imprisonable *offence* to park there without a small child, or even without a fairly large child. You can be childless, impotent and sterile and still park there in all legality.'

The monsteress had stuffed the bawling brat successfully into the pushchair and was now securely belting it in with a complex set of harnesses and trusses in preparation for the arduous, hazard-strewn trek to the health club entrance fully fifteen feet away. She straightened, turned and smiled with all the affection of a rabid Rottweiler and, in a startling burst of wit and originality, announced: 'Well, you can bloody well *wait*,' and trundled off with the screeching babe. She paused at the automatic doors and added, quite needlessly, 'You fat bastard.'

Well, now. The harpy bitch had gone just a *little* too far. She had pushed just that one too many of Grenville's buttons. And that was a big mistake.

Grenville squeezed back into his car and turned over the engine. He lifted the arm rest and rifled through the CD collection he kept in there, which was not a simple manoeuvre because it involved simultaneously twisting at the waist and bending, which hurt quite a lot and constricted his breathing, and twice he almost fainted and had to stop and catch his breath. But he found what he was looking for and slid it into the slot. He cranked up the volume as Steppenwolf chunked out the first chords of 'Born to Be Wild' and threw the gears into reverse.

He slammed into the 4x4 ferociously, almost giving himself whiplash.

There was a terrible crunch of metal and the target vehicle's alarm started blaring, as if it were wailing in pain. Grenville grinned wickedly and glanced up at his rear-view mirror, but the termagant's vehicle didn't seem to have moved very much. He twisted round – again, not a painless feat because it involved, well, moving – and looked through his rear window. The cronemobile didn't seem to have budged at all.

He slipped into first gear and, with the satisfying grind of slow vehicular damage, disengaged his car from the target vehicle and rolled as far forward as he could go, accidentally crunching into the bollard in front of him, then switched back into reverse again and slammed his foot on the accelerator.

This time there was a bigger crunch, and the uplifting chorus of much more damage, and his airbag blasted out of the steering wheel and almost smothered him. When the bag had finally deflated, he looked in the mirror again, but, again, the harridan's vehicle was still blocking his way. He got out of the car to inspect the damage.

The woman's SUV had not moved an inch. Worse still, it had not even sustained any damage to speak of. Some paint scratches on the front bumper were just about the only evidence of the encounter, and they looked like they were actually paint from Grenville's own vehicle, and might very well scrub off.

The rear end of Grenville's car, in contrast, had been almost completely stove in.

Perhaps he hadn't thought this through as completely as he might have done. Perhaps it had been a slightly foolhardy plan, attempting to budge what was, let's face it, the urban version of a Centurion tank, with a second-hand three-door family hatchback. Perhaps he should have waited for the red mist to subside before completely deciding on the wisest course of action.

He strolled to the front of his car. His front fender was bent and the radiator grille looked like a losing boxer's gumshield. Right. Now what was he supposed to do? Hang around until that dreadful woman emerged and clocked what he'd been up to? She didn't seem the type who'd let a major attempted assault on her property pass without comment. The police would doubtless be summoned and, although Grenville was morally in the right, he was, unfairly, legally culpable. He noticed the bollard he'd hit had been slightly dislodged, and the concrete at its base was cracked. Well, if he couldn't go backwards, he would have to go forwards.

He jammed himself back in the driver's seat. He switched off 'Born to Be Wild', because, quite honestly, he wasn't feeling all that wild any more, and since he couldn't recall anything in his collection entitled 'I'm An Idiot', he decided not to bother with music at all.

He disengaged the vehicles, wincing at the sound of what he now realised was even further major damage to his own car.

He rammed the bollard again, deliberately this time. He had to ram it twice more before it surrendered, by which point his bonnet was severely crumpled and steam and/or smoke was hissing out of it.

He trundled across the pavement by the automatic doors, which opened as he passed. He caught a glimpse of the blonde receptionist, who had finally put down her checklist and was wearing a truly bewildered expression. Grenville gave her the finger, aimed the car through another pair of bollards and almost made it without sustaining major destruction to both of the wings and a symmetrical set of deep double gouges along the entire length of both his side panels and doors.

He pootled off, whistling, for some reason, up to the barrier, at which point he realised he'd forgotten the security number in all the excitement. He drove through the barrier anyway, in the process losing his bonnet entirely and smashing his windscreen.

Yes, on balance, the health club had probably not been what you could call a 'good idea'. Well, at least he still had his diet to cling to. At least he'd managed to stick to that. At least he was losing weight. That was the main thing.

The health club was situated at the back of an entertainment complex, which had a cinema, a bowling alley, an ice rink and some restaurants. As he shuddered up to the exit roundabout, he noticed there was a sign for a drive-thru McDonalds, and giggled to himself. How insane was that? Siting a McDonalds next to a health club. And before he knew how it had happened, he was idling outside the drive-thru hatch and ordering two double sausage and egg McMuffins, both with hash browns, which he consumed with great delight and terrible guilt while he drove his smoking shell of a clown car one-handed towards the exit. He was just looping round the roundabout again and about to buy two more when he was saved from himself by the two policemen who placed him under arrest.

NINE

Jeremy was sitting in a helicopter.

And not just any helicopter.

Jeremy was sitting, if you must know, in the Prime Minister's private helicopter, which, incidentally, was flying somewhere. Specifically, it was flying Jeremy somewhere. Does real life get any hornier than that? Officially, of course, the Prime Minister didn't *have* a private helicopter. That might make him look like some kind of bloated, self-important plutocrat. Officially, it was a Government helicopter that anyone could use, theoretically. Only no one ever did, of course. It flew only when and where the Prime Minister wanted, and it only carried the Prime Minister and people the Prime Minister wanted it to carry.

The noise was breathtaking. The whole experience was breathtaking. Orgasmic. Shagtastic. He would have loved to call Derrian right then and explain why he was having to shout over the noise from the blades of the PM's chopper, but he'd been told he couldn't use his cellphone while they were in the air, more's the pity.

In the front, there were, perhaps unsurprisingly, pilots. Seated opposite him there was a woman. A fairly attractive woman, in Jeremy's professional opinion. She'd been there since he'd come aboard. She'd looked up from her laptop as he climbed in the cabin, nodded briefly and proceeded to ignore him. She didn't look like staff, so presumably she was a fellow traveller, heading for the same destination. He'd made several attempts to catch her eye. He was usually good at that, and there wasn't a whole lot of competition, but she seemed studiously uninterested. Jeremy wondered if was genuine uninterest, or if she was making a point of being uninterested, in which case his luck was very much in.

Jeremy had found that women often liked to show their interest by feigning uninterest. He had no idea why they would do that, but they did. Women often did the opposite of what you'd expect. You're talking to a woman, you're getting along fine, and it looks like it might be leading somewhere and then she mentions, almost carelessly, her boyfriend. Right away, your instinct is: she has a boyfriend, better back off, this is never going to happen. But you'd be wrong. She's not just mentioning her boyfriend to put you off: she's mentioning it to remind herself she has a boyfriend and she shouldn't be as attracted to you as she is. The boyfriend mention is her Alamo, my friend. Once the boyfriend is mentioned, you're on a cert.

Here's an even better one: a girl agrees to go to bed with you, but very firmly insists there will be no intercourse, which you both know is probably not true, but you go along with it anyway because you're a gentleman, and certainly you would never dream of having non-consensual sex. This day and age, you want the consent in writing, my friend, with at least three countersignatures from professional people of excellent standing, her mother and her father and, if practicable, all four of her grandparents, or you're a rapist.

So, she gets into bed with you, and in order to preserve the no-sex myth, she discards everything except her knickers. Well, that's money in the bank, buddy. That is, let's get real, a face-saving mechanism. 'Hey, I got into bed with this guy and stripped off and got into some serious foreplay action with him, but, ladies and gentlemen, I KEPT MY KNICKERS ON. Everyone knows that knickers are impenetrable even to the most agreeable and persistent penis. How on Earth we progressed from that innocent erotic enterprise to full, consensual intercourse is a bizarre mystery. And why we, furthermore, repeated this same, inexcusable act five more times in less than as many hours is so far beyond inexplicable, it beggars belief. I may sue those panty manufacturers. Their product should offer more sturdy protection.'

So, no problem if the girl was ignoring him. Especially if she was ignoring him deliberately. Bring it on, sister. Jeremy had stuff to do, anyway. Prime Ministerially allocated stuff. He could play the deliberate ignoring game, too. He took out the folder Debs had given him and worked his way through it.

Something changed in the chopper. Jeremy couldn't tell if it was the sound of the blades or the angle of attack. He looked out of the window. Yes, they were definitely descending.

There was some sort of camp below them. Like a holiday camp, or maybe a barracks. It was big. It was very big. They were already too low to take all of it in, but from above, the buildings all seemed to be laid out like giant Ferris wheels.

They landed on the large, white H in a circle, and the pilots cut the engines. Shame. Jeremy had wanted to race out, ducking under the blades through the dust storm they were kicking up, with someone shouting a greeting to him over the impressive din, as though he were not just a very important person, but a very important person in a hurry.

The woman put her laptop away, smiled at him and offered her hand. 'Jemma,' she informed him.

'Jeremy.'

'Nice to meet you. Didn't want to get into all that with the blades roaring. Worse than trying to chat in a nightclub.'

She'd been on a chopper before. 'Absolutely,' Jeremy agreed. 'Can't stand it either.'

They clambered down the steps from the chopper.

'And what are you doing here, Jeremy?'

'Oh, I'm just here to check the place out. Get the lie of the land, sort of thing.' At the behest of the Prime Minister of Great Britain, he wanted to add, but was worried it might sound a tad pompous.

'Well, obviously that's why we're all here. But what are you? A doctor? A lawyer?'

'I'm a Conceptuologist.'

'You're a what, now?'

'A Conceptuologist. I take ideas from Notion to Nation.' The girl was still looking blank. This was often the way, Jeremy found, when you tried to explain what it was you did to the hoi polloi. He smiled indulgently. 'Look, the word "concept" comes from the same root as conception. I nurture notions through their birth process. In a way, I'm a concept paediatrician.' And still blank. 'A concept marketer. I take concepts and find ways to accentuate their appeal.'

'You're in PR?'

That stung. 'Not really. I'm a Conceptuologist. What about you?'

'I'm a Knowledge Awareness Investigator and Dispersal-isator.'

Was she taking the piss? 'I'm sorry?'

She giggled. 'I'm a research assistant. I report to the Dietary Research Department at ULIST, which, in turn, reports to the Government.'

A research assistant. In other words, a student. Where was she getting her airs and graces from?

A man wearing a yellow hard hat drove up to them in an electric golf cart. He got out, nodded at Jeremy's companion and smiled. 'Jemma.'

She nodded back. 'Pete.' This was not her first visit.

He handed her a hard hat and turned to Jeremy. 'And you would be Jeremy Slake?'

'Jeremy Slank.'

'Sorry, Slank. The PR guy, right?'

Jeremy winced, but didn't correct him. What was the point? Pearls before swine. He smiled and took the proffered hard hat. It would seriously screw up his hairstyle, but it was doubtless compulsory. These days, you had to wear a hard hat to pick up a screwdriver. He'd seen men working on kerbstones on his street wearing hard hats, and he couldn't for the life of him figure out why. There seemed to have been no serious threat from above, unless someone was planning a suicide jump from a nearby rooftop, in which case the hard hats would, presumably, have been of scant use.

'I'm Peter Stone, Project Manager of this happy holiday home here. And I've been told to give you the full VIP tour. Is that OK?'

Jeremy said, 'Sure,' then realised the man had been talking to Jemma, who probably knew the tour by heart.

'That's fine with me, Pete.' Jemma smiled. 'I imagine there's been some changes.'

'Oh, yes. Some refinements, definitely.' Stone gestured for them to move off, and they did.

'OK, the stats: it's a four-hundred-acre site, with four planned phases. We've already completed phase one, and we're almost there on two. This fence skirts the entire perimeter, that's almost four miles of fencing . . .'

The fence was crosshatched wire, and sturdy wire at that, and it was at least twenty feet tall. Pretty much unclimbable, unless you were a circus acrobat.

Jeremy said, 'That is some serious fence, there. Is it electrified?'

Stone laughed. 'No. And there are no machine gun posts either. The intake here won't exactly be prisoners, but the regime will be pretty tough, and we don't want to encourage any potential quitters. We figure if they're fit enough to scale that fence, they'll be fit enough to leave.'

'Will there be guards on the gate?'

'There will be a security presence, but they'll be there more for stopping the ne'er-do-wells getting in than stopping the clientele getting out.'

'What happens if someone does escape?'

'They'll be chased by a giant rubber ball and suffocated. Look, Jeremy, it's not a prison camp. The people here will be morbidly obese. We're in a valley, and we're pretty remote. If one of them does try to bolt, they'll probably race thirty yards up the hill and collapse in a whipped-cream-deprivation coma. Let's take the tour.'

As they climbed into the golf cart, Jeremy finally caught the briefest glimpse of Jemma's knickers. Definitely *not* La Perla. Not even a thong. They were very businesslike low-rise shorts, less than a tenner for a pack of three from good old M&S, unless he was very much mistaken. Sturdy and practical, but that mattered not one whit. Jeremy conservatively reckoned they would be dangling from his bedpost before dawn.

TEN

Hayleigh resealed the magazine in its plastic wrapper and gave Jase just one last kiss. Hayleigh was a good kisser, in her own estimation. Seven or maybe eight on a scale of ten, she reckoned. She'd never actually kissed an actual boy quite yet – she'd never actually met an actual boy she'd like to actually kiss, if you want to know the truth – but she practised quite a lot: on her pillow, and on her hand, shaping the thumb and forefinger so they formed a very lifelike pair of lips. Plus, she'd seen an awful lot of screen kisses, so it wasn't like there was any big mystery. No big mystery, either, as to who the imaginary recipient of these practice snogs might be.

The letter from school was near the front of *Chick Chat*, wrapped in a plastic envelope of its own so it didn't get sogged from the food. The food was nearer the back of the magazine, sandwiched between a double-page spread on the pathetic manufactured boy band Cuz Weer Uz, who, in all seriousness, deserved everything they got, soggy food wise.

She was all ready to go now, with a few minutes before the call down. She opened her curtains to look out onto the dismal day. It was grey and wet out there, as it always seemed to be nowadays. Hayleigh, quite frankly, couldn't remember what the summer was like. The sun was struggling to cut through layer upon layer of stubborn cloud, and look: there was the moon. You didn't often see the sun and the moon in the sky together.

Hayleigh froze. It was a half-moon. Was it waxing or waning? That was the key question. If it was on the rise . . .

She rushed to check her diary. The thirteenth. She flicked back the pages. Crappy crud burgers! She should be on.

Hayleigh had started her periods a long time ago. She had been barely ten. Inside of a year, they'd become very regular indeed. You could set your watch by them. But lately, the last six months or so, they'd stopped. She was quite glad about that, really. They didn't seem to bring any particular benefits along with them, just unpleasantness and pains and some wild mood swings and pretty much nothing good after the initial novelty of Finally Being A Woman had worn off. But she was worried that if Mum found out, she might consider it another symptom of Hayleigh's Imagined Ailments. She might even have to face a grilling from a doctor and all kinds of psychiatrists and experts and wind up being force fed, which was the threat. She just couldn't bear to go through that malarkey. She still had a ton of weight to lose, and nobody seemed to understand that. Nobody seemed capable of wrapping their heads around that one at all.

She went into her drawer and took out the Swiss Army knife she'd slightly borrowed from Jonny's room, and flipped open the box containing the pink waterproof plasters she'd slightly liberated from the kitchen first aid kit. She dashed over to her door and cracked it open. She could hear Jonny rapping along to his terrible hip-hop music in the bedroom opposite. It was a fetching little ditty. Someone was going to 'shit on the bed, you son of a bitch'. Lovely. A Brahms chorale, perhaps? The Mormon Tabernacle Choir? Matins live from St Peter's?

Nobody else was around. Nobody likely to interrupt. She clicked the door closed and dashed over to her bathroom. No lock on the door, of course. Although she was unlikely to be disturbed in here, it could happen. Mum was fairly thought-less when it came to her children's privacy, and she might wander in without thinking to replace the loo roll, or the soap or some such thing, and if she caught Hayleigh doing this . . .

Quickly, then. She removed a sanitary towel from its packaging and sat down on the loo. She held the knife over her palm. No time for timidity, here. You have to be bold and decisive, otherwise it doesn't work and it hurts. A lot.

She made a smooth cut, about two centimetres long, precisely along her life line. If you cut along the lines, you won't leave too bad a scar. She squeezed either side of the incision. You needed quite a lot of blood for this to be convincing. She let it drip onto the towel. In the early days, she'd tried doing it with ink, but you could never quite get the right shade of red. Plus, ink didn't age in the same way as blood, and if the towels lay in the waste bin for days, as well they might, they just wouldn't be convincing. Besides which, ink smelled like ink, and blood . . . didn't.

She jumped as she heard her mother's foghorn summons. 'Come on, Hayleigh, we're late!' as if this were some kind of shock-horror newsflash. As if there were some morning they were not running late. She smeared the towel with the rest of the blood, then ran her hand under the cold tap until the bleeding seemed to have been stanched. She dried it quickly on the sanitary towel and applied the plaster. She dropped the doctored towel into the little metal pedal bin below her sink, then pressed on the wound and checked the blood wasn't leaking out. Excellent. Job done.

Just as she finished, the second, slightly more impatient shout rang up the stairs. Hayleigh ran out onto the landing calling: 'Coming, for God's sake!' and was halfway down the second flight before she remembered the magazine and had to spin round and double back, a manoeuvre that was guaranteed to provoke a minor curse of impatience from her waiting mother, but there was no avoiding that.

She grabbed *Chick Chat* and bounded down the stairs again. 'Forgot my mag!' She grinned, grabbed the school-bag her dad was proffering and stuffed the carefully packaged contraband inside with casual haste. Again, job done.

'You'd forget your head if it wasn't screwed on.' Her dad chuckled limply.

'It's not screwed on,' Jonny chimed in. 'She's a bloody

mentalist.' He started crabbing down the hall sideways in a wild exaggeration of Hayleigh's own movements earlier.

'Look at me, I'm Crab Woman. I'm the mighty Crab Girl. He spun and threw himself forward so he bodysurfed on the hall floorboards back towards the door. 'Weeeeee. I'm a crime-fighting idiot. I'm Moron Girl.'

Now, here's an odd thing. Although she wanted Jonny to die, and if she could have pressed a button that would make him drop dead on the spot right then, she would have had her thumb on it and been pressing like fury, Hayleigh actually thought he was being quite funny. She actually smiled.

Mum and Dad looked, quite frankly, baffled. If she had to speculate, Hayleigh would have guessed they were more worried about Jonny's sanity than hers.

Dad coughed nervously, 'Uh, Jonny . . .'

Jonny straightened himself at the door and struck a super-hero pose. 'I'm Mental Girl! I have the secret power to creep sideways down the hall.'

'That's great, Jonny.' Dad patted him on the head. 'But here, on planet Earth, we have to go to school right now.' And he shoved Jonny in the back, gently propelling him through the open door.

Jonny ran down the drive to the ridiculous eco-unfriendly 4x4, singing, 'Na na na na na na na na na na na na na na na na Mad Girl!'

Dad held out his arms to Hayleigh, so she was able, legitimately, to race past the mirror with her eyes on Dad and leap into a hug. One potential crinkle moment averted, thanks to Jase, then she pelted off to the car.

Hayleigh climbed into the ridiculously huge back seat of the gas-guzzling monster truck. She always allowed Jonny the dubious privilege of riding shotgun in the front, though it was technically her birthright as the eldest sibling. She didn't mind, because (a) it was easier to find a spot in a mirror-free zone back there, (b) any so-called 'erratic' behaviour on her part would be less noticeable and (c) it was slightly less likely Mum would lecture her in the rear position. Slightly. She also had fewer distractions and could concentrate on the wonderful advertising billboards that lined the route to school, and admire all those countless beautiful models and actresses with impossibly heavenly body shapes that Hayleigh could never dream of aspiring to in her wildest imagination.

Well, it had been a fairly typical morning, fraught with danger, anguish and near-death experiences, as per. But a reasonably successful one, so far. Calories consumed: zero. Fat intake: zero grams. Carbohydrates: nil points. In the minus column, of course, one ruined magazine, one small incision on the palm and . . .

Hayleigh's stomach somersaulted.

She had left the knife and the plaster box in her bathroom.

ELEVEN

The living quarters were prefabricated buildings, with very few frills. They were basically dormitories with a large sitting area attached. Jeremy assumed they were being taken around the 'show' barracks because there were a few incongruously lavish homely touches in what otherwise looked like a POW camp.

Stone was talking all the time in a more or less bored drone, depending on his personal interest in the facts and figures he was dispensing, interrupted by the occasional exchange with one of the many groups of hard-hatted workmen still labouring on the final touches. Jeremy hoped there would be some kind of handout at the end of the tour because he had no chance of remembering absolutely any of it.

The place was laid out with cold efficiency. Jeremy suspected the architect had been German. All the buildings were ruthlessly symmetrical. They were clustered into groups which led to a central point, like spokes in a wheel. The central points were like mini town squares. Each had a gym complex – each gym brutally stocked – a cafeteria, which was starkly over-lit and uninviting, quite deliberately so, Jeremy assumed. No venue for leisurely feasts or romantic tête-à-têtes, this. There were shops, mostly as yet unstocked, though the unit next to the gym entrance boasted a wide array of oversized jogging outfits and exercise suits in gaudy colours, and even had prices on display. The prices were marked in an unfamiliar currency, which Jeremy found vaguely disturbing.

'Uh, Pete: what are these prices? Jogging top 10g? Tennis racquet 1K?'

'Right. Normal currency can't be used here. Instead, residents have to earn credits in local currency. They earn those credits by losing weight. Each one has a fitness account and a credits card, which they insert at their daily weigh-in. You lose weight, your account gets credited. You gain weight, it's debited.'

That sounded a little draconian to Jeremy. 'So, you lose ten grams, you can buy a jogging top? You lose a kilo, you can get a racquet?'

'Exactly.'

'What if you're just not losing weight?'

Stone shrugged. 'Then you can't buy anything. Should be a great incentive.'

'So, what other kinds of shops will you have?'

'Oh, clothes shops, outsize clothes shops mostly, of course; electronics shops, you know, for iPods and step-counters, personal heart-rate monitors, that sort of thing. There'll be music stores, bicycle shops—'

Jeremy grinned. 'Sweet shops?'

'Definitely no sweet shops. No food shops of any kind outside the cafeterias.'

'And people have to pay for their food, too?'

'Not in so many words. They all have a food allowance, which is integrated onto their credits card. Their personal evaluator sets their daily diet limits, so it's virtually impossible to go off programme.'

Jemma interjected, 'I think you'll find that's a trifle optimistic. People being people, there's bound to be some kind of black market, some kind of peer-to-peer food trading.'

Stone nodded. 'We expect a degree of that, at least. But the way things are organised, someone's going to have to starve for someone else to overeat.'

'Unless,' Jemma suggested, 'someone starts smuggling food in. From the outside.'

'That's possible. Corrupt staff. It could happen. But nobody's allowed to eat outside the cafeterias, and everyone eats at set times. You get caught eating outside of that, you'll lose all kinds of privileges. And there are CCTV cameras everywhere.'

'Even in the loos?'

'*Every*where.'

'And who's monitoring them?'

'Each of these communal centres has a monitoring room at the top, each with a hundred and fifty screens, each screen divided into four. There are crews of ten monitoring officers, each on hour-on, hour-off shifts, and the rooms are manned round the clock. You can't wipe your backside here without it going on report.'

'Well, this is new.' Jemma looked grim. 'Big Brother is definitely watching us.'

Stone shook his head. 'We don't like the Big Brother reference. It really has negative connotations. This is not for public consumption. Jeremy – we really don't want this whole monitoring business mentioned outside of this conversation.'

'Don't worry. I'm not insane. I'm here to sell this idea.'

Stone brightened. 'Of course. That's good. Plus, if residents start overeating, we can assume they'll start putting on weight, lose credits and have nothing to trade. I think it's about as foolproof as a system can possibly get.'

Jeremy changed the subject. 'What about cinemas? TVs? I didn't see any screens in the living areas.'

'No TV. We definitely don't want to encourage couch potato-ism. What we're aiming for, really, is lifestyle change for the clients. Lifestyle change they can take home with them. There's a large cinema room in each communal area. We may show a movie one day a week, but it'll probably cost a lot of credits to get a ticket. Mostly, we'll be showing sporting events, which will be cheaper for residents. Of course, there are screens in the gym. You can watch Richard and Judy, so long as you're clocking up seven kilometres per hour on the jogging machine.'

'I like the lifestyle-change element.' Jeremy took out his notepad. 'That will definitely play.'

Jemma asked, 'What about books?'

Stone shook his head. 'Not as such. No bookshops, no libraries. Again, we don't want to be encouraging any kind of sedentary behaviour. Here and there, some in-house publications. Health education. Pro-exercise literature. That kind of thing.'

Jemma grinned charmingly. 'Why, Peter Stone, I do believe you mean "propaganda".'

Stone grinned right back at her. 'Hey, if trying to bring sick people to health makes me Goebbels, then hang me at Nuremberg.'

Jeremy finished scribbling. 'So what do the residents do all day?'

'Well, they exercise. They exercise a lot. At least two gym sessions a day. They insert their credits card into each workout station, and the levels and duration of each exercise are monitored. They're not allowed to leave the gymnasia until they've met the targets set by their personal evaluator, and they get double credits for everything over that. And they eat, of course. We've tried to make that particular experience as unrewarding as possible, for obvious reasons. The cafeterias are not an environment where many people would want to linger. The seats are uncomfortable – in fact, most of the seating in the village is deliberately uncomfortable – and the decor is unappealing. In a way, we're hoping we might engender a kind of negative Pavlovian response to eating in general, and we're hoping that response stays with clients when they leave.'

'Fit for life?' Jeremy offered.

Stone grinned and said with genuine admiration, 'You're good. That's a great slogan. Use it.'

'I will, don't worry.'

Jemma piped in: 'What about sex?'

Jeremy turned to her, quick as a whip. 'Not now, Jemma, there's people watching.'

Jemma laughed and punched him on the shoulder. That was good. That was a good sign.

Stone said, 'Actually, we want to encourage sex. It's terrific exercise, you know. We plan to have dances every night. Dancing is great exercise, too.'

Jemma asked, 'Alcohol?'

'No. No alcohol. No drugs. We're zero tolerance on that one. There will be therapy sessions for addicts, group and individual.'

Frankly, Jeremy thought that the prospect of morbidly obese people having sex without the aid of alcohol or drugs was extremely unlikely, but he asked anyway: 'And the people who do have sex, they'll be monitored on CCTV, presumably?'

'Unfortunately, yes. But those portions of the recordings will be wiped immediately.'

'Theoretically,' Jemma said. 'Human nature being what it is, though, you can't help thinking some of those sessions will show up on a security guard compilation video.'

Stone shook his head. 'Not a chance. Anyone tries pulling that number, they'll wind up doing prison time. Just for watching it.'

Jeremy said, 'Someone will have to watch them to wipe them.'

'That's unfortunate, I agree. But I don't see what we could do about it. Maybe we'll think about providing unmonitored sex zones, but off the top of my head, any exceptions like that will be open to massive abuse.'

Jemma nodded. 'Absolutely – people could cheat their way into the sex zones and have a full-on chocolate orgy instead of shagging. The dirty bastards.'

Jeremy loved a girl who talked dirty. 'What about work?'

'Well, at first there will be opportunities to volunteer for maintenance work and earn extra credits. General cleaning and so on. More opportunities for people with skills: electricians, plumbers and such. In the long term, though, we see no reason why the Well Farms can't be self-sustaining. They're all constructed on good farmland. We could have our own organic produce. Even chickens and dairy cattle. And farm work is hellishly good exercise. But that's for later. For . . . obvious reasons, I think.'

The reasons were not obvious to Jeremy, but Jemma was nodding, and he didn't want to look thick, so he gave a curt nod, too, praying that Stone didn't ask him what the obvious reasons might be. It seemed he'd underestimated Jemma, pigeon-holing her as a mere 'student'. She was clearly exceptionally bright, and Stone was paying her a great deal of respect. Obviously, the job title 'research assistant' had more cachet in the scientific community than it did in his own.

Their wanderings through the mall had brought them to an intriguing-looking shop not yet stocked: Rock Stop.

'You'll be selling musical instruments?' Jeremy asked.

'Absolutely.' Stone nodded. 'Electric guitars, basses, drums and such. We're hoping residents will form bands and play at the nightly dances.'

'Violins, clarinets . . . ?'

'No. Just rock stuff. The PM's a big fan of rock music, plus it makes the place a bit funkier. But none of that chamber music crap. Nobody ever got fit playing the bloody piccolo.'

'What about policing?' Jemma asked. 'I mean, a community this size, there's bound to be crime. Do you have an onsite police presence?'

Stone shook his head. 'Look, this is a voluntary community. We don't anticipate much in the way of serious crime. But we do have a relationship with the local police force. We have a panic button, and they undertake to be onsite within twenty minutes. Plus, we have our own security guards.'

'But they don't have the power of arrest? There's no detention cells?'

Stone shook his head again. 'It's a health farm, Jemma. When did you last see a SWAT team descend on Clivedon?'

'Well, I think you're making a mistake.' Jemma smiled grimly. 'A very big mistake indeed.'

TWELVE

Hayleigh was in a fugue of despair. How could she have been so careless? And today, of all days. Wednesday was cleaning day. Mum would almost certainly be in her bathroom at some point. Would she work it out? The bloody blade, the plaster, the sanitary towel? Would she put those things together and work it out?

Of course she'd work it out. Even dumb old dummkopf Lieutenant Randy Disher could probably work it out, low as he was in the detecting food chain.

So now she had to come up with a seriously convincing alternative explanation. She'd cut herself trying to shave her legs. With a Swiss Army knife? Well, that would make her look stupid, but it would be less of a disaster than being caught trying to fake menstruation. But then there was the telltale plaster on her palm. Would that cut have healed sufficiently by the afternoon? At least enough to cover it with make-up, assuming she could get hold of some make-up? And then she'd have to cut herself again on the leg and re-use the plaster from her hand. And if both wounds were discovered, then it might look like she was self-harming, like Bella Goodwyn in year five last term.

Maybe that wouldn't be such a bad thing. At least they didn't try to make self-harmers fat. They didn't force feed self-harmers, as far as Hayleigh was aware.

The Planetary Destroyer pulled up. Jonny leapt to his knees on his seat, said, slightly too loudly over the gangsta din from his iPod earphones, 'Thanks, Mum!' then swivelled round to face Hayleigh, chirped, 'Later, you mentalist,' and sprang out of the car.

Mum turned round. 'Would you like to get in front, Hayleigh?'

It wasn't a question. 'No, I'm all right here, thanks,' Hayleigh tried.

Mum patted the seat. 'Front. Now.'

Hayleigh clambered out of the car, slouched to the front and clambered back in again.

Mum smiled. 'That's better. Now I can see your pretty face.' She brushed Hayleigh's hair away from her cheek and smiled a mumsy smile. She slipped the Sport Utility Behemoth into gear and burned off a few litres of non-sustainable fossil fuel. 'I want you to have dinner with us all tonight, darling.'

Hayleigh tried not to let her expression slump, but she couldn't help it. 'Sure. No problemo.'

'I worry about you, you know.'

'I'm fine, Mum. Really I am.'

'And I want us all to have breakfast together.'

'Tomorrow? Sure.'

'Not just tomorrow. Every day.'

Every *day*?

'Don't look like that, Hayleigh. It's important family time. It's the one time we're all always around. We should all spend it together.'

And do what? Watch Dad find new, previously undiscovered areas to scratch? Thrill to the endless taunts and jibes the performing monkey-boy Jonny would hurl at her relentlessly? Well, that would be fun. That would make a fine start to the day. Or they could just load five chambers of a revolver and force her to play Russian roulette every morning. 'Fine. That'll be great.' Hayleigh nodded with a poorly forced grin. She would probably have to put up with this ridiculousness for the rest of the week, then the rule would relax and she could get on with her own way of living her life again.

That was assuming, of course, she survived the Swiss Army knife debacle.

THIRTEEN

The police intercepted Grenville's vehicle, if you could still call it a vehicle, on the entertainment complex roundabout. He hadn't spotted them in his driver's mirror because it had been tortured into a modern art sculpture by the exit barrier's surprisingly sturdy arm and was facing away from him; nor in his wing mirrors, because he no longer had any. He no longer had any wings. But he heard the siren very clearly through the gaping hole where his windscreen had been.

They overtook him and turned on their stop sign, and he pulled over obediently and waited in the car, because he seemed to remember the police don't like it if you get out.

After what seemed to Grenville an unnecessarily substantial interval, two uniforms emerged from the police car: one a ruddy-faced, squat man who turned out to be Scots, the other a tall, wiry man with close-cropped hair. They both looked very serious and threatening, and Gren was worried he might be in for a drubbing.

They ambled up to him, the radios on their lapels barking occasional nonsense, and crouched to his level at the driver's side window. The tall one tapped on the window and made a circular motion Grenville understood to mean he should wind his window down. Old-fashioned sign language, really, this day and age, Gren was thinking. Who manufactured cars with non-electric hand-operated window winders this side of the millennium? Might as well have mimes for turning over the engine with a hand crank. He pressed the electronic window button and the little window motor whirred and strained inside the door, but the window only budged a fraction of an inch or so and then juddered and struggled until he gave up.

Grenville made a helpless gesture with his hands and squeezed his lips into a suitably cowering apologetic expression. The ruddy Scot tightened his face and looked away, but Grenville couldn't tell if he was suppressing anger or merriment. The tall one straightened, took a step forward and leaned towards the windscreen gap.

'Are you aware, sir,' he asked with considerable gravity, 'that your rear licence plate bulb is out?'

And with that the Scot all but collapsed in a raucous fit of hysterical laughter, slapping his thighs. The tall one was trying not to snicker, but he wasn't making a terribly good fist of it. 'Would you mind stepping out of the vehicle, sir?'

Confident, now, that he wasn't facing a quick going over with a pair of telescopic truncheons, Grenville reached down to unbuckle his seatbelt, which set the Scot off again, and tried to open his door, but it seemed to be jammed solid. Horrified he might have to be winched out through the windscreen, he doubled his efforts and after two or three sturdy shoulder charges, the severely weakened door relented and came off its hinges completely.

Grenville climbed out of the car and walked noisily over the prone door, which rocked with each step, and jumped off onto the road as if it were the most normal thing in the world, and surely everybody did that, everywhere, pretty much every day, then strolled with what he hoped was nonchalant dignity around the car's smoking bonnet and onto the pavement.

Neither of the policemen seemed able to speak. Both were wearing tortured expressions, as if they were sucking incredibly sour boiled sweets they dared not spit out.

Grenville looked back at the remains of his car. It was, indeed, a comical disgrace. Charlie Caroli himself would not have been seen dead in it. No wonder the lad at the McDonald's hatch window had gawked at him so oddly.

The tall one had composed himself sufficiently to be capable, almost, of speech. 'Have some kind of . . .' He forced his lips together, but couldn't prevent a small series of farty noises escaping from his mouth. 'Have some sort of a prang, did we, sir?'

Right. This was what Grenville needed to complete his Perfect Morning. Two comedians in police uniforms taking the piss out of him in public and broad daylight. No, wait. Here was the crowning glory. A couple of passers-by seemed to have recognised him from the television and were recording his humiliation on their mobile-phone cameras for all posterity to enjoy at their collective leisure. Bring it on.

Now more angry than afraid, Grenville steeled his expression, drew himself to his full height and said, with hefty dignity: 'Is there a problem, Officers?'

That did it for Scotty. He literally doubled up in an uncontrolled guffawing fit, and couldn't stop for a good two minutes. His face had gone from ruddy to bright, shiny scarlet. He leaned on the tall policeman's shoulder, too weak from the laugh attack to support himself with any confidence.

Grenville did not react; did not move a muscle; certainly, did not smile. Bring it on, you blue bastards.

The tall one again calmed down first. 'I'm afraid, sir, I'm going to have to place you under arrest,' he announced, in all seriousness, though his voice was cracking.

Arrest? They were placing him under *arrest*? As if he was some kind of *criminal*? 'Arrest? What for?'

'For being a complete bloody *twat*!' Scotty-boy blurted, and went off on one again.

'You are not obliged to say anything . . .' the tall one said.

He was reading Grenville his rights. Grenville felt his head suddenly swell alarmingly. Heat rushed to his cheeks and there was a strange kind of wet buzzing in his ears. He could no longer hear the policeman's voice. They couldn't be arresting him. He had a show to do. He had to be at the studios in, what? Two hours. This had to be some kind of wind-up.

He snapped out of the funk when he realised Tall Boy was expecting some kind of response from him.

'I said: do you understand, sir?'

'There must be some kind of mistake, Officer, I'm not a—'

'Do you under*stand*, sir?' The policeman's words were slow and deliberate.

'But what am I supposed to have *done*?'

'Well, why don't we talk about it at the station, sir? In the meantime, would you like me to read you your rights again?'

'No, no. That's . . . I mean, if there's any damage, I'll be happy to pay—'

A weird barking noise leapt out of Rob Roy's throat and he sprayed the air with spittle. 'Any *damage*? You fucking demolished the East Finchley David Lloyd Centre in its entirety, you bollock-brained moron!'

'Leave it out, Moggoch,' the taller one said, but he couldn't disguise his grin. 'If you'd just like to turn around, sir.'

Turn around? Were they going to search him? Good God, this was all getting a bit too serious for Grenville's liking. He turned reluctantly, placed his hands on the shell of his derelict car and spread his legs. He was, indeed, being patted down.

What a mess. The car was a mess . . . everything was a mess. And all he'd wanted to do was take a spot of bloody exercise. Demolished the health club? He didn't think so. Knocked over a couple of bollards and snapped the arm off the exit barrier, which, in all seriousness, was doing the world a major favour, surely. Most of the damage he'd caused had been done to his own property. There was no law against that, was there? Unless he tried to claim it on his insurance, which he had absolutely no intention of doing. Imagine filling out that accident claims report. 'Inadvertently backed into a giant monster truck at thirty miles an hour, then inadvertently backed into the same truck at thirty miles an hour again, then accidentally knocked over three cast-iron bollards set in concrete as if they were skittles in a bowling alley after two or three attempts.' No, thank you. There would be no insurance claim. What, then, was his crime?

He felt the officer's hand grip his own firmly, and heard the disturbing clink of metal behind him. 'What are you . . . ?' The officer bent his arm behind his back, not painfully, but not gently, either. 'Are you going to . . .' He heard the metallic snap and felt the restraint close around his wrist. 'Are you handcuffing me?' Grenville hissed in distress and horror.

'Sorry, sir. It's just procedure.' He secured Grenville's other arm and snapped the second cuff closed.

'But what am I supposed to have *done*?'

The policeman gently pushed his shoulder and spun him round. 'If you'd just like to come this way, sir?' As if it were an invitation. As if Grenville had any choice in the matter, whatsoever.

He walked, slow and reluctant, to the police car. The oglers were still snapping away. Possibly, even, recording his tragic nightmare onto video. He felt like a drug runner or a serial killer, finally snared after months of manhunt. In fact, didn't those people get a blanket thrown over their heads to shield them from public scrutiny? Was Grenville not to be allowed even that small favour, afforded as a matter of course to mass murders and evil terrorists? Grenville turned his head and glared filthily at the photo-happy mob, creating a perfect image of hounded derangement which would make page five of three of the tabloids the following morning.

The police car was a Skoda. Dear me. Grenville couldn't possibly fit in the back of that, but William Wallace was holding open the back door, and the big lad was steering him towards it. 'Would it be a problem, Officers,' Grenville asked politely, 'if I sat in the front?'

The policemen looked at each other. It seemed to Grenville they were seriously pondering his perfectly reasonable request. At last, some ordinary human respect.

'I don't know,' the tall one said. 'What d'you think, Moggoch?'

The Scottish one bent his lips in an inverted bow. 'Don't see why not. Christ – why don't we let the bastard drive?'

He'd barely got the words out before he was seized again by a shuddering fit. They both went this time.

The Scotsman really did have to wipe the tears from his eyes. 'I'll tell you what, big boy, you are first-rate entertainment value. Get in the car.' He forced Grenville's head down and roughly shoved him into the back seat so Gren was lying face down laterally across it.

The laughing policeman knelt on the edge of the seat behind him. 'Sit up,' he barked.

But that, sadly, was an impossibility. With his arms pinned behind him by the handcuffs, Grenville had no leverage. The horrible truth is, a gentleman of Grenville's dimensions cannot lift himself with his stomach muscles alone, as if he were a teenage lad with a six-pack. In a sad, quiet voice, muffled by the seat, he said: 'I can't.'

'You what?'

Grenville lifted his head up and twisted his neck as best he could. 'I can't sit up.'

'Jesus.' The Scot grabbed his arm, and with Grenville's cooperation managed to manoeuvre him more or less upright. 'Comfy?' he asked, sardonically.

'Not really.'

'Right.' The policeman tugged at the seatbelt and tried to latch it, but it wouldn't reach. Not even nearly. 'Budge back a bit.'

Grenville tried to accommodate the request, but it was a doomed enterprise.

Beam Me Up Scotty tugged at the belt, pushed and prodded at Grenville's belly, then tugged again, enjoining

86

Gren to breathe in, cursing and muttering under his breath all the while.

'What's going on back there?' the tall one asked from the driver's seat.

'Can't get the bastard seatbelt on. Look! Won't go anywhere near him.'

The tall one turned and they both spent a few moments marvelling at this phenomenon, as if it were some inexplicable miracle, and perhaps they should be thinking about calling the Vatican to get it verified, which Grenville found not even mildly humiliating, though he did pray, quite fiercely, for a lightning bolt to strike him dead on the spot, and possibly the two police officers as well, but such gods as were listening extended him no such mercy.

'What are we going to do?' Moggoch asked.

'Forget it.'

For a tiny second Grenville thought that meant they were going to let him go, that his mighty bulk had been his salvation. But no.

'You're joking,' the Scot said. 'What if we crash? I don't want this bastard shooting through the windscreen with me sandwiched in between. They'd have to scoop me up with a bucket.'

'I'll drive carefully.'

'Shuffle over,' Moggoch ordered Grenville. 'Behind the driver's seat.'

Grenville shuffled. There was even less legroom behind the driver's seat, but all the protest had been driven out of him. This was ridiculous. He was a few pounds overweight, that was all, and yet here he was being made to feel like the bloody Elephant Man.

Robert the Bruce slammed the door on him and climbed into the front.

'What about my car?' Grenville asked.

Moggoch turned to him, his face a picture of delight. 'Your what, now?'

'My car.' He nodded at the wretched wreck of a thing. 'You're not just going to leave it there, are you? Shouldn't one of you drive it to the station?'

Rabbie Burns was chuckling quite openly. 'Don't you worry about that, sir. We'll send someone to pick it up.' He nodded to his companion. 'Put in the call, Micky. Get them to send someone from the Clown Division.'

LUNCH
Menu

A Disturbingly Green Kiwi Smoothie
Chickpea Cutlet with Some Kind of Wild Rice Crap

❦

Steamed Chicken

❦

Sloppy Porridge Crawling with Roaches

or

Steak Pie with Chips, Baked Beans and Gravy

or

An Unlucky Juicy Centipede

❦

Absolutely Nothing At All with the Merest Hint
of Apple

PHYSICIAN: He no doubt orders you to eat plenty of roast-meat.

ARGAN: No; nothing but boiled meat.

PHYSICIAN: Yes, yes; roast or boiled, it is all the same; he orders very wisely, and you could not have fallen into better hands.

ARGAN: Sir, tell me how many grains of salt I ought to put to an egg?

PHYSICIAN: Six, eight, ten, by even numbers; just as in medicines by odd numbers.

(Molière: *Le Malade Imaginaire*, 1673)

FOURTEEN

Jeremy scanned the food on offer in the institute cafeteria. The fare was, predictably, astonishingly healthy-looking. Which is to say, unappetising in the extreme. Brown rice, wholewheat pasta, limp-looking and therefore, presumably, organic salad items. Steamed and unseasoned vegetables. Nothing here had ever felt the gentle caress of a knob of butter, the tender sprinkle of a pinch of salt. Certainly, none of it had ever seen the inside of a frying pan. Neither, in any other circumstances, would any of it ever have seen the inside of Jeremy's stomach. But he was here, and he had to show willing. Trying not to sigh, he selected a re-formed chickpea cutlet with some kind of dry wild rice crap and a disturbingly green kiwi smoothie, and looked around for Jemma.

He spotted her, waving at him from a table she'd secured by the panoramic window looking out onto the gardens. She really was quite a decent looker. A good seven, maybe even an eight in her slap and Friday-night finery. Jeremy had long ago progressed past the stage of mentally undressing women completely. Now he tended more often to picture them padding around his flat with morning-tousled hair wearing one of his shirts. He found this much more erotic. In fact, it frequently involved mentally *dressing* women in more than they were actually wearing, which Jeremy considered a sign of his growing maturity.

'I couldn't find any ketchup.' He set down his tray and waited for directions.

'Ketchup?' Jemma gurned in a strangely becoming way. 'You'll be lucky, meladdo. There's sugar in ketchup. Pure evil. If you're lucky, every third Thursday you might find they put out some ethical fair trade organic sugar-free low-fat tomato sauce substitute in a perfume-bottle-sized portion. Other than that, you bring your own and hope you don't get spotted.'

'Still.' He prodded at his sawdust cutlet. 'It's all good healthy stuff.'

She took a bite of her chicken and winced.

Jeremy smiled. 'Not good?'

'Not anything. People used to say everything tasted like chicken. Now, even chicken doesn't taste like chicken. Nobody says things taste like chicken any more because they don't know what chicken tastes like. On top of which, this chicken is steamed. Steamed meat? It never had a chance of tasting like anything.'

Jeremy watched as she slipped a salt cellar out of her bag and shook liberal amounts of the deadly white crystals on the offensive meat. His eyes widened censoriously. 'Well, that's one way of doing it. Or you could just leave the chicken entirely and put a bullet through your brain.'

She looked up. 'So what now? You disagree with salt?'

He shrugged with his face. 'It's your life.'

'And I'm risking it by adding salt to my food?'

'Come on, now. It's a killer.'

'It's a killer?'

'Everyone knows that.'

'Everyone knows that? Really?'

Jeremy did not like the bite of sarcasm in her voice. 'Yes, Jemma. It's common knowledge.'

'OK, Jeremy.' She set down her cutlery. 'How's it going to kill me?'

She was shaping up to do battle. Jeremy sensed he was walking into some kind of trap.

'Blood pressure. Strokes. You should know that: you're the scientist.'

'I am indeed. I'm a scientist who's actually read the studies. And I can tell you there is no compelling evidence that excessive salt intake increases blood pressure, even by a tiny margin. Much less that such an increase would lead to strokes.'

'Oh, come on.'

'Here's the argument against salt. The theory starts with a plausible assumption: the more salt you ingest, the more water your body has to retain to maintain its sodium balance. Eventually, your kidneys respond by excreting more salt, which leads to a slight increase in blood pressure.'

'Well, there you have it.'

'The problem is, no studies have ever managed to prove that is what actually happens.'

'Now, I know that isn't true. I've seen studies quoted in Government literature—'

'I didn't say there are no studies which *claim* to prove a link. It's just that those claims are mostly scientific hogwash, where the figures have been massaged so crudely no one who believes in scientific methodology could take them seriously.'

'You're saying researchers actually made up the results? I mean, just plucked figures out of the air?'

'I always find this funny. You ever heard the Disraeli quote: "Three kinds of lies: lies, damn lies and statistics"?'

'Sure. Everyone knows you can make statistics prove just about anything.'

'I think you're right. Just about anyone knows that. Yet here you are, incredulous that respectable scientists might actually bend results to prove their case.'

'But other scientists check the results, don't they? I mean, that's how the process works, isn't it?'

'That is how it works, yes. And, mostly, a consensus is reached successfully. Just not in the case of salt. All the studies linking salt to strokes are disputed. They tend to use the Bing Crosby approach to data.'

'The what now?'

'The Bing Crosby approach.' She dropped her voice three octaves and delivered an impression of the crooner which was partly disturbing, but also partly sexy: 'Aaac-centuate the positive, eeee-liminate the negative. They just leave out the data that don't fit their conclusion. And so the link has never been satisfactorily proven.'

'But no one's *dis*proved it, either?'

She grinned. 'Depends who you believe. But no, not conclusively. It's actually one of the most fiercely contested arenas in all of science. And I'm really not sure why.'

'Well, if it's going to save lives, isn't it worth the fight?'

'Absolutely. But there's just as big an argument that reducing salt intake could cause more problems than it solves. If, indeed, it solves any at all.'

'It could cause problems?'

'Human beings *need* salt, Jeremy. We can't live without it. For instance, we need sodium to maintain blood volume. And salt is not just sodium. We need the potassium in salt for vasodilatation or constriction. We need the calcium in it for vascular smooth muscle tone. Even early civilisations recognised the essential nature of salt. What do you think "salt of the earth" is about? You know the word "salary" comes from Latin, from a time when Roman soldiers were actually *paid* in salt because it had a universal value, much more secure and cross-culturally acceptable than mere currency – in fact, in some cultures, it actually *was* currency; again, you've heard the expression "not worth his salt". In France, the imposition of the salt tax was a major factor in bringing about the Revolution . . .' She grinned. 'But now I'm ranting. Sorry.'

'But you're saying *less* salt can cause medical problems?'

'As I said, we need salt to live. Those men we saw, working outside?'

Jeremy nodded.

'It's winter now, but come the summer, they will each excrete around twenty-five grams of salt through their sweat in a working day. That's not counting what they excrete through their urine. They could not survive on six grams of salt per day. If they stick to Government guidelines, they could very well drop down dead. I hope to God they bring their own packed lunches.'

'Come on, now. Drop down dead? Don't you think that's slightly melodramatic?'

Jemma raised an eyebrow. 'You think? In the nineties, an eight-year New York study of hypertensive individuals found people on a low-sodium diet suffered four times as many heart attacks as those with normal consumption. Four *times* as many. That's exactly the opposite of what the anti-salt theory predicts.'

It was Jeremy's turn to exercise his eyebrows. Having put it off for long enough, he bit into the chickpea cutlet. It wasn't just bad, it was demonic. It didn't need seasoning as much as it needed exorcising. When he'd finally managed to swallow, he asked, 'So in what way is salt supposed to be good for us?'

'Well, amongst other things, it's vital for balancing the sugar levels in blood, the generation of hydroelectric energy in the body's cells, the nerve cells' communication and information processing, the absorption of food particles through the intestinal tract, the clearance of mucus plugs and sticky phlegm in the lungs, for clearing up catarrh and sinus congestion, it is absolutely vital to bone structure – salt shortage in the body can lead to osteoporosis; it regulates sleep, prevents gout, muscular cramping, varicose veins and spider veins. It's a very powerful, natural antihistamine. And two big relationship points here: it stops you drooling in your sleep and, most important of all, it's vital to the main-tenance of sexuality and the libido. Plus, it makes food taste better.'

Vital to the maintenance of sexuality and libido. Jeremy liked that. It definitely sounded like a come-on. He leaned forward. 'All right, so why has the Government spent literally millions on promotional campaigns to get people to consume less salt?'

Jemma shrugged with her eyebrows. 'Beats the crap out of me. Because they're idiots? Because they're advised by idiots?

Because they want to look like they care? Or maybe, and this is my personal favourite, because they like people to be scared about mostly everything. I really don't know.'

Well, she did go on a bit, this one, and she was certainly opinionated to the point of outright combat, but Jeremy decided it was probably worth putting up with the mouthiness to have a shot at getting inside those M&S low-risers. 'Tell you what.' He grinned. 'Pass the salt.'

FIFTEEN

Grenville was in a cell.

He was in a prison cell.

Grenville Roberts was doing time.

Technically, it was a holding cell, so it was not quite as well appointed, Gren imagined, as a genuine prison cell. Made of brick and concrete, it was painted a brilliant, relentless white. There was even a white brick partition separating off the toilet area. He was perched uncomfortably on a 'bed' that was more of a bench, really, again built out of bricks, topped with a smooth plank and with a folding foam-packed cushion for a mattress, such as might grace a steamer chair, thrown on top of it. He prayed he was not going to be forced to spend the night on it. Even if he managed to get most of himself on the 'bed' and maintain some kind of precarious balance all night with sufficient confidence to actually sleep, his back would never recover from the experience. Never. If he was forced to spend the night on this thing, come the morning you might as well just rip out his spine and throw it away.

How long had he been there? He looked at his wrist where his watch no longer was. It felt like three months, but it was probably less than an hour. If they could just process this ludicrous case and release him soon, he might even make the studios in time for the show.

They had removed all his possessions when they'd admitted him. He didn't understand what sort of threat he would pose if they let him keep his watch. Did they think he was going to open the case and use it as a digging tool to burrow an escape tunnel? He'd have to be in there longer than the Count of Monte Cristo just to scratch the outline in the concrete floor.

His watch, his wallet, his loose change, his keys, they'd taken the lot. They'd even taken his temporary David Lloyd Leisure Centre membership card, which they could probably keep. Grenville seriously doubted they'd be welcoming him back there with open arms any time soon. They'd also made him remove his trainers, which, as we know by now, was not a pain-free business, which invariably left him breathless and carried with it a serious threat of blacking out. And then, the crowning glory, what might actually rank as the cream of the humiliation crop in a day that had so far provided such a bumper harvest of them, and was yet barely halfway over: they had removed the elasticated drawstring from his jogging bottoms.

Now, just what did they think he was going to do with that?

Certainly, he couldn't have hanged himself with it. It was *elasticated*. Even if he'd been able to find some kind of protuberance in the ceiling to tie one end to, which there wasn't – these people weren't fools, you know: after the first few thousand cell-hanging suicides they'd stopped installing light fixtures that were potential gallows – but even if there had been something to secure a noose to, and he'd then looped the noose around his neck and managed to kick the chair away from under him, he would have simply wound up bouncing endlessly around the room like a mad bungee jumper at a punk concert. The worst damage he could have done to himself was bang his head on the ceiling a few times.

So he had to walk to the cells barefoot with one hand holding up his trousers. Fucking madness.

They had read him his rights, again, and Moggoch had described the arrest, leaving out, of course, his own sardonic remarks, but reporting absolutely everything Grenville had done and said. He was being charged with Criminal Damage under the 1971 Criminal Damage Act and Driving Without

Due Care and Attention. He'd been offered his phone call, and it had taken him quite a long time to try to decide who best to call. His first thought, oddly enough, had been his ex-wife, but he'd rejected that impulse. Wouldn't she just have loved that? Grenville banged up. She'd still be laughing next Christmas. As he thumbed with increasing desperation through his mental Rolodex, he'd realised a terrible, terrible thing.

Grenville Roberts had no friends. Nary a one. How the hell had that happened? He *used* to have friends. Good friends. And he'd kept many of them all the way to his thirties. But, gradually, they'd all got married and childrened-up, and moved around the place. And they'd kept in touch, at least at first, but then less and less, until, finally, they'd all become more or less strangers. By way of substitution, he'd acquired new friends, mostly the parents of his daughter's friends, as a matter of fact, but there wasn't the closeness there: no shared experiences; no time spent together in the trenches of youth. There was no one he felt was close enough to call and tell he was under arrest.

In the end, the most important thing was letting the production team know he might be missing today's recording, though he really didn't want them to know quite why, and he couldn't think of a suitable excuse. Besides, what if The Girl answered the phone, as well she might? Grenville could live without that particular delicious humiliation, thank you very much, on this day so rich in them.

His agent, then.

It was unfortunate that his agent had to find out about this silliness, it being fairly early in their professional relationship, and this being a unique aberration in Grenville's behaviour, and he didn't want Seth thinking he made a habit of throwing berserker rages in health club car parks, but there was nothing else for it.

He'd asked for a phone book, because he didn't know the number off by heart just yet, and he'd met with more law-enforcement derision. What did he think they were? Bloody Directory En-bloody-quiries? Did the desk sergeant *look* like one of the moustachioed tossers from the 118 adverts?

So that was that. Your one permitted phone call could only be made to phone numbers you had committed to memory. Since Grenville only actually knew two numbers – his ex-wife's and his own – he was, quite frankly, fucked. He wasn't going to let them get away without paying for a phone call, though, so he rang himself up and left a long message on his answering machine, which was mostly an abusive and bitter diatribe about the astonishingly poor standards of law enforcement in this country in general, and wild speculation about the immediate ancestry of one Scottish law enforcement officer in particular.

He'd also been offered a choice between contacting a solicitor he knew, or availing himself of one of their own duty solicitors. He only knew one solicitor: the one who'd handled his divorce, a certifiable moron whose monumental incompetence was only matched by his magnificent flair for fiction when it came to billing. So Grenville opted for the duty solicitor, who would doubtless turn out to be equally incompetent, but had the twin advantages that he would turn up sooner and he'd be charging precisely nothing.

He'd been fingerprinted, photographed and had a DNA swab taken, which entailed a pretty policewoman inserting a sort of elongated ear bud into his mouth, not all that unpleasant an experience, actually. It had been a long time since a pretty girl had touched his mouth.

But he was now in the system. Any crime, anywhere in the country, and Grenville Roberts would be one of the names that popped up on the database. Any car crime, any criminal damage, and Grenville Roberts would doubtless be hauled in for questioning and sweated under the lights for hours on end. He might as well get to like it here because it looked like he was going to be a regular visitor. Perhaps he should have his address book tattooed on his body, so he never got caught out at the phone-call stage again.

They'd asked him if he was Muslim, which seemed a bit cheeky, but it turned out they were just trying to ascertain his dietary proscriptions. Just how long were they planning to keep him here? He'd told them he was on the GI diet plan, which had just produced more merriment and derision.

He shifted his weight on the brick bench, the edges of which were cutting into his thighs, quite cruelly. How much longer before they would come and collect him? Surely the solicitor should be here by now? Surely someone was free to interrogate him? Perhaps they could only find two nice cops and were waiting for a nasty cop to become free. Perhaps they'd forgotten him altogether, and he really was destined to spend the next fourteen years in this cell, like Edmond Dantès, in which case he should probably get on his knees and start scratching at the concrete with his fingernails. The journey of a thousand miles, after all, begins with a single step.

Mercifully, there was a noise at his door. Grenville stood. The door was a solid-looking thing, with a thick glass window in the top half – Grenville assumed the glass was unbreakable, and he certainly had no intention of trying to test that theory just as yet, though precisely what proportion of the fourteen years might elapse before he was driven to try breaking through it with his bare forehead remained to be seen.

There was a face at the window, looking through at him. The face had a uniform under it.

Below the window, there was a wicket; a sort of metal chute which was a conduit for supplying the cons (which is how Grenville now thought of himself) with sustenance. A tray appeared in the wicket, and the voice on the other side announced that it was lunch.

My, my. Luncheon was served. La-di-dah. Waiter service, too. The Wormwood Scrubs Hotel, if yew don't mind.

Grenville approached the repast with some trepidation.

What unspeakable Dickensian gruel awaited him under the aluminium heat cover? Sloppy porridge crawling with roaches? Texan grits dotted with bluebottle carcasses? Dried biscuits alive with wriggling maggots?

He lifted the lid cautiously, then lifted it off completely. It was a fairly appetising-looking pie. Chips were piled liberally beside it. There was gravy, and there were beans.

And, as far as he could recall, his GI diet forbade Grenville from eating any of it.

He couldn't remember, with absolute certainly, the list of forbidden foods – perhaps he should have that tattooed on his body, also. Clearly, he was going to have to spend a great deal of time in tattoo parlours should he ever regain his freedom. But he could say, with a fair degree of conviction, that pies were not permitted, and he knew for a fact he was not allowed chips or beans. Perhaps he could lap gently at the gravy, but he doubted it: it almost certainly contained flour.

He carried the tray over to his bed anyway. He didn't want to look like he was refusing food or being awkward and uncooperative in any way. There was a fruit juice, probably from concentrate, which, unless he was getting mixed up with the Atkins, was also denied him. He'd been on this diet for an entire week now, this morning's insane breakfast excepted, and he was just beginning, he thought, to feel some benefits, and he was damned if he was going to backslide again.

With a strength of purpose and resilience of will he found extremely admirable in himself, he sat back on the bench again, the food tray as far away from him as humanly possible. He tried not to be distracted from his introverted misery by the taunting aromas the repast was hurling his way, but his strength of purpose and resilience of will were not quite as strong, purposeful or resilient as he'd first hoped.

He was hungry. He hadn't been hungry before the food had shown up, but now, it turned out, he was absolutely bloody ravenous.

He thought he would try one chip. A single chip wouldn't

blow his diet, now, would it? He wasn't put on this planet to sit around starving to death, was he? He wasn't supposed just to wait in his cell, ignoring perfectly edible food, and then later be forced to scrabble around on the floor trying to trap an unlucky juicy centipede and gobble it down greedily like Papillon, on Devil's Island. Better a chip than even the juiciest of centipedes, in his opinion.

It was not a bad chip. Grenville knew his chips, and this was not a bad one. He, personally, preferred frites, slightly thinner, crisper on the outside, and this was a thicker chip and not quite crisp enough on the outside, but floury and lush inside, and it would probably be improved by a small splash of gravy, so he took another chip and barely dabbed it in the gravy, being careful not to contaminate it with the tomato sauce from the beans, which, let's face it, was almost pure sugar, and, indeed, the gravy did complement the chip delightfully. Out of professional courtesy, he thought he should at least see what was in the pie. He took up the plastic knife and fork, wondering, vaguely, if he should be thinking about somehow secreting the knife away so that later he might in some way be able to tool it into some sort of 'shank' for personal protection in the exercise yard, and cut into the pie.

The pastry was admirable. Firm, yet crumbly. And the pie was minced beef and onion, which was one of Grenville's personal favourites in the whole of pie creation, bested only by steak and kidney pudding. Plus, of course, he could probably eat it with impunity, so long as he stuck to the filling only.

He lifted the tray onto his knee, removed the lid, and in less than seven minutes the entire meal was just the memory of a smear on the plate.

SIXTEEN

It was lunchtime before Hayleigh could attend to the contraband secreted away inside *Chick Chat*. There had been no morning break because Mr Madders (guess what his nickname was) had given the whole class a detention because Daniel McWeaver-Boastcroft had let off a terrible fart, which smelled so, so bad that Maddo had thought it was a stink bomb and wanted the culprit to own up, but Daniel was just too embarrassed, and so the whole class suffered. Hayleigh didn't blame Daniel, though. Owning up to a fart so deadly that people at the back of the class were actually suffering third-degree burns and radiation poisoning would have been a massive humiliation from which his reputation would never have recovered.

She slipped into the loo and, mercifully, found an empty cubicle right away. Working quickly, she dealt with her lunch first. She squeezed the banana (a hundred and forty-three calories) out of its skin and into the plastic bag, and emptied the carton of semi-skimmed milk (200ml, ninety-six calories) down the loo. She unwrapped the tuna and mayonnaise baguette (a whopping five hundred and thirty-five calories, not to mention twenty-three grams of fat) and crumbled it over its wrapping, which she then smeared with some of the filling. Incredibly, there was *another* sandwich in the lunchbox. Was Mum trying to *kill* her? This time, it was ham and cheese (five hundred and fifty-seven calories and a heart-stopping twenty-seven grams of fat). Again, she removed the wrapping and, rather cunningly, she thought, crumbled half of the sandwich over the wrapping, and left the other half intact. She didn't have to pretend to eat *everything*, did she?

Leaving half a sandwich would be even more convincing. Ha ha. Detect *that*, queen of detectives. She disposed of the cheese and onion crisps (a hundred and eighty-four calories), again down the loo. Crisps got soggy and went down when you flushed, unlike bananas which were, quite literally, un-sinkable. They should have made the *Titanic* out of bananas. She gingerly removed the Mars Bar (two hundred and ninety-four calories, I don't think so) from its wrapping and laid it beside the banana.

And there, at the bottom of the lunchbox, was Hayleigh's Lunchtime Nightmare. An apple. A big, red, juicy apple. Fifty-three calories of fruity hell.

You can't just empty out an apple. You can't just cut it up. You have to leave a core with teeth marks in it. She'd tried giving apples away before, but people got suspicious if you followed them around while they ate it, and then scrabbled around in a bin to recover the discarded core. You could get called a loony for that kind of behaviour, if you weren't careful.

There was nothing for it. Best get it over and done with. She sat on the loo, held the bag under her mouth and tried to psych herself up for the unavoidable horror. The smell of the banana was starting to make her feel nauseous. She took the plunge and bit into the apple. A big chunk. She spat it out into the bag immediately and carried on spitting and spitting and spitting. Yuck. Yuck. Yuckety yuck. She bit off another chunk and spat. This time, she really thought she was going to puke. She leapt off the loo seat quickly and spun round so her head was over the bowl, but all she did was some dry heaving.

When she recovered, she sat down again. She was sweat-ing. God, she couldn't go through with this. Maybe that was enough. Maybe the apple looked pretty close to eaten by now. She looked at the apple, but it was still almost intact.

Well, she'd come this far . . .

In the end, she managed to create a reasonably convincing-looking apple corpse with five more bites. It took her almost twenty minutes.

She put all the remains back in the lunchbox, opened the cubicle door and peered out. She was lucky, there was no one around. She dashed over to the waste bin and dumped the plastic bag, which was, basically, a calorie bomb that could have fed the whole of Ethiopia for fifteen years. Then she took out *Chick Chat*, removed the cover, took out the dangerous blue letter and dumped the mag and the putrid breakfast remains in the bin. Sorry, Jason.

Then she crossed over to the drinking faucet and washed her mouth out for five minutes, until she could barely taste the apple, and locked herself back in the cubicle.

What a rigmarole! What a stupid rigmarole! If only people didn't stick their bloody noses in her business, she could live a normal bloody life. She could not *wait* till she was old enough to leave school. Could not *wait*. To leave home, even. It would be sad, yes, but at least she'd be able to call her life her own.

She opened the envelope. She didn't have to steam it, or anything. If the contents were benign, she could pretend it arrived tomorrow, and she opened it, thinking it was for her; that it was a book token she'd been expecting for house points or something.

It was not benign.

It was from Mrs Mellish, the bitch.

'Dear Mr & Mrs Griffin, I am writing blah de blah daughter Hayleigh blah de blah growing concern yack yack yack fainted in gym class.' What?! She hadn't *fainted*. She'd felt a bit dizzy, that's all. And sat down on the floor for a bit. Lay down, actually. Quite hard. But that was just to catch her breath, for heaven's sake. That wasn't *fainting*. But, oh no, old Melon-head wouldn't let it go. She'd wanted her to go to the *hospital*, as if she was going to die, or something, but Hayleigh was having none of that. The nurse had been called, and she had examined Hayleigh, and taken her pulse and her temperature, when really all she wanted was to sit down on her own and catch her breath. But no, the nurse had to use everything in her silly bag, including that blood pressure armbandy thing that actually hurt a bit when it was fully pumped up.

And then there had been Dark Mutterings between the nurse and the Melon bitch, and Hayleigh was sent to lie down on the nurse's couch and get some rest. In the middle of the morning. Like she was some kind of toddler. Like this was some kind of pre-school Montessori nursery, and she needed a mid-morning nap. She almost asked: 'Where's my little mini bottle of kiddie milk, then?' but she was worried they might actually *give* her some. She'd lain down for an hour or so, and then returned to her classes, feeling great, and thought that was end of that.

But at the end of the day, there had been That Little Chat, which had involved some very wild accusations and exceedingly strange questions and although Hayleigh fended off absolutely all of the mad rantings calmly and rationally, she had got the feeling this ridiculous problem wasn't going to go away.

And she'd been right. How right had she been? Rightly, rightly right, in case anyone were remotely interested. Right in the subjunctive, in case anyone were interested precisely how right she had been. There could be no righter right than expressing one's rightness in the correct grammatical mood. All of which rightness wafted airily above Mrs Mellish's dismal monkey brain. Eee ee eee. Hayleigh went back to the, quite honestly, inarticulate letter. '. . . fainted in gym class.' Lie. 'Blah de blah nurse expressed concerns yack yack malnourished . . .' What? Lie, lie, lie. Well, Mrs Mel-bitch, you have so tripped yourself up there. Hayleigh? Malnourished? Yeah, right. Malnourished as a pregnant rhino. Malnourished as a giant walrus in a fish farm. '. . . malnourished blah diddly blah eating disorder.' Well, there it was. The nub of the thing. People think if you're overweight, you must have an eating disorder. When, in actuality, Hayleigh didn't know anyone else in the entire *world* who ate more sensibly than her; who kept a better eye on her fat intake; who was more aware of the calorific values of foods. '. . . disorder quack quack quack sure you have some concerns yourselves . . .' and more of the same wild, deranged nonsense, on and on and on. 'Please call and arrange a time when you are both available blah de blah some urgency.' Right. Brilliant. What, in fact, was urgent here, Mrs Melon Tart, was that Mrs Melon Nipples got some brain surgery very fast. A total brain transplant, preferably. That was what was urgently required here. A brain transplant from a disturbed chimpanzee might improve her powers of rationality. An urgent total brain transplant with a single-celled pond amoeba would practically transform the dreadful woman into a close approximation of a humanoid.

Well, there was only one place for that letter, and she was sitting on it. She wished she wanted a crap so she could wipe her bum with the hateful thing first, but she didn't. Truthfully, she couldn't remember the last time she'd performed that particular function. She flushed the filthy letter away along with the milk and soggy crisps and the dirty blue envelope.

Thank *God* she'd intercepted it. All hell would have broken loose at home if it had arrived when she wasn't there. She couldn't even bear to think about the devastation it would have wreaked.

She checked the bowl. Everything had gone. She flushed it again, anyway. Crisis averted. Job done.

SEVENTEEN

Grenville was sitting in an interview room of Hornsey Police Station, waiting for the nice and the nasty cops to turn up. He was waiting with the duty solicitor, who was costing him nothing, and he certainly seemed to be getting his money's worth. He wondered if there might not be some sort of annual competition to select the dickheadedest solicitor of the year. He certainly hoped so. He had two dead certs he knew for sure would absolutely *walk* it. He would clean the bookmakers *out*, baby.

This latest candidate was Charles Whitman. Like the poet, he'd said, though Grenville was unaware of any poet named Charles Whitman, and then he'd laughed, to let Gren know it was some kind of joke, which it wasn't, not by any stretch of the imagination, even if there had been a poet named Charles Whitman. Look: if he really did have a poet's name, say his name was 'Thomas Stearns Eliot', and he'd said 'like the poet', in what way could that be construed as comedic? It *was* like the poet. It was *exactly* like the poet. Where's the joke? So, right away, Grenville knew he was dealing with an idiot, and he was already beginning to regret not calling in that robbing incompetent leech from Wank, Wanker and Wankstain, Solicitors-at-Law, Est. 1983.

He'd asked for Grenville's version of the events leading to his arrest, but he didn't seem to pay nearly enough attention, interrupting him on no less than four occasions to take phone calls on his mobile, each time holding up his hand, flipping open the phone and saying: 'Sorry, I have to take this one,' then wandering off to the far end of the room. He didn't seem even vaguely interested in the unspeakable behaviour of the Gorgon woman, which was Grenville's only possible mitigation, and appeared to concentrate instead on what he kept insisting on referring to as Grenville's 'rampage' through the car park, no matter how many times Gren corrected him. If he started calling it a 'rampage' in court, the daft bastard, they'd lock Grenville up and throw away the key. It was an unfortunate set of incidents. It was a regrettable overreaction to inhuman provocation. It was foolish, yes. It was irresponsible, undeniably. A rampage it was not.

While he waited for the latest vital phone call to conclude, Grenville picked away at his training shoes, which had been returned to him for the duration of the 'interview', forcing him into further unnecessary painful manoeuvrings. For some reason, they weren't afraid he was going to unthread the laces and fashion them into some sort of garrotte with which he could strangle himself while he was in the interview room, but he was seriously contemplating using them to choke the life out of Charles Whitman, the non-poet name-sake. They had not, however, returned his watch, for fear, no doubt, that he would crack it open here and use its base as a mini shovel to dig his way out of the interview room, but there was a clock on the wall, and by now his absence would definitely be causing headaches at the studios. They'd probably assumed he'd been in some kind of accident, which, actually, would be a much better state of affairs than their knowing the truth. He might get someone to put his leg in plaster once he got out of the interview, and feign having been in a crash. Yes, that would be infinitely preferable. He thought he could pull that off. Hobble around in a cast for a couple of weeks. He certainly had the car wreck to back up that little yarn.

The production team were probably phoning around hospital accident and emergency rooms right now. He wondered how The Girl would take the news. Would she be worried for him? Would she be beside herself with grief, imagining the worst? Would her wonderful breast flood with relief every time she found out he wasn't languishing in intensive care in each hospital she phoned?

Whitman finished the latest phone call, doubtless destroying the life of another of his hapless clients in the process, and returned to the table.

'Sorry about that. Couldn't be helped.' And he laughed again. Grenville replayed both sentences a few times in his head, but couldn't dig a joke out of either of them. 'Now,' Whitman consulted his notes, 'at the end of your rampage—'

'It was *not* a rampage.' Grenville said it quietly, but firmly, hoping that this might be the best way to communicate with this chimp, hoping that might be the technique by which information might penetrate his consciousness. It had better be. The only other option left open to him was to somehow get hold of a hand drill, trepan straight through the dreadful man's skull and tattoo the words directly onto his frontal lobes with his own fountain pen.

'Sorry, I keep saying that, don't I? What should I call it?'

'Do we have to call it anything? I did some things I wish I hadn't. They don't have to be grouped together under a single name. We don't have to call it "Assault on David Lloyd Leisure Centre 13". We don't have to call it "The East Finchley Three-Door-Hatchback Massacre". We don't have to call it anything.'

'Fine. At the end of your . . . I'm sorry, I keep on wanting to say "rampage".'

'Resist that urge. I beg you.'

'At the end, you drove through the exit barrier, snapping off the arm.'

'That is correct. Yes.'

'May one ask: why?'

Grenville rubbed his hand over his face. 'It's complicated. I did it because it really shouldn't have been there.'

'It shouldn't have been there?'

'It served no discernible function. It just stopped people from leaving the car park, and nobody knows *why*.'

'I see . . .' Whitman said in such a way as to let Grenville know he didn't see, at all.

'You're supposed to punch in a security code, but they let everybody know what the security code is. Does that make any sense to you?'

'Not really. Did you know the code?'

'That was the reason I went back and parked in the parent and toddler space. To find out the code.'

'And you didn't find it out?'

'I did find it out.'

'I see . . .' Whitman said again, but he didn't, and who could blame him? 'And that was the end of the . . . of the . . . can we call it a mêlée?'

'No.'

'A fracas?'

'Shut up.'

The door to the interview room opened and a woman in a police uniform with man's trousers strode in. She'd been the one who'd taken Grenville's DNA swab earlier. She had one of those asymmetrical hairstyles: short on one side, but with a long lop-sided fringe that tended to flop over her left eye. Quite fetching, in his opinion. Grenville craned round, hoping that she might be the nasty cop, which would be a bit erotic, in his opinion, which perhaps might give an indication of the extreme poverty of his current sex life, but no one else came in behind her.

She smiled at them without humour and said: 'I'm Detective Constable Redmond. I'll be conducting this interview. She put a very, very hefty folder on the desk. Was that just Grenville's case? Surely not. Surely that must be the file on all as yet unsolved cases since the inception of the Bow Street Runners. How had they generated so much paperwork on him in such a short space of time? Good Lord: they couldn't have had that much evidence against Slobodan Milošević.

'We'll be recording this on tape, and your responses will be admissible. Do you understand?'

Grenville nodded. One detective? How was this going to work, then? Was she going to be nice, or nasty? Or was she going to do both? Was she going to pull some sort of crazy, bipolar manic depressive routine – slapping him gruffly with one hand, then offering him a cigarette with the other?

She started the tape, said her name, the date and time and named the others in the room, and then opened her folder. She read out the arresting officer's report, which, as Grenville had suspected, made the police out to be shining knights of public service who never took the piss out of anyone, or at any point fell helpless to the floor with derisory laughter. They had received a call that criminal damage was being committed, et cetera. There was a matter-of-fact description of Grenville's arrest, which omitted the entire seatbelt fiasco, but Gren didn't mind that. There then followed some witness statements, including one by a Mrs Curtiz, who turned out to be the crone who'd started it all. The witness statements were more emotionally charged than the police report, and Grenville didn't come off very well at all. He was squirming in his seat by the time Officer Redmond had finished.

She looked up. 'Do you agree those are accurate reports of the events?'

Grenville squirmed again. 'Well . . . up to a point. There are one or two places where—'

Redmond held up her hand. 'Let me stop you there, Mr Roberts, just for a second.'

Walt Whitman chirped in. 'Detective, I think my client should have an opportunity to explain his rampage. Don't you?'

Brilliant. Grenville shook his head and looked down at his laces. Why could you never put your hands on a good trepanning drill when you really needed one?

'And he will, Mr Whitman,' the detective acknowledged.

'Believe me, I'm doing him a favour. I thought it might be in his best interests if, before he said anything he might regret, we all sat down and watched the CCTV footage first.'

EIGHTEEN

After lunch, Jeremy and Jemma drove around the Well Farm in the golf cart Stone had allocated them, but, frankly, there was very little to see. Just dozens and dozens of the wheel structures, all identical, all with the same central community mall, with the same gym, the same shops . . .

'Little boxes,' Jemma said glumly, 'made of ticky-tacky.'

Jeremy nodded. 'They are a touch depressing.' It would need a genius photographer to make this place look inviting in the brochures. 'Wait a minute . . .' He checked through the folder Stone had given him. 'Yes. There's a map. There's a nature walk,' he tapped the map, 'here.'

'Right.' Jemma nodded. 'Now if only we knew where we actually are . . .'

'Good point. Well, it's north. Head north.' He looked up for the sun, oriented himself and pointed left. 'Thataway. Then left at the first ticky, and right at the next tacky.'

The nature walk, it turned out, was well signposted, and they found it easily. As Jeremy climbed out of the cart, he heard Jemma laugh. He turned. 'What?'

'Brilliant.' She giggled. 'Look at that.' She pointed to a big sign: 'Nature Walk'. And underneath a more temporary sign: 'Under construction'. Jeremy laughed, too.

There was a large map by the entrance, offering a selection of walking trails. Green route for the beginner, blue route for the advanced walker and black route for the more sturdy souls. Jeremy, not a hiker by nature, suggested the green route and, to his relief, Jemma concurred.

It was peaceful in the woods, and they walked quietly at first, listening to the birds. Most of it was, in fact, natural, but they did occasionally happen upon some artificial improvements to nature: a man-made pond, as yet unfilled, with the promise of a small waterfall above it; a freshly cut clearing, its destiny as yet obscure; and Jeremy saw an electrical wire dangling from a tree, which turned out, on inspection, to lead to a cleverly concealed camera.

'Great. The Hills Have Eyes.'

Jemma shivered. 'Does this place bother you at all?'

'What? The woods?'

'No, the whole place. Doesn't it make you feel uncomfortable?'

'Well, it's not designed for comfort, is it? In fact, it's mostly designed for *dis*comfort.'

'That's not what I meant. Well, actually, it is partly what I meant. It's all just a bit too draconian: deliberately designing the eating zones to be unpleasant. No comfy chairs anywhere. TV only if you exercise like mad.'

'Sure, it's a little heavy on the tough love,' Jeremy said. 'But desperate measures for desperate times.'

'Well, it worries me. It worries me a lot. There's something about the whole attitude here. They're too . . . confident. Too sure they're right.'

'What did Stone mean when he said they weren't going to start people farming for "obvious reasons"?'

Jemma smiled grimly. 'Because they don't want the public to think of these places as "work camps". That's their nightmare, right now: that people will start comparing them to Concentration Camps. That would kill the project stone dead before it could get off the ground.'

Yes, it most certainly would. You would not get a great many people volunteering for Concentration Camps. Definitely not a good idea, then, to go with the slug line: 'Fat – The Final Solution'.

They strolled on and came across a stream. It might have been a romantic moment but for a cluster of workmen, who seemed to be stocking it with carp. For some reason, the men were wearing hard hats. Again, why did anyone need hard hats to handle goldfish? Were the carp psychopathic? Were they armed with clubs, or something?

'The thing is,' Jemma plucked a reed from the banks of the stream, 'I'm pretty sure they're not right.'

'Not right about what?'

'About any of it, quite frankly. Look, they have this bee in their bonnet about obesity being an epidemic and a major health hazard and the biggest threat to human longevity in the twenty-first century, and I don't know exactly what they're supposed to be basing it on.'

'What are you saying? There *is* no obesity epidemic?'

'Look, for a start, there's very little evidence that being overweight is as terrible for your health as it's made out to be. In actual fact, it's much, much unhealthier to be even a few pounds *under*weight.'

'You're joking.' Jeremy looked around nervously. Were there microphones as well as cameras in these woods? This was heresy in these parts. Blasphemy, almost.

'I joke not. It's true across the board, but especially in older people. Over sixty-five, underweight is a killer, but being overweight, even by as much as forty pounds, actually *improves* their life expectancy. Quite dramatically, too.'

'I'm not sure that's right.' Jeremy wondered if they were far enough away from the stream stockers not to be overheard. He quickened his pace.

'Well, I am. And I do have the advantage of having actually *glanced* at the statistics. But, OK, I don't want to argue with you. I can email you the references when we get back, if you like. But let's say there *were* an obesity epidemic, and it *did* put the population in mortal danger. What on Earth would you do about it?'

'Well . . . this.' Jeremy waved his arms. 'You'd help people to get thinner.'

'Fine. The problem is: short of radical surgery or perma-nent starvation, it's incredibly difficult to lose weight and then sustain that weight loss. Diets don't work in the long term. They pretty much all work at the beginning, but over the long haul, they just don't. If they did, everybody would be able to lose weight, and I'm pretty sure very few people actually *want* to be obese. I'm pretty sure there are very few obese people out there who haven't had a serious stab at dieting already. Ninety-one per cent of successful dieters regain their original weight within a *year*. And almost always, they actually become *heavier* than when they started. I have yet to see a study that follows what happens to the other nine per cent, but I'll bet the attrition rate over a decade is pretty high. The chances are these "Well Farms" will actually wind up harming people.'

Now Jeremy was really getting nervous. He pretended to scratch his forehead, as if shielding his face from any prying cameras might somehow help. 'Surely, if diets don't work, it's because people stop sticking to them.'

'Look, we've been attacking this "problem" for over a century now, and getting precisely nowhere. We've spent billions upon billions researching the causes and cures of "overweight", and it's become clear that most of our assumptions are pretty much, if you'll forgive me, fatuous. Take calories. Calories are a measure of heat energy. In dietary terms, they refer to the amount of heat energy the body needs to generate to eliminate particular foods. You know this, right?'

Jeremy nodded.

'Well, the theory is, fundamentally, calories in, calories out. If you expend more calories than you take in, you lose weight. You take in more than you expend, you put weight on. Sounds blatantly obvious. So obvious it's been accepted and acted on for over a hundred years. The problem is, the calories in/calories out theory treats the human body as if it's a machine. What's more, it treats all human bodies as if they're the *same* machine. And after a century of research, it remains unproven. The calorie equation doesn't seem to hold true. The simple truth is, telling people to lose weight by eating less and exercising more is unproven and probably just plain wrong, and, in actual fact, probably quite dangerous.'

'What, so now we shouldn't even exercise?'

'That's not what I'm saying. Exercise is great. It's bad to overdo it, but moderate regular exercise will definitely have a beneficial effect on your health. Just don't expect it's going to help you lose weight, that's all.'

She was saying all this quite matter-of-factly, as if she was utterly unaware that she was systematically attempting to demolish the logic behind the entire enterprise on which they were now employed.

And, of course, Jemma being Jemma, she didn't stop there. 'Look, even if you fly in the face of all these arguments and insist that being fat is unhealthy, you are then leaping to the conclusion that a fat person who loses weight will automatically assume the health characteristics of a naturally thin person, which is not necessarily the case. Here's an example: bald men don't live as long as hirsute men, in general.'

Jeremy ran hand through his hair, involuntarily. 'Is that true?'

'As I say, in general. It's probably because they have higher levels of testosterone, which appears to lower life expectancy. Now, nobody in their right mind would suggest that giving bald men hair implants would somehow bestow on them the same life expectancy as a naturally hairy man, now would they?'

'Of course not, no.'

'But we're making precisely that logic error when we try to make fat people thinner. Unfortunately, nobody's ever conducted a study to test whether such a transformation does affect people's life expectancy in a positive way.'

'Why not?'

'Because nobody knows how to turn fat people into thin people.'

NINETEEN

Soooo. They had recorded Grenville's entire non-rampage on closed-circuit cameras. The whole thing.

That was probably not very good.

He hadn't seen any cameras. But then, he hadn't been looking for them. What was it with this car park? Were they secretly running the Royal Mint from some obscure corner of it or something? They had more security than Heathrow Airport, Belmarsh Prison and the Crown Jewels room of the Tower of London combined. Grenville had probably been lucky not to get mown down by some guard in a camouflaged machine gun post armed with a Kalashnikov, or speared with a pike by a hidden Beefeater.

For the benefit of the audio tape, Redmond announced that she was starting up the video.

The show started with Grenville parking in the crèche space. The camera, of course, was perfectly placed to capture every single detail. It was shooting down from a high angle directly onto the scene, the lighting was good, the focus was superb and it was even in colour. Trust Grenville's luck to pick a day when Stephen Spielberg was directing the CCTV cameras.

As Grenville disappeared into the leisure centre, the 4x4 pulled up.

Now, Grenville started thinking this might be a good thing, after all. Now everyone would see the intolerable provocation he'd been subjected to. Now they would understand. Now he would be vindicated. Bring it on.

He watched himself emerge from the building. He looked like he was already in a fairly foul mood, which was odd –

he didn't remember that. And then the interchange with the Medusa began, only, damn it, there was no sound. Well, of course. Why would Grenville be thinking he might actually catch a break?

Worse still, the camera was slightly behind the woman, shooting over her left shoulder whenever she faced Grenville, so most of her venomous expressions and the more frightening of her Gorgon looks went unrecorded. In contrast, Grenville – and why would it have been any other way? – was in full view at all times. And it didn't look good. He thought he'd been a lot calmer, a lot more collected and reasonable than this. It didn't look like he was calm, collected and reasonable. It actually looked like he was a short-tempered vicious bully harassing a harmless mother who was struggling to protect a helpless infant. That's what it looked like. There had to be some way to prevent this footage being played in court. Surely there was some clever lawyerly loophole that could render it inadmissible. Grenville shot a quick glance at Ezra Pound, who actually seemed to be enjoying the show. He looked like he might reach into his briefcase at any moment and produce a bag of popcorn. Grenville would *definitely* have to get another lawyer.

Then the show really hotted up. They got to the start of Grenville's not-a-rampage. The first impact looked amazingly insane. He was truly grateful, now, that the footage had no soundtrack. It was a monstrous collision that rocked the 4x4 and all but stove in the back of his own car. The second impact was, if anything, worse. Forget Spielberg, this *had* to have been directed by Quentin Tarantino.

Then there came the bollard-busting sequence. He had rammed the bollard many, many more times than he'd remembered. He must have blanked that bit out. It took about ten attempts to knock it over. He'd then dragged the dead bollard under his car and onto the pavement. He had no recollection of that bit whatsoever. Then there was the squeezing the car through the space between the remaining bollards bit. When you saw it from this angle, you could plainly see the car was never going to fit through, not even nearly, and, although there was no sound, Grenville found that the mind could not help but conjure up the dreadful screech of tortured metal as the smoking car crunched through.

Well. That was that. It wasn't good, it was pretty damning, obviously, but at least he was about to tootle out of the frame, and that was a small blessing. But no. Oh, no, no, no, no. Mercy me, no. The shot *changed*. Tarantino had, presumably, yelled, 'Cut!', the shot hand changed and they were now looking down at the exit barrier. Again, the lighting, the angle, everything was perfectly in place to capture Grenville's wreck of a clown car trundling up, smoke and steam a-billowing from his ruined bonnet.

And he hadn't stopped, as he'd imagined, to try to remember the security number, he hadn't even slowed down, just kept right on trundling towards the barrier, and – Jesus H. Christ! *That* looked bad. That looked very bad indeed. The windscreen warped and crumbled and then shattered into billions of fragments, the bonnet buckled and wrenched itself clear of the car and the security barrier went flying through the air, spinning, in what looked, to Grenville, suspiciously like slow motion, *directly towards the camera*. Forget Tarantino. This work bore the unmistakable hallmark of the master of disaster, John Woo. And Grenville found his mind was dubbing on its own soundtrack: the gigantic smash of the glass and the tinkling of the falling shards and a sort of lazy whump, whump, whump as the arm spun languidly through the air towards the viewer and, yes, the barrier's arm smashed into the camera and the screen went dead.

Well. Perfect. Academy Awards all round, Grenville was thinking. Best Action Movie, Best Horror and the coveted trophy for Most Convincing Impression of a Deranged Berserker for his own mantelpiece. He'd better start writing his acceptance speech.

He looked around at his not-the-poet lawyer, hoping his previous impressions of the man might have been misbegotten. Hoping that, now the man was in the arena of his professional expertise, he might somehow find another gear, that he might somehow turn out to be Atticus Finch in disguise. That he would lean forward and say to the detective, with a confident smile, in the soft tones of an educated Southern gentleman, 'Of cowahse, you realise, Ma'am, that undah tha East Finchley Leisure Centre Code of 1862, and the Barnet District Penal Act of 1736, not one single frame of this sorry little brouhaha is admissible in a cowht of lawah. So, if that's all the evidence you have in this mattah, you might cayuh to return mah client's personal accoutrements, way-upon the payuh of us will be compelled to take our leave of youah delightful companeh.'

Instead, the man was moronically staring at the blank screen with his mouth open, like some poor, lobotomised creature from the very deepest cellars of Bedlam. When he finally gathered the few shreds of what only the most generous observer might call his 'wits', he turned to Grenville and said: 'Well, if that's not a rampage, I don't know what is.'

TWENTY

Hayleigh kept her eyes straight ahead and tried to walk as upright as possible as she passed through the school gates. Technically, she wasn't allowed to leave the school environs at lunchtime – that was a privilege reserved for Year Eleveners – but she often got away with it. If you didn't make eye contact with anyone and the teacher on duty was distracted, or just plain lazy, and you did it with confidence, you could usually pull it off. Today, she simply couldn't afford *not* to pull it off. She had made an unbreakable promise to a certain Mister Jason Black, and they would have to throw an animal capture net over her and shoot her with elephant tranquiliser darts to stop her from keeping it.

She crossed the road carefully and made a beeline for the newsagents. All that nonsense with the apple and whatnot had left her very little time to accomplish this desperately important mission and get back in time for, ugh, gym class.

There was a handwritten sign on the door, and very poorly handwritten it was, too: 'only TWO school kid Allow in the shop'. It annoyed Hayleigh for very many reasons. Which two school kid were allowed in the shop? Did these two blessed individuals know who they were? And why only them out of all the school kid who might want to spend money in the shop?

She didn't have time for such speculation now. She opened the door, and the bell rang. The Mumbling Man behind the counter looked up, but didn't smile, of course, then went back to fiddling with his pricing gun, like he was Wild Bill Hickok cleaning his six-shooter, only, from what Hayleigh knew about how much he charged here for a small pack of Kleenex, the pricing gun was probably a much deadlier weapon than anything ever dreamed up by Messrs Smith and Wesson.

She scanned the magazine racks. There was a picture of Courteney Cox Arquette on the cover of *OK!*, looking divine, as usual, in a low-cut red dress. She had a fabulous cleavage, and yet you could clearly see practically her *entire* ribcage. How did the woman do it? Big boobs, skinny body. You have *got* to take your hat off to that kind of dieting genius.

And there he was, on the cover of *Chick Chat*. And look, he was on the cover of *Teen Talk*, too. Could she afford both? She dived into her purse, and yes, she had enough, so long as the Mumbling Man accepted the one euro coin, which, she believed, he was compelled to do by European Law, or the International Court of the Hague or Amnesty International or some such. She grabbed the mag, and, wait a minute, who was that on the cover of *Teen Talk*, arm-in-arm, no less, with Jason? Staring dreamily into his eyes? Could it be that total cow Amyline from the dreadful girls' band Gurlz Banned? And what was the headline? 'Jase & Amyline: Some Kinda Lurve?' I think not. I think that belongs deep in the realms of notness, high atop the palace of notitude.

She put the magazine back, of course, gingerly, as if its cover had suddenly turned toxic. She wouldn't be spending the euro coin right now, and she certainly would never be spending *any* coins on that particular periodical ever again in history, not even if they put out a special Big Boys Cry edition with a hundred posters of all the band butt naked. She took *Chick Chat* to the counter, and it wasn't until the Mumbling Man asked if she was all right that she realised she was crying, quite profusely. Some of her tears drooled off her chin and onto the *Evening Standard* early edition, still bundled and bound with string by her feet, and made quite a loud plop.

She nodded and fished up her cardigan sleeve for her hankie.

Silly. She was being silly, and she knew it. She couldn't expect Jason to be a complete Benedictine monk until he met her, now could she? Of *course* other girls were going to try to snare a dreamboat like Jason. Of *course* he'd feel flattered by their attentions, even if they were really ugly, talentless slags. She might as well get used to it.

She blew her nose and collected her change. The Mumbling Man asked her again if she was all right, and she said she was fine and thanked him. Odd, he'd never said two words to her before. When did he turn into Care Worker of the Year?

The shop door jangled and she stepped onto the street. The fresh air, laden as it was with gasoline fumes and carbon monoxide, felt good anyway. It cleared her head. She had been *very* foolish blubbering like that, like a pathetic schoolgirl. The whole Amyline slash Jason business was almost certainly a publicity stunt, anyway. For sure, in fact. Engineered, no doubt, by their respective weaselly managers. Of course it was. And Jason probably hated every minute of the dreadful photo shoot. It was probably purgatory for the poor lamb. Every minute of it. She hoped they hadn't made him pretend to *kiss* the sour-faced *vache*. That would be *too* cruel.

By the time she'd got to the kerb, all was forgiven. She could never stay mad at Jason for long. Not even when he'd done that stupid stuff with the drugs and punched that photographer. She looked up at the school clock, but couldn't quite focus at first. She rubbed her eyes. Blimey, it was one-thirty already. Disasterama.

She crossed the road just a little too quickly, and a man on a moped had to swerve to avoid her. He braked screechily a few yards on and started yelling all kinds of vile things at her, but Hayleigh didn't stop, just carried on running through the gates, past mad old Madders on playground duty, who also started yelling at her, but she just kept running, and, out of the corner of her eye she saw something impossible, but no, that could not be, and she couldn't stop to check, but, of course, she had to, so she slowed slightly and turned her head and stopped altogether and turned and froze and was instantly transformed into a citizen of Gobsmackville, Arkansas.

Because there, on the quadrangle, parked right next to the awful Ms Davies' truly awful pink Smart car, was her mother's 4x4.

DINNER
Menu

Cabbage Soup
Steamed Fish with Bok Choi That Tastes Like
Cabbage Soup

~

Meat- and Taste-Free Chilli

~

Mixed Grill without Chips and Peas

~

Definitely No Rhubarb Crumble or Custard

~

Glucose, Saline & Liquidized Snickers Bar Cask
with Just a Soupçon of Morphine

'I find no sweeter fat than sticks to my own bones.'
(Walt Whitman: *Leaves Of Grass*, 1885)

TWENTY-ONE

Well, Grenville was thinking, that was one mystery cleared up. That was why there had been no need for any good cop, bad cop routine. They knew full well they wouldn't have to coerce any kind of confession out of him. They had him bang to rights, in flagrante, DVD available in all good stores from Monday.

He stirred uncomfortably in his chair. 'Soooo. What happens now?'

DC Redmond flicked back her fringe. 'Here's the thing: all this stuff, plus your statement, will now go to the Crown Prosecution Service, and they'll decide whether or not to prosecute, though, given the evidence, I don't think they're going to pass this one up. Then, normally, we'd agree bail and release you, and you would appear in Magistrate's Court, probably tomorrow morning.'

Grenville didn't like the sound of that. There was a big, invisible 'but' hanging over that sentence.

'However,' Redmond went on, 'Mrs Curtiz is very nervous that you might try to interfere with her, and that—'

'What?!' Grenville screwed his face in disbelief. 'Inter*fere* with her? I wouldn't touch the bloody woman with a diseased leper's dick.'

'She feels intimidated by you, and she is the chief prosecution witness, and given the somewhat violent nature of the offence, we have to take her seriously.'

'It looked a lot, lot worse than it actually was.' Grenville pointed at the blank screen. 'I'm fairly sure that footage has been doctored, because that is *not* how I remember it at all.' He looked around at his legal representative for some kind of back-up, here.

'It did look fairly violent.' He shrugged.

Thank you, Atticus.

'I'll talk it over with my colleague,' Redmond went on. 'Since you have no previous record, the balance may well be in your favour.'

'And otherwise?'

'Otherwise you'll have to spend the night in the holding cells.'

A whole night in that dreadful cell, on that dreadful excuse for a bed? Grenville turned to Whitman and was astonished to see quite how impassive and unperturbed he appeared to be about this latest horror. 'Are you going to stand for this? Are you going to let them bang me up overnight?'

'Well, I hardly think that's going to be—' and the bastard's phone went off again. He held up his palm, picked the mobile up with his other hand, flicked it open and checked the caller ID. 'I'm sorry,' he said, 'I have to take this one,' and started to rise from his seat.

Something inside Grenville snapped. He was mad as hell, and he wasn't going to take it any more.

He leapt up and grabbed the phone roughly. The raw power generated by a combination of Grenville's weight and momentum astonished them both, in fact, inadvertently sending Whitman crashing back onto his chair, which went tumbling backwards to the floor. But Grenville didn't stop there. He arced back his arm and hurled the offending mobile hard against the far wall, where it impacted with a satisfying crack and broke into several pieces.

Something flashed at the edge of Grenville's vision and he half-turned just in time to see Detective Constable Redmond leap onto the table and hurl herself at him. He had no time to react, other than to spit out the words: 'What are you doo—' before she crashed into his ribcage, hurling him backwards. He smashed through his own chair, painfully, splintering it into firewood, and walloped down onto the fragments, hard. He would probably still be picking the splinters out of his arse in his late seventies.

The policewoman was on top of him. It had been a long time since Grenville had actually had a woman kneeling over him, and he wished the circumstances might have allowed him to enjoy the moment, just a little, but she did something skilfully painful to his arm and wrist that forced him to roll over onto his front and more jagged slivers of erstwhile chair dug into entirely new parts of him. He felt the cuffs snap around his wrists again, and then Redmond stood up, breathless.

Grenville managed to roll onto his back again.

The room appeared to be devastated, as if a poltergeist army had suddenly swept through it. It didn't seem possible that this amount of destruction could have been wrought in so short a time. Chairs were broken, or scattered on the floor. The table had been tipped over, spilling tape recorders and paperwork all over the place. Whitman was still sitting on his chair, with its back on the floor, looking up at the ceiling, his briefcase contents spilled around him. It was a nightmare. Grenville praised the Lord they hadn't been videoing this little interview. He would have been Alcatraz-bound for sure.

'What,' he said to the panting detective, 'was all that about?'

'I think that was about you kissing goodbye to the bail option.' Redmond swept her hand through her hair. 'Unless your learned counsel disagrees.'

Whitman, who still seemed to be in some kind of shock, shook his head in the negative, without taking his eyes from the ceiling. 'See that?' he said. 'That was another rampage.'

With great difficulty and great pain and, nonetheless, great dignity, Grenville hauled himself into a kneeling position and then to his feet, handcuffs notwithstanding. 'And you, you bastard,' he nodded at the idiot solicitor, Alan Sugar style, 'you're fired.'

TWENTY-TWO

Hayleigh could hardly focus as she struggled into her gym gear, which she had to do with a towel draped over her so the other girls couldn't see how truly gross her body really was, if you hadn't guessed.

Her mother, here at the school. *In the middle of the day.* What could that mean? Hayleigh's fevered brain raced around, desperately searching for some possibly benign explanation for such a potentially nightmarish combination of unlikelinesses. Maybe Hayleigh had left something in the car? Or at home? Some piece of homework, perhaps? But no, she couldn't come up with anything. Perhaps Mum herself had forgotten to put something in her lunchbox. A two-hundred-pound bar of Galaxy chocolate, maybe, to supplement the million-calorie banquet she'd already laid on. Hayleigh doubted that. She must have arrived at the end of lunch, or Hayleigh would surely have noticed the car on her way across the playground.

She finished dressing and hung up the towel. Most of the rest of the girls were already in the hall. There was just Sasha Patak, sitting on the corner of a bench, making a meal of pulling on her trainers because she hated gym class, absolutely hated it, poor thing. Think, Hayleigh, *think*! A family accident? Perhaps Jonny had broken his arm or something. That would be a good scenario. That would be a *great* scenario. Only, why would that bring her mother here, now? Had Hayleigh forgotten she had some sort of dentist appointment or something? No, Mum always arranged those kinds of things for the half-term break, to make them doubly horrible, thank you so very much. She kept running through increasingly unlikely possibilities – Mum was applying for a job as a teaching assistant, a dinner lady, a janitor

– anything was better than contemplating the alternatives that were actually likely.

She ran out into the hall without enthusiasm. To her horror, Mrs Mellish wasn't there.

Hayleigh's stomach performed an impressive series of somersaults. Oh, please, please God, don't let Mum be talking to Mrs Melons. In the absence of supervision, the girls had mostly broken into chattering clusters and the boys had started larking about. It would only be a matter of minutes before the whole gym class civilisation broke down, and they'd be in *Lord of the Flies* country.

To distract herself, Hayleigh grabbed a netball and started shooting. She was a pretty good shooter, and she almost, almost lost herself in it. She was just about to score a winning penalty goal for the England Olympic team in Beijing when suddenly the noise level in the room dropped to almost zero. Hayleigh turned and saw Mrs Mellish walking towards her across the hall. And Hayleigh's mother was walking in her wake. The dreadful Mellish must have phoned her. Which was probably an infringement of Hayleigh's human rights. Crappy poo puddings. She would *not* have liked to have heard that conversation.

And now they were united against her. They were coming for her, and nothing could stop them.

Well, this was it.

The Big One.

The Perfect Storm.

There was the fan, there was the shit.

And Hayleigh was going to get covered in it.

Mrs Mellish shouted out some brisk commands to the class, and the kids all started running, with various degrees of conviction, in laps around the hall.

Hayleigh threw down the ball and ran over to join the lappers, running in the opposite direction, obviously, from Mrs Mellish, her mother and the disasters they were trying to inflict on her.

Mrs Mellish yelled out for her to stop, but she pretended not to hear. It was a dismal ploy, doomed to failure, which would, at best, buy her thirty more seconds of freedom, but it was all she had, and she seized it.

And Hayleigh didn't really know what happened next. One minute she was in full flight, like a desperate stallion that had leapt from its corral and was making a hopeless bolt for freedom, and the next she was lying on the gym floor, her mum crouched beside her, with Mrs Mellish gone, and the rest of the class staring down at her with very strange expressions indeed.

Mum was talking. At least, she looked as if she was talking, but it was very soft, and Hayleigh couldn't quite hear her. Hayleigh raised her head and looked around, trying to get her bearings, and caught sight of her right leg in her jogging bottoms, which was bent at a very curious angle, like one leg of a swastika, as if her knee was on backwards, like Jonny sometimes posed his Action Man. Only it looked as if her leg wasn't bent at the knee. Wow. It looked like it should have hurt, but it didn't. She looked at her mum, puzzled, for some kind of explanation that would make sense, but, oddly, it looked as if it was Mum who was actually in pain. Her cheeks were streaked with tears, and she was wearing a bitter little kind of tight, tight smile.

Hayleigh tried to speak, to reassure her mum that she was all right, and there was nothing to worry about, when a bright white lightning bolt shot all along her frail little body, and stabbed into her brain, and she blanked out.

And, mercifully, she didn't wake up again until the ambulance was almost at the hospital.

TWENTY-THREE

Jeremy and Jemma endured dinner in the cafeteria. Jeremy opted for cabbage soup, which appeared to be nothing more than slightly warm water with cabbage in it, and steamed fish with bok choi, which tasted like warm water with cabbage in it, and he was grateful he could borrow Jemma's salt. Jemma opted for a meat-free chilli, which turned out to be not only free of meat, but free of texture, spice and taste.

There was no dance that night, of course, and no lecture to attend. There was, in fact, absolutely nothing to do. They both had plenty of work they could attend to, however, so they said their goodnights and went to their respective dorms. So much for Jeremy's amorous ambitions.

They each had an entire dorm to themselves. Jeremy sat at the table in his living area for an hour or so, transferring his notes and thoughts onto his laptop, but the chair was so infernally uncomfortable, he couldn't take it any more. He stood up and checked his watch. It was barely eight-thirty. Could he seriously go to bed before eight-thirty? He hadn't done that since he was seven years old. But the only alternative would be to go to the gym, and he could hardly start pumping iron in his Emporio Armani suit and Versace shirt. He could wear his sleeping T-shirt, but then it would get all sweaty.

He could go for a walk, he supposed, but he'd really done enough walking for the day. Besides, there really wasn't anywhere to walk *to*.

Bed, then. At least he'd be up early to delight in whatever passed for breakfast in this hell hole.

He moved into the dormitory. God, it was depressing.

Presumably, residents were not to be encouraged to spend too much time in here, either. He sat on a bed, which was, predictably, exceptionally uncomfortable.

Maybe he could improve his comfort level by stacking another mattress on top.

In the end, it took a pile of four mattress before the bed was remotely sleepworthy.

He went into the bathroom, which was large and reasonably well equipped. There was a shower section, with a rank of five shower heads side by side. He fought off an image of five morbidly obese people soaping each other up, then went into one of the five WC cubicles. He was just undoing his belt when he remembered the CCTV cameras. Then he remembered that the toilets were equipped to weigh everybody's waste, and he lost the urge to take a dump.

He consoled himself with the thought that the loos were doubtless designed for minimum comfort levels, too, and it would not have been a relaxing experience in any way, shape or form. He stripped to his waist, washed and brushed his teeth, then went back to the dorm.

He pulled on the Well Farm T-shirt he'd blagged from Stone for sleeping, then, ever mindful of the cameras, he climbed under the covers and tugged off his trousers.

Eight-thirty. He doubted he'd get any sleep, thinking about the CCTV which might or might not have been recording his every move. Damn it, he couldn't even risk a quick hand shandy.

Sometime around two in the morning, he finally dropped off.

He didn't wake until he heard Jemma knocking at the dormitory door. He sat up in a panic, not quite remembering where he was. In some kind of hospital ward? An army barracks? A youth hostel? He tried to get up but he'd forgotten about the mattress stack, mistimed his landing and tumbled roughly to the floor, banging his head quite nastily against his bedside drawers.

'Jeremy? Are you all right?'

He suppressed several swear words and called back: 'Fine. I'm fine. Be out in a sec.' And scrabbled around trying to find his trousers. Where the hell had he left them?

Jemma knocked again. 'Are you sure you're all right?'

'Absolutely. One hundred per cent hunky-dory.' The trousers had somehow gotten themselves tangled in the bedclothes. His beautiful Emporios, rumpled beyond recognition. 'Just coming,' he called.

He made the mistake of trying to tug on his trousers whilst simultaneously walking to the door and fell over again, this time catching his chin on a bedpost. He thought he might actually have blacked out for a second or two, because the next thing he knew, Jemma was bending over him with an expression halfway between concern and amusement. 'Jeremy?'

'I'm fine.' He tried to stand up, to regain some small iota of decorum, but realised his trousers were still round his knees, and fell over again. He seriously hoped the CCTV cameras weren't running. This entire episode would definitely make the Christmas bloopers tape. He grabbed the trousers, tugged them up and stood, running his hand through his hair and grinning broadly as if that was all it would take to restore his dignity. 'Morning,' he said brightly, as if this was how he normally started every day: a full-blown slapstick performance with his trousers round his ankles.

'What's happened to your face?'

Jeremy's hand shot up to his forehead, where a nasty, painful bruise was starting to swell. 'Had a bit of a tumble.'

'A bit of a tumble? You look like the losing finalist of an Ultimate Fighting bout.' Jemma scanned the dorm. 'You were here on your own, weren't you? I mean, you weren't sharing with a gang of Nazi skinheads or anything, were you?'

'Tripped and fell is all.'

'Well, we'd better get going. Helicopter leaves in fifteen minutes. Don't suppose you mind skipping breakfast.'

Jeremy definitely did not mind skipping breakfast. He wanted out of there as soon as possible. He wanted real food. He wanted bacon. Greasy bacon. He wanted eggs. He wanted a dump. But more than anything else, he wanted privacy.

Stone chauffeured them to the helicopter pad in his golf cart. He gave them both a VIP goodie bag, full of Well Farm literature and knick-knacks, shook their hands and said his goodbyes.

The chopper flight back to London seemed infinitely less glamorous than the outward trip, but at least Jemma was more inclined to chat. They had to shout over the noise of the blades, of course, so the conversation was necessarily simplified, which, with Jemma, was a mercy.

'Listen,' Jeremy yelled, 'I've been thinking about what you were saying.'

'Which bit of it?'

'All of it. Are you going to recommend they close the project down?'

'God, no. Not that they'd listen anyway. They'd probably have me shot.'

That was a relief. This gig would be the making of Jeremy, and he didn't want any negativity kiboshing it before he even had a chance to shine.

'No,' Jemma reiterated. 'They've invested billions in it. They're not going to stop now. Certainly not on the say so of a low-life research assistant from ULIST.'

'But you think it's a bad thing, all in all?'

'It's definitely a bad thing for the poor sods who sign up for it. Dangerous, even. Completely against the Prime Directive in medicine: first, do no harm.'

'So you don't feel guilty, just standing by and letting it happen?'

'I'm not Joan of Arc, Jeremy. I know when I's beat. I think they'll figure out the whole thing's a disaster before they do too much damage. People will simply stop coming when the word gets out the regimen's a flop. When the clientele dry up, the farms will close down quietly and expensively and get turned into holiday camps and theme parks. Plus: there are upsides.'

'Upsides?'

'These farms will represent the biggest controlled experiment in history into how obesity actually works. They'll generate humongous amounts of data. It's a fantastic, unprecedented opportunity to finally lay all kinds of dietary myths and nonsense to rest. God, we might even find out how to actually *cure* some dietary illnesses, and wouldn't that be an unexpected bonus? We might even find the causes of overweight are genetic, or psychological, or even viral.'

Jeremy nodded. He was wondering if he could use this particular plus in his pitch, but couldn't see how it would play very well, letting people know they were, fundamentally, signing up to be guinea pigs, and paying for the privilege.

The chopper set down at London City Airport, which of all of London's airports had the advantage of actually being in London. Jeremy was slightly disappointed; he'd had visions of setting down in some sort of high-profile area, where the incoming passengers might be famous people, or at least politicians. He offered to share a cab with Jemma, but she was heading back to the university, in the opposite direction.

If Jeremy was going to make a move, it was now or never. 'Look, I might need to pump you for some facts and figures and suchlike. Have you got an email, or a phone number I could reach you on?'

Jemma fished in her bag and pulled out a business card. 'Why don't you come over on Friday for dinner? I can cook you some food that actually tastes of something.'

Jeremy grinned. 'Great.'

Jemma grinned back. 'I don't think my boyfriend will mind.'

The boyfriend mention! Money in the bank. It was all Jeremy could do not to leap up and click his heels. It was all he could do not to tug his Versace shirt over his head and run in tight little circles of joy with his arms aeroplaned out.

The boyfriend mention.

Ker-ching!

TWENTY-FOUR

There's a ruined church spire in Hiroshima – or was it Nagasaki? Grenville couldn't remember which – that had been twisted into a tortured corkscrew in an instant by the sudden, terrible fury unleashed by the first atomic bomb, and has been preserved there as a testament to the power and the folly of which man is capable.

That spire was precisely the same shape as Grenville's spine this morning.

He had endured a night on the brick bed bench from hell, or at least, mostly on it. He'd had to get up a few times, just to make sure he still *could* get up, and he'd rolled off it at least three times, to his knowledge. Possibly more. He'd been in such a ragged state of exhaustion by the wee small hours, after the trials and tribulations of the day, he may very well have fallen off it eight or nine times, more, because when he finally awoke, he was lying on the unforgiving coldness of the concrete floor.

His hips, his back, his arms, his arse were all potted with painful and probably ugly bruises. If he'd stripped off, he'd probably find he looked like a giant, overweight giraffe. Lovely. He'd probably be in better shape if those two coppers actually had set about him with their truncheons. He'd still be in pain, but at least he'd have a decent shot at a lawsuit.

He arched his back, which cracked like Chinese New Year, but so painfully he was unable to derive any relief from the procedure, and he sat back down on the torture bench.

What a day. A day he'd laughably started out thinking of as his 'health' day. Grenville shook his head, incredulous, and immediately wished he hadn't.

The interview had concluded with him being virtually frogmarched back to his cell by two burly police officers, as if there were some sort of major risk he would run amok, handcuffed and barefoot – yes, they made him remove his shoes yet again – and single-handedly destroy the station. Yet all he'd done, when you boiled it down, was grab an idiot's phone and thrown it against the wall: a fairly minor act of harmless retaliation that was more than justified, under the circumstances. He'd done it before to a sous chef in his own kitchen – in fact, he'd disposed of that phone in a bubbling pot of court bouillon, and, yes, they had used the bouillon later in the service to poach the turbot in – without any repercussions whatsoever, yet here it led to his being denied bail for the utterly insignificant crime of hurting his own car, and manhandled into a prison cell like he was Hannibal fucking Lecter. On top of which, you could now add a second act of Criminal Damage to his charge sheet. And because they had removed the drawstring, and his hands were cuffed behind his back, his trousers fell down no less than three times en route to the pen, which was such a gross indignity, it wasn't even amusing to the police officers, who pretty much found everything about him amusing.

He'd stewed in his cell for hours on end. He found time passed a lot more slowly when you didn't have a watch. Maybe he'd stop wearing a watch. He'd feel like he was living longer.

The wicket had delivered dinner. After the guilt and horror of the previous two meals that day, Grenville had absolutely no intention of eating it. He'd dutifully collected it and set it on the floor in the toilet area without even lifting the lids – there were two dishes this time. But the minutes ticked on, and there was nothing else to do in this hell hole, so he'd got up again and peeked. Mixed grill. Good grief. You could eat like a lord in here. Who said crime didn't pay? Well, mixed grill, that was all right, GI-wise. He could eat meat with impunity, more or less. He just wouldn't have the chips or the peas. And he certainly would not be having that rhubarb crumble and custard, no way on God's good Earth.

He looked over at the tray now. Both of the plates were sparkling clean. The boredom, and the desperate urge for comfort, had defeated his finer ambitions.

His fucking health day.

And this morning, he was going to court. He was going on trial. DC Redmond had said he was entitled to call somebody to arrange for a change of clothes, if he so desired, but there was no one. He could, he supposed, have called his ex-wife, but he decided the potential for humiliation in that far outweighed the humiliation of turning up in court in his smelly jogging clothes.

The door rattled, and DC Redmond was standing there. Grenville must have looked even worse than he'd dreaded because she actually took a slight step back when she saw him and her expression was fairly close to the expression adopted by the Bride of Frankenstein when she first laid eyes on the groom.

Yeah, well, you try spending a night in the hole, lady, and see how you look to greet the morn.

She escorted him to the front desk, where, once again, his trainers were returned to him, and he had to put them on, while everyone in the station, apparently, just had to watch. There must have been some sort of regulation compelling them. He wished there wasn't always someone looking when he was forced to do that. When he was done, flushed and breathless, they also returned his elasticated drawstring.

'What, in the name of all that's holy, am I supposed to do with that?' Grenville asked, but the desk sergeant just shrugged. And then Redmond cuffed him again, though this time his hands were in front of him, which was a marginal improvement, at least.

He made a stab at re-threading the drawstring as he was led through some corridors towards the back of the station, but it was hopeless. Hopeless. It would have been hopeless even if he hadn't been cuffed. You needed a safety pin or something to re-thread a drawstring, and they weren't likely to grant him that mercy, were they? They weren't about to hand a known berserker a weapon of mass destruction like a safety pin. He could have gone through that police station like Schwarzenegger in *The Terminator* with a *safety* pin. It would have been *Assault on Precinct 13* all over again. A bloodbath. Bodies everywhere.

He gave up and stuffed the drawstring into his pocket, and shuffled on, clutching the waist of his joggers.

They reached the back door and Redmond signed him over to a uniformed Group 4 guard, and handed over the cuffs keys.

The Group 4 man – were you supposed to call them 'officers'? – made him hold his cuffed hands out, and, yes, magnificently, his joggers fell directly to his ankles, right in front of Delectable Constable Redmond. Super.

Group 4 just left them there while he removed the cuffs, then they banged heads as they both stooped to pull up his jogging bottoms. Or rather, Group 4 banged his riot gear *helmet* on Grenville's unprotected head, which left him momentarily stunned, and then the bastard pulled up Grenville's trousers for him. What was going through his tiny mind? You don't pull another man's trousers up for him, not ever. Not even if you've just had a homosexual liaison with him on Hampstead Heath. You certainly don't do it without his permission. Your tailor doesn't even do it. The only person who's permitted to pull up your trousers for you, in your entire life, is your mother. And she has to stop doing it *well* before you're four years old. Grenville was praying Redmond hadn't hung around to witness this particular escalation in his humiliation, but, of course, she was still standing behind him, waiting for her cuffs back. If there truly was a God, and Grenville ever got to meet Him, he was going to give Him a fucking good kicking, and that was for sure.

He was shepherded up a small set of metal steps into the

waiting prison van. Inside were two ranks of cubicles, each about half the size of the average toilet cubicle, with a small bench seat in each of them. Surely they couldn't be expecting Gren to occupy one of those? He would never fit in there, and even if he did, they'd never be able to get him out again. But, yes, that was the intention he deduced from the witty push in the back from the Group 4 man.

He squashed himself into one, uncomfortably, and looked up.

There was another man in the cubicle opposite staring at him with what Grenville could only assume was murderous hatred.

They'd put him in the van with a bunch of hardened criminals.

TWENTY-FIVE

Hayleigh opened her eyes from some very, *very* strange dreams. It wasn't quite dark, but it wasn't quite light, either. The room was illuminated by an artificial yellowish glow, and that was the first oddness.

Oddness number two: she had no idea where she was. She was in an unfamiliar bed, but she didn't remember having made any arrangements for a sleepover. Plus, as far as she could tell, there was no one else in the room. And when you have a sleepover, you really don't do much sleeping, not until the early morning, and you wake up in broad daylight. She did, however, have something close to the sleepover sore throat and hoarse voice, normally the result of copious amounts of laughing and talking, but this felt different, in some way. Her throat was drier than it had ever been in her life, as if someone had spent the night attacking it with Mum's crème brulée blow torch.

She looked around for water. There was a vase by the bed with flowers in it, and Hayleigh seriously thought about emptying them out and glugging down the entire contents of the vase, that's how thirsty she was. Fortunately, there was a plastic water jug just beside it, and an empty glass. She started to reach over for it, when she realised that, oddness *numero trois*: there was something in her arm.

Something *in* her arm.

She looked down at it. There were three thin rubber tubes running down from some plastic bags which were dangling from a sort of white metal coat hanger, and another tube attached to a box with a digital read-out on the other side of her bed. And all of these tubes were attached to a huge needle that was taped against her arm, just below the elbow, but on the other side.

She was in some kind of hospital.

What was she doing in some kind of hospital?

Oh, the leg. She'd hurt her leg, she seemed to remember.

She lifted herself onto her elbows to check the damage. And what was this, now? It wasn't only the rubber tubes that were attached to her. There were wires taped to her chest and, she felt with her free hand, to her temples. What was going on? Were they turning her into some kind of Borg or something? And, oh God – a tube was stuffed *completely* up her nose.

A wave of cold horror flooded through her entire body.

They were force-feeding her.

They were deliberately trying to make her fat.

That was totally in violation of her European Human Rights.

Well, they'd picked the wrong gal to mess with this time, me ol' buckaroo. With some urgency, because Lord knows how many calories per second they were pumping *straight into her veins*, where they would cause the absolute maximum damage in the quickest possible time, she tore off the tape and carefully tugged the needle out. It was a very long needle, and she almost fainted a couple of times, whether from the actual pain, or just the thought of the pain, she wasn't sure, her head felt so fuzzy, but eventually she got the evil thing out and let it drop to the floor, where it could spit out its poison with impunity.

Now it was the turn of the nose tube. Heaven alone knows what damage that was wreaking to her figure, second by wicked second, but it was coming out right now, believe me. She gave it a gentle tug, trying to ascertain just how far up her nose they'd stuffed it, and she gagged and started dry-heaving so violently she thought she might actually choke to death right there and then.

The tube went all the way down her *throat*. It might even

possibly go all the way down *directly to her stomach*! What bald-faced, unexpurgated malice! It was a very thick tube, too. They were probably pumping the most fattening foods possible straight into her. Probably a liquidized version of the legendary Snickers Bar Cake, *the* most calorifically lethal foodstuff in the history of the world.

Well, that tube was coming out right now, or Hayleigh would choke in the process. Either way, this madness ended now.

She tugged again, but hardly got any of it out before the gag reflex kicked in again, and she seriously thought she wasn't going to recover from this one. Finally, it stopped, but it left her weak and breathless, flooding with tears and on the brink of unconsciousness, and she just had to rest for a couple of minutes.

She must have dropped off to sleep again, because the next thing she knew, the evil fattening tube was not her primary concern. She was snapped back to reality again by the bona fide *Guinness Book of World Records* Worst Pain Anybody Has Ever Felt, Ever.

Check it out, it's definitely in there. Hayleigh Griffin's leg. Page two thousand and seventy-four.

It felt like someone had splintered her leg with an axe, and just kept on chopping. She wanted to scream, but she couldn't. Her mouth was too dry from the tube of evil. She thought about pouring a glass of water, and how sad was that, to need a glass of water just to be able to scream, but the mad woodsman swung again, and a tiny squeal did manage to squeeze itself out of her this time.

Mama mia, her leg was *caning*. She had to die right there and then, please God, because this was unbearable, and there was nobody to make it stop. There was nobody to save her.

But there was somebody. The best somebody, as it turns out.

That tiny squeal had been just enough. It wasn't loud enough for the nursing sister, sitting at a desk just outside

Hayleigh's room, to identify, competent and caring and efficient as she was. Even if she'd heard it, she'd probably have thought it was a bed spring squeaking, or a chair leg moving across some flooring. But it was plenty loud enough for a mother to hear. Plenty loud. Even thirty feet away down a corridor. Even engaged in the most distressing conversation of her life with a psychiatric specialist, and even though her heart was breaking and her world was falling apart around her while all she could do was stand by helplessly and watch it happen, she heard that squeal all right, and she knew *exactly* what it was, and she said nothing, because that would be wasting time, she just turned around, dropped the paper coffee cup some well-meaning idiot had pressed on her and *ran*, leaving her husband and the psychiatrist staring after her, bewildered. Oh, she ran. You will never see running like this. She would have flown, if she could. For all we know, she did.

She crashed into the room, and saw Hayleigh writhing on the bed, and saw immediately that the precious tubes were dangling free and not in her precious daughter's arm. She yelled for a doctor, and the ward sister was already in the room beside her, saying, 'Oh my God, the morphine!' and they both dashed over to the bed, the nurse to the side where the tubes were and the mother to the other side. And while one disinfected the needle and jabbed it back in again, the other held her daughter's hand and mopped her brow and tried to pour her love into this tortured little girl, every last drop of it, using a method that not even mothers knew they knew, and no scientist would ever understand, and prayed that she could have the pain instead.

Every last drop of it.

PART TWO:

Sixteen Days

'Here's the smell of blood still.
All the perfumes of Arabia will not sweeten this little hand.'
(Shakespeare: *Macbeth*, Act V scene i)

TWENTY-SIX

They'd wedged him into a cubicle from which there was no escape, in a van quite literally packed with hardened criminals who were utterly unhampered by restraints of any description whatsoever. There was a guard sitting by the door, but what use would he be if a van riot broke out and everyone decided to pile into Grenville? Would he even care? He wasn't even a proper, trained police officer. He was an employee of a security firm, and probably cheaply employed at that. Let's face it: he'd probably failed the police entrance exam. He probably failed it because he was an idiot who pulled up other men's trousers for them, unbidden, amongst many other reasons. He wasn't about to wade in with his dismal truncheon – selected not for its effectiveness or its sturdiness but solely for its magnificent cheapness – into a psychopathic mob, bent on gang-raping a defenceless over-weight guy, braying at him to squeal like a pig. They might as well have thrust a spit up his backside and stuffed an apple in his mouth. Still, at least when they'd all finished having their brutal way with him, he'd have someone to pull his trousers back up.

Grenville stopped looking at the sociopath opposite. These were prison rules, now. No eye contact. He thought he might enjoy studying the sides of his cubicle for the duration of the trip, but he was wrong. Someone had etched the words 'I goin to kill you' on it in a very ragged hand. Marvellous. Nothing quite as scary as a grammatically incorrect death threat. And what tool had been employed in this etching? It didn't look like it had been scratched in with fingernails, or, if it had, then those fingernails would, themselves, constitute

155

deadly weapons. Someone had somehow smuggled some kind of sharpened tool into the vehicle. Hell, they probably all had. It was probably standard practice if you were a regular visitor.

The first stirrings of claustrophobia could no longer be ignored, now. Grenville was not a serious sufferer. He hadn't, in fact, experienced claustrophobic feelings at all before the weight had started piling on. But it gets to be a genuine threat, when you reach a certain size, that you might seriously manoeuvre yourself into a spot from which you really cannot extricate yourself. It's a real danger, and from such things a phobia can form. He was beginning to sweat, and his hands were starting to shake. He felt he might vomit, even. That would be good. That would help his case no end. To be led into court jiggering like a victim of St Vitus's dance, with great dark damp patches under his armpits, puke stains down his jogging-top logo, smelling strongly of sweat and vomit and Lord knows what other bodily excretions. It had been a serious mistake not to swallow his pride and ask his ex to fetch a change of clothing. But then, come to think of it: how would she have got into his flat? How would anybody? The entire arrest procedure was not designed to accommodate single, friendless men who didn't have phone directories tattooed on their bodies.

He twisted round painfully, given the confines of his cubicle, the Henry Moore sculpture that was now his spinal column and the problems he had twisting round even under perfect conditions, so he could look out of the window behind him, and perhaps find some succour in the evidence that someone, somewhere was living a normal life.

The glass was tinted, so he could see out, but passers-by could not see in. And there it was: rush-hour London. People scurrying about, smelling of too much aftershave and cologne, with Starbuck-coffee breath. Normalcy. God, he wanted to be out there with them, with nothing more to worry about than being slightly late for work. They had no idea, those blissfully normal people, how unbelievably lucky they were. No idea.

He was only just below the stage of screaming abdabbery by the time the prison van pulled in at the rear entrance of Highbury Corner Magistrates Court. They were herded from the van – yes, herded: what were they now, but animals? – and handed over to a real policeman. Grenville never thought he'd be so glad to encounter one again, and less than half an hour after he'd been wishing to see them all writhing in the mighty conflagration of hell's own ovens for all eternity. He was cuffed again, but this time he managed to pin one side of his jogging bottoms with his elbow, and so was spared the indignity of having the entire criminal fraternity of North London inspect his sweaty boxer shorts.

He was led down yet another dingy corridor, and once again compelled to remove his trainers – what, in the name of all that was holy, did the Metropolitan Police have against footwear? – and deposited in yet another cell.

This one, incredibly, was even less well appointed than the last, and even smaller. It made his previous cell look like the presidential suite of the seven-star Burj Al Arab hotel in Dubai. This one didn't have a window. It didn't even have a loo, which, seriously, was currently a fairly desperate requirement for Grenville, whose bowels had been considerably loosened by the trip in the convict carrier. It had the obligatory torture bench, though it was not quite as generous and opulent as the one on which he'd spent a small part of the previous night.

He sat down on it anyway. There was nothing else to do. He prayed his case would be heard soon, because another hour or so in this purgatory, and he would start seriously thinking about attempting bungee suicide with the elasticated drawstring the careless fools had let him bring into the cell in his pocket.

And his prayer was answered. Maybe God was genuinely scared of the kicking Grenville had promised Him. He was taken from the cell, and even given a chance to freshen up before he was led to the court, uncuffed, clean, and trainered-up, where he met his legal representative, one Charles Whitman.

Whitman nodded and didn't smile or crack one of his famous non-jokes.

Grenville just stared in disbelief for several seconds, unable, even, to utter the words: 'Excuse me, Atticus, but didn't I sack you?' But finally, he managed.

Whitman looked around for someone named Atticus, then turned back. 'I didn't think you meant it. I thought it was in the heat of the moment, as it were. With the red mist clouding your . . . uhm . . .'

'No, no. I really did mean it. In all honesty, I don't think I've ever meant anything I've ever said before with more passion or commitment.'

'Oh dear. Whoops, sorry about this, but there *is* no-one else. You'll just have to make do with little old me,' and he chuckled at that little nugget, let me tell you. 'Unless you'd like me to get the case adjourned until you can bring in your own counsel?'

Well, Grenville had a serious decision to make here. Postponing the case might very well entail a return to the holding pens for heaven knew how long. And more jogging-bottom disasters. And more shoe removals than you could shake a stick at. And he would probably have to stay in the same clothes all the time, since there was no one on the entire planet Earth he could call to fetch him a change. And another trip in the rape wagon – no, two trips, at least. And at least one more night on the torture bench, possibly more, and as far as he was aware, medical science had not yet arrived at a suitably advanced state where spine transplants were commonplace.

On the other hand, he was being represented by Dylan

Thomas, here, whose undisputed idiocy could not be concealed for an instant, even by the thick veil of a mother's love. Assuming, that is, he was indeed of woman born, and not crafted by a deranged scientist from a collection of human dingleberries that had been somehow brought to life in an accident with lightning, which seemed infinitely more likely. Having his case pled by this incompetent dunderhead might very well lead to a considerable stretch in a *real* prison. By nightfall, Gren could very well be lying in the loving tattooed arms of a neo-Nazi axe murderer who'd claimed him as his bride.

It was a tough call.

But he had the scent of freedom in his nostrils. Standing outside the courthouse in the open air had given him a taste of it, and he wanted it so badly, he couldn't bear the thought of one more second in captivity. In his mind, he was already in the familiarly comfortable cocoon of his own living room, showered lemon clean and resplendent in the flowing folds of his beloved kaftan, tucking into a GI-friendly yoghurt, shaking his head wistfully as he chuckled to himself about the whole lunatic affair, which had so very quickly become just a sepia-toned memory. Which, incidentally, is precisely where he would have been almost twenty hours ago were it not for the sterling legal talents of this nincompoop, and he would have been spared most of the more extreme of his tribulations.

He just wanted the damned business over with. 'Fine.' He nodded.

'Fine, you want a postponement?'

Grenville closed his eyes shook his head. Life must be a wonderful, thrilling mystery, every waking moment, to this goldfish-brained moron, who seemed, literally, to understand nothing, ever. 'No. I'd like you to represent me.'

'Good, then let's get this over with and get you out in circulation again.' He cracked open his briefcase. We just have to—' And his phone went off. He held up his hand, flicked open the brand-new mobile and checked the caller ID. 'Sorry,' he said, 'I really need to—'

'No, you don't,' Grenville said with murderous calm. 'You really don't.'

Whitman looked into Grenville's face and finally understood something. 'You're right.' He smiled. 'It can wait.' And he flipped the phone closed and turned it off.

The trial was nothing like Grenville had imagined. There were no impassioned pleadings, no clever witness interrogations – and were you wearing your prescription spectacles at the time of the incident? – no objections, Milud. Nothing clever or, in fact, interesting. He himself was not even called to the stand. The charge was read out, Grenville's genius lawyer simply pled guilty, which, surely, Washoe the chimpanzee trained to use sign language could have done, statements were read, and Whitman asked for clemency, on the basis of Grenville's previous unblemishedness, which, again, Washoe the signing chimp could have accomplished with ease. Grenville was fined two thousand five hundred pounds for his work in the car park, and subjected to a compensation order of five thousand pounds. He was fined a further one thousand pounds for the police interrogation room shenanigans, with another compensation order in the amount of six hundred pounds for the furniture damage there, which seemed a bit steep; it wasn't as if the chairs that had been smashed had been priceless Queen Anne antiques. In fact, a quick trip to IKEA could have refurnished the entire station for a little under forty quid. The magistrate also felt duty bound to pass on the advice of one DC Redmond that Grenville might consider some anger management therapy.

And that was that. He was a free man. He was a much poorer free man than he'd hoped, but that couldn't be helped.

He shook Whitman's hand, such was his relief.

Whitman smiled, and said, 'Well, I think that went well,

under the circumstances,' and apparently there was another hidden joke in that sentence, too.

It seemed like a lot of money to Grenville. He asked Whitman what would have been the maximum fine he could have expected.

Whitman had to check. 'Let me see: maximum fine of two thousand five hundred, and compensation order in the amount of . . . five thousand pounds.'

'So, wait: you're saying I was given the maximum possible fine?'

Whitman kept staring at his book. 'I suppose you could look at it like that.' He chuckled.

What other way was there to look at it? The dozy bastard, far from being free, had cost him over eight grand, one thousand six hundred pounds of which were unarguably directly attributable to him, personally. Free? It would have been cheaper for Grenville to hire Rumpole of the Bailey and Kavanagh, QC to defend him in tandem. But he said nothing. As he turned to go, Whitman coughed and said: 'There is just one, final thing . . .'

Grenville turned and Whitman handed him a slip of paper.

'It's a . . . small matter.'

It was a bill for a mobile phone.

Perhaps Grenville ought to take up DC Redmond's suggestion, after all.

He stepped out into the free air and sucked in a great lungful of freedom. The traffic fumes at Highbury Corner never tasted sweeter. He glanced at his watch. Not quite ten a.m. He could treat himself to a nice, GI-compliant breakfast on Upper Street or he could head straight home. He decided on home. He could freshen up, call the studios and be back in the saddle, recording his show this afternoon, with nobody on the production team any the wiser, and very little damage done, all things considered.

He headed happily for the Tube station, passing, en route,

the news stand. A billboard caught his attention out of the corner of his eye. He turned and stared at it.

Bold as you like in that crazy fake felt-tip scrawl was the slug line: 'TV CHEF IN CAR PARK RAMPAGE'.

TWENTY-SEVEN

Jeremy got off the Tube at Leicester Square and walked through Soho, up Wardour Street and turned right onto Broadwick Street. On the corner, at the intersection with Lexington Street, he found the pub. It was quaint and Olde Worlde, clad in good polished wood, with Victorian-style lanterns bathing the name in a warm golden glow in this early winter twilight. The name was 'John Snow'. Not 'The John Snow Public House' or 'The John Snow Inn', just plain old 'John Snow' in gold letters, repeated on both façades and again around the curve on the corner. It looked like a sturdy old place. It looked like Jack the Ripper might have sunk a few flagons in there. Jeremy checked his breath, then touched his hand to the armpits of his Paul Smith shirt and sniffed his fingers. Satisfied he was, indeed, a world-class sex machine, he tugged open the door and went in.

It was fairly busy, as most of the pubs in the area would be at this time of night, even on a Wednesday. City workers and media folk, reluctant to go home for various reasons, flocked to the wine bars and ale houses of Soho, and kept them busy from about lunchtime to midnight. You go into a pub in Soho in the afternoon and it's empty, there's probably something seriously wrong with it. Definitely do not try the chilli.

Through the crush he saw Jemma, sitting at a table, studying the *Evening Standard* intently, occasionally marking it with a pen. He fought his way over to her, to see if she wanted a drink. She smiled, very nicely, when she looked up at him, and she not only already had a drink, she'd got him one in, too. Carlsberg Extra Cold, if that was all right. Which it was. Jeremy sat and sipped.

'Nice pub,' he said.

'You've never been before?'

'Didn't even know about it.'

'I wanted to meet here for an interesting reason.'

'Are you OK, Jemma? Only you sounded funny on the phone.'

'We'll get to that.' She smiled. 'First, let me tell you about John Snow.'

Jeremy raised his eyebrows, intrigued, and sat back with his pint.

'In the mid-eighteen hundreds, the most serious disease round these parts was cholera. It was extremely contagious, extraordinarily nasty, incurable and almost always fatal. At the time, we didn't understand anything about the ways contagious diseases were communicated. Conventional wisdom was they were passed by the inhalation of vapours. John Snow was a local obstetrician – he was actually a pioneer in anaesthesia – and he had a different theory: he thought cholera created poisons in the human body that emerged in the vomit and faeces, which were then passed on in water supplies contaminated with these products. At the time, there were lots of alternate theories flying around, and his was just one of many.' She paused and took a sip of wine. 'Anyway, there was a massive cholera outbreak in 1854 in the Soho area, and Snow got his chance to test his theory. He made a note of all the cases in this area, and worked out that almost all the victims drew their water from a standpipe just outside this pub. So he removed the pump handle. *Voilà!* The epidemic stopped.'

'Amazing.'

'There's a replica of the standpipe outside. You probably saw it on your way in.'

Jeremy nodded. He hadn't.

'It was one of the most sensational intuitive leaps in medical history, and it changed the future. It saved millions of lives. Millions. Removing the Broad Street pump handle is up there with the discovery of penicillin.'

'So you're saying, in the middle of the nineteenth century, people were drinking water contaminated with raw human sewage? With vomit and shit?'

'Hard to believe, I know, but it wasn't until around twenty years later that local authorities were legally compelled to provide safe, clean water. And it all started outside this pub.'

Just over a century before Jeremy was born, people living in the greatest city of the greatest empire the world had ever seen were literally drinking piss laced with diarrhoea. 'Shit,' he said, involuntarily.

'So Snow became the founding father of a new branch of medical science: epidemiology. And if he could see what they do with it today, he'd be spinning in his grave.'

'What d'you mean?'

'I'll tell you,' she pushed forward her empty glass, and smiled, 'when you bring me back an Oyster Bay merlot.'

Jeremy jostled his way to the bar, and returned with their drinks. He didn't particularly enjoy being lectured to by Jemma. Not that he wasn't interested in the stuff she told him. It just didn't seem to put the relationship on the correct footing, for his liking. It made him seem stupider than her, which he probably was in her chosen field. Still, she seemed to need to talk, though he doubted what she really needed to talk about was John Snow and the Broad Street pump.

'Epidemiology,' he reminded her as he sat down again.

'Right. Chapter two: Austin Bradford Hill. He does not have a pub named after him, to my knowledge. Just after the Second World War, it transpired that lung cancer cases were fifteen times more frequent than they had been twenty-five years earlier, and no one knew why. Hill was a professor of medical statistics, and the Medical Research Council asked him to look into the lung cancer escalation. Now, at the time, pretty much everyone smoked. Smoking was not thought to present any kind of danger at all. In fact, some adverts actually promoted some brands as having health benefits. Hill and his team conducted a massive trial on forty thousand doctors over the course of eleven years. He did it by post. They found that, on average, seven of the non-smoking subjects died each year from lung cancer per hundred thousand, compared to a hundred and sixty-six smokers. That represents *twenty-four* times more risk for the smokers. It was hailed as a major breakthrough, and again, it changed the world. Unfortunately, not for the better.'

'Of course it was for the better. Who knows how many lives that saved?'

'Well, it may have saved lives. Probably saved quite a few, in fact. But the repercussions were definitely not healthy. For a start, everyone now believes that cigarettes cause lung cancer.'

'Well, they do. It's on cigarette packets, isn't it?'

'It is. If you can actually *find* a packet of cigarettes, this day and age. Everyone believes it. You hear that somebody has lung cancer, your first question is: were they a heavy smoker? But the truth is, all Hill proved is that smoking cigarettes is *linked* to lung cancer.'

Jeremy shrugged. 'Pretty much the same thing, isn't it?'

'No, it's a completely different thing. You remember that example I gave you about bald men not living as long as hairy men?'

Jeremy did, and again the reference caused an unwilled movement of his hand through his hair. 'Sure.'

'All that shows is that baldness is linked to a reduced life span. It does not suggest that baldness *kills*, that if a hairy man shaved his head, he'd be shortening his life. Baldness is not the mechanism. The mechanism is probably high testosterone levels. All Hill's results demonstrate, at best, is that smoking *may possibly* be connected to the mechanism that causes lung cancer. To this day, nobody knows what that mechanism might be.'

Jeremy wished she'd stop bringing up that particular example. He was fairly convinced he was blessed with more than his fair share of testosterone. 'Twenty-four times more likely, though? That's more than "may possibly".'

'It's an impressive figure, sure. But it depends how you look at the numbers. If you present them another way, they show that ninety-nine thousand, eight hundred and thirty-four smokers out of a hundred thousand do *not* contract lung cancer. That's over ninety-nine point eight per cent, and there were good scientists at the time who were asking why *those* figures weren't considered when the results were evaluated. In any event, the results were accepted, the conclusions drawn and a monstrous bandwagon was created.'

'I'm not sure I follow you.'

'For a start, it gave governments the green light to start interfering in our lives, in our behaviour and our habits – all in our own best interests, of course. It sowed the seeds of the Nanny State. Everything from "don't smoke" to "don't drink", "don't spank your children", "don't use salt". Researchers everywhere wanted to get famous like Hill, and they all started panning for gold, trying to find their own route to the spotlight. They resorted to researching the looniest things: the precise shape of the perfect female bottom, for instance – it didn't matter: anything to get them a grant and a shot at the top. Worse, they lowered accepted scientific stand-ards in a desperate attempt to wring some tiny significance out of their wretchedly insignificant results. From Hill's twenty-four-times-increased risk, you now only have to prove a risk is less than *twice* as likely and you'll get published.'

'What? So if it had turned out that two smokers out of a hundred got cancer, and only one non-smoker, that would count as proof now?'

'The figures on passive smoking are even worse than that. And that's after undesirable results have been winkled out and discarded. Which is why you can read an article claiming that tea causes testicular cancer one day, and tea protects against testicular cancer the next. The way standards have eroded in epidemiology, if you try hard enough, and play dirty enough, you can prove that just about anything causes just about anything else.'

'That's insane.'

Jemma nodded. 'And those are not the only demons that flew out of Hill's Pandora's box. Tort law was born. American lawyers started prosecuting the tobacco companies, winning billions in tort cases, and whenever another link between disease and a product was "discovered", on they'd move like locusts. And we, of course, are pathetically following their lead. It also gave birth to the single-interest fanatic groups, such as the Soil Association, Consensus on Salt and Health, and Action on Smoking and Health: groups who weren't interested in balanced arguments or genuine research or serious discovery. All they wanted was to prove their case, and so they funded their own "research", the entire aim of which was to give them the results they wanted.'

Jemma stopped her diatribe and leaned back in her chair. 'I surely can talk, can't I?' She grinned.

'You surely can at that. But it is interesting. And scary, too.'

'It's just that I am a scientist, and I love science. And I hate to see it being strangled this way.'

'Ok. But I'm pretty sure you didn't invite me here just to teach me about cholera, vomit water and the evils of epidemiology.'

'No. Well, actually, that was part of it. I sort of need you to understand those things. To understand where I'm coming from.'

OK. Sounded like Jeremy was finally starting to get somewhere. Sounded like a prelude to something intimate. 'And the other part?'

'I'm off the Well Farms project.'

'What? You've been taken off the project?'

'It's much worse than that. I've been given the total heave-ho. The Spanish fiddler.'

'You've been fired from the university? Jesus. How did you manage that? I thought you had to practically kill somebody to get fired as a research assistant?'

'You practically do.'

'So, who did you kill?'

Jemma shrugged. 'I didn't get a reason, Jeremy. I got in this morning, my stuff was in a box and they pretty much told me to fuck off. They said I needn't bother to hand in my thesis.'

'That doesn't make sense. I mean, I don't know you all that well, but I imagine you're pretty good at your job.'

'I'm very good at my job. They wouldn't have put me on the Well Farms project if I wasn't good at my job.'

'So you've got someone's back up, then?'

'Maybe.'

'An old flame? Someone's, uhm, amorous attentions you've rejected?'

'Nope. If it was that kind of thing, they'd have had to give some sort of explanation. Some reason, even if it was a spurious one. They'd be terrified of a tribunal. They hate that kind of publicity.'

'What, then?'

'I think they got pressure.'

'Who from?'

'It can only be from the people who are funding the Well Farms research project.'

'But isn't that . . . ? Wouldn't that be . . . ?'

'The Government, Jeremy. That would be the Government.'

TWENTY-EIGHT

'What about this one?'

Hayleigh glanced over. Her mum was holding up a picture of Charlie from Busted. Yeah, right, she wouldn't even use that to wipe her derrière, thank you so very much. She shook her head.

Mum clucked, disappointed. 'I thought you liked him.'

Yes, about three years ago. When she was a *kid*, for heaven's sake. Busted weren't even *together* any more. Old people. You can't live with 'em, you can't chop 'em up with an axe, stuff their torsos into a suitcase and sling it in the river.

'I'm not doing very well with this, am I? Wait – how about this one? Dominic what's his name from *Lost*? You like him, don't you?'

Hayleigh shook her head again. Dominic Monaghan was cute, agreed, and there had been a time when he might have warranted a fairly respectable position on her wall, or on her computer's screensaver, but she had limited space here, and Dominic was not quite of sufficient lushness to make the cut.

'You can't *just* have pictures of Jason thingumabob, Hayleigh, darling. It's just not healthy.'

Hayleigh was, it seemed, destined for a fairly lengthy stay at the hospital. She had been given official permission to personalise one wall of her room, so long as such personalisation did not cause any damage to the decor, if you could call it decor, and Mum had offered to help her do it. But, in fact, she was just making the whole enterprise take twice as long, at least, with her ill-informed suggestions. Charlie from Busted? Good God, was he still *alive*, even?

'Ah ha!' Mum pronounced with delight. 'Michael Chad Thingy. I *know* you like him.' She brandished the picture triumphantly.

Chad Michael Murray. Yes, he had been Hayleigh's previous crush, and she still had a soft spot for him. And that was a good photo of the old dreamboat. It might just qualify. Hayleigh nodded grudgingly and held out her hand. Mum crossed over to her wheelchair and handed her the magazine.

Hayleigh scrutinised the poster. It might very well be acceptable. She took out her clear plastic ruler and measured it. It could be no larger than half the size of Jason's smallest poster. Anything bigger would have been a clear and blatant challenge to Jase's unquestionable domination.

Her mum looked on, clearly baffled and trying not to show it. Well, if she thought this was obsessive-compulsive behaviour, she should take a look in Livvie Davidson's bedroom some time. That place was literally a total *shrine* to Wentworth Miller. She had a Wentworth *altar*. Really: with candles and everything. She even had a box she claimed held a lock of Wentworth's hair she'd bought on eBay, which Hayleigh doubted very much was authentic since she'd never seen a picture of him where he actually *had* any hair, and no way José would Livvie let anyone actually look inside the box to verify its colour. No room on *those* walls for secondary crushes, let me tell you.

Yes, the Chad Michael Murray pic was correctly dimensioned. It could go in that gap over there, near the corner and low down, of course. She pointed out the spot to Mum, who went to work with her scissors.

Hayleigh had a metal plate in her leg. Can you believe that? An actual metal plate, held in by metal screws. She had a girder inside her. Can you even begin to imagine what that would do to her body weight? She probably weighed more than a London bus already. A London bus full of passengers, in fact. On top of which, they were now force-feeding her. Well, not exactly. They were forcing her to *eat*, which, if anything, was worse. If she refused, the deadly nose tube would be re-inserted and they would be free to pump anything they felt like directly into her stomach, and that had happened twice already, which was quite enough of that. So eating was the lesser of two very evil evils.

And Mum was there at every single meal. Watching every single morsel on every single forkful. Didn't she have a home to go to? Hayleigh shuddered to think what the house would look like by now, with Dad and Jonny running the ship. You probably had to burrow your way in through piles of rotting garbage and ancient pizza cartons. And Jonny would doubtless be making full use of the opportunity to explore her bedroom, rooting through her most private things like a pig in the undergrowth. There was a lock on her five-year diary, but it was a fairly flimsy one, and Jonny had almost certainly worked out how to pick it by now. Her most intimate secrets were probably being posted on his blog site as we speak.

No, wait. *Mum* would have taken her diary. Of course! And pored over every inch of it with a Sherlock Holmes-style magnifying glass. How could she have been so dumb as not to work that one out? That's probably how she knew Hayleigh had a thing for Chad – there was an entire page in there where she'd practised signing Hayleigh Michael Murray, just to see what it looked like.

Well, the joke's on you, Mum. Most of it, the reportage of Hayleigh's actual activities, was *faked*. Period pains, faked. Food eaten, faked. Tales of carefree fun, faked. Bouts of depression, unrecorded. She wasn't a fool. She wasn't about to risk that kind of stuff falling into the wrong hands. The worst she'd find, the only genuine stuff, would be some embarrassing poetry and song lyrics and florid prose, mostly dreamy speculation about the J boy.

'Here?' Mum asked, holding Chad's picture in a primo position, dead centre of the wall. Hayleigh shook her head and pointed again to the correct spot. Mum moved it over, but it was still too high. Hayleigh waved her hand to indicate it should be lower. Mum found the correct spot and looked at her expectantly, and Hayleigh rewarded her with a curt, tight nod.

The cow bag wasn't expecting Hayleigh to actually *speak* to her, was she? They could lock her up in this purgatory. They could force her to eat. They could fatten her up like a biblical calf. They could not make her enjoy one single millisecond of it. She would cooperate as far as it was necessary to avoid worsening her pitiful plight, but that's all they were getting, and not one iota more.

And then, the dreaded moment. Mum was balling up a blob of Blu-Tack when the orderly arrived with the food trolley.

Mum beamed brightly, as if the Queen of Sheba had walked in with her entire entourage, and said in a voice utterly choking with enthusiasm: 'Oh, look, Hayleigh. Lunch!' She would have used exactly the same intonation if the Lord of Hosts had suddenly appeared on the bed with His heavenly chorus of cherubim and seraphim.

Lunch. Well, whoops a dee! Set off the firecrackers and roll out the orchestra.

And Mum clapped her hands like a lovelorn schoolgirl. 'What's on the menu today, Benjamin?'

And the orderly made a great big pantomime of raising the lids covering the plates, as per bloody usual, like he was the maître d' at the Ritz, and faking a swoon in the sweaty steam that rose from under them as if everything on offer was really ambrosia and nectar, the Food of the Gods, instead of the filthy slop it actually was.

'Well, today, mes dames, we have ze chicken fricassee,' Benjamin intoned in his dreadful fake French accent, 'or ze fish and ze chips.'

'That looks fantastic. I'm *starving*. I think I'll have ze fish and ze chips, zank you. Fish is so good for you, isn't it, Benjamin?'

'Oh, *oui, oui, oui*. It's so good for you, it should probably be illegal.'

Why did they have to go through this dismal charade every single bloody meal? Did they really think she was so simple-minded she would *fall* for this pathetic little panto? Did they think the surgeons had removed her *brain*?

'Which d'you want, Hayleigh? Yummy chicken or scrummy fishy?' Mum asked, foolishly forgetting Hayleigh could only nod or shake her head in response, and so offering two consecutive choices could only elicit a stonewall stare.

'Would you like chicken, darling?'

Well, now, let me see. Would you like us to beat you to death with this delicious hammer or would you prefer us to smash your brains out with this vitamin-enriched crowbar? Tough call. The fish, if you could get away with leaving the batter, was probably the lowest in fat and calories, but then there were the lethal chips and, unmentioned, peas. The chicken was fairly low in fat (it wasn't actually fricasseed, either, it was grilled) but it came in a God-knows-what chasseur-type sauce, *and* there was mash, deadly mash, and carrots.

No, that sauce could *not* be trusted. Hayleigh shook her head.

'The fish, then,' Mum said to Benjamin, because, of course, Hayleigh could not be allowed to refuse that. Hayleigh no longer had any will of her own, in case you were wondering.

'Excellent choice, ladies. And from the dessert menu? The rice pudding is really, really nice. Honestly.'

Mum glanced over at Hayleigh, but she knew better than to even try to offer her that particular death threat. She turned back to Benjamin. 'I think we'll have the fruit salad. It is only lunch, after all.'

'Another good choice,' Benjamin said. 'It's fresh. I know because I opened the tin myself.'

The two adult clowns found this a very funny joke indeed.

'I'll see you in my dreams, girls,' Benjamin said, as per bloody, and waved and went, praise de Lord.

Hayleigh looked down at her hands. They were clutching the arms of the wheelchair so tightly, the knuckles had gone bright white. And this wasn't even the worst bit. This was just the light-entertainment *prelude* to the worst bit.

Mum brought over her tray and hooked it into its slots on the wheelchair. She'd even set a flower in an Orangina bottle on it. 'Would you like some orange juice?' she asked, knowing full well the answer would be in the negative. Hayleigh didn't even bother. 'Water, then.' Mum sighed. She crossed to the bedside table, poured a plastic glassful and set it down on Hayleigh's tray. Hayleigh knew this was another charade, Mum pretending to be disappointed she would only drink water, because it wasn't just plain water. There was stuff in there. You could taste it. Once she'd caught a glimpse of a bottle of it in Mum's bag, and she'd just managed to read the words 'fortified' and 'calcium' before the *vache* had managed to snap the bag shut, so no one was fooling no one here, milady. Hayleigh tipped it away and replaced it with tap water whenever she got the chance, which was not nearly often enough for her liking.

She'd agreed she needed calcium. Apparently it was mostly calcium deficiency that had weakened her bones, blah blah, made sense. Boring but true. Well, fine. She'd agreed to take the supplements *in tablet form*, just to keep the peace, so long as she was allowed to read the label listing *all* the ingredients, of course. But it didn't stop there. They were always trying to sneak it into her diet in one way or another. Every morning – *every* morning, mind you – they made her drink an entire glass of milk. That was one of the very worst bits of the day, which was invariably made up completely of bad bits, one after the other. At first, they'd tried to give her full-fat milk. Full-fat milk. What was that about? A drink that boasted in its very name that it was full of fat. Well, she'd put her good foot down on that subject, and no mistake. She'd demanded skimmed, and they'd settled on semi-skimmed, as a compromise, but it was still an ordeal. The thing about milk: it tastes hideous even when it's fresh. If you take your time drinking it, sipping infinitesimally tiny amounts, with long breaks in between, it actually gets worse. After an hour or two, it turns into stale yoghurt. It's like sucking down a spittoon. And if you complain about that, they just go and get you a fresh glass, and the whole thing starts *all over again*. The only, the absolutely only way to get through it was to imagine Owen Wilson in *Starsky and Hutch* is sitting on the bed in that daft cowboy disguise, saying, 'Do it! Do it!' in that silly voice, and you just do it, down as quick as you can, glug, glug, glug, and pray you don't throw it all back up immediately, so you have to taste it twice.

Well, once you've gone through that, and you've taken the tablets, you'd think that would be enough, but no. They just had to try to sneak some fortified water down your gullet, too. There's such a thing as too much calcium, people. We've all gone calcium crazy, here. When she got a chance at a computer, she would definitely look up the symptoms of lactose intolerance on Wikipedia, to see if they were easy to fake.

So, now they were all set for the Battle of Marathon that was lunch.

Mum pointed her wheelchair at the window, so she could enjoy the full, unremitting bleakness of the view, and sat at the table with her own tray. And the deal was: mouthful for mouthful. It could, and often did, take hours. More than once, they had still been at it when dinner arrived. Insane. Is it not possible, not ever, to, once in a while, not feel all that hungry? Does everybody *always* have to have the appetite of a starving dog at a butcher's bin?

But the rule, amongst many, many rules Hayleigh was obliged to observe if she wanted to escape the Snickers-bar-cake drip, was you have to eat at least two-thirds of the food on your plate. And you have to have at least one mouthful of everything. Everything. If a cockroach inadvertently wandered onto your plate, then woe betide it: it would have to be eaten.

Mum was poised over her own plate with her knife and fork primed, watching Hayleigh's every movement with scrupulous intensity.

Hayleigh prodded her food with her knife. Where to begin with this little banquet of horrors? Well, obviously, not the chips. The chips would definitely be constituting the bulk of her leavable third. Why did almost every meal come with some form of potatoes? Potatoes weren't really food. For a start, they weren't vegetables, they were tubers. Second, they belonged to the deadly nightshade family, and in Hayleigh's humble, anything with a family name of 'deadly' should probably not be eaten. They don't often quote the 'deadly' part on restaurant menus. Hmm. Wonder why? Third, they contained nicotine. Really. A portion of mashed potatoes was like spending a night in a smoky room. Why didn't they just give her a nice Havana cigar and have done with it? And last, but not least, the calories. The sheer audacious *calories* of the damned things. But she wasn't supposed to even think about calories. That was another of the many bizarre rules in the *Alice in Wonderland* world of Hayleigh Griffin.

A scoop of peas, perhaps?

No.

Couldn't face the peas just yet. They were so sweet, it was hard not to imagine you were chewing down on nuggets of pure sugar. You have to surprise yourself with the peas, and you can't actually chew them at all. You have to *mime* chewing, and swallow them whole. Not for the first mouthful.

Better get on with it. She cut into the deep-fried batter, trying not to shudder, and lifted it clear of the white fish inside. Hot and pungent steam blasted up from it, and Hayleigh tried not to smell it, but she was too late. She fought against her natural reaction, which was, quite frankly, to hurl the entire contents of the tray at her mother, then race her wheelchair out of the room, down the corridor and not stop till she reached Bolivia, where she would seek political asylum. She didn't react at all. Just kept her head pointing down at the plate and looking out of the top of her eyes at Mum, who had cut into her own batter, and was now waiting to mimic Hayleigh's next move.

God, woman. Get a *life*!

Hayleigh lifted a flaky chunk of the fish and set it down on another bit of the plate, away from the killer batter.

It was extremely tiring, this whole business. She felt like lying down and sleeping for a month. She took a sip of the poisoned water, and stared down at the fish. OK. Nothing else for it. Might as well get it over with.

She dug into the fish with her fork and lifted it clear of the plate. She raised it towards her mouth, but when she saw it close up, she realised it was far too big, so she put it back on her plate, and cut it in half.

'Hayleigh, darling, *please*. I'm starving.'

Then *eat*, woman, eat. Who's stopping you?

She raised the loaded fork to her mouth and put the fish inside. That act was quite exhausting enough, thank you, and she didn't have the energy just yet to chew, much less swallow, so she had to let it lie there on her tongue for a little bit while she gathered her resources.

And plop! A big tear rolled out of her downcast eye and onto the plate. Marvellous. Now, under regulations, presumably she'd have to eat that, too. Brilliant.

Just how long could she put up with this insanity?

Not much longer, that was for sure.

Not much longer.

TWENTY-NINE

Grenville sped along Friern Barnet Road in a natty little sports car. It was fairly cold and sharp out, but it was bright and dry, and he had the roof down and sunglasses on, and he was feeling good. Nothing like the wind blowing through the remnants of your hair and the roar of a straining engine to give you a sense of freedom.

On the seat beside him, riding shotgun, was a slim, hardback copy of *Caging Your Furies – Seven Simple Steps To Managing Your Anger*, by a Dr Alan Roth. He hadn't had chance to do more than skim through it, as yet, but he'd already picked up some techniques that sounded like they might be useful. Grenville didn't really think he had an anger problem, but looking back on the events of the previous day he had to admit he could perhaps have handled one or two things slightly better, possibly. Rage was quite a commonplace emotion in a professional kitchen. You couldn't really be a head chef and a shrinking violet. But sometimes it could get out of hand. Tom Aikens, when he was a wunderkind cooking at Pied-A-Terre in Charlotte Street (his signature dish, then, was pig's head: to die for) supposedly got sent home for pressing a commis' hand on a hot plate, and, since he refused to accept he'd done anything to apologise for, he never went back. Grenville had never done anything quite so outrageous, but he'd had his strops, that was for sure. Still, he no longer worked in a professional kitchen, and he had no intention of ever doing so again, so it was probably time he put that side of his nature behind him.

He checked the speedo and raised his foot slightly off the accelerator. That was one of the techniques from the book.

Always go five miles per hour slower than you have to. If you're in a rush, you're in a rage. He'd hired the car. His own was a write-off, it goes without saying. He'd have to buy a new one, but he wouldn't have time until the weekend at the earliest, and instead of a bog-standard saloon, he'd decided to treat himself to something with a bit of zip and glamour. Plus, with the roof down, a convertible is much easier to get into. You don't have to bend almost double and crush each and every one of your internal organs just to cram yourself behind the damned steering wheel.

He wasn't quite sure how he'd managed to wind up with that joke of a hatchback in the first place. That had been his wife's runaround, but, thanks to the sterling skills of his ruthless legal team, he'd got that in the divorce settlement and his wife had wound up with his Jag. She'd also kept the house and half the shares in his restaurant, the business he'd built up with the sweat of his own brow, by the way, but that had counted for nothing. Grenville had been forced to sell his half just to get somewhere to live, so, effectively, his wife had come away with everything they'd owned together: the house, the Jag, the restaurant, and he'd come away with a crappy six-year-old hatchback and a poky little flat in North London. He still found it hard to wrap his head around quite how all that had happened. It's not as if the divorce had been his fault. It was his ex who'd done the extramaritals – with his sommelier, the Frog bastard. She was the one who'd been boffing the help.

There was the Law, and there was Justice. It would be nice if they got to meet once in a while.

Grenville thought the whole car park business would probably never have happened if he'd been in the Jag. People respect a Jag. The crone would have thought twice before double parking an XK8.

So he needed a new car, and he might even splash out on a decent one. He couldn't really afford it, what with the fines and everything, but his career was going reasonably well. He had a book, or at least a third of a book, out, and that was selling. There was talk of another book for next Christmas. His agent was making noises about getting his own series, all to himself, on a mainstream channel. So he could probably push the boat out just a little bit. Nothing too extreme: certainly not a Jag. Maybe an MG. Were they still making them? Otherwise, if he just replaced the hatchback with a similar model, he'd be forking out about fifteen, sixteen grand in total just to be in exactly the same position he'd started in the previous morning, and that seemed unpalatable.

This little Toyota wasn't bad, as a matter of fact. Might check out the second-hand prices on one of these.

He swung in through the entrance to Elstree Studios, and had a small delay at the security barrier – here, amazingly, they had a security barrier that stopped people getting *into* the car park – because he didn't have his official sticker, which was on the windscreen of his other car, which was now scattered to the four corners of the Earth. But the guard was a decent human being, who recognised him, on top of which Grenville had his laminated studio pass, so the barrier was raised and he parked in his usual spot, the whole endeavour concluded without so much as an angry gesture. Thank you, Dr Roth.

He got out, easily, and looked up at the sky. Didn't look like rain, so he decided to leave the roof down. Then he'd be able just to leap straight in after the show, like Patrick McGoohan in *Danger Man*, and whiz off. He picked up the book and popped it in his recipe folder – didn't want anyone catching sight of that, thank you very much – then he locked the car with its electronic key fob and walked jauntily over to the production offices.

He hadn't phoned ahead. Given the tabloid reports, he couldn't face making such a phone call. They'd probably tried calling him, probably tried several times, in fact, but the digital tape, or whatever it was, on his answering machine had been completely used up by his own diatribe from the police station. He'd had a good giggle at that. He'd decided it would be best to brazen it out. He could make light of the whole affair in front of everyone, play it down, and any gossipy nonsense would probably be over and done with by the time the cameras started rolling. He might take a bit of a ribbing from the other presenters, but that was to be expected. He could live with that.

He poked his head around the door of the *Cook It, Change It, Dig It!* office and said 'hello', just to see The Girl, really, but The Girl wasn't there, just the production accountant, who barely lifted her eyes from the log books to acknowledge him.

He sauntered off towards make-up, and there She was, La Femme, the vision of loveliness, coffee mug in hand, emerging from the kitchen area. Grenville smiled and nodded 'Morning' at her, but she was looking at him very strangely indeed, and she kept on looking at him strangely even when he'd passed her, and that was worrying. That was not a good thing. There was always some flirtatious banter between them. Always. There was something very disturbing about that look she'd given him. Almost as if . . .

Almost as if she hadn't expected to see him.

He popped into make-up, and there was something even more worrying. Because sitting there, in the make-up chair, being worked on by Liz, the ancient make-up girl, was Bob Constable of *Ready, Steady, Fuck It Up* fame.

Now, why would they need another celebrity chef on the show?

Constable saw him in the mirror and grinned warmly. 'Grenville. How you doing, mate?'

'I'm good,' Grenville said. 'Yourself?'

'I'm champion, lad. Let's catch up when I'm finished in the chair.'

'Yes,' Grenville said. 'Let's do that.'

And he went off to look for a producer to kill.

THIRTY

The John Snow seemed to have got very hot and crowded all of a sudden. Jeremy leaned in closer and lowered his voice. 'The *Government* got you fired?'

Jemma thinned her smile. 'It's the only thing that makes sense. I mean, out on my ear, no names, no pack drill. Someone must have been leaning on the department. Someone with a lot of clout. I've tried calling a couple of people I thought were my friends there, but no one will talk to me. I'm a non-person. I've been Photoshopped out of the picture.'

'Jesus! Why?'

'I think it was Stone.'

'Peter Stone?'

'I think they had the cameras on us all the time.'

'The *cameras*?' Jeremy almost gagged, and then said, 'Jesus!' again.

'And I think the cameras must have been miked, which is pretty unusual, don't you think?'

And all Jeremy could do was break the third Commandment again.

'I need another drink,' Jemma said, fishing a purse from her bag and rising. 'Same again?'

'No, no. Let me get it. You're out of work.'

'Don't be so daft. I'm not a pauper yet.'

Left alone at the table, Jeremy began, rather selfishly, to worry about himself. What had the cameras and the microphones caught of him? He couldn't think of anything he'd done that was particularly subversive or offensive, with the possible exception of his one-man re-enactment of the Three

Stooges stage show in the dormitory. He'd handed in his work on the Well Farms project on Monday, as he'd been asked, and it had been, in his humble opinion, good work; very good work. All his best people had pulled out all the stops and worked the weekend and burned the midnight oil with him, and they'd come up with a first-rate campaign plan. A winner, no question. But he hadn't got any feedback, yet, and this was Wednesday, and he had expected *some*thing by now.

He rewound and replayed their Nature Walk conversation, but no, as far as he could recall, it was Jemma who'd done all the talking, which seemed to be the norm in this relationship, and he'd just nodded politely and chipped in now and then.

He jumped when Jemma came back with their drinks.

'Sorry.' She grinned. 'Didn't mean to startle you.'

'I don't know what you're so bloody chirpy about. Of all the things you want to do before you're thirty, getting on the Government's shit list does not rank highly.'

Jemma shrugged. 'Not a lot I can do about it, is there?'

'But why? What did you say that would cause them to – ?'

'I was off-message, Jeremy. That's all it takes with this bloody lot, isn't it? With the "my way or the highway" brigade.'

'So what are you going to do?'

Jemma tapped the *Standard*. 'I'm going to get another job. I've got an odd feeling I'll find it quite hard to get another research position at any university. At least at any university this side of Kuala Lumpur. You got any positions going, Jeremy, in the conceptuological industry?'

'Come on, even if they did get you fired, they're not going to blackball you. That's crazy.'

'Maybe you're right. Maybe I'm being paranoid. I just think, if they were behind my dismissal, and I can't come up with anything else that makes sense, they're not going to want me anywhere I might spout my poisonous treachery and get listened to. In any event, methinks I should be polishing up my bartending skills, just in case.'

Jeremy shook his head. 'I'm not buying it, Jemma. There's got to be another explanation.'

'I'm open to suggestions.'

'But it doesn't make *sense*. Well Farms . . . it's a benign programme. At least, it's *intended* to be benign.'

'I don't know. I've been thinking about it, and I'm not sure I believe that any more.'

'Come on, Jemma: they're only trying to improve people's lives. To *save* lives, for crying out loud. They might be misguided . . .' and the instant that left his lips, Jeremy regretted saying it. He doubted they were being bugged in there, but Jemma's paranoia was contagious. A lot of faces in the pub crowd were starting to look oddly out of place to him, and that man at the table opposite hadn't touched his pint or turned the page on his newspaper since he'd sat down, as far as Jeremy could work out. Perhaps they should think about going somewhere else. Like the planet Mars, perhaps.

And, naturally, Jemma chose this particular moment to launch into another one. 'If they really wanted to save lives, they could do a lot of things that would be easier and cheaper and would actually have a chance of working. They could easily do it in hospitals, just by forcing the staff to *wash their bloody hands*. One hundred thousand people a year contract infections just by *being* in hospital. Really. Just by lying in a hospital bed, you have a one-in-ten chance of getting seriously ill, because the standards of hygiene are now at about the same levels as they were in the Crimean fucking War. Why? Because the cleaning of the wards is farmed out to the lowest bidder. We have higher levels of MRSA and other antibiotic-resistant super bugs than anywhere else in Europe. We are killing five thousand people a year just by *admitting* them to hospital, and contributing to another fifteen thousand deaths, mostly because of bad fucking laundry practices. Now, even by the Government's own pathetically inept reckoning, passive smoking is supposed to be responsible for one thousand deaths a year – it isn't, by the way, and there is not one shred of non-dubious evidence that it's responsible for so much as a cough – but, even by their own reckoning, it doesn't get *close* to the devastation being wreaked by MRSA, yet they spend billions on advertising and force draconian laws through parliament to combat the one, and do absolutely bloody nothing about the other. Can you even begin to explain to me how that could possibly make sense? It's so bizarre, even Lewis Carroll wouldn't use it.'

Jeremy was looking around the pub nervously throughout most of this latest harangue. What did that man at the table opposite find so bloody engrossing on that particular page of that particular newspaper? Was he committing it to memory? And why had he bought that bloody pint if he didn't want to bloody drink it? 'Jemma, you really don't know when to stop, do you?' he said, trying to lighten up her mood.

'No. No, I don't. And I think that's one of my most beguiling features, don't you?'

Jeremy had to smile. She certainly was a feisty one, he'd give her that.

She leaned in closer and lowered her voice. Jeremy could smell the liquorice aroma of the red wine on her breath. 'Jeremy, you're the only person I know who's still on this project that I can even remotely trust.'

'*If* I'm still on the project.'

'Of course you're still on the project. *I'm* the stupid bitch who can't keep her mouth shut. I want you to watch out.'

'Watch out for what?'

'I don't even know. I don't think these farms will wither and die, like I imagined. I think they'll go on. I think they'll mutate, in some way.'

'Mutate? Into what?'

'Into something bad. Something very bad indeed.'

THIRTY-ONE

Extract from *Caging Your Furies – Seven Simple Steps To Managing Your Anger*, by Dr Alan Roth.

We all of us get angry. Anger is a natural, healthy emotion, which spurs us on to react against injustices. Even Jesus Christ got angry. Remember the banishing of the merchants from the temple steps? (John, 2:13-25.)

But while anger is valid, temper is not. The techniques in this book are devised to help you harness your anger and channel it positively, *without ever losing your temper*.

This is an overview, and all of these techniques outlined below are explained and expanded later in the book. I urge you to read it thoroughly. These are powerful techniques, and must be used properly. However, it is my intention to set out my stall in such a way that by the end of this introduction, you will already have grasped the fundamentals that will enable you to grab back control of your temper gremlin, and, therefore, your life.

Ask Yourself: Is It Anger I'm Feeling?

When you find yourself in a situation where your gorge is rising, ask yourself if you are right to be feeling anger, or is anger in this situation an unreasonable and inappropriate response?

Don't Lose It

We often talk about people being beside themselves with rage. What we mean is they are no longer reacting as they normally would. They are reduced to the role of onlooker in their own life. It's vitally important to maintain control of our responses, in all situations. Below are some techniques to avoid 'losing it'.

1) Walk Away

This is the first and most powerful anger management tool. If you remove yourself from the scene, even for a few moments, you dramatically improve your opportunities to find the correct response to a situation.

2) Buy Some Time

I don't advocate the old chestnut of 'counting to ten'. It might work the first few times, but it rapidly loses power and becomes a meaningless exercise. Sometimes, counting to ten can actually *build* your anger. A more advanced tip is to memorise a short poem you like, one you can recite to yourself in your head. It can be anything: a Shakespeare sonnet, an amusing limerick, anything that makes you feel good. It's especially powerful if it makes you laugh. When you feel the blood rising, repeat it to yourself, mentally. You'd be surprised how often this can diffuse a potentially confrontational situation. And if at any point you feel that poem is no longer working for you, find a new one. It's important to keep it fresh. I have reproduced a selection of suitable pieces at the end of this book. It's not, as some of the more unkind detractors of the first edition cruelly suggested, merely 'a dismal way of padding out a thin pamphlet with painfully few ideas and absolutely no new ones into a sellable-sized volume'. It's valuable. It's probably saved lives. Use it. (My own current favourite is 'There Was a Young Woman from Philly'. I had to use it quite a lot when I read those reviews, let me tell you!)

3) Reproject

Try imagining the person on whom your anger is focused is someone you love. It's hard to feel hatred for your dear old grandma, much less punch her lights out!

4) Slow Down

What's the rush? Racing from one place to the next is creating unnecessary stress in your life. If you're in a rush, you risk a rage. Set off earlier. Always try to drive five miles an hour slower than you think you have to. If you're walking, don't just put your head down and try to cover the distance. Stroll. Saunter. You'll find it improves the quality of your life quite dramatically. Enjoy the journey. Smell the roses!

5) Avoid Your Triggers

Many of us find certain situations or people repeatedly cause us to lose our tempers. It's important to recognise them and, wherever possible, avoid them. It might be an obnoxious work colleague. It might be rush-hour traffic. Sometimes it may be difficult to avoid them altogether, but I have found in almost every circumstance it's possible, at the very least, to minimise your contact with them. If it's the traffic, for instance, think about leaving home earlier. If it's someone in your office, contemplate moving your desk – it's usually possible. Failing that, think about moving to another branch, or even another career!

6) Don't Feed The Monster

Sometimes our misplaced anger is the result of outside stimulus. Some people only get angry when they drink alcohol, or a certain type of alcohol, or a certain amount. Cut it down, or cut it out altogether. If you use recreational drugs that consistently induce anger in you, the answer is very simple: stop. It's illegal anyway, unless you're Dutch.

7) Walk Away

I know, I know, this is the same as the first technique, and I'm not including it again because, as some fools have suggested, I can't actually think of seven different techniques to satisfy my publisher's remit, but because it's *so* valuable, I felt honour bound to include it twice. If you're facing a situation where you can feel yourself losing control, get out of there. Don't walk, run. Or at least saunter quickly!

In the following chapters, we will explore all these techniques in much more detail, and I have included several case studies which illustrate the concepts, and show us how my temper-control course has improved countless lives. In most cases, just reading this book properly will help you wrest back control of your life, and keep your Furies where they should be: caged and under your command. In some of the more extreme cases, however, a more personal consultation may be required. Check out my website, which lists my current seminar program. If you would like to become a fully licensed Roth Anger Counsellor, log on for details of online courses and franchise details.

Take your time with this book, and enjoy it.

And remember: don't be an onlooker in your own life.

Dr Alan Roth *

---

* Dr Alan Roth is not a medical doctor, and has never claimed to be one.

THIRTY-TWO

Hayleigh was in her psychiatrist's office. Oh, yes, hadn't you heard? Standard procedure for a broken leg, regular visits to the nut doctor. Endless hours of dull, dull dullness. You'd better not break *two* legs round these parts, me old cock sparrow: they'd probably lock you up in the loony bin and throw away the key. They'd probably tie you up in a strait-jacket and shoot one million volts of electricity into your brain.

She was sitting in silence as usual. Hayleigh had, quite literally, not said one single word in any of their sessions. For the first three sessions, neither had the psychiatrist. They had simply been seminars of silence. In fact, by her fourth visit, Hayleigh had almost started to look forward to the break from her mother's endless prattle. A tiny little oasis in the desert of Hayleigh Griffin's existence.

But the nut doctor had caved and started talking. He'd tried, at first, asking questions, but Hayleigh had no intention of answering any questions, ever. Under the Geneva Convention, she was required to give her name, rank and serial number, and that was all. And since she had no rank or serial number, as far as she was aware, and since they already knew her name, she was not obliged to say anything at all.

She had talked at first, when she came out of the swoon after the operation. She'd *had* to talk to defend her corner in the food-regulations negotiations, but once they were settled and set in stone, she had not said one word, not one single word to anyone. She was on Talk Strike.

So the nut doctor had given up his interrogations, and that had been that for session four.

In session five, however, he'd tried a different tack. He'd started talking *at* her. He'd obviously got his ammunition from *la grande vache* herself, because he seemed to know an awful lot of intimate information about her. Hayleigh managed to shut most of it out. She just had a nice chat with herself, thank you very much. The occasional barb penetrated, though. She did realise, didn't she, that everybody was only trying to help her? Yeah, right, they were torturing her for her own good. If she didn't start eating properly she could cause herself serious damage. Does this face look bothered, mate?

And, gradually, she'd been able to phase out his voice, so now, by what must surely have been session one million and seventy-five, it was nothing more than a background hum. White noise.

But then he said something she could not tune out. Something so outrageous, it could probably give you a heart attack, and you could drop down dead on the spot.

What he said was: 'Would you like to meet Jason Black?'

To hear that name, coming from her tormentor's lips, sent Hayleigh's head spinning. Her stomach started flopping around like a freshly landed fish. She tried not to react, but he must have seen her stiffen, because he carried on with the filthy business, and there was triumph in his tone.

'I mean, I'm not sure we'll be able to swing it, but I can get in touch with his people, give it a shot. Would you like that, Hayleigh?'

She could feel her own face colouring with fury. To drag Jason into this hideous business. How dare he? The one, the only decent part of her life. The safe haven she kept in her head. They'd reached into her most private place and violated it. The filthy, filthy bastards.

'I mean, you'd talk to Jason, wouldn't you?'

Stop saying his name! She shook her head violently. It wasn't talking, but it was communication. She hated herself for handing him this tiny victory, but this had to be stopped. It had to stop now.

'He's probably got a busy schedule, but he might agree to pop along.'

Hayleigh was fighting back tears. She would not give him the satisfaction. She tried to concentrate on the Litany. Jason Black. Age twenty-two. Born in Cheadle, Manchester. Birthday: September 25th. Star sign: Libra. Favourite colour: purple. Fave food: beef burrito. Biggest luv: haven't met her yet (natch!) Most embarrassing moment: going on stage without trousers . . .

But it wasn't working and she couldn't stop the tears now. And the nut doctor knew he had done a bad thing finally, because he was apologising and asking what was wrong. Well, here's what's wrong, Mr Psycho: when you're a prisoner in a tower, when your every waking moment is torture, and your gaoler even sleeps on the sofa in your room, and you aren't left alone for more than three minutes in a week, you need something to cling on to, I'll tell you that much. You need some kind of *hope*. Because this is unbearable, and somebody, *somebody* has to come and rescue you. There has to be somebody out there who just might steal in, in the dead of night, and whisk you up in his strong, brave arms and carry you away. Because you're a prisoner of conscience, you're a princess in a tower, and we all know they need a handsome prince, there has to be a handsome prince out there for every princess prisoner, doesn't there? And when you start talking about inviting the prince over for tea and bloody biscuits, you're shattering a dream, you're stealing a person's hope. Because somebody has to come to the rescue, and if not Jason, then who?

If not him, then who?

And then Hayleigh felt a terrible coldness invade her body, as if she were back on that dreadful drip again, only this time they were filling her veins with pure ice.

Nobody was going to come.

There would be no rescue.

She'd known it all along, really. It was a stupid, immature

fantasy, when you faced up to it. She hadn't really been fully aware she was clinging on to it with such intense desperation. It had just been there, at the back of her mind, dreamy and opaque. It never had a chance of standing up to scrutiny.

And suddenly, she felt more weary than she had ever felt in her life. She just couldn't go on. It was as simple as that. She had no struggle left in her. She barely noticed her mum was pushing her down the corridor back to their cell. Back to the unbearable routine.

She couldn't take it any more.

And there was only one way out.

THIRTY-THREE

Grenville finally tracked down the producer. He was cowering in the edit suite, the stuck-up spineless snake. His face fell for just an instant when he first saw Grenville, but he recovered quickly and made all the right facial moves to give the impression he was delighted to see him.

'Grenville.' He crocodile-grinned. 'We didn't know whether or not to expect you.'

'Why? I work here.'

'Well, with all that . . . you know . . . business yesterday. We thought you might want to keep a low profile for a wee while.'

'Oh, that was all blown out of proportion. It was nothing, really. You know how the tabloids are for making a mountain out of a molehill.'

'For sure, for sure.' The producer agreed too quickly and nodded just a little bit too enthusiastically for Grenville's liking.

'Soooo. What's Bob Constable doing here?'

'Bob? Oh, did you bump into him? Yes. Well, he stepped into the breach for us yesterday, as t'were, and we couldn't get hold of you and your agent didn't seem to know where you were, so we sort of . . . Look, I might as well tell you. He's your replacement.'

'My temporary replacement, you mean.'

'Uhm. No. He's your replacement, full stop.'

Right, Grenville. Steady on, now. Try the Happy Poem.

There was a young sous chef from Hitchin . . .

'You cannot be serious.'

'I'm sorry, Grenville. I really am.'

'Bob *Constable*?'

'We were lucky to get him at such short notice.'

'But Bob *Constable*?'

'What's wrong with Bob Constable?'

'What's wrong with Bob Constable is he's not fit to lick my backside.'

'Bob's a fine cook.'

'He is not a fine cook. He's an idiot. I am a Michelin-starred chef. Bob Constable cannot even spell the word "Michelin".'

'Well, we'll just have to agree to disagree on that, Grenville.'

OK, Grenville. Walk away. 'Hang on. Can you just excuse me for a second? Will you just excuse me for just one second?'

The producer looked slightly baffled, but nodded his assent. Grenville stepped out of the room and into the corridor.

There was a young sous chef from Hitchin

Whose wife was consistently bitchin' . . .

This was unbe-fucking-lievable. Cunt bloody Bobstable? Yes, it was anger he was feeling, and yes, it was appropriate, and no, he wasn't beside himself. Right.

Grenville strode back into the room. 'I'm shell shocked, here. I really am. I mean, why? Because of that stupid non-sense in the car park? I mean, there's no such thing as bad publicity, is there? It's not as though I went on a five-day three-in-a-bed cocaine binge orgy with a former *Blue Peter* presenter.'

'No, it's not just your rampage—'

'It was *not* a rampage.'

'If you say so. No, it wasn't just because of that. I'll be blunt. We've been getting pressure from the network. They think you're bad for the image of the show.'

'Bad for the image of the show? In what way am I bad for the image of the show?'

'Well, your . . .' The producer looked him up and down. 'Your size.'

'My size? You're sacking me because I'm overweight?'

'Not in so many words, Grenville. They've been looking for an excuse to replace you for a bit, now, and that . . . business yesterday: you handed it them on a plate, basically.'

'You're sacking me because I'm fat?'

'You present an image the network doesn't want associated with their cookery output.'

'In other words, they don't want a fat chef on their channel.'

'Your words, Grenville, not mine. Look, I've been honest with you. I could have said it was because of your rampage, not that it was a rampage, but I didn't. I told you the truth.'

Grenville was actually feeling dizzy with rage. He could feel himself swaying. He tried to reproject. He tried to imagine the man was, in fact, his sainted grandmother, but it was no use: no matter how hard he tried, the bastard still looked like an ugly shit you wouldn't want to find in your toilet bowl. Time to walk away again.

'Will you excuse me again, just for a sec?'

And again, the producer looked a little bewildered, but nodded, and Grenville stepped out of the room again.

There was a young sous chef from Hitchin
Whose wife was consistently bitchin'.
Without any bluster . . .

And sod this for a game of soldiers. Grenville stormed right back into the edit suite. 'Can you even do this? I mean, I've got a contract. Is this even legal?'

'Yes. There's a morality clause. The network lawyers say it's cast iron. Check with your agent, if you like. Run it by your own lawyers.'

Grenville didn't think he'd be running it by his own lawyers. He wasn't convinced his own lawyers could even read. 'So that's it? Just like that, I'm gone?'

'I'm sorry, Grenville. It's been a privilege working with you. I'm sorry it had to end like this. If it were up to me—'

'But what about the book?'

'What book?'

'The next *Cook It, Change It, Dig It!* book, for next Christmas.'

'Well, presumably Bob will be doing that.'

'Can he write?

'There's no need to be like that—'

'No, seriously. I'm not even sure he's got opposable thumbs.'

'Look, I don't want to be mean, but you're not exactly the world's greatest cookery writer yourself, are you?'

'What? What do you mean?'

'Oh, nothing. Let it pass.'

'No. I can't let that pass. You made an assertion that is the *exact* opposite of the truth. I want to know what you meant.'

'I mean, seriously: ten pages on how to boil an egg. It's a bit—'

'It was not ten pages.'

'Ten pages, Grenville, on how to boil an egg.'

'That's including illustrations, though.'

'Perhaps. But ten pages? Everybody in the world knows how to boil an egg.'

'Only if they've read my recipe.'

'Are you suggesting you're the only person on the entire planet who knows how to boil an egg?'

'Of course not. Nico Ladenis can probably do it, too, you cocky little moron.'

'Right, Grenville, I think you should go now, before this starts getting nasty.'

'It's already gotten nasty, mate. It got nasty when you stood there and fired me for being a big fat bastard.'

'Do I need to call security?'

'You can call who the fuck you like, you suppurating little shit. Call your mother and make her apologise for not aborting you.'

The producer picked up the phone. 'I'm calling security.'

Grenville stormed out. He had to. He was on the brink of punching the dick-wad to within an inch of his life, and he had a criminal record now, so that would never do. Besides, what would Dr Roth have to say about that?

There was a young sous chef from Hitchin
Whose wife was consistently bitchin'.
Without any bluster,
He killed her and trussed her . . .

Right, he'd handled that confrontation much better. Apart from the abortion remark and the 'little shit' remark, he'd pretty much kept his cool. He'd practically been dignified.

He was furious, but, surely, he had every right to be furious. They had fired him, not because he was untalented or incapable of doing the job, but simply because he was too fat.

He strode past the production office, valiantly resisting the urge to dive in and scream a host of abuse at anyone who happened to be standing about, which was symptomatic of the new Grenville, who was not an onlooker in his own life, who was in complete and total control of himself, but just before he hit the exit door, he wheeled round without stopping, threw open the production office door and yelled, 'And fuck the lot of you, right up the backside!'

Unfortunately, the only person in the room was The Girl, so great, another brilliant triumph for Grenville Roberts, and another bridge down in flames. Sterling work. He was burning more bridges than Operation Market Garden.

Outside, it had started to rain, quite heavily, in fact, and Grenville relished it. He really needed it to help him cool off, but then he reached his car, and, of course, he'd left the roof down.

He unlocked it with the beeper and opened the door. A good two inches of water cascaded out onto his trousers. How was it possible that so much rain could have collected in so small an area in such a short space of time? It was as if every single raindrop had been deliberately funnelled into this one spot. Look out, God, for there's a mighty kicking a-coming Your way.

He squelched into the fabric seat and turned on the engine. How did you get the roof back up? The girl at the Hertz office had shown him, but he couldn't remember now. He looked in the glove compartment for the manual, but it didn't seem to be there.

Stuff it. He just had to get out of here. He gunned the engine and reversed into a large concrete pillar.

There was a young sous chef from Hitchin
Whose wife was consistently bitchin'.
Without any bluster,
He killed her and trussed her,
And served her up, roast, in his kitchen.

He looked around nervously for CCTV cameras, and, yes, of course, there was one pointed directly at him. He waved at it.

He drove out of the car park at ridiculous speed, frankly, and with the rain driving into his face, he was partially blinded, so it wasn't until he hit the first set of traffic lights on Friern Barnet Road that he noticed there was a security barrier wedged firmly in his radiator grille.

He reached into his folder, pulled out Dr Roth's book and hurled it with some considerable venom out of the car. There was an old lady sheltering from the rain under a greengrocer's canopy. The book hit her smack in the middle of her face, and she went down like a coal sack.

THIRTY-FOUR

Well, now. Jeremy Slank finally had Jemma in his den. And the game was more than afoot, Watson, the game was almost concluded. From this position, he rarely failed to achieve closure. Very rarely indeed.

She'd eschewed his offer of supper when they'd finally been turfed out of the John Snow, but accepted, to his great surprise, the offer of a nightcap back at his gaff. Jemma, predictably, had not stopped talking all throughout the last-orders bell – thankfully the proprietors either hadn't sought a late-night license as yet, or had no interest in invoking it on a midweek night – the repeated cajoling of the bar staff and the donning of overcoats. She probably carried on while Jeremy had visited the loo.

She had continued talking while he snagged a cab, all throughout the taxi journey and all the way up to his flat. She was still talking now, sitting on the sofa, while he poured them both a substantial glass of very decent red wine. He usually got very good results with champagne, but he suspected Jemma was a cut above that, and spot it for the blatant ploy it was.

'The big problem,' she was saying as he handed her the glass, 'is actually how to define obese and overweight. For years, doctors used a standard established by an insurance company, of all things: the Metropolitan Life Assurance Company – the MetLife weight tables actually used to appear on most commercial weighing scales. But it was a thoroughly inadequate system, and when it transpired that MetLife weren't actually using their own scale to evaluate insurance risks, the whole thing was abandoned, and a replacement had to be found.'

She took a big glug of wine. All this talking was making her thirsty, and Jeremy was thinking that might turn into a problem soon. She'd had, what? At least a bottle and a half already. He didn't want her reaching that state of inebriation where her judgement could be said to be impaired and he would cross the legal line from seduction to date rape. He would have to make a move fairly soon.

'So, about twenty years ago, they started using BMI, body mass index, an equation devised by a Belgian epidemiologist in the nineteenth century, Adolphe Quetelet. And you thought you didn't know any famous Belgians.'

She laughed, just a little bit too loudly. The balance was beginning to tip. Jeremy reached out and took her hand gently in his. She didn't pull away. She didn't seem to notice, as a matter of fact. She must have thought it the most natural thing in the world. So far, so fine.

'It's a very simple equation,' she went on, smoothly, 'your weight, in kilograms, divided by the square of your height in metres. If you have a BMI below 20, you're underweight, 25 to 30, you're overweight, over 30, you're clinically obese. These definitions are pretty arbitrary at best. They don't in any way take into account the proportion of your body weight that is made up of fat, which is the real measure.'

Now was the time. Jeremy leaned forward and placed his lips on hers. She did respond this time. She kissed him back, but affectionately, not passionately, almost as if she barely noticed it. It was not, in Jeremy's considerable experience, a 'first kiss' kiss. Very odd indeed. He didn't press it, just leaned back slightly and let her carry on. Which, of course, she did, as if nothing unusual or remarkable had taken place at all.

'Now, remember, this is the measure the Government uses to define obesity, the measure they use to set the so-called "Fat Tax", the measure they will be using as a criterion for the Well Farms. But under that definition, almost all American footballers are obese. Not overweight, mind you, but *obese*. Even the quarterbacks. Some of the wide receivers, the fittest athletes on the planet, men who can sprint to Olympic standards in full football armour, carrying a ball, are actually defined as "morbidly" obese. It's insane.'

Jeremy really wished she'd stop talking about the Government. Especially in his flat, thank you very much. He decided he'd make one last move and then give up. He leaned forward again and lightly began undoing the buttons on her shirt. She seemed to have reached the end of this particular rant, and there was a danger of an awkward silence, of all things, which would be very bad timing indeed, so Jeremy said: 'Well, isn't that just the exception that proves the rule?'

Damn, he was having trouble with her buttons, which wasn't like him. She looked down at his fumbling and lightly brushed his hands away, and Jeremy assumed that that would be the end of that. Major disappointment, of course, but these things happen. You live to fight another day.

But that was not the end of that. Far from it. Instead, Jemma carried on undoing the buttons herself. She'd obviously simply got impatient with his fiddling clumsiness. Well, now, this was shaping up into something special.

'The exception that proves the rule?' She snorted. 'I love that one. What can that possibly mean? You have a hypothesis, someone presents evidence that flatly contradicts it, and that's supposed to prove your case? How does that work, then?'

She tugged her shirt off, laid it over the arm of the sofa and in the most matter-of-fact way, reached around behind her back and unhooked her bra.

'The exception, dear boy, does exactly the opposite. The exception *disproves* the rule.'

She leaned forward and shucked off the bra and, just like that, her breasts were free. It wasn't exactly a striptease worthy of Gypsy Rose Lee, it wasn't exactly sensual in any way, more like someone undressing for a swimming gala, or in a Top Shop changing cubicle, but it *was* an undressing and the boobies were out, baby, in all their bouncy glory. Without pausing for Jeremy to exploit this opportunity to enjoy the visual splendour of them, much less the texture, taste or weight of them, she leaned forward and started undoing his belt buckle. Sweet Lord in heaven above, this was strange.

And, of course, she carried on talking. 'I mean, anyone who uses that hoary old chestnut can't have thought about it for thirty seconds. It involves a total misunderstanding of the word "proves". In that phrase, it's used in an old form that's pretty much obsolete these days.'

And Jeremy's zipper was down and his penis was hauled out. Over the top, lads! Up and at 'em!

' "Prove" used to mean "test", basically. The exception *tests* the rule. The exception *challenges* the rule.'

She was running her hand up and down his shaft, gently but skilfully. She had a talent for this work, that was for sure. She was efficient and unhurried, not like the majority of girls who go for speed and strength to achieve the goal, and try to tug the damned thing out by the roots. And then she knelt down before him, still talking, and lowered her head towards his erection.

'And if you can't come up with a convincing thesis to explain the exception, matey pie, then your theory is utterly and totally blown.'

As Jeremy himself was about to get utterly and totally blown. And best yet, she would surely have to stop talking with that monstrosity in her mouth. Surely. Things were certainly moving along nicely now. From first kiss to tits out for the lads to gob job in what? Two minutes? Less? Slightly forward, wouldn't you say? Not that he was complaining: Jeremy liked a girl who got right down to business. He was all for it. He just wouldn't have put Jemma in the first-date oral sex category. In many ways, the orals was more intimate than just plain straight sex.

Her lips, deep red from the wine, were hovering over his tip now, and he really ought to stop things for a second and don a rubber, but she didn't seem in the slightest bit bothered about such niceties. She probably had a few thousand theories about why condoms were unnecessary, or dangerous even, and in any case, Jeremy was not about to subject this particular gift horse to any kind of dental scrutiny right now.

And she stopped. She froze within millimetres of his straining Iwo Jima monument and looked up at him, horror in her features. 'Oh my God. What am I doing?'

She pulled her hand away from his penis as if she'd suddenly realised she'd been holding a giant stick of primed Semtex, which, let's face it, was pretty much the truth, leaned back and covered her breasts with her arms. 'Jeremy, I'm so sorry – I thought you were Keith.'

Keith? Who the fuck was Keith?

'Well,' Jeremy said gruffly, 'you've started, so you'll finish. I mean, surely?'

Jemma turned and scooped up her bra and shirt, one-handed. 'I'm so sorry. I must have had more to drink than I thought.' She raced over to his bathroom and paused at the doorway, and turned. 'Really, really sorry, Jeremy. Really.' And she disappeared inside.

Jeremy leaned back in the armchair and looked down at his rampant cock in disbelief. What was he supposed to do with that? It would be hours before he could stuff it back into his trousers. Perhaps he could poke it out of the window and hang his washing out to dry on it. Perhaps he could paint the knob end orange and pretend it was a Belisha beacon. It certainly felt like it was glowing.

In the end, he opted to force it back against his belly and, very carefully, strapped it in place with his belt, then tugged out his shirt to cover up the entire construction.

He was dizzy and disoriented with lust. He'd been working all weekend to hit his deadline, and he'd slept from Monday afternoon all the way through to Tuesday afternoon, and he'd had no opportunity, up until now, to vent his pent-up sexual energy, so he was just about as primed as he had been at any time since puberty. To be led so far up the path to release and then stopped was, quite frankly, physically dangerous. There was a serious threat that some part of his apparatus might actually explode.

Jemma emerged from his bathroom, fully clothed and freshened up. 'I think I'd better go,' she said.

'Don't be silly—'

'No, really.' She took out her mobile. 'Have you got a cab firm you use?'

'Well, if you're absolutely sure—'

'I am.'

Jeremy nodded at the pin board by his front door. 'There's a cab firm on there, and an account number. I'll call them if you like.' He was hoping she'd turn down his offer, because he wasn't sure he'd be able to walk over to the phone without snapping his belt.

'No, no. I'll do it.'

'Just quote the account number and you won't have to pay.'

'I'll pay. Don't worry. I couldn't let you pay. Is this your address?' She tapped an envelope on the pin board.

'That's it, yes.' Jeremy struggled to his feet. 'I just have to . . .' He nodded towards the bathroom.

'Of course.' She held her mobile to her ear and turned to face the pin board.

He made his way slowly to the bathroom, leaning forward to minimise the strain on his belt, for fear a sudden movement might result in his garrotting his own penis. He finally made it and closed the door behind himself.

That had gone well. He staggered to the sink and tenderly undid his belt. The penis sprang out, undaunted by the experience, still enthusiastic and keen for action. He ran the cold tap over it – he swore there was a hiss and some steam when the water first hit – but three minutes of icy drenching failed to dim the wilful beast's eagerness. It was still straining at the leash, raring to go.

He thought about manually achieving conclusion with a spot of DIY, but it seemed a dreadful waste. He remembered reading somewhere that you only generated a finite amount of semen in your life, and he really didn't want to waste what must have been at least half of his lifetime supply in such a tawdry, solo enterprise. On top of which, there was a very real risk he might clog up his sink. Try explaining that one to the Dyno-Rod man.

He finally calmed down to a semi-erection, but all of that cold water, and all that lager and wine, had made him want to pee, very badly. He tried forcing his pecker down over the loo, but couldn't achieve a suitable peeing angle without considerable pain, so he stood just inside his shower cubicle and pointed at the tiled wall opposite. Mistake. It was as if he'd turned on a riot-control water cannon. The awesome power he unleashed splashed right back at him off the tiles and doused his Emporio Armani trousers and his Paul Smith shirt fairly thoroughly. Some of it even hit his face.

He managed to stop. He wedged his todger in the shower door and finished his pee in that curious situation, safe from the splash-back, though it was a bit late in the day for that. The damage had been done.

When he'd finally subsided sufficiently to tuck himself away and sponged himself down and rendered himself as presentable as he was likely to get, he stepped back into his living room.

Jemma was gone. She'd left a note on the pin board. Jeremy crossed over and read it.

'Sorry, sorry, sorry. Can you ever forgive me? I'm a terrible person. If you don't absolutely hate me, please give me a call and I'll' and there she'd scribbled something out. It looked like 'make it up to you', and instead the missive went on: 'take you out to dinner one night. My treat. Jemma xx', and, as an afterthought, she'd put an asterisk after 'night' and added 'with Keith'.

Jeremy sighed. Dinner with Keith. He could hardly wait.

He wondered if it might not be too late to call someone up to help him unload the terrible burden lolloping around in his testicles, but it was. Two-thirty in the morning, almost. He could probably persuade Susie to come along, but the request would smack of desperation, surely. Or worse still, would be an indicator that he had stronger feelings for her than he actually did, and might impel their relationship along to a place he didn't want it to go. To wit: it might actually become a relationship.

No, he'd call it a night and sort it out tomorrow. As he headed towards his bedroom, he stopped at his work station and decided to check his emails. There were a few, some from the office, quite a few junk. He had to laugh. No, Jeremy Slank definitely did not need Viagra tonight, my friend. And there was another one.

And, unless it was a wind-up, it was from the office of the Prime Minister of Great Britain.

It was very short. It said: 'J, Well done. Great stuff. Can't thank you enough. Cheers.' And there were two letters at the bottom. They happened to be the initials of the nation's leader.

THIRTY-FIVE

So, there was just one question remaining. How to do the dirty deed?

Being hospital-bound, and in the constant company of the Cow Detective, Hayleigh's options were limited. No opportunities to throw yourself in front of a bus or a Tube train, for instance. Her room was high enough off the ground to contemplate a defenestration, but the windows were suicide-proofed, which she found odd – didn't people tend to go to hospital to get better? – and, on top of that, it would be quite a tricky business manoeuvring her girdered leg out of it, anyway. She didn't know enough about electrocution to guarantee a successful attempt with that particular methodology, and it never seemed a pleasant way to check out when they did it on television shows. Plus there was that awful death scene in *The Green Mile*. No thank you.

Hanging was out. You have to do fairly complicated height-to-weight-ratio mathematics to make sure you break your neck right away, so you're not just left dangling there, slowly choking to death, and Hayleigh hated maths. She was unlikely to be able to get her hands on a gun, which would have been quick, at least, and any pain involved would be over relatively quickly.

Pills or knife, then? She was in a hospital, so she could, theoretically, get hold of either. Pills would probably be better: they would probably hurt less. But you have to know the right pills. She doubted she'd be presented with much of a choice in the pill department. She'd probably have to swipe them off a trolley she passed in the corridor or something like that. There was no guarantee they'd be deadly. What if she swiped some vitamins or something and actually made herself *healthier*?

Hayleigh allowed herself a little giggle at that. In a weird sort of way, planning what she mentally referred to as her 'finale' was quite fun. In a *very* weird sort of way, of course. It was a project, and it occupied her mind, and helped her get through the worst of the day. Lunch that afternoon had been, if not actually enjoyable, then at least bearable, and it had been done with in record time.

Mum looked over from the table where she was tapping away at her laptop and smiled at the giggle. She probably thought Hayleigh was showing signs of improvement. Little did she know. Later, in the unlikely event she ever managed to wrangle a moment's solitude, Hayleigh might allow herself an evil-villain laugh in honour of the irony. 'Mwah ha ha haaa!' This truly was the secret of all secrets.

So, back to business: she was leaning in favour of the knife. She could definitely get hold of a knife. It would probably need to be something a bit sharper than a regular dinner knife, though. She'd actually passed a tray of surgical instruments that very morning, while Mum was wheeling her out for the daily fresh-air nonsense, and spotted a wicked-looking scalpel in there. She couldn't grab it in full view of *La Vache*, of course, but the opportunity would present itself again. Making the cut would require courage: you can't be wishy-washy and indecisive in these matters or you wind up like Emmalina Dawson, in a great deal of pain, with hideous scars on your wrist that mark you out as a complete emo, and constantly under the unblinking eye of parental suicide watch, so you never get another peaceful moment to yourself for the rest of your entire life. You have to be bold and sure-handed. Make sure you find an artery, and there's no going back.

She favoured doing it in a warm bath, which is what the Romans used to do. You just slip away, then, all warm and dreamy, hardly even noticing it at all. But, of course, nothing being straightforward in the life and troubled times of Hayleigh Griffin, they didn't let her *take* baths, with her leg and all. She just got a disgusting bed bath every three days from her mum or a nurse, during which you had to try like fury to go somewhere very far away in your head, which was not always easy. Sometimes even the Jason litany (extra-long version) didn't help.

But, presumably, when the opportunity to do the deed presented itself, she would be out of range of the Ever-Watchful Eye, and she'd be able to find a bath somewhere in the hospital and run it. She'd have to keep an eye out for bathrooms. Maybe she could ask an orderly or a nurse in a way that appeared innocent, and wouldn't set alarm bells going off in the heads of certain personages who need not be named. She'd have to think about that.

But the success of all of these schemings hinged on one thing: getting away from Mommie Dearest. Well, she'd just have to be patient, that's all. The dreadful woman would have to go home sooner or later. She would have to. Even if it was just for a night. Dad was always banging on at her to spend a night in her own bed, for the sake of her health: the sofa in Hayleigh's room was giving her a bad back. So far she'd refused, the stubborn old cow bag, but she couldn't hold out for ever, surely? Of course, if she did relent, Dad would doubtless be substituted, tag-team style. But that would be fine. She could get away with murder on his watch. She might even get away with suicide.

The big question remaining was: should she leave a note? That was a tricky one. Presumably, Mum and Dad would be upset, and a note might ease their distress a bit. On the other hand, she'd have to write the note beforehand, and, knowing herself as she did, that would probably entail several drafts before she got it just right, all of which would be potentially damaging evidence, if discovered, that may even thwart the entire finale. It's not even as if she were left alone at any time: Mum even accompanied her to the loo, lifted her on and made her leave the cubicle door open, to make sure she wasn't throwing up or some such thing. Dignity was not a major feature of Hayleigh's daily routine. The only time Mum left her side was when she needed the loo herself, and she always managed to time that to coincide with the appearance of an orderly or a nurse.

So a note would be risky. She had heard much talk, in the wake of the Emma Dawson incident, that suicide attempts are cries for attention. Well, that was the precise opposite of what Hayleigh wanted. Attention was what she was trying so desperately to get away *from*. She would leave a note only if she had time, and write it at the absolutely last minute. In the meantime, she could start composing it in her head. Something elegant and tragic. A poem would be inappropriate. Something prosaic, though, and dignified.

'Hayleigh, darling?'

Hayleigh looked over at her mother. She wasn't off Talk Strike as yet, but that was on the cards, certainly. She needed people to start dropping their guards a bit, and it would be difficult to achieve that without speaking. She would pick her moment to break her silence; a moment when she could secure the maximum advantage from it. For the time being, simply paying attention when *la grande* spoke would be considered breakthrough enough.

Mum smiled, predictably. 'You seem to be feeling a bit better.'

Hayleigh shrugged with her eyebrows.

'Would you mind terribly if Dad came to stay with you tonight?'

Would she *mind*? It was all she could do not to leap out of her wheelchair and perform *Riverdance* in its entirety, encores included. She sucked in her cheeks to contain an involuntary grin that didn't want to go away, and shrugged casually with her eyebrows again.

'It's just, well, Jonny's missing me, I think. And I wouldn't mind a night on a proper mattress, to be honest.'

Delicious. Jonny, a plague and a pestilence all his life, might very well turn out to be her salvation.

She smiled another shrug and bent back down to the maths exercises she was pretending to be working on – oh yes, it's not enough to be a prisoner in a living hell, they give you stacks of quadratic equations in case you might actually be enjoying a minute of accidental happiness – and tried to keep the grin sucked in while she mentally hummed the Big Boys Cry version of 'Tonight's the Night'.

THIRTY-SIX

Excerpts from the book: *Cook It, Change It, Dig It! –The Whole Lifestyle Makeover Show.*

Cook It, Change It, Dig It! burst onto your screens this year, and what a splash it made! Our expert team worked wonders turning families' lives around. With dandy Leroy Burton-Blunt on decor, delicious Sámmi Greene in the garden and super-chef Grenville Roberts in the kitchen, we really made a difference to the homes we visited! Now you can use all the top tips from our experts to make the changes you would like to see!

Enjoy this book, and don't forget to watch the next series!

Simon Falter

Simon Falter (Series Producer)

BACK TO BASICS

Hi, Grenville Roberts here. What we found in many of the homes we visited was that people were too often buying pre-packaged foods for their families, and hardly ever cooking from scratch. While that's all very well once in a while, it's not a good basis for a family diet. Warming things up is not cooking. What follows on these pages is good, old-fashioned home cooking, and not fancy-Dan, once-in-a-lifetime dinner party recipes –

the bookshelves are groaning with those types of books: what I'm offering here is good, nutritious food people actually like to eat every day.

HOW TO BOIL AN EGG

This is from the first show I did. The Warburton family confessed to being absolutely useless at cooking, and they practically lived out of the microwave. Which is a great shame. Simple, basic cooking skills used to be passed down the generations as a matter of course, but now, sadly, convenience has overridden that tradition. Let's see if we can't get it back.

Eggs are a magical ingredient in cookery. They provide the basis for many alchemical transformations, where substances change properties and texture. They bind oil and vinegar in mayonnaise. The whites fluff up and stiffen for meringues and soufflés. You can boil them, poach them, scramble them, fry them and whip them and they come out a different way every time. Eggs provide all the amino acids essential for human nutrition. Now, neither you nor I know what amino acids actually *are*, but we know we need them, and you get them from eggs. One-sixth of the egg is protein. The yolk provides iron, sulphur and vitamins A, B_1, D, E and K, and they're reasonably low in calories, if you care about these things.

For boiling, you need your eggs as fresh as possible. That way, the yolk will stay suspended perfectly in the dead centre of the albumen. There are several ways to check how fresh your eggs are.

Eggs lose volume during storage, so a fresh egg is heavier, with less of a gap inside between the white and the shell. You can test for freshness by dropping an egg into salted water: less than three days old, it will sink to the bottom; up to a week old, it will float halfway up. If it floats all the way to the top and lies on its side like the victim in the opening segment of an old *Quincy* episode, it's only usable as a stink bomb. Alternatively, break a raw egg onto a plate. If the yolk stays in the middle of the white and stands tall and proud, it's fresh. If it's a week old, the yolk will lollop apathetically to one side, and the white will be less thick. If the yolk is barely held by the albumen, it's been around for a couple of weeks. If it's bright green, you've accidentally picked up a lime instead of an egg, or you've found an egg left over from my fridgeless student days, in which case put in a call to the bomb-disposal squad. Obviously, both these freshness tests are difficult to perform in even the most accommodating supermarket, so check by feel and sight. If the egg feels full, it's fresh. If you hold it up to a very bright light and it's transparent in the middle, it's fresh-laid. If it's transparent at the ends, it's a stink bomb. The final, and, actually, simplest method is to check the sell-by dates, if you can trust them. An egg has a natural lifespan of twenty-one days – that's how long it takes for a fertilized egg to produce a chick. Older eggs have their uses: scrambling, omelettes, of course, and older egg whites are actually better for making meringues and soufflés, but for boiling, freshness is paramount. Store them in your fridge, pointy side down. An egg stored at room temperature degrades more in a single day than a refrigerated egg does in a week. I don't know why they don't refrigerate them in supermarkets, but they don't.

Besides being graded by size, eggs in the UK have to pass certain quality standards, though, in practice, anything less than a Grade A is only fit for throwing at Deputy Prime Ministers. Grade A batches must have less than four per cent of the eggs cracked, and no more than one per cent of them should contain blood spots, which is mightily reassuring. Grade B are less fresh and may have been refrigerated or preserved. Alarmingly, there are such things as Grade C eggs, which are deemed fit only for food manufacture. Oh, good. How many bloodspots can they have, then? How many cracks? How old can they be? Do they come in boxes that still have those slogans from the 1970s – 'Go to Work on an Egg', and 'E for B and Be Your Best'? Think of that next time you buy instant custard powder.

So, fresh Grade A eggs, free range if you can possibly afford it, and large ones. These timings here are specifically for large eggs. Besides the eggs, you'll need a pan of boiling water, a jug of some kind, a slotted spoon and an accurate timer. Don't bother with so-called egg timers, they're useless. Get a digital timer: they're not expensive and they're more accurate than their wind-up counterparts. And make sure you test the alarm on it before you buy. I had to replace one recently because it gave everyone in the kitchen a cardiac arrest every time it went off.

Eggs, remember, are one of very few foodstuffs we consume that are actually designed by nature simply to be food (the whites, at least). The whites are also, interestingly enough, one of only two ingredients in the average kitchen that are alkaline – the other is baking powder.

Take the eggs from the fridge and place them in a jug of cold water. If any of them start giving off bubbles, the shells have tiny cracks in them. Take them out and use them for something else. They'll crack in the pan otherwise, and you'll have a mess on your hands, as well as a wasted egg.

Put the jug containing the survivors in the sink and turn on the hot tap. This will gradually bring the temperature of the eggs up to the point where plunging them into boiling water won't crack them.

Set the timer for four minutes and fifteen seconds.

With the slotted spoon, transfer the eggs from the jug to the pan of fast-bubbling water, as quickly as possible, then start the timer.

Now you can make your toasty soldiers, if you like. When the alarm goes off, turn off the heat and get the eggs out as quickly as you can, transferring them back to the jug, and then run them under the cold tap for a few seconds. This stops them cooking and makes them easier to handle. And now all you have to do is put them in egg-cups and eat them. You can even peel them at this point: tap firmly all along the shell, roll them firmly on the work surface, but not so firmly you squash them, and the shell will peel off easily. Either way, you'll find the eggs are perfect every time with this technique. If you want a slightly firmer boiled egg, such as you might use in a tuna *niçoise* salad, set the timer for seven minutes. If you want a proper hard-boiled egg, the yolk of which you can rub through a sieve to make an accompaniment for caviar, or use as the basis of a 'safe' fresh mayonnaise, thirteen minutes is perfect. Anything longer than that and the yolk starts to discolour to an unappealing greeny black tinge around the edges.

So far we've only been talking about hens' eggs, of course, but there are several other types of bird eggs you can boil. Quails' eggs used to be fairly commonplace in restaurants, mainly because of their daintiness, which fitted in well with the Nouvelle Cuisine madness that swept through the country in the eighties. Not really worth bothering with in everyday cooking, frankly. Ducks' eggs, however, are a real treat. They're easier to get hold of than you think. Just ask your butcher.

Let's move on, then, to boiling duck eggs . . .

THIRTY-SEVEN

Grenville was climbing the stairs of the Century Club in Shaftsbury Avenue. It did have a lift, but because the footprint of the lower floor wasn't as big as the space upstairs, the elevator shaft didn't go all the way down, and then, when you got to reception and signed in and they told you your agent was in the upstairs bar, just one floor up, you could hardly summon the lift rather than mount one more flight of stairs, now, could you? And so what was the point of the lift? Grenville had never seen anyone actually use it.

The problem with climbing stairs is that you exert a force on your knee joints forty times your body weight. When you're Grenville's size, that's a lot of force. That's probably enough force to move a small mountain five feet to the left. So don't be telling him that climbing the stairs is good exercise. It may be good exercise if you weigh as much as a single, normal human. When you weigh almost as much as two normal humans, it hurts. Pretty much all exercise hurts. If you are of average dimensions, imagine exercising with another you clamped around your body. Imagine yourself clinging onto yourself, onto your front, arms wrapped over your shoulders, legs wrapped around your waist, like some brain-dead, limp succubus. Imagine going jogging carrying that bastard.

Grenville carried his own succubus up the second flight of stairs. His agent was sitting at a table in a raggedy armchair. London clubs like raggedy furniture. They probably hack away at it with a carving knife just to get the right degree of raggedness. This club was, what? Five years old? Seven? The chairs looked like they'd been there for generations.

Seth rose from the chair when he saw Grenville, and he shook his hand and hugged him warmly with his other arm. Which, when Gren thought about it, was the most physical affection he'd been shown by another person since his divorce. Since long before his divorce, in fact. Unless you could counted DC Redmond kneeling on his chest, which you probably couldn't.

'How are you doing?' Seth asked sincerely.

'Good.' Grenville nodded. 'I'm good. Obviously, I've been better.' Obviously. He'd lost his livelihood, and very possibly his career, he'd acquired a criminal record and a reputation for rampage, was in a financial hole to the tune of seventeen thousand pounds, if you factored in buying another crappy hatchback – all thoughts of zip and glamour were now out the window – and paying the excess on the insurance of the Toyota he'd practically totalled. And he no longer had the Christmas book to look forward to. Yes, he'd been better.

'Well,' Seth beckoned towards the waiting staff, 'let's see what we can do about all that.'

Grenville sat, ordered a virgin Mary, and they got down to business. 'Have you talked to the production company?'

Seth nodded. 'I've talked to them a lot. We're not going to get much comfort there.'

'No chance they'll take me back?'

'Not really, Gren. Did you really call him a "suppurating little shit"?'

'It's possible.'

'I did manage to get some dosh out of them. Not a king's ransom. Four shows' worth of fees, and I had to do a lot of arm twisting and legal threatening just to get that, believe me. They've pretty much got us over a barrel.'

'Can we sue?'

'It wouldn't be worth it, even if we had a case, which I seriously doubt—'

'Seth, they sacked me for being overweight: surely that's discrimination. Surely a tribunal—'

'They'd never admit to that. Plus, can you imagine the publicity you'd get? You'd come off looking pathetic, even if you won. If you weren't white, if you were a woman, if you were a Muslim, even, anything, they wouldn't have dared chance it. But you're Caucasian, you're a man and you are, bluntly, a fat man at that. You have absolutely nothing going for you.'

'Right, then.' It stung Grenville, having someone come right out and call him fat, even though there was no denying it. He *was* fat. Face it. Suck it up. 'Onwards and upwards. Whither now?'

'Look, I've been talking to the Beeb. They are interested in you. They like your style, they like your talent, they like your cooking. They like your approach, cooking stuff that people actually want to eat instead of all that la-di-da dinner party baloney. Stuff people actually *can* cook. That's all good.'

'So, what? They're thinking about giving me my own series?'

'It's definitely on the cards. I pitched your title at them: *Grenville's Staples*, and they loved it.'

'There's a "but" coming here, isn't there?'

'There is a but, I'm afraid, Grenville, and it's a fairly big but.'

'Go on.'

'They want you to lose weight.'

'Jesus.'

'I know. They didn't come right out and say it, but your size is clearly a problem for them.'

'Jesus.'

'It would be a big break for you, Gren. Your own show, mainstream, prime time. Your own book deal. *Strictly Come Dancing*. It would be the making of you.'

'I know, but—'

'But, Jesus. Yeah, I know.'

'How much weight?'

Seth shrugged. 'They're just concerned that people don't want to be told what to eat by a guy who's blatantly overweight. Just a few pounds, I suppose. A couple of stone. Four or five stone, that's all. I mean, Brian Turner isn't exactly Jennifer Aniston, is he?'

'Five stone?'

'Five stone, tops.' Seth nodded. 'Maybe six.'

'Do you know how hard that would be? Do you know how long it would take?'

'It's not going to be easy, Gren. But I don't see what else we can do. We're going to hit the same brick wall wherever we go.'

'What about the two fat ladies? They were fat.'

'That was then. That was a different time. This is now. Fat's not cuddly any more.'

'I mean, I am on a diet. I'm doing that GI nonsense. It's not been going too well recently, what with one thing and another, but . . . six stone?'

'Possibly seven. I think we need to go more drastic than the GI diet.'

'Drastic? How drastic?'

'Well, liposuction, that kind of thing.'

'Liposuction? I tell you, Seth, I've seen that operation. It's a fucking nightmare. They treat you like a slab of meat. They ram this giant prong in you like they're cutting up a beached whale. And it lays you low. And it hurts. And you don't lose all that much weight anyway. Plus it leaves a scar.'

'Well, there's other types of surgery. They can remove part of your bowels . . . I know, you're pulling a face, I wouldn't fancy it either, but we have to explore all our options.'

All *our* options. It wasn't the agent going under the knife, was it? Or did he have to lose ten per cent of his own bowels as part of their contract?

'Or . . .' Seth toyed with his drink swizzle. 'There's stomach stapling.'

'Stomach stapling?'

'It does get results. Six, seven months, you'd be back in shape.'

Stomach stapling. Grenville's staples. 'I have thought about it, Seth. I've thought about it long and hard. I don't know if I can face it.'

'Well, think about it some more, will you? It does seem to be about our best option. I've got another client, swears by it. Turned Sharon Osborne's career around.'

Grenville stared into his own drink. He snorted a laugh. 'You know, it used to be people wanted their chefs fat. You've heard of Brillat-Savarin, the great French epicure? He would always check out the kitchens before he ate, and if the chef was too skinny, he'd walk right out of the restaurant.'

'Like I said, Gren. Different times. Shall we eat?'

Seth got up and headed out towards the restaurant. Grenville hauled his life-sapping succubus out of his chair and followed his agent out without enthusiasm. One of the chefs scurried past him towards the kitchen with a hot dish. You could have threaded the skinny bastard through a needle. Different times, indeed.

THIRTY-EIGHT

It took for absolute ever to get rid of Mum. She kept having second thoughts, not to mention third, fourth and fifth thoughts; then she had to go over every nanosecond of Hayleigh's routine with Dad, down to the finest minutiae, which had produced, incredibly, a ten-page print-out from her laptop, and then she went over it again. Then she made him swear all kinds of holy oaths that he would not deviate from the routine by a single letter, and all the time Dad was reassuring her and urging her to be gone, almost as much as Hayleigh was, inside her head. Finally, with a weary sigh, she shucked on her coat and slumped out of the room, Jonny buzzing excitedly around her like the planes at the end of *King Kong*.

She looked like a nervous wreck, the woman. Hayleigh had no idea why. Dad smiled broadly at her. 'Looks like it's just you and me now, honeybun. What d'you want to do? Oh, wait . . .' He consulted his list then looked at the clock. 'You've had dinner, right?'

Hayleigh nodded.

'Fancy a DVD? I got a couple of crackers from Blockbuster. We can play them on the laptop.'

Hayleigh shook her head. She needed Dad to get as bored as possible, which shouldn't be too difficult.

'Sure? I've got Jack Black's new one.'

Hayleigh shook her head again.

'Tell you what. I'll put it on. You don't have to watch it if you don't want. You can read or whatever.'

Damn. It would be hard not to watch a Jack Black movie. It would be harder still not to laugh.

Dad slipped the DVD out of its cover. 'Hayleigh . . .' The chirpiness had gone from his voice now. 'I wish you'd start talking to us. For your mother's sake, at least. It's breaking her heart.'

Hayleigh shrugged. Then she licked her lips and said, 'OK.'

Dad froze, bent over the laptop. 'Excuse me?'

Hayleigh shrugged again. 'Fine, I'll talk.'

'Seriously?'

'Whatever.'

'Can I hug you?'

'No.'

'Can I call Mum and tell her?'

'No.'

'Please, Hayleigh. It'll make her day. It'll make her *year*.'

'Only if she promises not to come back tonight.'

'Absolutely.' He took out his mobile feverishly.

'You can't use that in here.'

'Oh, right.' He looked around and found the phone on the wall. 'Can we use this one?'

'It's internal.'

'Damn!'

'There's a payphone down the corridor.'

'Great. Have I got any change? Yes. Right. D'you mind if I leave you for a couple of seconds?'

'Whatever.'

And he dashed out of the room like a dog after a bicycle made of sausages.

Well, that had been even easier than she could possibly have imagined. She released the brake on her wheelchair and rolled towards the door. She was just trying to work out the geometry of how she might peek down the corridor without her leg girder poking out of the door, which involved some fairly convoluted manoeuvring, when Dad dashed back in again.

'She's going to want to speak to you.'

'God! I'll talk to her tomorrow.'

'Promise?'

'Cross my heart,' Hayleigh smiled wickedly, 'and hope to die.'

'All righty.' And he dashed off again, then dashed right back. 'Are you sure I can't hug you?'

'I'm absolutely certain.'

'Fine.' And he was gone.

Hayleigh counted to twenty, then wheeled around again and peeked out backwards. Dad was at the payphone. It wasn't ideally placed for her purposes – he had a clear view right down the corridor – but it would have to do.

Hayleigh set off in search of a knife.

She didn't hurry. Even though there was a good chance Mum would do her nut when she realised Dad had left his post to call her and send him racing back in again, she kept it cool. Hurrying around, looking like you're somewhere you're not supposed to be, that just attracts the wrong kind of attention. You just move confidently, and if you're looking for something, you do it so it doesn't look like you're looking.

She wheeled past an orderly's trolley and stole a glance. As far as she could tell, it was just cleaning stuff. There might be bleach on there, and bleach was pretty poisonous, wasn't it? But it didn't matter, because just as Hayleigh wheeled by, the orderly herself popped out of the door. She recognised Hayleigh, and looked surprised to see her on her own and out of her room. 'Are you OK?' she asked, suspicious.

Hayleigh gave her a what's-your-problem-you-loony look and nodded. She could feel the orderly's eyes burning into her back as she wheeled on, but she didn't look round, just kept on going.

There were surprisingly few unguarded trays of miscellaneous surgical equipment lying around. None, in fact. Didn't they ever do any operations in this hospital? There was a door to what looked like it might be a storeroom of some kind, but when she cautiously paused to try the handle it was locked. Not necessarily a bad thing: if they locked it, there might be a cornucopia of dangerous stuff in there. Apart from the locked possible storeroom, she exhausted the options on this particular corridor very quickly.

Of course! They didn't do any operations *on this floor*. She had to go to another department. Surgical or Accident and Emergency, for instance. Now she had a choice: try to get to the lift, and explore another floor, and risk Dad finding her absent and raising all kinds of hullabaloo and perhaps even tracking her down, which would result in interrogations, and a security clampdown, possibly even the dreaded Return of the Mummy, or going straight back to her room right away, and live to die another day.

She decided to go back. There was even a possibility she might not even have been missed. But that was not to be.

Dad was standing in the doorway to her room looking round frantically as she turned the corridor towards him.

'Hayleigh! For God's sake! Where have you been?'

She brazened it out. 'Loo.' She said it matter-of-factly, as if going to the toilet alone was the most normal thing in the world. Which, of course, it was for everyone else over the age of three.

It worked. Dad looked confused. He looked around for his instructions. 'But I thought . . .'

Hayleigh pressed home her initiative. 'Did you get through to Mum?'

And right away, he let the whole escape-attempt business drop, just like that. Mum would have smelled a rat, and she would have questioned Hayleigh like Jack Bauer in 24 for hours on end until she'd winkled out the truth. But Dad just let it go. Easy peasy, lemon squeezy. 'Yes. You should have heard her. Honestly. She was crying buckets. She had to pull the car over. I think she'll sleep well tonight, I really do. Are you sure you don't want to call her tonight? It would mean the world to her.'

'Tomorrow,' was all that Hayleigh said.

So, in one easy, bold assault, she had broken through the walls of her prison. She could now expect to make unaccompanied trips to the loo more or less at will.

Dads. Bless. Like shooting fish in a barrel.

THIRTY-NINE

Grenville studied the menu without enthusiasm. The food at the Century was good, and under normal conditions, diets permitting, he would have loved to try the veal and kidney pudding with sweetbreads, but it would hardly be politic to be ordering suet pastry in light of the circumstances – *stomach* stapling? Jesus – and, though he had a fondness for offal, all that talk about bowel surgery had put him right off internal organs all together. He opted for a salad, which was a wretched thing to do in a restaurant where there were skilled hands in the kitchen, but what choice did he have?

Seth, the thoughtless swine, ordered the veal and kidney pudding and a glass of wine. Grenville opted, naturally, for water. What a good boy. Grenville shook his head and, not even realising he was speaking out loud said: 'Bowel surgery?'

'There is another alternative.' Seth pulled an A4 envelope from his briefcase.

What was this now? Was there something beyond stomach stapling and bowel removal? Some new technique that was even more drastic? Bombardment by gamma rays that melted body fat, perhaps?

Seth handed him the envelope, smiling. 'You know I always save the best till last.'

'What is this?'

'You've heard of these "Well Farms" the Government's opening?'

'Yes, of course.'

'They're looking for high-profile celebrities to be part of the initial intake. Quite smart, really. It would be perfect for you.'

'What's in it for me?'

'You mean besides the thanks of a grateful nation?'

'Besides that, yes.'

'Some good positive publicity – which, let's face it, you could use right now – the opportunity to lose a lot of weight and get fit and healthy, plus a regular newspaper column.'

'Come again?'

'That's right. A dieter's diary. Pretty good money, too. Again, not a king's ransom, but it'll get you by. It's not as though you can actually spend money in those places, anyway.'

Grenville grinned. 'You're a sneaky bastard. Bowel removal. Bloody hell, you had me going there.'

'No, honestly – I was serious. It's something to bear in mind if all else fails. But this is certainly a more palatable option, wouldn't you say?'

'It's brilliant. Lose weight, get fit and get paid for doing it. What could be better?'

'My thoughts exactly.'

'So, how long would I have to stay?'

'Well, that's sort of up to you. Until you hit your target weight, in an ideal world.'

'But Seth – that would be months and months. Possibly over a year.'

'But you'd walk out to fame and fortune, my boy. Your own show, book deals, your own range of cookery utensils, a supermarket ad deal, even. The world would be yours for the taking. Plus, you'll be in the best shape of your life.'

Grenville thumbed through the brochure. 'It looks a bit Spartan, Seth. Is there a VIP bit?'

'I don't think so. I could speak to them about that.'

'I mean, these are *dormitories*. It'll be like *Tom Brown's Schooldays* for fat men. I'd want my own room, at least.'

'I'll have a word. But my instinct is, they'll want you to slum it with the general population. Your experience will have to be the same as everyone else's if you're going to give a public account of it. Just think of it as if you're a contestant on *Big Brother*. Or, in your case, *Very Big Brother*.'

Another fat remark. Grenville didn't even bother feigning a smile. 'Hmmm. What if I hate it?'

'I wouldn't hate it, if I were you, Grenville. That would put a real spanner in the works. They're not going to sit back and let you trash-talk people out of taking up their initiative, are they? They'd kick you out quicker than boiled asparagus. If I were you, I would find it a thoroughly salubrious and uplifting experience.'

'Can I sleep on it?'

'Of course. But don't take too long. The launch is coming up, and they want firm commitments before the end of the week. Personally, I don't see how you can turn it down.'

'No. I don't think I will. It's just . . . it's a pretty big commitment, that's all.'

'Of course it is. Just be sure you make the right decision.'

Grenville nodded.

Seth reached into his briefcase again. 'There is just one more piece of business I'd like to get out of the way before the food arrives.' He produced another envelope and handed it to Grenville. 'I've asked around, and this is supposed to be a really good course.'

Grenville slid out yet another brochure. This one was extolling the virtues of a Roth Anger Management seminar.

'There's one starting Friday,' Seth said. 'Three days. You should think about it.'

And that was all that was said on the subject. Which was lucky, because otherwise Grenville might have rolled up the brochure and shoved it unceremoniously up Seth's backside and blown the 'Flight of the Bumble Bee' up his rectum in double time.

The meal was taken up with gossip and chat, with Grenville looking enviously at Seth's food while he munched his way joylessly through the vegetation on his own plate. By the time it was over, Gren had made his decision: he would be a

Well Farm inductee. The economics of it were irresistible. He could even rent out his flat for the duration. He wouldn't have to buy another car right away, either. It was a win-win situation. In any case, what were his alternatives? Go back, cap in hand, and beg his ex-wife for a job in his own restaurant? His own restaurant, where the cuckolding git of a Frog wine waiter would technically be in charge of him? Seth congratulated him on his wisdom, paid the bill and left.

When he'd gone, Grenville ordered the veal and kidney pudding for himself. It was truly delicious. A triumph. And then – why not? He was about to embark on a regime of deprivation for untold months – when he finished it, he ordered another one.

FORTY

The insides of Hayleigh's cheeks were very sore indeed. They had watched the Jack Black movie, and, while it wasn't his best by a long chalk, it was pretty damned funny, and so she'd had to keep biting her cheeks to stop herself laughing out loud. It was particularly hard when Dad went into one of his legendary howling fits, literally throwing himself about on the sofa, pounding it with his fists with tears in his eyes and laughing directly at her, challenging her not to join in. She had actually started shaking a bit at that point and had to turn away and pretend to drink some poison water.

The movie was over now, mercifully, and it was just after half-past nine, which was fully thirty minutes after the designated time in the Wonderland schedule for Hayleigh to lie in bed and pretend to go to sleep. Madness. Dad had popped the DVD back in its cover and was looking around for the *Obergruppenführer's* list.

Time to make the move.

As if it were the most natural thing in the world, Hayleigh started wheeling herself towards the door.

'Hang on,' Dad was saying. 'Where's the list?'

The list was down the back of sofa, where Hayleigh had stuffed it when Inspector Clouseau here had gone on his own toilet stop. It wasn't going to stay hidden for ever, because she'd had to leave some of it poking out so it looked like it might have worked its way down there accidentally. But she'd reckoned it might buy her a little time, and she was right. She carried on wheeling.

'Hang about.' Dad was lifting up the cushions. He'd find it in a second. 'Where are you going?'

'Loo.'

'Well, I'll come with you.'

'Dad, I'm perfectly capable—'

'I'm coming with you, and that's that.' And he grabbed the handles of the wheelchair and took over.

This was not going according to plan. 'Dad, please, this is embarrassing.'

'Sorry, mate,' he said in a terrible cod cockney that made Dick Van Dyke's attempts in *Mary Poppins* sound like pure genius. 'More'n my job's worth.' And then, to show off the mighty extent of his full repertoire of uselessness, had a go at Leslie Howard as Sir Percy Blakeney from the *Scarlet Pimpernel*, one of their favourite 'together' movies: 'Now, milady, whither the *salle de bain*?'

Slight problem, here. The loos were just by the payphone. Dad had, of course, seen Hayleigh returning from her pretend visit from the opposite direction. She pointed towards the payphone and hoped he wouldn't notice. He did.

'Hang on. I thought they were the other way?'

'They have them at both ends of the ward,' Hayleigh lied, praying he wouldn't check that out. He seemed placated.

'We seek 'em here, we seek 'em there, we seek those lavvies everywhere . . .' Dad hardly ever talked in his own voice when he was with Hayleigh. He probably needed psychiatric help, the poor man.

He pushed her to the loo door, turned around and started backing into the door.

Hayleigh almost died on the spot. 'Er, what are you doing?'

'I'm supposed to go in with you.'

'No way.'

'Mum said—'

'I don't care what she said, you are not going in there with me. It's probably illegal.'

'But you need help, don't you?'

'It's a disabled toilet. I can manage, thank you.'

He was confused, poor thing. 'Hang on.' He looked around. 'At least let me find someone to go in with you.'

'Dad, I'm *bursting.*'

There was nobody about. Nine-forty in a hospital ward is like four in the morning anywhere else.

Dad called out: 'Hallo?' quietly, so as not to disturb the slumbering sickies, which sort of defeated the object, really.

'Dad!'

'Wait there. Just for a sec.'

'I'm going in.'

'Just wait. Please. Just one minute.' And he scooted off down the corridor, looking for the night duty nurse.

Hayleigh wheeled herself into the loo.

She had no plan. If she was to achieve anything here, she'd have to improvise, and she'd have to do it quickly. There was no telling how long it might take Dad to track down someone who'd be free to supervise her, or how long it would be before he gave up and came in himself in total defiance of probably several European Court of Human Rights laws.

She looked around the room. There *was* a bath, but she wouldn't have time to use it now. There was nothing sharp, though, as far as she could tell. At least, nothing sharp enough to do the business. But then, triumph! There was a long mirror over the rank of sinks. She could break that and maybe produce a cruel enough shard. Nice irony there, mirrors being a long-term enemy. But could she do it quietly enough not to be heard outside? If she tried and failed, the jig would be up, and she'd be in permanent lockdown.

She wheeled herself up to the paper towel dispenser and tugged free a huge wad of towels, which she started wrapping around her fist. They might just be enough to muffle the crash.

When she'd finished her makeshift boxing glove, she wheeled herself over to the part of the mirror that was furthest from the door and wrangled the chair round to try to find the best angle from which she might launch a decent attack, but it was useless: the sink was in the way.

She would have to stand.

She slipped the brake on and grabbed the rim of the sink.

She took a deep breath and tried to haul herself out of the chair, but she'd never tried it before on her own, and it took more effort than she'd anticipated, not helped by the reduced grip inflicted on her by the paper towelette boxing glove.

She fell back on her seat, and her plastered leg struck the underside of the sink, causing her not inconsiderable pain. But the pain was all right. The pain was good. It helped her focus.

She glanced around at the door. She heard nothing outside. Good.

She unravelled the glove quickly and tossed it into the sink. She gripped the rim again with two good hands and hauled.

And up she came.

At last, she was standing on her own one foot.

She swayed, dizzily. She felt so weak. Astonishingly weak. Like a new-born kitten. An angry butterfly could have dive-bombed her to the floor with ease.

Well, there was no time for weakness. She wrapped the towelettes around her fist again: not easy when you had to stand balanced on one leg like a flamingo, while the other leg was feeble and sore and weighed an absolute ton. But she was determined and resilient and she got it done.

Gripping the sink with her left hand, she turned her head away from the mirror and steeled herself for the punch. She was Maggie Fitzgerald from *Million Dollar Baby*. Go, *mo chuisle*. Yes, boss. And she swung. This would, of course, mean another seven years' bad luck, but that was hardly going to matter now, was it?

She hit the mirror with what she considered to be a fairly mighty blow, but the towelette boxing glove just squeaked across the surface. All she'd managed to do was clean the bloody mirror. Brilliant.

Come on, *mo chuisle*: one more shot to the chin. Yes, boss. She closed her eyes, turned her head away and swung again. Not so much of a swing this time; more a straight-ahead punch, like a karate blow she'd learned from Jonny practising on her. And she made good contact, and twisted her fist on impact, and yes, all those years as a makeshift punching bag for her pesky brother had not been wasted because there was a cracking sound, but it hurt her fist quite a lot and she was fairly convinced she might actually have broken her wrist, but she didn't yell out, or make any kind of sound whatsoever, because that could blow the whole thing.

She opened her eyes and turned to inspect the damage. At first she couldn't see any, but that wasn't right, because she had definitely heard a crack. She wondered for a second if it might have been her own wrist she'd heard breaking, but no: if you craned in quite close to the mirror and stopped trying to blur out your own reflection like you were looking in one of those 'Magic Eye' books, you could just about make out a hairline crack, threading its way diagonally across the mirror.

So the mirror was weakened, at least. One more blow should do it. Just one more, *mo chuisle*. Yes, boss. Yes, boss. But her hand was hurting quite a bit. It was certainly badly bruised. Try as she might, she could no longer form it into a fist. Could she do it with her left hand? The mirror *was* weakened, after all. It might not take very much at all to bring it crashing down.

Breathing quite heavily, partly from the exertion and partly to try to shut out the pain – she was already on painkillers, of course, so what she was feeling was probably just a small percentage of the actual pain – she unwrapped the towelette glove to transfer it to her left hand. Her right hand was quite a mess. She was surprised that bruises could come out so quickly. Didn't it usually take a few hours before they went purple? Ah well, it *was* Jason's favourite colour.

She started wrapping up her left hand, holding onto the sink rim with her elbows. It was slow going, balanced awkwardly as she was, and her right hand didn't want to cooperate very much; it was about as useful as a lump of Play-Doh. She was getting worried, now, that if she damaged her left had, too, she might not have sufficient dexterity to carry out the dirty deed at all. Perhaps it would be best to try to break the mirror with a series of light taps along the fracture. Yes, that might do it. In fact, it might be best to wrap the towels around her right elbow, then, come what may, she'd still have one good hand left, at least.

But did she have time?

How long had she been in here alone, now? She did find that the painkillers could distort her sense of time. It seemed to her she'd been in the bathroom for absolutely ages, and even Dad would be starting to get suspicious. She glanced round at the door again and listened, frozen like a deer.

She decided there wouldn't be time. Not if she wanted to smash the mirror without detection and then do the deed without risking interruption. The mirror was cracked already. She'd made a start. Perhaps next time she could smuggle in a heavy blunt object to finish the job, so she wouldn't have to hurt her hand again.

She ran the taps, just in case anyone was listening outside. She should have done that from the start, probably, to mask the sounds. In any case, her timing was impeccable, because at that precise second, the door was flung open and Dad stepped into the bathroom, looking confused and flustered.

'Daad!' Hayleigh admonished.

'Sorry, babe: couldn't find anyone. What are you doing?'

'What's it look like? I'm washing my hands.'

'But you're . . . you're standing up.'

'It's the only way to reach the taps properly.'

'No weight on that leg, they said. No weight for six weeks.'

'I'm not putting any weight on it, am I?' She dried her hands on the bunched-up towelettes, as if that was why she had them, which turned out pretty neat, really. She tried not to put any pressure on her injured hand, but it was fairly tender and the slightest touch was like cracking it with a toffee hammer. She fought the impulse to wince, though. This had to look natural and normal in every way. She threw the bunched-up towelette ball into the bin. Goal! And then lowered herself back into her chair. She wanted that to look natural and painless, as well; as if she did it all the time, did Dad but know it. But she could only support herself with her left hand, so it was quite tough, and her arm was shaking with the strain quite visibly.

Dad let her go so far, wanting to allow her her dignity, but she couldn't quite pull it off without letting out a squeak of effort, and he rushed over to her and helped her back down.

'Thanks,' she said, quite angry with herself for showing weakness.

'I don't want you getting out of that chair again, all right?'

'Fine. I'll sleep in it, shall I?'

'Don't get lippy with me, you monkey. Mum will probably slaughter me for letting you do that.'

He started to wheel her towards the door. Hayleigh managed to keep her right hand hidden under the folds of her hospital gown.

She'd have to wait till later, till Dad had dropped off to sleep. She could do that. She could lie awake all night if she had to.

FORTY-ONE

Grenville was trying not to think of the discomforts and minor humiliations that had already been inflicted on him on the trip to the Well Farm. He was trying to focus, instead, on the bright future that was awaiting him. A future where he was slim again. Off The Peg. Touch your toes. Admire your own penis. Where you could bound effortlessly up stairs two, or even three, at a time. Throw everything even slightly Day-Glo out of your wardrobe. Get out of a chair without any involuntary grunting. Sit *down* in a chair without involuntary grunting. Take a bath without fear of being stranded there for days like a whale in the Thames. Have sex without fear of crushing your partner. Tie your shoelaces without fear of fainting. Turn, suddenly, and look over your shoulder without the risk that dozens of shafts of pain might go shooting through your internal organs, as if you were being assaulted by the massed ranks of the English archers at Agincourt.

There would, of course, be months, many long months, before all this could come to pass. And there would be deprivation, discipline and hard work. There would also, it appeared, be stupidity, ignorance and incompetence to deal with along the way. But it would be worth it.

The launch had all the hallmarks of a disaster happening in slow motion. In the first place, the celebrity vanguard had been picked up from their various residences in London in minibuses for transportation to a photo shoot in a Government building in Whitehall, which meant senseless hours added to the journey. Grenville would have happily made his own way, and it would have taken about an eighth of the time, but the organisers didn't want to risk anyone not turning up, and they didn't want to splash out on individual cabs for everyone, so that was that. And he, of course, had been the first one to be collected.

And of course, the minibus was too small. It would have been adequate for transporting regular-sized, Off-The-Peg skinnies, but the seats were a crush for a bunch of gruesomely overweight celebrities. Seatbelts wouldn't fasten. Elbows ground painfully into inflated abdomens. The more people they picked up, the more the internal temperature in the vehicle rose alarmingly, making everyone sweaty and grumpy, and hardly in the best frame of mind for posing for publicity shots. Grenville was wearing his chef's jacket, as requested, and soggy dark patches were already starting to form under his armpits, and, presumably, on the small of his back. Smashing.

And, naturally, when the full complement was finally on board, the minibus broke down. They easily exceeded its maximum load, and first there was this terrible metallic grinding as the exhaust was forced onto the road surface, but the idiot driver didn't think of stopping and perhaps disembarking one or two of his passengers for pick-up by a back-up bus, or some such. Oh, no. He kept on going with sparks flying out of his undercarriage, defying his passengers' protestations, and the mass horn power of London traffic, until the rear suspension snapped entirely, and irrevocably, stranding them all perfectly at Hyde Park Corner, the busiest, most aggressive and dangerous road intersection in the entire Western world.

Only then had the slack-brained donkey radioed in for back-up. And, of course, the back-up had taken over an hour to arrive, with everybody stuck in the broken-down bus, because to leave would have been to court death by traffic. And, obviously, the back-up had been an absolutely identical minibus, which Slack Brain had tried to cajole them into, as if, somehow, this one might somehow magically accommodate them all. But Grenville and a couple of the others finally rebelled and, amidst protestations and all kinds of jobsworth threats, had hailed a black cab and made their own way to the destination.

The photo shoot had been planned to take place on the roof of the building, some forty-eight floors above the ground, and the lifts had been very small indeed. A quick calculation of the permitted acceptable poundage in Grenville's head led him to the conclusion that even two of the celebrities in the lift at one time would run the danger of exceeding the maximum load, and he suggested they all went up one at a time, individually, but the PR girl was already way behind schedule, and the safety plaque on the lift advised that four people at any one time would constitute an acceptable load, so she compromised with three. Grudgingly, and with a certain degree of trepidation, Grenville had taken the first car, along with a former breakfast TV presenter and a losing *Big Brother* contestant, who weren't quite so rotund as the bulk of the celebrities. It had been a squeezed and claustrophobic journey, with the elevator car groaning and grinding disturbingly at times, but they'd made it safely enough, and climbed the last two flights of stairs to the roof terrace without too much pain and breathless complaining.

The occupants of the second car were not so lucky, and Grenville and his fellows were left shivering on the roof, with a couple of dozen other overweight celebs whose minibus journeys hadn't proved quite so disastrous, for another forty minutes while the rescue operation took its course. That lift was closed down and the rest of the celebrities were compelled to use the one remaining lift, one at a time, and the whole operation took another hour.

And just as they were finally set up, and the photographer had at last managed to get everyone to smile, however unconvincingly, and framed them spectacularly against the London skyline, the building's Health and Safety Officer had broken the whole thing up because they were contravening about one hundred and thirty-seven H&S regulations, including not wearing hard hats, overalls and safety harnesses, which would have made a very strange publicity shot indeed. Grenville didn't understand why they had to wear hard hats under the open sky, anyway. What was likely to fall on their heads there? The planet Mercury, perhaps? Old bits of Russian space station? Nothing, certainly, that a hard hat would offer convincing protection against. And they also, it seemed, en masse constituted an excess load for the roof, which was hard to believe since there was a helicopter landing pad up there.

So they'd all been trooped off again and had their photos taken in an office, all crammed together to try to accommodate some small section of the skyline through the window behind them, but, quite frankly, the shot could have been taken anywhere. Because of the confined space, the photographer had to use a fisheye lens, which would make everyone look even fatter than they were, especially on the periphery, where Grenville was. He would have bet good money that the caption appearing in the papers along with the shot would be 'Never Have So Few Weighed So Much', and he'd have won, too.

So, after very much ado about absolutely bugger all, quite frankly, they were all bussed back down to the ground, one at a time in the single remaining elevator, except for one or two brave souls, including Grenville himself, who decided to take the emergency stairs.

And waiting for them outside was a small fleet of minibuses ready to transport them all to Norfolk, identical to the one that had broken like an Airfix model on the way to the shoot.

But the mess had been sorted, overspill buses had been provided, and they were now on their way to Norfolk, in slightly more comfort, air conditioners on full blast, and there was just a chance things might proceed smoothly and without further cock-ups.

Because, so far, all in all, the whole enterprise looked set to make the launch of the skyscraper in *The Towering Inferno* look like a hats-off, rip-roaring, runaway success.

FORTY-TWO

It was the pain that woke her up. Her leg was caning, as usual, but her right hand was hurting, too, and it took her a few seconds to remember why. She looked over at her bed-side clock. Five-ten a.m. Normally she would have pressed the button to summon a nurse and get her pain management meds, but not this morning. She had other plans.

Dad was snoring quite volubly on the couch. She had tried to stay awake, to outlast him the previous night, but he was having none of it. He was poring over Mum's list of instructions like he was cramming for his GCSEs or something. He'd probably memorised it, which would not be a good thing. It might mean that the laxities she'd fought so hard to win yesterday would all be lost. She'd managed to stay awake until he'd finished that business, but then he'd slipped the other DVD into the laptop and started watching it with his earphones in. It's extra hard trying to stay awake when you're pretending to be asleep, and Hayleigh must have finally succumbed.

But the pain, her new friend, had given her a shot. You might think that ten-past five is very early in the morning, but not so in a hospital. In a little over forty minutes, the day would be starting. Hayleigh had no idea why hospitals arranged the days in this cockamamie fashion. Perhaps someone thought it was inherently healthier to have your breakfast at six and go to bed at nine. Perhaps they wanted to make hospitalisation such a miserable experience that people couldn't wait to vacate their beds and get back home to have breakfast at a civilised time, and still be awake in the evening at the same time as most ten-year-olds.

Still, she had a window. She had to get out of bed and into her wheelchair without disturbing Dad. No small order.

She looked over at him again, and, finally, she seemed to have caught a break. He'd gone to sleep still wearing his earphones.

The wheelchair was on the wrong side of the bed. It would have been better if it had been on the door side, so she didn't have to wheel past Dad to get out. Hayleigh cursed her lack of forethought. She wondered, briefly, if she might try lifting it over the bed and setting it down on the other side, but abandoned the notion fairly quickly. It was a heavy monstrosity, and even if she could lift it, given her current, pathetic, fairy-like weakness, the procedure would likely cause more ruckus than it prevented.

She felt another twinge in her leg and then a twinge in her hand, as if each pain centre were vying for her attention. She looked at her right hand. The bruising was a deep purple now, verging on black, but the swelling seemed to have gone down. She tried flexing it, and made a fairly successful fist without too much agony. There was probably nothing too wrong with the hand. She knew she had some kind of blood problem, something to do with platelets, so that probably accounted for the odd colouration. She'd probably hurt it when she'd first hit the mirror and not realised because of the meds, otherwise she'd never have been able to land that second blow. See? Pain has a value, sometimes. Stops you doing stupid stuff. Even something as awful as pain has its upside.

She pushed the wheelchair back out of her way and inched over to the side of the bed, timing her movements to coincide with each snore. When she got to the edge, she swung her good leg over the side.

So far, so good. Unfortunately, she hadn't worked out a plan beyond this point. She had to get into the wheelchair, obviously, but she couldn't afford to let her bad leg just fall off the bed in its own good time. For a start, it would hit the ground hard enough to wake even the most comatose earphoned snorer. On top of which, it would cane like hell.

She managed to grab on to the arms of the wheelchair from behind herself, and with slow, jerky movements, she got her bottom resting on the seat, with most of her bad leg still on the bed. From that position, she could lift up the plaster cast with both her hands and lower it onto the wheelchair leg rest.

She was actually sweating when she'd finished.

She looked over at the clock again. Five twenty-three. Not good. The morning shift orderlies would be brewing their demonic tea very soon.

Still, she couldn't hurry. This would probably be her last chance before *la vache* came back on watch. She wheeled past Dad as gently as she could, but just as she was almost by him he jerked and yelled out and even opened his eyes and looked straight at her for a brief second. Hayleigh realised with horror that she had actually managed to run over his dangling foot in slow motion. Genius. Incredibly, though, he didn't seem to wake completely, just yelped and snorted and turned over.

Hayleigh waited, frozen, not daring to breathe for what seemed like the length of a double maths lesson, which was longer, in terms of Relativity, than the entire Mesozoic era. When she was finally convinced he was still asleep, she rolled on.

She needed her heavy, blunt object. She'd had time to plan what she'd use as she'd lain in her fake sleep last night. Like all the best ideas, it had been practically staring her in the face all the time. Over in the corner of the room, propped behind her locker, were a pair of as yet unused crutches. They had been there so long, you stopped even noticing them. It would be the most natural thing in the world to take them to the bathroom with her. No one would look twice. There was even a clip on her wheelchair designed to house them.

She'd also had time, lying there, to compose her note in

her head. She'd been through several versions, most of which were downright embarrassing. You do not want your final words in this world to have you blushing in the next. She'd settled on something short and slightly wistful. It did the job, and didn't make her seem foolish. But, glancing at the clock, it might well be the note was a luxury she could ill afford. Still, she scooped up her exercise book and pen anyway.

It was five twenty-seven when she rolled quietly out of the room, crutches snug in their retainer. There was a light on to her right, down the corridor, past the payphone. The night nurse was probably there, doing her sudoku puzzles. She'd have been up all night, and Hayleigh doubted she'd be in much of a mood for patrolling, but her station was perilously close to the bathroom.

Hayleigh rolled through the doors towards the nurse's station and risked a quick peek. Deserted! That could be good, and it could be bad. It would have been nice to know where nursey was, frankly, so there could be no nasty surprises. At least she wasn't here and practically *guaranteed* to hear the mirror smash, though.

Hayleigh rolled towards the bathroom and was just about to go through the door backwards when she heard the toilet flush. Well, now we knew where nursey was.

Hayleigh looked around frantically for a hiding place. There was a chance that the night nurse wouldn't realise Hayleigh wasn't supposed to be out on her own, but if she did – and given the insane diligence of Mommie Dearest, everyone in the hospital had probably been issued with the ten-page list of Hayleigh's schedule – it could mean ruination.

There were no good prospects for concealment in the corridor, and the next bend was too far away, so Hayleigh had no option but to retreat. She headed back to the nurse's station, in the hope there might be somewhere nearby she could hide and wait till the nurse moved off to make a cuppa or something, if she ever did, but it was too late. She could hear the bathroom door opening and the clip-clop of those ugly, practical shoes the poor nurses had to wear, and the plan was now well and truly scuppered.

But no. The shoes were clip-clopping *away*, down the corridor towards the kitchen. Nursey was going to make her cuppa right now. That would give Hayleigh a good five minutes at least in which to do the deed, and she was almost certain to be unheard and uninterrupted.

She waited until the last clip had clopped, then wheeled excitedly towards the bathroom and reversed in through the door.

Her heart was beating like one of Jonny's stupid electro dance tracks. She was actually elated.

First things first. She rolled straight over to the bath cubicle and started running the bath. That might, again, prove to be a luxury she could not afford, but there was no harm in having the option, was there?

She moved over to the mirror and quickly checked the fissure was still there. It would be just Hayleigh's luck if some eagle-eyed maintenance man had spotted it and replaced the mirror overnight. That would have been just absolutely bloody typical. But no. The crack was there. Ha, ha. The mirror crack'd.

Now, would she get a better swing at it standing up? Probably not. She could probably do the job just as well from her wheelchair. Plus it would be quicker and involve less pain.

She unhooked one of the crutches and tested the heft of it on her palms. It was surprisingly light, disappointingly. Probably aluminium or something. Still, it ought to be enough to do the business. The top bit, the bit you slip round your lower arm, was a sort of flimsy plastic three-quarters of a circle. Below that was a grip covered with leather, or, knowing the NHS, some sort of cheap leather substitute. The other end had a rubber tip on it. Which end would be best? The handle bit was probably heavier, yet, paradoxically, it was also softer.

Hayleigh suddenly became aware of the sound of the wall clock ticking. Five forty-two. What was she wasting time for? Was some part of her deliberately making her indecisive, trying to put off the inevitable?

She held the tip end, manoeuvred herself into optimum position and swung.

The crutch just slid across the mirror. She swung again, much harder this time, downwards, not laterally, and to hell with the noise.

The grip of the crutch bounced right off the mirror and flew out of her hands, crashing into the cubicle door behind her.

Hayleigh yelped in frustration and wheeled herself over frantically to retrieve it. What the hell did they make the mirrors out of in this place? Tungsten steel? The hall mirror she'd broken at home had smashed with the first blow, and had been totally obliterated in four or five. This bloody mirror could survive an impact from a speeding train. She leaned over sideways and picked up the errant crutch. It was only at that point she realised she needn't have wasted the time: she could simply have unhooked the second crutch. Was she really deliberately trying to sabotage herself? Well, whichever part of her psyche was responsible for that bit of nonsense had better buck its ideas up. This was going to happen, and that was truly final.

She rolled back to the mirror and was surprised to see the whole thing was covered in hairline cracks. All it took was a couple of little light prods with the rubber tip and a whole segment collapsed, tinkling into the sink and onto the floor with the absolute minimum of noise. Like fairy laughter, really.

Hayleigh wrapped some towelettes around her hand and rooted in the sink for a suitable shard – she didn't want to accidentally cut herself before she deliberately cut herself, now, did she?

She found a very cruel-looking fragment indeed that

would do the job nicely, thank you so very much. It curved wickedly, like an Arabian assassin's dagger. She tried a practice cut – more of a tentative poke, really – on the fleshy part of her left palm, just below where her fake period wound was healing nicely, and was delighted to see a thick glob of blood emerge with hardly any pressure at all. This would definitely do the trick.

Holding the shard carefully in her toweletted right hand, she wheeled herself over to the bath cubicle. It was five forty-seven.

FORTY-THREE

The future's bright. The future's Slank.

Jeremy was sitting with Anton Deleware, the CEO of the entire organisation, the biggest name in the conceptuological industry this side of the Saatchi empire, and he was talking to him not as an employee, but as a partner.

The work on the Well Farms project had been a triumph. It had meant working virtually around the clock for two weeks solid – a project this size would normally have a lead-in time of six months at the absolute minimum, and Jeremy had to assume that whoever had been given the assignment originally had screwed it up, somehow, and he'd been hurled into the breach at the last moment. It had been a monumental task, but the budget had been large enough, and Jeremy had been good enough.

And it had been received with such rapture at Number Ten, it had been the making of Jeremy Slank. They were, at this very moment, on their way to meet the big man himself at the launch of the country's first Well Farm in Norfolk. They were travelling not in a limo or a roller: nothing so crass, but in a top-of-the-range Hummer, surely the coolest and classiest mode of transport ever devised by man. Jeremy himself was looking as cool and classy as humanly possible in a brand-new Armani suit. None of that Emporio garbage for the likes of him, thank you so very much. He wasn't, technically speaking, a full-blown partner of Conceptua yet, but it had been offered, and now he needed to get an accountant and a lawyer to sort out the legal niceties. They'd pretty much had to offer it to him, really. Once word got out about his work on the Well Farms project, rival companies would be head-hunting him like Congo pygmies.

And yes, he was on his way, once again, to meet the Prime Minister, who was now practically his email pen pal. True, he'd only received the one email from the great man as yet, but, theoretically, he could now engage him in electronic correspondence any time he wanted to.

He really wished he could have called Derrian on his cellphone right now, but it would have been too crass. Old Man Deleware notoriously didn't even own a mobile, and he was known to sneer on them as chav accessories, so Jeremy had switched his off for the duration of the journey.

This was almost certainly one of the three greatest days of his life so far. What's more, it was the third one in as many weeks. There was, in fact, only one thing missing from his life that would make the whole thing perfect.

That bloody woman. Try as he might, he couldn't stop thinking about her. He'd picked up his phone several times over the past few days and selected her number from his contacts, but he always wound up hitting the stop button before the dialling was complete.

It was this Keith business. He didn't want to wind up in some tawdry *ménage à trois*, where he started hanging around with them, going out to dinner and suchlike, with Keith eyeing him suspiciously all the time, quite rightly, and even if he did eventually manage to sleep with Jemma, there would be guilt and fallout and general unpleasantness. He'd been there before, quite frankly, and he wasn't in a hurry to go back. He really was on a hiding to nothing, and it would be better off all round if he could just put her out of his mind completely and forget about her.

Only he couldn't.

He'd tried dates with a couple of his other squeezes, but he'd ended up having to fake a headache, believe it or not, on both occasions, and not even the prospect of extremely dirty sex with Susie could awaken his enthusiasm.

He was barely eating. Worse, he couldn't even bring himself to engage in DIY. He'd tried several times, but just lost interest halfway through. A night out with a few of the lads, usually a one-way ticket to oblivion and blissful forgetting, hadn't even worked. No matter how many pints he threw back, he couldn't seem to get even mildly drunk. In the end, he'd begged off that evening too, before the curry, even, to howls of ribald derision. Unheard of. What was wrong with him? Was he – saints preserve us – in *love*? This rake, this roué, this latter-day lounge lizard, this bounder, this cad? Surely not.

He'd certainly been acting like a lovelorn schoolboy. He'd even Googled her, for crying out loud, and had actually come across her online blog.

Naturally, most of her blog entries were rants about the shortcomings of epidemiology and such – Jeremy doubted, now, they'd been monitored at the Well Farm; all anybody had to do to assess Jemma's convictions was check out her blog – but there was some personal stuff in there, too. She even mentioned him, obliquely, in one or two of them. He'd found out stuff about her background and her family, and generally felt he was getting to know her better. And the more he knew, the worse it got.

There was a picture gallery, and he'd spent more time gazing at that than was healthy. She took a good picture. There was one that had shocked him, the first time he'd laid eyes on it. It looked like a picture of her on holiday, kissing her dad. But it wasn't her dad, of course, it was that bastard Keith. He was practically bald, and his beard was greying at the edges, as were the remnants of his Friar Tuck hairstyle. Which implied, of course, that the cradle-robbing bastard probably had a surfeit of testosterone, which was a hideous thought. On the bright side, though, it also implied he was heading for an early grave. Well, he couldn't head there fast enough for Jeremy's liking.

But a couple of things had happened recently that had interesting implications. First, in her latest blog, she'd mentioned that she'd been having Relationship Troubles (her capitalisation) and kept going on about how all men were bastards, which, he hoped, didn't include himself.

Old Man Deleware did not go in for small talk, thank God – that would have made the journey a terrible slog. He spent most of his time reading, with funny little quarter-lens glasses perched on the end of his elegant nose, or dictating stuff to his personal assistant. Occasionally, he would pass a document or file over for Jeremy to peruse, and now and then he asked for his opinion on artwork or copy, so the journey passed pleasantly enough.

They arrived at the Norfolk Well Farm in good time. The place had a much more finished look about it than when Jeremy had first been there, almost three weeks ago, now, so someone had been working very hard. There was quite a high level of security at the gates, including some armoured police visibly sporting some serious-looking machine guns. Jeremy imagined they were not there to hunt down any of the enrolees who chickened out and tried to make a bolt for it, but rather to ensure the Prime Minister's safety.

They were waved through quite quickly and headed for the stadium, where several TV crews were in fairly advanced stages of setting up. There was a VIP hospitality marquee, and the Hummer's driver set them down there. As Jeremy was crouching to get out, Old Man Deleware tapped him on the elbow.

'Here you go, Jeremy,' he said, offering him an ornate silver box, like a trinket box, or a decorative business card case. 'Enjoy yourself, lad. Have a care with that, it's pure.'

'Thank you, Anton.' Jeremy slipped the case into his pocket.

Deleware nodded slightly. 'You've earned it.'

Jeremy stepped out of the Hummer. He was hoping it was just a business card box. Some kind of valuable antique in recognition of his achievement. It was unlikely, surely, that the distinguished Anton Deleware, pillar of the Establishment and on the very brink of knighthood, would be slipping him some drugs, in full view of armed policemen. Surely.

He didn't have chance to think about it. They were whisked into the tent by a couple of exceptionally beautiful hostesses wearing very fetching little black dresses and plied immediately with champagne.

FORTY-FOUR

The bath was filling up nicely. Hayleigh swooshed the water around with her left hand, to check the temperature. It was slightly too hot, not that it mattered an awful lot when you thought about it, but she turned on the cold tap anyway. It would have been nice to have some bubble bath, but there was none, just some stinky NHS soap you could scrub with all your life and never work up a lather. It was probably for the best, really. The soapy bubbles would probably get into the cuts and that might hurt.

The bath was designed for disabled access, but the design assumed there would be some kind of able-bodied assistance. Hayleigh rested the assassin's dagger on the rim by the taps, unravelled the towelette glove, then wheeled herself back and locked the cubicle door. There could be no interruptions now. There was a big gap below the door, though quite what it was there for was a bit of a mystery. Still, no orderlies were likely to crawl on their hands and knees to peer in, were they? And even if they did, all they'd be able to see was a girl lying peacefully in a bath. No, she was safe enough.

The note, then?

Why not?

She took out her exercise book and found a clean page that didn't have the impression of an algebraic equation on it. That's the last thing you want on your suicide note. She took out her fountain pen, which was a beautiful Mont Blanc Dad had bought her for passing her entrance exam, and he'd lied to Mum about how much it cost, because Hayleigh had looked it up on the web and it was insanely expensive. She'd started to wonder if it was some sort of spy pen or something, that could see through walls or shoot tiny heat-seeking missiles, but no, it was just a pen. She unsheathed the nib and screwed the lid onto the other end.

'Dear Mum and Dad,' she wrote, and then added: 'and Jonny'. She hadn't intended to include the brat at all, but it seemed a bit cruel when you really came down to it, and she was feeling quite magnanimous. 'Please don't be sad. This is the best thing for everyone. I am in a happier place, now.' And she signed it with her best celebrity practised autograph signature, 'Hayleigh R. Griffin'. The instant she'd done that, she regretted it. She didn't need to sign her full name, did she? Would they think it might be some other Hayleigh floating in the bath like Ophelia? A Hayleigh T. Griffin, perhaps? Still, what was done was done. She didn't have time to write a thousand different versions, and there was nowhere to hide the rejected drafts anyway so she'd just wind up looking silly.

She tore the page out of the book carefully and laid it on the chair.

She went back to the bath and swooshed the water round again. Still a bit on the hot side, but that was probably best. She turned the taps off. The only sound, now, was the water lapping. All that was left to do was climb in the bath and get it over with.

So why wasn't she doing it?

She glanced over at the note on the chair. She couldn't help thinking about that last line. Would she really be in a happier place? She was suddenly hit by a terrible, terrible bleakness. What if there really was nothing? Absolutely nothing at all, not even darkness. Somehow, she had managed to conjure up exactly what nothingness felt like, and it was the most awful thing she had ever experienced.

She spent heaven knows how long trying to shake the feeling of emptiness from her gut. When she finally came out of it, she was shaking. That was a weird interlude. How many precious minutes had it eaten up? She couldn't see the wall clock from inside the cubicle. Was it worth risking a peek?

No. It wasn't going to help, was it?

She gripped the big handles on the bath with both hands and hoisted herself out of the chair. How was this going to work, then? Bad leg in first? No, that wouldn't do – she'd have to put her weight on it at some point, and that was a definite no no. Good leg first? No. The bad leg would be supporting her. She might manage it if she used the crutches, but she hadn't had any instructions on how to use them as yet, and the whole thing could easily end in disaster. The only option, it seemed, was to go in head over heels. There would probably be a big splash, and her bad leg might well crack the other side of the bath with quite a bit of force, but there was no helping that. It might do some serious damage, but it's not as though she was ever going to be using it again, was she? Damn! It was hurting already in anticipation. She wished there was some way she could get her hands on her pain meds. They would make the whole procedure infinitely more bearable. She braced herself and got her balance so that she was exactly on her tipping point, sucked in a deep breath and held it. She hated dunking her head underwater, but there was no avoiding it. She hoped she didn't crack her head against the bath . . .

Now, wait a minute.

She eased back and breathed out again. That might actually be a better way of doing it. If she could somehow guarantee knocking herself out and drowning while she was unconscious, she wouldn't have to go through all that hideous violent wrist-slashing rigmarole. If she aimed to land heavily, smack on her head . . .

No. This was foolish. Changing horses midstream. Always a mistake. She was just putting off the inevitable. She had a plan, she should stick to it. Frankly, this whole business with the bath was just getting in the way.

She lowered herself back into her wheelchair and started

winding the towelettes round her hand again. She could do the business, then just let her arms dangle in the bath as her life ebbed away. Super.

She wound the towelettes around her right hand slowly, almost ritually. This was to be her last act on the planet Earth, and she meant to do it with as much dignity as possible. She took up the assassin's dagger like a high priestess about to perform a sacrifice and turned her left hand over so she could see the veins in the wrist. She had planned to do both wrists, so she could die twice as quickly, of course, but now, thinking it through, that might not be possible. Would she still have the use of her left hand once she'd sliced through it? What if she severed some nerve endings or something and rendered it useless? Plus, if she did it right, blood would be geysering out of it all over the place. She could hardly cut her right wrist with her right hand, now could she? Perhaps she could hold the dagger in her mouth. Oh well, best to get it over and done with.

The cruel shard hovered over her wrist. She caught a glimpse of her ugly reflection in it. Her tongue was sticking out of the corner of her mouth. No point in hesitating. She raised the dagger just a little bit, but she couldn't make the downward thrust. She tried to conjure up Owen Wilson in his silly Texan outfit, but he just wouldn't come. He just wouldn't sit on the corner of the bath and say 'Do it!' in that stupid voice. Very well, then, thanks so very not at all, Owen, she'd just have to do it on her own.

She raised the dagger again. Both her hands were shaking. She really needed to be her own hero, right now. She needed to do this one, brave thing.

She heard the outside door open, and froze. It was probably just a nurse or an orderly. She'd let them do their business and . . .

Somebody called her name.

It was Dad.

He didn't sound bothered, or worried or anything. Just

calling out to see if she happened to be in the loo, more like. All she had to do was stay motionless and stop breathing for a little while.

'Hayleigh!' he called out again. 'You in here?'

She heard his footsteps and the clanking of the loo cubicle doors as he checked them. And then the outer door opened again. Was he gone? Was that it? But no, somebody else had come in. There was another set of footsteps: lighter, faster.

'Is she in here?' It was *Jonny's voice*. Crappy poo burgers. That meant the Scorpion Queen was back, too. Well, of course she'd be here before six o'clock in the morning. Of course she'd be up before the lark, raring to get back to business, her instruments of torture all polished and shiny after a good night's rest. Still, it wasn't over yet. All Hayleigh had to do was stay calm and cool, and not move until they gave up and left, which, being men, they surely would soon.

'Bloody hell!' It was Dad. 'What's happened to this bloody mirror? Hayleigh?'

Still. Be still.

'Hayleigh? Come on, Jonny. There's another loo at the other end of the corridor.'

Ha! And just another few seconds of stillness . . .

But she heard Jonny's footsteps racing towards the bathroom cubicle, and he skidded and slid into the partition. She glanced back at the door, and there was Jonny's head poking under it, looking up at her.

'You,' he said, 'are an absolute mentalist.'

FORTY-FIVE

The VIP tent seemed extremely VIP indeed to Jeremy. There were quite a few definite A-listers in evidence, and Jeremy was enjoying rubbing shoulders with the great and the good.

Then a buzz went around the marquee and Jeremy turned to see the Prime Minister and his entourage sweep through the room, meeting and greeting rock stars and movie stars and comedians as if they were all dear old friends. He moved swiftly, but politely, the smile never leaving his face, and in no time at all he was offering Jeremy his hand and his smile. Jeremy didn't doubt for a second the great man had absolutely no recollection of who he was, but then, astonishingly, he turned and introduced Jeremy to his wife, and then spent quite a while explaining how magnificent and talented Jeremy had turned out to be, and had single-handedly rescued this entire operation from imminent disaster. Jeremy, of course, made the expected modest protestations, but inside, he was so excited he thought he was going to be sick on the spot.

And that wasn't the end of it, by any means. The Prime Minister then tapped him on the shoulder and said: 'Come on then, Jeremy. Let's get our show on the road,' and nodded to the Secret Service bodyguards that Jeremy was OK, and he found himself part of the very select few who constituted the Prime Ministerial posse. *Our* show. Blimey.

They swept into the stadium and mounted the stairs to the podium where the speech was going to be delivered. Jeremy found himself actually standing next to the Prime Minister. His wife on his right-hand side, Jeremy on the left. Unbelievable. Jeremy looked around. There was a very healthy press turn-out. Very healthy indeed, this far out in the sticks. He had, indeed, done a sterling job.

There was a slight pause in the proceedings before the PM took the short step up to the podium. Jeremy noticed the great man was surveying the assembled mass of the overweight with some amusement. He was humming, softly. 'Dum, dum, dum, dum . . .' Jeremy recognised the tune, but he couldn't place it for a second. Then it hit him. The Prime Minister was humming a tune from *Dumbo.* The tune was 'Pink Elephants on Parade'.

Then the PM stepped up to the podium, to rapturous applause. Jeremy heard the applause echoing in the stadium sound system. Was it, in fact, being sweetened by recorded applause? Unless the audience had all been fitted with personal microphones, what other explanation could there be? He could see the red light on the TV cameras in front of him and the monitor below it.

And Jeremy Slank was in the shot.

Jeremy Slank was on national TV.

In fact, this was probably going to be shown around the world.

Jeremy Slank had gone global.

His mouth dried up, suddenly and inexplicably, and it was hard to keep smiling. He felt like he might be swaying. He tried to focus on the auto prompt on the camera, and that worked, because he was surprised and delighted to see the speech he'd written personally had been used almost in its entirety. The only bit that appeared to have been changed was the last line. Jeremy had written something about the rest of the world soon wishing they could be 'as fit as a Brit'. He thought the change that had been made was significantly inferior: it was basically an indirect insult to the volunteers. Still, the PM's speech writers had to do something to make it look like they were worth their salaries.

Then it was all over. The PM waved, there was more

digitally augmented applause and the entourage swept on to a photo opportunity.

Jeremy followed the Prime Minister along the line of celebrity volunteers, like royalty at a cup final. It was a pretty poor haul of celebs, that was for sure. He hardly recognised half of them, and the ones he did recognise were mostly has-beens or never-weres. But notice had been short, and overweight celebrities are, ironically, notoriously thin on the ground. Jeremy shook hands with all of them. He did know Grenville Roberts – someone had given him the *Cook It, Change It, Dig It!* book for Christmas because he was such a hopeless cook, and he now used the boiled eggs recipe all the time. He was going to mention it, but Roberts looked dangerously grumpy, and hadn't he recently gone on some kind of rampage of destruction in some car park or other? Jeremy decided not to risk it.

The posse moved off again, this time heading for the helicopter pad. The PM was now in conversation with one of his assistants, and Jeremy thought his moment in the spotlight was over, but then the assistant dropped back and said the Prime Minister wanted a quick chat with him.

Jeremy caught up. The Prime Minister signed some documents, on the move, and then turned to him. 'Good work, Jeremy. Great work. That went very smoothly. Are you going to the launch party?'

It had been Jeremy's idea to split the launch between Norfolk and London. A lot of the press and most of the celebrities would be too lazy to make the trip to the frozen wastelands beyond Watford Gap, where there be dragons, and this way they could get two stabs at coverage.

Jeremy nodded. 'Absolutely, Prime Minister. Of course.'

'Come with us, then, in my . . . in the ministerial chopper. I've got an interesting proposition for you.'

Jeremy was staggered. 'I'd be honoured, sir.'

'Good.' The PM nodded, and turned again to his assistant. When they reached the helicopter, Jeremy hovered at the periphery of the group: he imagined there was probably a strict pecking order, and he didn't want to clamber aboard out of turn and make some massive protocol faux pas.

As he started to mount the steps, a Secret Serviceman stopped him. 'I'm sorry, sir. I'm afraid I'm going to have to search you. I'm sure you understand.'

Jeremy nodded, stepped down and spread out his arms, and it was only at that moment he remembered the silver box Anton had given him.

It was too late to stop it now, to make some kind of excuse and beg off the helicopter trip altogether: the Secret Serviceman had already started patting him down.

FORTY-SIX

The brochures had not done the Well Farm justice. Not even nearly. As soon as the minibus passed through the entrance, Grenville was looking out for the gas ovens. The armed police manning the gates did nothing to dispel the impression that they were, at the very least, entering a modern-day version of Stalag Luft 4.

The mood in the bus was not good, already. They'd been driven for hours, marched around, trapped, rescued, steamed, chilled, herded, and nobody had thought to offer them refreshment. Worst of all, they were in Norfolk.

There had been a series of arguments en route, and almost a fight with the driver when he'd refused a request from a gone-to-seed erstwhile rugby player to stop at the motorway services for some water, at the very least. But the driver had his schedule, and the dehydrated female once-upon-a-time children's TV presenter who was close to coma would just have to suck it up until they reached their destination.

They'd all been calmed down by the promise of sustenance on their arrival at the Farm: a promise that turned out to be as hollow as a chocolate Easter egg. They were, instead, driven directly to a sports stadium in the centre of the facility and herded out onto the pitch.

And what a sight met their eyes as they emerged from the competitors' tunnel. Fatties, fatties everywhere. A veritable sea of the overweight flooded the stadium pitch. The celebrities were marched to the front of the crowd for another photo opportunity. Hard to believe, but they actually had been given VIP treatment, and spared heaven knows how long of the wait that had been inflicted on the hoi polloi, the huddled masses, the uncelebrated.

The stadium seating was mostly empty. The massed ranks of the press were all assembled at one end, and digital cameras were clicking away, all trying to get the most amusingly humiliating shot of the throng of tubbies. Grenville would have staked his house that some tabloid wiseacre would caption the picture 'Wouldn't It Be Blubbery'. The PA announced the arrival of the Prime Minister, who made a mercifully short speech, thanking them all for being pioneers of the country's fantastic fitness initiative, which would soon be mimicked around the globe, but never, of course, bettered. He ended with hope that soon, every last one of them would be 'Fit to be a Brit', which Grenville thought was a bit of an insult, implying they were currently unfit to claim citizenship of their own nation.

The celebrity gross were then hurried out of the stadium to yet another photo opportunity, this time with the PM himself. He spoke to each of them, individually, though with his face directed away from them in order to accommodate the cameras, and through the grimace of his constantly forced rictus of a smile. He said to Grenville that he hoped they could pose together again very soon, for a before and after picture, and without waiting for a reply moved on to a failed contestant from a pop star talent competition, who, everyone really knew, had lost the final precisely because she'd been too fat. It was a good job he hadn't waited for Grenville's reply, too. It was a good job for both of them.

And after that, the press hullabaloo moved on elsewhere. The celebrities were all left in the hands of a young woman who appeared to be made of plastic, and was wearing a sports top labelling her as a 'Well Farms Fitness Consultant', who told them they were moving on, now, to induction, at the head of the queue as befitted their superstar status, she added brightly. Grenville couldn't tell if she was taking the piss or not. He guessed not. That would have required some native intelligence, which the walking Barbie doll failed on all subsequent occasions to demonstrate.

The superstars followed her as she walked off, rather too briskly for everyone's liking, towards the gym complex. To their collective horror, it soon became apparent they'd be expected to walk all the way. And it was a long way. It was after four p.m. now, and none of them had been offered so much as a glass of water since breakfast. Stomachs were growling, sugar levels were dipping and tempers were fraying quite dangerously. One former weather girl was crying openly, and others were on the brink.

Grenville jogged as best he could to try to catch up with the wretched woman, and explain the seriousness of the deprivation that had been foisted on them quite unnecessarily, but she'd kept up her pace, oblivious that most of her charges had fallen rather seriously behind – a couple of them had actually given up and were sitting on the floor in quiet despair – and Gren couldn't catch her. He'd tried yelling for her attention, but his breath was short, his mouth was dry and she didn't seem to possess anything as sophisticated as attention, in any case.

Finally, they reached the gym complex. The unspeakable plastoid woman was waiting for them, sporting an air-hostess-advert smile, and she chided them for being 'slowcoaches'.

Grenville sucked it up. As politely as he could, and in words even a plastic blonde might understand, he explained the situation. The woman was surprised. She'd been under the impression they'd all partaken of the buffet in the VIP tent. They'd missed lunch, she explained, but dinner would be served at six, and she led them to a drinking fountain that wasn't working.

Dinner? Six o'clock? Six o'clock was not dinner. It was high tea. Was this to be the regime Grenville had subscribed to? Was everyone in the camp expected to acquire the eating habits of an octogenarian?

Barbie tried to lead them upstairs for induction, but the

broken drinking fountain proved to be her Arnhem, and she actually had to be rescued by Grenville and the rugby player from a choking headlock a has-been soap star superbitch was trying to throttle her with.

After that, they did get their water, at least, and a couple of plates of dried-up crudités, salvaged, no doubt, from the VIP reception, whose attendees had had the good sense to give them a wide berth.

They proceeded, then, to induction. Grenville was allocated his Personal Fitness Manager, who was also made entirely of plastic. He endured, once again, all the usual measurings and the weighings and the blood pressure armband. But there were other, more rigorous assessments, too. He had to give a blood sample and a urine sample and, oddly, a DNA swab. Couldn't they get your DNA from your blood or even your piss? His lung capacity was measured. He was given an electrocardiogram. He was put through his paces on a variety of machines, one of which, a sort of ski slash step machine, which simulated, for some reason, walking up stairs, only backwards, he couldn't work at all. This had thrown the android, who had to put something in the box on her form, but no matter how much she cajoled him, Grenville couldn't even complete a step. Either he was altogether too heavy for it, or the requisite muscles had never developed in his legs. In the end, rather than prolong the torture, she agreed, with ridiculous reluctance, to fill in the box with a question mark, but she was less than happy about it.

He rowed, he cycled, he jogged, all on simulators, and all still in his chef's jacket. And this, mind you, was the superstar VIP treatment. At the end of it, he was awarded with a printout of his new exercise regime, a personalised diet chart and his shiny new Well Farm credits card.

Finally, he was reunited with his happy troop of tubby failures, and they were handed over to a 'Residential Consultant', who had clearly been squeezed out of the same nozzle as the other two Well Farm employees, who checked them all off on his clipboard and led them to their accommodations.

And, of course, they were expected to walk. And, of course, their guide set off like the starting gun had been fired at the Camptown Races, and he had to win this one or die. Were they under instructions to force march their charges at blistering speeds, these plastic parodies of people? Were they under the impression they were leading a bunch of seven year olds who were just bursting to run everywhere? It had been a long, hard, gruelling day, and there were mutinous – and even murderous – mutterings. Mercifully for the guide, their residences were not too far away.

And as soon as Grenville stepped through the door, he wished he was back in his detention cell in Hornsey Police Station.

What looked like a reasonably comfortable, if sparsely furnished, communal living area in the brochure was, in fact, more like an army barracks after a mortar attack. It was depressing beyond belief. Two tiny sofas, two Spartan tables and a scattering of very uncomfortable-looking chairs were arranged randomly around, and that was it.

Grenville approached their guide. 'Have we been robbed?'

'Sorry?'

'Has some bastard come in here and nicked all our furniture?'

The guide looked puzzled and consulted his clipboard. 'No.' He shook his head. 'No, I think this is the full checklist.'

'This is the *full* checklist, is it?'

The guide consulted his clipboard again. 'Yes, sir, it's the full checklist.'

'How many people are supposed to live in this billet?'

'Eight.'

'There are only six chairs.'

'Two of them are sofas.'

'They might be sofas for Kate Moss. Can you imagine two of us lot squeezed into one of them? Are we trying to get into

269

the *Guinness Book of Records* or something? My armchair at home is bigger than both those sofas put together.'

The guide smiled brightly. 'Well, we don't plan to have you doing a lot of sitting. We're not here to turn you into couch potatoes, are we?'

The rugby player emerged from the dormitory. 'Have you seen the bloody beds? You couldn't fit my bloody dick on one of those.'

The guide held up his hands and appealed for calm. Any complaints or problems they might encounter could be dealt with in the morning, once the induction process was over for everybody. Then he read out the list of the celebrities who were billeted to this particular hovel.

'Excuse me.' Grenville approached the guide again. 'Are you saying this is a mixed-sex dormitory?'

The guide again consulted his clipboard. 'Yes. Yes it is. They all are.'

There were howls of protest from the women inmates. Grenville held up his hand. 'Ladies, I'll deal with this, calmly and politely.' He turned to the guide. 'Are you out of your fucking tree, you brain-dead little turd?'

'Now, there's no need for that kind of—'

'There's *every* need for that kind of. You are going to reallocate the rooms, right now, my friend, this very instant, and you are going to put the women in one hovel, and the men in another.'

'I'm afraid I can't do that.'

'You can't do that? Why would that be? Because you're too simple-minded? Because such a demanding endeavour as crossing out a couple of names on your clipboard and replacing them with other names is so far beyond your capabilities, it might cause your pond-life brain to explode with exertion?'

'I don't know what you're getting so upset about. I mean, they do it in *Big Brother*, don't they? Don't you want to share a bedroom with a few lovely ladies?' He wriggled his eyebrows suggestively. 'You know, sex is one of the best exercises—' But he never finished the sentence, on account of Grenville's face being pressed so dangerously close to his own, they were on the verge of kissing.

'Listen to me very carefully, you obnoxious chitterling,' Grenville said quietly, 'because your very life depends on your response. We are not zoo animals. We are not a bunch of fucking pandas. We will not be herded into mating units for your amusement and delectation. So, one last time: are you going to allow these "lovely ladies" some small portion of dignity and reallocate the rooms, or are you going to spend the next three days shitting bits of undigested clipboard?'

The guide looked down at his clipboard again. 'I think that can probably be arranged, sir.'

'I think it probably can, yes.' Grenville stepped back. The rugby player slapped him on the shoulder. Gren had handled that well. He had marshalled his anger and used it to good purpose. Dr Roth would have been proud.

The guide's cheeks were glowing red. He made a few scribblings on his clipboard and announced the new men-only guest list. 'OK, the rest of you come with me. You'll just have time to freshen up and change for dinner.'

The guide stepped towards the door, clearly keen to get the hell out of there, but Grenville called him back. 'Whoa! What are we going to get changed into?'

'Come again?'

'Where's our luggage?'

And again the idiot consulted his clipboard. What the hell was written on there? The Complete and Utter Guide to Everything? 'Didn't you bring it with you?'

'It was in the minibus.'

'Ah.'

'Well, can you get someone to fetch it for us?'

The guide glanced nervously at the door, as if he was assessing his chances should he have to try to make a bolt for it. 'Not really, sir. The minibuses have all gone.'

'They've gone? What d'you mean, gone?'

'They dropped you off, and then they . . . went.'

'Well, surely someone unloaded our bags first?'

The guide looked down at the clipboard, then back up at the smouldering Gren, and back down again, as if it might bring him solace in this, the hour of his great need. Maybe it would. Maybe he had the Twenty-Third Psalm or Desiderata written on it. 'Let me check that for you, sir. Will that be all right? If I go and check it right now?'

'It will be all right if you come back with our luggage. If you don't come back with our luggage, then it definitely won't be all right, and I will hunt you down like the dog you are, skin you alive and turn *you* into luggage. Will *that* be all right?'

The guide nodded winsomely. 'I'll see what I can do,' he said and strode briskly out of the room.

FORTY-SEVEN

Jeremy glanced around nervously, trying to assess his probabilities of making an effective bolt for freedom, but it was ridiculous. Was he really going to try running away from armed professional killers? Even in the unlikely event he managed to avoid taking a bullet or seven to the back of the head from them, the place was swarming with armed police and SWAT teams with military-grade weaponry. Was there, possibly, a worse place in the world to be carrying Class A drugs? Jeremy doubted it. Had he known, Old Man Deleware? Had he guessed this might happen? Did he have advance information? Was he deliberately setting Jeremy up? The old stag, destroying the young upstart in the herd before he got too big to be dealt with? That would make some kind of hideous sense.

Jeremy was trying not to sweat, but that's not possible. Your sweat glands have a will of their own. His mind was racing through all the possible outcomes of this search that might *not* somehow result in his arrest, humiliation and imprisonment. Perhaps the Secret Serviceman might not find the box. Unlikely: he was a member of the elite bodyguard of the leader of the nation. It was a fair bet he'd be pretty good at his job. Perhaps he'd find the box, and consider it too small to be of concern. Possible, but not probable. He was likely to be exhaustively thorough. Perhaps, then, the box was innocent and innocuous. Jeremy hadn't had the opportunity to check its contents. That was probably his best bet. But hadn't that bastard Anton said something about its being pure? Could he possibly have been referring to the silver the box was fashioned from? Dubious, at best.

The Secret Serviceman straightened, and for a blissful moment, Jeremy thought it was over and he'd got away with it. But no.

'Can you just show me what you've got in that pocket, sir?'

Jeremy deliberately misunderstood and went for the wrong pocket. Desperate, really.

'The other pocket, if you don't mind, sir?'

He wouldn't be calling Jeremy 'sir' in a minute. In a minute he'd be calling Jeremy a stupid, dozy bastard. A perp. A crim. A lag. Jeremy took the box out of his pocket and handed it over.

What an idiotic way to end up. One minute, basking before the world press, at the top of his career with a glittering future beckoning him, a favourite son, standing on the left hand of the country's most powerful politician; the next, handcuffed, disgraced and ruined. They would throw the book at him for this, surely. Seven years or so in prison were unlikely to improve either his looks or his job prospects in any significant way. The tragic irony was he didn't even use the bloody stuff, himself. He'd tried it once, and it had rendered him impotent. For him, cocaine was the equivalent of chemical castration, so he'd never touched it again. That bastard Deleware. That cunning, evil bastard. Well, Jeremy would certainly have plenty of time to plan his revenge. Plenty of time.

The agent turned the box over in his hand and peered at Jeremy over his shades. He opened the box and looked inside. Jeremy couldn't see into the box from his angle. The agent peered at him again and snapped the box shut.

This was it, then. Goodbye, cruel world. He rehearsed a few dismal explanations, all of which were unlikely to buy him leniency. It wasn't his box. He didn't know what was in it. He thought it was sherbet dab. Pathetic.

The agent jiggled the hand that was holding the box, as if he was trying to assess its precise weight, and then handed it back to Jeremy.

'All right, sir.' He nodded. 'You can climb on board now.'

Puzzled, and almost dizzy with relief, Jeremy thanked the man and mounted the steps. Were the contents of the box indeed innocuous? Had Anton given him a completely innocent gift? Jeremy started to feel guilty about doubting the old man.

The Secret Serviceman caught up with him on the steps and whispered in his ear: 'Christ almighty, lad. That little lot should make the party go with a bloody bang.'

FORTY-EIGHT

JEMMA BARTLET'S BLOG, MARCH 16TH.

I'm afraid it's going to be another ranty blog, faithful readers. I'm having Relationship Troubles, I'm hating my new job, and then there was this new advert on the TV for an overpriced yogurt drink that has been proven to dramatically lower cholesterol. *Proven*, mind you. *Dramatically*, if you don't mind. So, all in all, it's been pretty much the week from hell.

Let's get this cholesterol nonsense sorted once and for all. I'm quoting here from Ancel Keys, Professor Emeritus at the University of Minnesota. This is what he said as far back as 1997: 'There's no connection *whatsoever* between cholesterol in food and cholesterol in blood. And we've known that all along. Cholesterol in the diet doesn't matter *unless you happen to be a chicken or a rabbit.*'

The italics are mine.

Nothing you can eat or drink can possibly have any impact, whatsoever, on your cholesterol levels. And Ancel Keys is not just any old Professor Emeritus: he is the leading proponent of the cholesterol theory on the entire planet.

We'll get back to that in a minute. First, let's look at what bastards men are: they are all bastards. Every last one of them. QED.

Having reassured you all of my rigid adherence to clinical method and my unbending scientific impartiality, let's get back to cholesterol.

We all know that high cholesterol levels are linked to

heart disease, right? Actually, no. Not right. The truth is: after the age of fifty, the lower your cholesterol level is, the lower your life expectancy.

I'm going to say it again, and I'm going to put it in italics, because, well, someone should: *After the age of fifty, the lower your cholesterol level is, the lower your life expectancy.*

In fact, a falling cholesterol level sharply increases your risk of dying from just about everything.

We really ought to be thinking about how to raise our cholesterol levels, not lower them.

But, surely, saturated fats are bad for us?

Think again. No study has ever shown reducing saturated fats in the diet reduces heart disease. In fact, a fifteen-year study in Finland found that businessmen on low-sat.-fat diets were more than twice as likely to die of heart attacks than those who weren't.

So how is cholesterol supposed to cause heart disease? Well, take a deep breath, here's the science bit: cholesterol cannot actually enter the bloodstream directly: it's not soluble. Instead it gets packed into little spheres called lipoproteins which are then released into the blood. So you don't actually have a cholesterol level, in fact. What you have are levels of various lipoproteins. What we now think of as 'bad' cholesterol is contained in low-density lipoproteins, or LDLs. I don't want to make this too complicated, as some men might be trying to read it, but to cut a long story short, LDLs are produced from VLDLs (very low . . . etc.). What produces an excess of VLDLs is eating carbohydrates, and what reduces the production of them is eating fat. Hmmm.

Anyway, the theory, if you can dignify this nonsense by calling it that, is that the LDLs somehow magically pass through endothelial cells into the arterial wall itself where they form arterial plaque. How they manage this is still an unexplained mystery. The veins, remember, are pretty much identical to arteries – when you perform a heart bypass, you substitute the damaged arteries with veins (which then, incidentally, suddenly become susceptible to plaque formation). Why does cholesterol only start causing plaque when it reaches arteries? Why doesn't it fog up the veins?

The current, lunatic theory runs something like this: LDLs head towards the arteries where they somehow force their way through cell walls and self-detonate like some crazy suicide bomber. It's hard to imagine anyone could come up with less credible scientific hogwash than that.

The whole cholesterol theory is an absolute farce, and was dismissed as 'the greatest scam in medical history' by Dr George Mann in the *New England Journal of Medicine*, way back in 1977.

So why does it persist? Why does the medical establishment still flog this dead horse of a theory, which is, and let's not mince words here, *exactly the polar opposite of the truth*?

Well, our old friend vested interest is at work here. They're flogging the dead horse because people are still buying it. The market in cholesterol-reducing statins alone is worth in excess of £20 billion a year. People have won Nobel Prizes on the back of it. And how else would you sell those dreadful margarines unless you could convince people spreading converted petroleum on their toasty soldiers was somehow healthy for them?

And why else would you buy those crappy overpriced yogurt drinks?

And, by the way: did I mention that all men are bastards?

FORTY-NINE

Jeremy Slank was sitting in the Prime Minister's private helicopter, only this time, the Prime Minister was sitting in it, too.

What's more, he was sitting in the Prime Minister's private helicopter, with the Prime Minister and enough seriously illegal drugs in his pocket to satisfy the cravings of even Tony Montana at the end of *Scarface*.

The Prime Minister, who never seemed to stop working, was busily approving documents, reading proposals and making executive decisions for most of the trip, and it was only when Jeremy began to recognise some London landmarks that the PM found a moment to spend with him.

When the great man sat down next to him, Jeremy suddenly felt as if the box in his pocket had actually started to glow. He was genuinely worried it might burn his leg. 'Once again, Jeremy, magnificent work at ridiculously short notice. Sorry we had to spring it on you like that, but we had, uhm, a bit of a policy dispute with our last PR mob, who shall remain nameless.' He turned to share this golden nugget of a gag with the rest of the chopper, and though they couldn't possibly have heard him over the whupping of the blades, they recognised the purpose of the winsome smile and laughed, dutifully, anyway. He turned back to Jeremy. 'And we were left with our pants round our ankles, rather. You pulled them up for us, Jeremy, you pulled them up.'

Jeremy was slightly uncomfortable with the imagery, but he just shrugged modestly. 'I'm glad I could be of service, sir.'

'What that means, Jeremy, is that you are now our go-to guy. I've got another project for you, and it's a biggy. I want you to undertake the re-branding of the National Health Service.'

The re-branding of the NHS? That would be worth millions upon millions. Jeremy struggled very hard to keep his expression serious and intelligent, when all he really wanted to do was clap his hands, giggle uncontrollably and blow idiot, bubbly raspberries of delight.

'The NHS is becoming a bit of an albatross for us. People are starting to perceive it as a failure, which it is not, of course. It is, in fact, the envy of the world. We want you to realign that perception. You'll have a massive budget and pretty much carte blanche. This is big for us, Jeremy. Very big indeed. If it's not handled well, it could be an election killer. What d'you say? Will you be my go-to guy?'

Jeremy nodded. 'Frankly, Prime Minister, I'd cut my right hand off for that opportunity. In fact, I'd even cut off yours.'

The PM threw his head back and laughed raucously, and slapped Jeremy on the back. 'Excellent, Jeremy, excellent. Look, I'll get Dan over there to give you the full brief. You're going to want to tour some hospitals and so on. When you've done the groundwork and gathered your data, why don't we meet up and chat about where you might take it?'

'That would be wonderful, Prime Minister.'

'Oh, you can drop the formalities when we're off-camera, Jeremy. Most of these vagabonds and reprobates just call me "P".' And he turned round once again to share this jest with the assemblage of vagabonds and reprobates, who, once again, unless they had been bionically augmented, couldn't possibly have heard, but, once again, did their duty anyway. He turned back to Jeremy. 'Why don't we do it one weekend at Chequers? I'll get Dan to sort out a date with you. Would that be cool?'

Jeremy smiled and nodded. 'That certainly would be cool.' And he tried out his shiny new privilege: 'It would be very cool indeed, P.'

FIFTY

'Hayleigh?' Dad knocked politely on the cubicle door. 'Are you all right in there?'

'I'm fine.' She had to think quickly now. If they started putting two and two together, they'd come up with a hundred and fifty-seven, and any prospect of any kind of freedom henceforth would be a fond and distant dream. But all was not lost, not just yet. First things first, she carefully let the assassin's dagger slip into the bath. Mistake. Horribly, you could see it quite clearly on the bottom. In fact, if you were standing so the light struck it, you couldn't help but see it. It couldn't have landed shiny side down, now, could it? Of course not. Either she had to retrieve it, which was probably not possible, or she had to murk up the water somehow.

'I'm just washing my hair,' she yelled, and, hauling herself out of the chair, she dunked her head in the water.

'She's got a paper boxing glove on her hand!' Jonny yelled. 'The bloody loony.'

Crappy crap pudding. She couldn't do much at all if the pesky brat was going to scrutinise her every move.

Fortunately, her father came to the rescue. 'Get off the floor, Jonny.'

'She's a nutter, Dad.'

'Get off the floor. You'll ruin your uniform.'

'Barking, she is,' Jonny said, but he got up anyway.

There was no shampoo, of course. Nothing so straightforward in Hayleigh's wretched existence. All she had was the dreadful NHS soap. She unwound the towelettes, dunked the soap bar in the bath and started rubbing it in her hands to try to work up some kind of lather. It took a while, and it was awkward, balancing on one leg, and her purple hand was caning beyond belief, but bubbles did start forming eventually. Not nearly enough to serve her purpose, but when she rubbed her soapy hands through her hair, and dunked her head in the bath again, the water did start to cloud over, quite a lot. Her hair must have been fairly filthy. One more lather should do it.

'Hayleigh!' Dad was starting to sound impatient now. 'Come on, babe. I'm already waist-deep in unspeakable quagmire for letting you out of my sight.'

'Nearly done!' Hayleigh yelled back. She managed one more lather-up and dunk, and the deadly shard was no longer catching the light, as far as she could tell. She lowered herself back into the wheelchair and looked round for a towel, but, naturally, there was no towel. Did you honestly expect anything different? She grabbed the towelettes, but they didn't do a very good job of drying her hair. They collapsed into soggy fragments after just a couple of swipes.

'Hayleigh,' Dad called, 'if you don't come out pronto, I'm sending Jonny in after you.'

Oh, poo pie. That would be disasterama. The ugly little tic would find the dagger, for sure. He had some kind of homing instinct for weaponry. But wait, maybe she could turn this to her advantage. 'I need a towel,' she yelled.

At least one of them would have to go off and fetch a towel. Yes. Hopefully, even, both of them.

'Hayleigh, are you telling me you went in there to wash your hair, and you didn't take a towel?'

'I know. Thicko, aren't I? Forget my head if it wasn't screwed on.'

Which, of course, was Jonny's cue: 'It is most definitely *not* screwed on. It never *has* been screwed on. It probably drops off altogether when she's in bed.'

'Jonny,' Dad said, 'go and fetch your mother. Ask her to bring a towel.'

No, no, no. We could not have the Chief of the Chief of

Detectives herself, in person, at the actual scene of the crime. That would never do. As Jonny's footsteps raced pell-mell out of the room, Hayleigh wheeled quickly over to the door, slid back the lock and opened it. 'Never mind. I'll dry it in the room.' She smiled her winningest smile.

'You're soaking,' Dad said. 'You'll catch your death.'

'Not if we hurry.' Hayleigh wheeled past him, trying to urge him to follow with telepathy. But her telepathic powers were clearly not up to the job because Dad peered into the bathroom and saw something.

'Oh, Hayleigh,' he said, recrimination in his voice. 'Look at that.' And he started walking towards the bath.

Hayleigh wheeled back to the cubicle door, and tried to keep the anxiety out of her voice: 'What? What's up?' She glanced round anxiously. How long before Mrs Monk arrived on the scene?

'This,' Dad said, and, rolling up his sleeve, he stooped and dipped his arm in the bath. He pulled it out again and held up the plug. 'You can't just leave the water for someone else to drain.'

'Excuse me? Wasn't it you who was telling me to hurry up?'

Dad was still looking into the bath.

'Come on,' Hayleigh urged. She had to get him away from there. 'I'm shivering, here.'

'Right.' Dad seemed fascinated by the swirling bath water, but he managed to drag his eyes away from it and padded back towards her, just as Jonny burst into the room with a towel, but, as far as Hayleigh could tell, no Mother in tow.

Jonny held up the towel and grinned proudly. 'Nicked it. Nicked it off a trolley.'

Hayleigh held out her hand – the undamaged left one, of course – for Jonny to pass her the towel, but, predictably enough, Jonny decided it would be infinitely better to sling it with maximum force straight into her face.

'Thank you,' Hayleigh said sweetly. 'You arsehole.'

'Welcome, bitch ho.'

Hayleigh started drying her hair. The towel was good cover for her bruised hand. Dad was staring at the mirror now. You could just about see the cogs in his brain clanking round. 'Hayleigh, tell me honestly, now: did you do that?'

Hayleigh looked at the mirror as if the massive damage she'd inflicted on it was somehow hard to spot, as if it didn't look at all like a jumbo jet had flown straight through it. 'Did I do what?'

'Of course she did it!' Jonny shrilled. 'She's always doing it. She hates mirrors. It's all part of her complete and utter mentalism.'

'Shush, Jonny, let Hayleigh speak.'

Hayleigh hung her head and nodded.

Dad shook his head sadly. 'Oh, Hay. We are going to have to get you back in with that therapist.' And he started wheeling her out of the loo.

She'd got away with it! Unbelievable. Jonny himself had furnished her with a completely credible alibi, bless his rancid little socks.

She was still towelling her hair when, halfway back to her room, she noticed her exercise book jammed down beside her hip, and suddenly remembered she'd left the suicide note on the bathroom chair.

She had left the suicide note on the bathroom chair.

Thank God Dad hadn't spotted it.

Stupid, stupid cow. What now? She couldn't just leave it there, could she? She'd signed the bloody thing with her full name, middle initial included. Why had she done it? She'd always known the note could turn into a liability. She ran through the text of it in her mind. Could she possibly spin it into something innocent? No, whichever way you looked at it, it was pretty unambiguous. She had to go back and retrieve it. And she had to do it right now, before Mommie Dearest got wind. She slammed on the wheelchair brakes. 'Hang on: we have to go back.'

'What?' Dad was irritated. He was doubtless already in for several painful lashes from the tongue, and he probably had a good idea of how the news of Hayleigh's latest mirror assault would be received in certain quarters. 'What *now*, Hayleigh?'

Rather than give him the opportunity to refuse permission, or, worse still, send Jonny scurrying back for it, she spun the wheelchair round, released the brake and headed off back towards the bathroom at such a lick, she probably left tyre burns on the corridor floor. 'Forgotten something,' she called back.

'Is it your head?' pig dog brother yelped in delight. 'Did you forget your head, you bloody spazmo?'

'Jonny,' Dad chided. 'You're not to use that word.'

'What word? Bloody or spazmo?'

'Neither,' Dad said.

Hayleigh glanced back. Dad was following her, damn it, and Jonny was dancing around him like Dash from *The Incredibles*. She just couldn't get enough speed out of the wheelchair to maintain a sufficient lead, especially since she had to reverse into the bathroom. She thought about going through head on and opening the door with her bad leg, but the lack of pain management meds in her system made that option untenable: she might very well pass out from the pain, and all would be lost. And she was so close, now, to getting away with the whole business, she didn't dare risk it.

Dad caught up with her at the door and took control of the chair. 'What is it you've forgotten?'

'I left some homework on the bathroom chair.'

Dad sighed, angrily, and pushed her towards the cubicle door, which was still ajar. Hayleigh saw the note immediately. She hadn't even had the foresight to leave it upside down. She reached over, grabbed it and stuffed it into her exercise book.

'You brought your homework to the bathroom?'

Hayleigh shrugged. 'Something to do while I waited for the bath to fill.' And at that moment, she glanced over at the gurgling, draining bath and caught a glimmer of a sparkle as the light hit the mirror shard in it.

She dropped her towel so Dad would have to bend over and pick it up. She looked up. The water was agitating the mirror fragment, and the reflection was darting about the ceiling like Tinker Bell.

Dad handed her the towel, and Hayleigh grabbed it off him. He started to turn towards the bath, so she launched the wheelchair towards him and caught him a savage blow to the shin.

'Bloody hell, Hayleigh!' He reached down to massage his leg.

'You can't say that word,' Jonny admonished, 'you spazmo.'

'Sorry, Dad. I'm trying to hurry things along here. Are you OK?'

'I'll live. Let's go, then,' Dad said grumpily, and wheeled her out again, limping slightly.

Crisis averted. Hayleigh clutched the exercise book to her chest. She would still have to dispose of the note, of course, and, since she would now be under the Ever Watchful Eye for the foreseeable future, she could only think of one way to do that safely.

She wondered, briefly, how many calories there were in a sheet of exercise book paper.

FIFTY-ONE

It wasn't until P and his coterie had availed themselves of all the photo opportunities, sipped drinks, rubbed shoulders and left the party that Jeremy finally got a chance to examine the contents of Anton's silver box. He stole into the lavatory in the club's VIP lounge. Outside, rock stars, pop stars, footballers and supermodels were really starting to party now the headmaster had left the building. He cracked open the box.

Now, Jeremy was not an expert in these matters. Far from it. But he knew, from Grenville Roberts' recipe for Victoria sponge cake, what ten grams of baking powder looked like. There was easily double that amount of powder in the box. Easily. Clearly, Anton hadn't intended it for his personal use alone. It was there to make the party go with a bang, as the Secret Serviceman had predicted. Was this how the big boys played it? It all seemed terribly seedy to Jeremy. What next? Pimping?

The lavatory door flew open and Jeremy snapped the case shut, guiltily. A young man and a young woman entered noisily and started necking quite seriously, running their hands up and down each other's bodies. Jeremy recognised them, not by name, though, but he knew they were both from manufactured pop groups. The woman was from Gurlz Banned, and the bloke was from Big Boys Cry. They were really getting into it, clearly oblivious to him, and when the lad's hand started tugging down the girl's thong, Jeremy thought he ought to make his presence known.

'Steady on, now, chaps. We'll all be wanting some.'

They didn't break off their foreplay. They didn't even seem

embarrassed. The bloke just peered over the girl's shoulder and grinned at him. 'Wait your turn, innit? Wait your turn.' Then he spotted Jeremy's box, and that distracted him from his amorous endeavours. 'You got some naughty salt, mate?'

Jeremy had been on the brink of flushing the bloody stuff down the loo. He shrugged. 'I do indeed have some naughty salt. Would you like some?'

'Fuck me, yes.' His eyes were wide and he literally panted like a dog.

Having none of the paraphernalia of druggery, Jeremy tried to tip out a couple of lines' worth onto the marble sink top, but misjudged and a big pile cascaded out.

The bloke's eyes got even wider. 'Fuck me. Are you serious? That's half of Columbia there, innit.'

Jeremy shrugged again. 'Be my guest.'

'Right.' The bloke rubbed his hands. 'We are going to seriously partayyyy. Amy, fetch the girls.'

She tottered towards the door on shoes that were designed to enhance the shape of her legs for photo shoots – and they did a very successful job of that, Jeremy thought – but were impossible to walk in.

'Don't tell anyone else, though, innit.'

Amy nodded and left.

'Right.' The bloke rubbed his hands again. 'Let's get stuck in.' He patted his pockets. 'Fuck. Got a credit card?'

Jeremy took out his wallet and handed over his Amex. He'd considered using his Tesco card, but didn't think that would give quite the right impression.

The bloke chopped himself a generous line with Jeremy's Amex. 'Right.' He patted himself down again. 'Got a tenner?'

Jeremy took out his wallet. He only had twenties. He didn't suppose it made much of a difference.

'Cheers, innit.' He started rolling the note into a tube. 'Ain't got no cash, innit. Fuckers give us two hundred and fifty squid a week spending money. Can you credit it? Two hundred and fifty. Three number ones on the trot, they give us fucking spends. Hardly pays for the ganja.' He bent to the marble, and Jeremy looked away.

The bloke snorted mightily, then threw back his head and yelled: 'Fucking, fucking, fuck, fuck, fuck.' He looked round at Jeremy. 'That is some top fucking straight, innit.' He offered the rolled up note to Jeremy.

Jeremy shook his head. 'Maybe later.'

'What's your name, mate?'

'Jeremy.'

'Jeremiah.' The bloke grinned. 'I is Jase, innit?' and he held out his hand palm down. Jeremy shook it.

Amy burst back in, giggling. Two of the other gurlz from her banned tottered in after her in their ridiculous heels, each carrying two bottles of champagne. Amy turned and locked the door. Jeremy was beginning to wish he'd known that possibility had been available to him.

'Here you go, girls.' Jase waved at the coke mountain, generous host that he was. 'Fill your boots.'

The girls all took a noisy snort. It turned Jeremy's stomach a little. It seemed a bit degrading, in his opinion. Porcine. The sort of thing you really ought to do in private.

When they'd all filled their boots, Jason took another trip on the merry-go-round, and went back to his foreplay attack on Amy.

The other two girls turned their attention to Jeremy, running their hands up and down the lapels of his jacket and licking their glossy lips.

'What d'you think, Justine?'

'I think he's well cute.'

'Shall we do him?'

'Get his cock out. Let's try him on for size.'

Justine knelt and started unzipping his flies, while the other one grabbed his neck and rather artlessly thrust her tongue down his throat.

Well, this was it. A dream come true. A threesome. A classic end to an epic day. And the girls were, no doubt about it, stunningly gorgeous. It was, after all, what they'd been hired for. They might not be the classiest women on the planet, or, by a very long way, the most intelligent, but they were, visually, stunners.

And what man wouldn't, in Jeremy's position?

It turned out, in fact, that Jeremy wouldn't.

Justine was still fiddling with his zipper when the other one finished her tonsil assault and stood back to lift her top over her head. Looking down at the fumbling girl on her knees suddenly caused a flashback to slam into Jeremy's head. He stepped back and said: 'Sorry, girls. I hate to be a party pooper, but I'm spoken for, I'm afraid.'

Justine didn't even look fazed. She stood up and said: 'Sure?'

'I'm disappointed, but I'm sure.'

'Cos, if we're not your flavour, Jase'll sort you. Won't you, Jase?'

Jason, who was currently on the receiving end of a very slurpy blow job from Amy, grinned and said, 'No worries, mate. I'll blow you, if that's your cuppa.'

Jeremy thanked them all, but assured them that was definitely *not* his cup of tea.

And while Amy worked away on Jason, the other two girls engaged in a snogging session themselves, in their underwear. La Perla, it was, too. Whether it was for Jeremy's benefit, or whether that was really *their* cup of tea, was unclear. Certainly Jeremy was beginning to regret his noble stand, and it was a relief when Jason finished his business with a noisy yell of, 'He doesn't want *that* one back!', zipped himself up, grabbed Jeremy's Amex card and said: 'Top-up, anyone?'

Jeremy had to hang around until they'd worked their way through the mound, just so he could get his Amex card and his money back – these superstars of pop didn't have a credit card or a note of the realm between the lot of them.

There was much raucous fun. The four of them did a rendition of Three Dog Night's 'Joy to the World' in his honour, though most of them didn't know the words, or, it would appear, the tune. The notion that these people made their living from singing was very hard to swallow. Either the recording engineers were geniuses, or someone else did the singing for them.

Jeremy made his excuses, they all swapped mobile numbers and he left them in the loo singing, for about the fifteenth time, 'Jeremiah was a Bullfrog'. It wasn't getting any more melodious with practice. He thought about leaving them the rest of his stash, but the truth is, the idiots might very well have killed themselves with it. They didn't seem to be capable of wrapping their juvenile minds around the concept of 'enough'. He took the box with him. He'd probably flush it away when he got home.

He left the club and stepped out into the sharp night. Some waiting paparazzi debated whether or not to snap him, but decided not to waste the space on their compact flash cards. It had been one hell of a day. He signalled one of the waiting cabs.

So that was sex and drugs and rock 'n' roll then, was it? As far as Jeremy was concerned, they could keep it.

PART THREE:

March 21st

MENU DU JOUR

Pan-fried Foie Gras with Sauternes Jelly
Lobster Thermidor

❧

Chicken Nuggets with Chips and Broccoli

❧

Absolutely Nothing At All

'There is nothing conventional about wisdom.
There is nothing common about sense.'
(Rob Grant: *Fat*, 2006)

FIFTY-TWO

Something was afoot. Something was definitely awry.

In the bleak wasteland that Hayleigh's life had become since the failed finale – a limbo land where you weren't actually dead, but you couldn't say you were actually living, either – the dull, endless routines were constant and never changing. There wasn't even a weekend to look forward to, there was just a featureless nothing, with the days all melting together into one giant, congealed, ugly lump. She had given up the whole euthanasia business altogether, for the duration of her imprisonment, at least. She just could not, when it came right down to it, face the sheer *violence* required. When she'd planned it, the final act had seemed clean, almost serene, and dignified. But it was not. It was actually a slasher horror movie. It was *Scream*, which she wasn't supposed to have seen, but, in the days when she'd been allowed sleepovers, there was always somebody's brother who had a forbidden DVD, or more lax parents who didn't seem to care about a movie's certification. And, given the opportunity, how could you *not* watch a movie with diet goddess Courteney Cox Arquette in it, gruesome as it was?

Compliance was the watchword. Hayleigh was complying. She had quite simply run out of struggle. She did what was asked of her in a switched-off, distant kind of way. She resumed her visits to the nut doctor. She listened to him. She even answered his questions, and responded to his probes in a polite, if detached way. She ate her meals, joylessly and without appetite, but she ate them. She'd stopped worrying about what was on her plate. She simply pretended it was all astronaut mulch. Sausages, potatoes, custard: it was all the same to Hayleigh. They could have fed her cowpats dipped in rat poison and she wouldn't have noticed. The first few days on this compliance regime, she had thrown up after every meal, involuntarily, and that had caused great consternation and gnashing of teeth, but then she'd settled into it, and what went down her gullet now had the good manners to stay down.

And she felt like an astronaut, too: floating in zero gravity slow motion through a featureless fug of infinite space; waking, eating, eating, eating and then sleeping. She was no longer on Talk Strike, but she hardly ever spoke, anyway, outside of the nut doc's office. What was there to say? Mum, of course, chitter-chatted away to her, but she might as well have been talking to a coma victim. Hayleigh was, she had no doubt whatsoever, going slowly, inexorably insane.

But now, something was happening. Something that might actually be, lawks a'mercy, interesting.

First, this fella had come into her room. He was really quite lush, although Hayleigh didn't normally go for older men, and he was *ancient*. He must have been pushing twenty-seven at the very least. He had a very nice suit on, and the best haircut she'd ever seen in real life. Most of the male hospital staff seemed to get their coiffures from the same barber stroke butcher's shop that must clearly have been caught in some kind of time warp and could only provide haircuts directly copied from her Gran's 1954 Gratton catalogue. He'd smiled at her (fab smile, fab teeth) and asked her about her Jason wall. She'd blushed (silly cow) and answered him, and then he'd beckoned Mum, and they'd gone out of the room.

Hayleigh hadn't been able to catch the full gist of their conspiratorial whisperings, but Mum had come back into the room trying very hard not to look excited at all, but Hayleigh knew her better than that. They were, after all – don't vomit, now – roomies. Hayleigh asked her what it was all about, but she'd just said she wasn't sure, and it would probably turn out to be nothing at all, but then El Lusho had popped his head in the door, nodded and gave Mum the thumbs up, and she *really* started trying not to look excited.

And now, the strangeness was being compounded. Mum had wheeled her to the bathroom and washed her hair, with actual shampoo. The mirror, mercifully, had been repaired by now, and she wasn't sure Mum had even been told about the incident. Certainly, it had never been mentioned since.

Then, curiouser and curiouser, Mum had wheeled Hayleigh back to her room and blow-dried her hair for her. She hadn't had her hair blow-dried since she'd been carried in through the hospital doors, almost three weeks ago.

And then Mum had helped her get dressed. In *clothes.* She'd been so used to wearing the standard-issue white hospital gown with a humiliating slit up the back, she'd forgotten what clothes felt like.

And then lush mush had come back with a Boots the Chemists bag which had actual grown-up make-up in it, which is normally the sole province of the sleepover because Dad doesn't approve of you wearing make-up in case it somehow turns you into a woman, and Mum had started putting it on for her.

All the while, Hayleigh was badgering her, trying to wheedle out of her just exactly what was going on, and all Mum could say, when she managed to stop grinning like a lunatic, was that it was a surprise, and she'd find out soon enough.

And when Mum had finished with the slap: foundation, blusher, eyeshadow, lip gloss, the full monty, and even some Chanel eau de toilette, she stood back and admired her work, and declared that Hayleigh looked absolutely beautiful, which, unless one of the surgeons from *Nip/Tuck* had somehow sneaked into the room without her noticing and secretly performed major facial reconstructive surgery, Hayleigh seriously doubted.

And then it happened.

As long as you live, you will never guess who came bounding into the room.

Seriously, you would have a heart attack and die right there and then.

FIFTY-THREE

Jeremy was wandering randomly along the corridors of the London Royal Hospital. He'd been taken on several official tours of several institutions, but he knew better than to believe the dog and pony shows those bullshit artists put on for him. He was, after all, king of the bullshit artists. So he'd done some research of his own. It wasn't difficult. Security in most hospitals was close to non-existent, except on a few post-natal wards. And what he'd found, quite frankly, appalled him. There were endless corridors lined with trolleys that had been re-designated as 'beds' in order to hit Government targets, and many of them had very sick people on them. The staff morale was just about flatlining, from the surgical consultants to the Eastern European cleaning staff, who had one half-hour break for their lunch, without pay, of course, and nowhere to eat it: nowhere to sit down, even, and they were paid like Dickensian chimney sweeps. The whole edifice of the National Health Service was crumbling visibly, and here he was with instructions to paper over the cracks.

Well, it wasn't his job to be winkling out the truth. He wasn't a scientist, he wasn't a journalist. His job was to make his employers look good. His job was spin. Although you didn't call it that any more, the word 'spin' having acquired negative associations. What you did was: you realigned perceptions. You didn't lie – you wouldn't last long in the industry if you actually out and out lied – you adopted the . . . what had Jemma called it? Dean Martin? No, you adopted the Bing Crosby approach. You accentuate the positive and eliminate the negative, and don't mess with Mr In-Between. He smiled at the memory of her singing that in her scarily convincing baritone, with her face all contorted.

What the NHS needed was billions of pounds. What the NHS needed was to put doctors back in charge and hurl the budget-leeching administrators out of their high office windows. What the NHS was getting was Jeremy Slank, some plaster and paint, a flash new logo and a few million for advertising.

It didn't make him feel good, but it was his job, and he would do it, and do it well. After all, with his new partnership slice of the action, and his own ridiculous fees, this contract alone would make him very comfortably a millionaire before the end of the year. On top of which, he just might be able to slip in some positive changes. They needed to stop farming out the cleaning contracts and bring that particular service back in house. That wouldn't cost an arm and a leg, and it would actually save lives. Maybe, if he did a good enough job, he could have a decent shot at selling that option.

And then he'd seen her. The wraith. This young girl – it was impossible to tell her age accurately – so thin and frail it looked like a strong wind would snap her in two. Her eyes were sunk in her head in dark hollows. She looked for all the world like one of the children sheltering under the robe of the Ghost of Christmas Present in the cartoon version of *A Christmas Carol*: the girl named 'Hunger'. She was in a wheelchair, and someone who loved her had painstakingly coloured in the plaster cast around her leg in purple felt-tip. Of course, she looked very poorly, but it wasn't that that broke Jeremy's heart when he looked at her. It was her eyes. They looked so fierce and proud and defiant. As if she was a healthy kid trapped in the body of a frail one. It was as if she needed someone to rescue her. As if – and Jeremy had no idea why this word popped into his head – as if she needed a hero.

Then he'd seen the montage on her wall, and recognised that idiot from the launch party. Maybe he could do something for her, after all. Not be her hero, exactly. Just organise a little something to brighten her day.

He made the phone call.

'Jase?'

'What up, dude?'

'It's Jeremy. Jeremy Slank?' Confused silence. 'We met at the Well Farm launch party last week, remember?'

'Sorry, man, I was well wasted, innit?'

'I introduced you to my friend, *Charlie*?'

'Oh, right. With you. The Bullfrog, innit? How's it hangin', mate?'

'Good. Look, are you around? In London, I mean?'

'Yeah. I is chillin' with me posse, innit?'

'Look, I know it's a big thing to ask: could you possibly get over to the London Royal Hospital?'

'I dunno 'bout that, mate. I is well busy, innit. We is writing a song, innit.'

Jeremy smiled. This bloke couldn't have written his name in the ground with a stick with someone else guiding it for him. He could hear the sound of a PlayStation game in the background. 'I appreciate that, Jase. It's just, there's this girl here, and she's pretty sick and all, and I think a visit from you might—'

'You want me to do her?'

'*Do* her? No. She's just a kid. And she's pretty ill.'

'You know me, mate, I'll fuck anything.' There was raucous laughter from the posse.

'I hate asking for a favour, but it'll only take half an hour, and it would mean the world . . . If you could just see her, you'd be here in a flash.'

'You got any of that good gak?'

'Jesus. This is a cellphone, dude.'

'Sorry, innit.' And he adopted what Jeremy could only imagine was Jason Black's interpretation of how a normal human being with an actual IQ might speak: 'Would your delightful friend Charles be in attendance, Jeremiah, what ho?'

Jeremy shook his head. He'd have to get a cab back to his pad. Lucky he hadn't remembered to flush the bloody stuff away. 'Yes, Jase. Charlie will be here.'

'That is bear good, amigo.'

Jeremy assumed this was some kind of positive response. 'You'll come over, then?'

'I am out of the door as we is speaking.'

'Top man. Meet you at the lifts on the fifth floor in an hour.'

'Sorted.'

Jeremy met Jason at the lift. He was flirting with a nurse when the doors opened, and not too successfully if the nurse's expression was any guide. Jason gave Jeremy a big smile and offered his hand, palm down, for a handshake.

'Bullfrog, ma man. You is looking cooking.'

'You too, Jase,' Jeremy lied. The bloke looked and smelled like he hadn't washed in a week, or changed his clothes in twice that time. It could well be so: he was probably on a constant 24/7 party. In fact, wasn't that . . . ? Yes. He was still wearing the same shirt he'd worn at the launch party: a neat, fitted pale yellow shirt with blue and red vertical stripes. Didn't they have an entourage, these people? Surely they had someone looking after their wardrobe, at least? Or did that only happen higher up the pop food chain? He was, naturally, sporting the obligatory wannabe rock star shades, though the hospital lighting was dim at best. 'She's just down here.'

'Whoa, whoa, whoa. What about the naughty salt?'

'Well, I thought you'd want to see her straight.'

'I ain't been straight in five years, mate. I hate straight. I need the naughty salt to *get* me straight.'

Jeremy looked around, then dug into his left-hand pocket and discreetly palmed over the silver box.

Jason shook his head. 'No, no, no, man. You always give with the right hand, and receive with the left, innit.'

What? Bloody druggy nonsense. Jeremy swapped hands, thereby doubling his risk of detection and passed the case over.

'Wicked.' Jason pocketed the box deftly. He licked his lips. The prospect of the drugs was literally making him drool. 'Where's the nearest, ah, facility?'

Jeremy nodded in the direction of the loos.

'Want to come with?'

'Not right now, thanks.'

'Your loss.'

Jason swaggered off like he was holding a watermelon between his thighs. Was that how the cool kids walked now, or was he just recovering from pile surgery?

Jeremy waited. And though the lavatories were a good twenty yards down the corridor, he could actually hear Jason snort, followed by an unintelligible yell, a 'fuck me sideways' and a cowboy 'Yippee!'.

Jason emerged seconds later, looking considerably happier. He took a few regular steps towards Jeremy before he remembered how he was supposed to walk, and resumed his swagger.

'That is some serious blow, Jeremiah. That is uncut and straight from the coca plant.' He held out his right hand, palm down, to return the box.

Jeremy shook his head. 'Keep it, mate.'

'Seriously?'

'It's yours.'

'Fuck *off*! This must be worth, like, a grand, man, innit.'

'You're doing me a favour.'

'You is my number one go-to guy, Bullfrog.'

'Don't mention it.'

'Listen, if I call you, can you get me—'

'I'm not a dealer, Jase.'

'No offence, innit.'

'None taken.'

Jason looked at the box, then slipped it into his pocket. He rubbed his hands. 'Right then, where's the ho?'

Jeremy tried not to wince. 'Down here. Her name is Hayleigh.'

'Right. Like the motorbike, innit.'

'No, that's Harley.'

'Whatever.'

'This way.' Jeremy nodded down the corridor and turned.

'Hang on, mate.' Jason opened his mouth into a big 'O' shape and started making a series of bizarre choking noises deep in his throat. 'Kukkrrrrrk, kukkrrrrrrk . . .'

'Are you all right?'

Jason nodded but kept on making the choking noises anyway. Jeremy looked round, worried, to see if there was a doctor or a nurse nearby who might rush to the rescue if Jason had a fit or something.

Jason spoke, but his voice rattled from somewhere down low in his windpipe. 'Shit, man, I think I anaesthetised me throat.' He put his hand on Jeremy's shoulder for support and bent his head. He kept on making the choking noises, 'Kukkrrrrrk, kukkrrrrrrk, kukkrrrrrrk,' as if someone was trying to throttle the life out of him. What if he choked to death? What if he OD'd? What if he dropped down dead right there on the spot with Jeremy's drug stash on him?

But he finally stopped choking, gave a massive snort and straightened up. 'Like I said, mate. That is *good* blow.' His face was red and he was sweating, and none too fragrantly, either. Jeremy offered him some cologne, but Jason said he was 'chill' and they moved off towards Hayleigh's room. There were white specks on Jason's shirt, but Jeremy couldn't tell if they were renegade grains of coke or just common or garden dandruff. Hopefully, the kid would be too blown away at meeting Jason to scrutinise too closely.

Just before they got to the door, Jeremy stopped and nodded to let Jason know this was the place. Jason nodded back, gave one final sucking snort and swaggered into the room.

Jeremy heard him say: 'Whassup, Harley?' in a loud,

showbiz bluster, then pushed himself off the wall to leave. He hadn't got halfway down the hall when he heard a cry of 'Wait!' and Carla, the girl's mother, came racing after him. He turned and smiled at her. He couldn't make out what her expression was supposed to be saying. Her mouth was all twisted, like she was biting the inside of her lip. Was she going to hit him?

'You, mister, are some kind of wonderful.' There were tears pooling in her eyes.

'No sweat,' Jeremy said. 'Really.'

'I think you must be an angel or something.'

'I'm anything but that, Carla. All I did was phone a friend.'

'All you did was very possibly save that little girl's life, did you but know it.'

Jeremy could only smile. He had absolutely no idea what you could say in reply to that sort of thing. He fished in his jacket pocket. 'Listen, you'll let me know how she gets on, won't you?' He handed over his business card. 'Give me a shout when she's well enough to go home?'

'Jeremy Slank.' Carla sniffed. 'You will be guest of honour at her twenty-first birthday, and you'll be on my table, by my bloody side, at her bloody wedding.'

Jeremy nodded. 'It's a date, then.' He smiled again and turned to go again.

'Just one second, Mr Angel. You are not getting out of this building without suffering the biggest, sloppiest, blubberiest kiss you'll ever have to endure in your life.'

And Jeremy let the woman kiss him on the cheek, very sloppily indeed, and even held on to her for a bit while she sobbed helplessly all over his Armani-clad shoulder.

FIFTY-FOUR

It had been unbelievably exciting when he'd first come in, and he got her name slightly wrong, but never mind that, he was there *in the flesh*, and she thought her heart was going to burst out of her ribcage and go racing round London and complete the Marathon all on its own. She literally could not speak. She must have looked like she was a brain-dead vegetable, with her mouth lolling open, and, for all she knew, dribbling drool. But he bounded up to her, his arms wide open, with his big, dimpled grin all over his face, and took her face in his hands and kissed her sloppily on the forehead.

And he *smelled*. Wow, was he ripe. Well, fair enough. He'd probably been working round the clock in the studio, be-cause the new album was a bit behind schedule, and he'd taken time out to visit Hayleigh in person, so she wasn't going to hold a little thing like a dizzying stench of body odour against him.

He sat down, then, on the couch, leaned back flamboy-antly, arms thrown wide, lifted his head and sniffed back the vilest gurgling snort Hayleigh had ever heard in her life. And that, in all seriousness, was the *high* point of the encounter.

He spent the next five minutes just lolling there, his right leg crossed over his left, forming a triangle, just staring at the ceiling. Then he finally snapped out of it and looked down and gave a little start, as if he was surprised to find her there. He snorted again, and asked her what she was in for. Hayleigh smiled coyly and pointed to her leg. He stared at the leg for a ridiculously long time.

'Purple, innit,' he pointed out, ingeniously.

'Can you guess why, Jase?'

'No, mate, innit. Is it coz your surgeon was the artist formerly known as "Prince"?' And he laughed at that for about twenty minutes, which turned into a very strange kind of coughing fit, with his mouth shaped into a giant oval, and his face going redder and redder and odd little choking sounds coming from somewhere deep in his throat. Hayleigh looked round at her emergency button. She thought she might need to summon a crash cart. 'Fuck me,' he said when he finally recovered. 'Sorry 'bout that, babe. Got a touch of the flu, innit.'

Hayleigh did her best to pretend nothing very odd had happened. 'It's your favourite colour, Jason.'

'What is?'

'Purple.'

'Is it? Fuck me.' He glanced round at the decorated wall, and jumped. 'Fucking hell, man. I'm the fucking wallpaper. What is that about?'

Hayleigh squirmed in her chair. She noticed a thick glob of snot had started dribbling from his nose. Jason, intent on studying his tribute, seemed completely oblivious. To everything.

He turned back towards her and, once again, seemed shocked to find someone else in the room with him. 'Fuck me sideways, gel. You is one scrawny bitch, innit?' The snot had now drooled all the way to his lips. Still staring at her, Jason stuck out his tongue and dragged the giant glob into his mouth with it. He chewed, thoughtfully, for a while and then swallowed it down. 'I like 'em with a bit more meat on, innit?' Then he wiped up the rest of the mucal debris from his upper lip with two fingers and *sucked them clean.*

Hayleigh was beginning to feel nauseous.

Jason's left leg started juddering quite violently. It was impossible to tell whether or not the movement was voluntary. He held up his wrist and looked at it. He was not wearing a watch. 'I best get going, innit.'

Hayleigh nodded. She was quite relieved. She'd been starting to feel a little bit frightened.

Jason put his right leg down and slapped his hands on his thighs. The left leg was still going strong. 'Well,' he said, 'I best get going, innit,' again.

But he didn't get up. He just sat there, hands on thighs, one leg doing a single-handed *Lord of the Dance*, pulling a series of very strange expressions with his face, wrinkling his nose and wiggling his lips as if he was trying to exercise his teeth. 'Well,' he said, finally, 'I best get going, innit.' And he stood. 'You get better, now, yeah?'

Hayleigh nodded.

'Here.' Jason fished in his back pocket and pulled out an unmarked CD case. 'This am our new album. Not quite finished the mix yet. That is well rare. That is well precious, mate. The record company ain't even heard that yet.'

He handed Hayleigh the case. She opened it excitedly. It was empty. She held it up to show him. 'There's nothing in it, Jason.'

'Shit. Must have left it in the machine, innit.' He stood there awkwardly for a moment. 'You want me to sign it for you?'

Hayleigh nodded and handed him back the case. She couldn't have given a toss whether he signed it or not. The stupid thing was cracked anyway, from where he'd been sitting on it. Whoops a dee, an empty, cracked blank CD case. By this time, though, she just wanted to get rid of him.

He patted down his pockets several times. 'Got a pen?'

Hayleigh turned and wheeled towards the table and picked up her pencil case, but when she turned round, Jason was already at the door. 'Later, babe,' he called back at her, and, as an afterthought, added, 'And put some fucking meat on you, innit? I like a bit of arse meself.' He made a crude grabbing motion with his upturned hands, and he was gone. He'd taken the broken CD case with him.

FIFTY-FIVE

Grenville rolled out of bed like he was tumbling down from the Cross. He literally had to roll. After – what? A year? Eighteen months? No, wait: after four nights on that mattress, his spine had quite simply turned to jelly. And not nice jelly, either. Extremely painful jelly. Jelly with razor blades in it. He couldn't have straightened up if he'd tried.

He looked at his watch. Five forty-five. Brilliant. He'd managed to sleep through fully fifteen minutes of the obnoxious alarm that was piped into your room and didn't stop until you rose. How did they do that? How did they know? He was on the floor now, on his hands and knees, but obviously that didn't qualify as actually being up because the klaxon was still blaring at full volume.

With a great effort of the will, he reached up to the bedpost and hauled himself painfully into an L shape, his head resting against the post. Still the klaxon blared. He lifted his head and yelled: 'I'm *up*, you filthy bastards. This has *got* to count as being up.'

But he was not rewarded with the silence he craved. He looked around. The former rugby player was still asleep. Admirable. World-class sleeping ability, that. Hats off, mate. Grenville staggered to the shower room, like the Crooked Man walking his crooked mile.

Why they had to wake up at five-thirty in the morning anyway was a bizarre mystery to Grenville. Was there something intrinsically slimming about getting up before the milkman? Did it somehow aid the reduction of subcutaneous fatty deposits, keeping the same hours as a three-month-old baby? He turned the showers on, knowing from bitter experience that it would be another fifteen minutes before they were sufficiently hot not to induce frostbite in your extremities, or kill you from shock, and you then had a window of five minutes before the eco-friendly energy-efficient solar panel heating system gave up for the day.

He staggered over to the washbasin and cleaned his teeth. He was growing overly fond of cleaning his teeth. It was the only time in the day he experienced flavour. Cleaning his teeth was literally the best meal of the day. He showered and had a stab at drying himself with the smallest bath towel he had ever seen. He'd complained, on the first day, that they hadn't been given any towels at all, but the Residential Consultant had assured him that these were the bath towels and not, as Grenville had wrongly assumed, face flannels.

That was one of fully fifty-seven complaints lodged by Grenville and his roommates on the first day. The following morning, some wag from administration had stuck an A4 sheet above their door with the legend 'Heinz Lodge' etched upon it. Grenville didn't mind that. It showed at least that someone, somewhere within this administration, had at least the faint stirrings of some kind of wits.

Six of the beds had broken during that first night, spilling their occupants quite painfully. A one-hit-wonder ex-pop star had been stabbed clean through the upper arm with a large shard of wood from the splintered frame, and had to be choppered to hospital. And he hadn't even been the first of Grenville's lot to go. The former breakfast TV presenter and the losing *Big Brother* contestant had gone straight after dinner: just walked out of the dining hall, through the gates and kept on walking, they didn't much care where. Grenville had badly wanted to join them. The food had been utter swill. No, wait, at least swill had flavour. Pigs climbed over each other to get to it, did they not? Somehow, the magnificent swill-master plying his demonic craft in the kitchens had managed to remove even the vaguest hint of taste from every last morsel on offer. There was no seasoning, there were no sauces. Everything was steamed or boiled. Everything. Even the meat. Steamed chicken. Unbelievable. But he'd sucked it up and stuck it out. There was a lot at stake for him here. And he was, undeniably, losing weight. Starvation would definitely do that for you.

That didn't stop him complaining about the food, though. And even though it seemed to be getting him nowhere, he carried *on* complaining about the food, on the official forms provided, after every single meal, at very great length and in very great detail.

In a day or so, he would have to start writing his newspaper diary column. He would find it very hard to put a positive spin on the experience so far. Very hard indeed. Perhaps he should think about starting it today. It would require a gift for fiction he had not tapped since his A-levels. He unhooked his dressing gown and pulled it around his damp body. It was labelled extra large. If he tugged hard and held it tight with both hands it could just about stretch to cover one of his nipples. His stomach, his tackle, his remaining nipple and everything north and south was left dangling on display for all the world to see. Thank merciful Christ he'd made a stand about the mixed barracks.

Their luggage had finally shown up yesterday, and that had been a good thing. Grenville had spent the first two days and nights in his chef's jacket and trousers, which, after eight full-on gym sessions, countless table tennis games and a knackering stroll through the nature walk had begun not just to smell, but actually to evolve. He had earned enough credits to buy a new outfit, or even two – he had lost over ten pounds already – but he'd be buggered if he was going to blow that on more hideous Day-Glo sportswear when he had brought perfectly good hideous Day-Glo sportswear of his own, if only the dozy bastards could find it. No, Grenville was going to save up his credits till he could afford something big. Like an escape helicopter, for instance. Or an AK-47 to use on the Hell Farm mattress supplier.

You were only allowed one suitcase, however – Lord knows why – and he'd been unable to fit his own dressing gown in it – that is, if he wanted to bring anything else at all. He'd tried wearing the standard-issue dressing gown back to front, but it was so tight around the neck that if he sat down and accidentally trapped the wrong part of it under his buttocks, he wound up strangling himself.

By the end of day three, Grenville and Geoff, the rugby player, had been the only remaining occupants of Heinz Lodge. Geoff hadn't left because he had nowhere to go. His wife had kicked him out when she'd found out about his mistress, and then his mistress had kicked him out when she'd found out his wife had kicked him out, because he was no longer enticing as a single man who spent the entire day and night drinking beer and watching sports. Geoff was there for the duration, come what may.

Grenville hadn't left because he had staying power. He was not a quitter.

He went back into the bedroom to put on his exercise gear. He left a puddle trail behind him because the com-plimentary towelling slippers were, inevitably, three sizes too small. When you have great fatness thrust upon you, the excess load causes your feet to spread inexorably. Grenville had achieved full-grown adulthood with a shoe size of nine. Now he needed twelves. He wasn't even Off The Peg in the footwear department. The klaxon was still going off, and Geoff was still asleep. Incredible. Half an hour of it. Was he just asleep, or was he dead? Grenville waddled over – he still hadn't worked up the courage to straighten up just yet – and leaned over to check Geoff was still breathing. He was. He must have jiggered himself out yesterday watching the test match, poor bloke. Five hours of constant peddling was enough to take it out of anybody.

Grenville got dressed. Even under normal conditions this process demanded strange, uncomfortable contortions. Doubled over like a hook, it was close to impossible. It took

313

ten minutes. The incessant klaxon made it even more enjoyable than usual. The armpits on his freshly laundered T-shirt were dark and damp by the end of it.

Gren waddled to the living area, leaned his back against the hilarious *Borrowers* sofa and in one swift, brave movement straightened his spine. It sounded like the photographers' flashbulbs going off on Oscar night as the Rat Pack and their entire entourage strolled along the red carpet. Flashbulbs went off in Grenville's head, too. He couldn't see for three full minutes. He might have screamed, but he couldn't hear himself above the klaxon.

When he'd recovered sufficiently, and convinced himself he wasn't actually crying, he stepped out into the chill dawn.

The Stalag street lights were on, and the sky had a purple glow about it. Very pretty, that. Perhaps that was something he could mention in his column. Although it would be hard to ascribe the quality of the sunrise to the administrators of the Well Farm, it was, at least, something positive.

He started jogging towards the gym centre, but stopped after three steps with a mild cramp and just walked instead. The klaxons were still going off in several of the hovels he passed. Signs of a rebellion brewing?

Although the attrition rate had been extraordinarily high in the celebrity huts, as far as Grenville could see, it had kept to a reasonable level in the rest of the camp. He assumed most of the remaining inmates weren't quite so free to make their choices. Perhaps they could ill afford not to stay. Perhaps they'd rented out their homes for the duration, as Grenville was preparing to do. Perhaps they had nowhere else to go. He knew for certain that those on the dole would cease to receive benefits if they quit. But that didn't mean they were prepared to sit back meekly and take whatever the camp kommandants threw at them.

The whole enterprise had been undertaken with astonishingly little foresight. All the fixtures and fittings had been designed and bought by normal-sized people, with a breathtaking inability to project what the requirements of the oversized might be. The chairs, for instance, were not only uncomfortable, they were instruments of torture that required balancing talents normally only encountered in the circus to be put to their intended purpose. They were impossible to use for anything except hurling at Residential Consultants. The beds had all needed replacing at Lord knows what cost because they were not merely too small and uncomfortable, they were potentially lethal. The turnstiles in the gym had to be removed because people kept getting trapped in them. It was a nightmare.

A farm employee was tending the immaculate lawn outside the centre. The first daffodils of spring were showing their heads in the beds that lined the path. That looked pretty, too. He could mention that. Nice lawns, lovely dawns. Great.

Although he was already ravenous, Grenville decided to clock up a few minutes on the rowing machine. This was partly because the rowing machines were the most comfortable seats in the entire sorry complex, and his backside sorely needed the respite, and partly in order to rack up some more valuable credits, which he now decided would be best spent on a surface-to-surface rocket launcher with which to dispatch the kitchen swill-meister.

He put his card in the slot and rowed. So far he must have rowed the equivalent of a transatlantic crossing. If he kept this up, in a month or so he'd look like Stretch Armstrong.

He finished his session and retrieved his card. The cards were precious, here. You couldn't do anything without them. Seriously, you even needed your card just to open the toilet door. You literally couldn't take a dump without your card. He scanned the notice board. Tonight's movie was to be *Shallow Hal.* Superb. A comedy with Gwyneth Paltrow dressed in a fat suit for us all to laugh at. Was somebody actually *trying* to foment a riot?

Today's inter-lodge football tournament had been postponed until further notice, unsurprisingly. Yesterday's had been a bloodbath. You can't take people who haven't done any serious exercise since Bobby Darin last topped the charts and expect them to survive a full-blown football tournament. A *table* football tournament would probably have produced a crop of career-threatening injuries. As it was, there had been countless strains, seven broken bones of various severity, five concussions and two heart attacks before the competition had been called off. The emergency helicopter was getting more exercise than the lot of them put together.

At the point of starvation now, he climbed the stairs to the cafeteria. Such was his hunger, he was almost looking forward to breakfast. Almost, but not quite. Although the cafeteria was fairly crowded, there was none of the conversational buzz that usually fills the air in eating establishments. Perhaps it was too early in the morning for people to be feeling chatty. Perhaps everyone was too depressed to talk.

Grenville saw, to his intense disgust, that the seating problem had still not been sorted out. He tracked down the duty Residential Consultant to give her a good barracking. Either she was a new girl, or the others had all requested transfers to other blocks on the estate, specifically to avoid Grenville's tongue, leaving this poor, unwitting wretch right in the firing line, the cowardly bastards.

'Excuse me, miss. I was under the impression that something was going to be done about the seating, as a matter of urgency.'

She smiled and looked down at her clipboard. 'Really? I don't have any record of a problem with the seating.'

'Well, look around you. Can you not see a problem?'

She looked around her. She did not particularly see a problem.

'I'll give you a clue, shall I? Haven't you noticed that people are standing up to eat their breakfast?'

'A lot of them are, yes.'

'*All* of them are, yes. Why do you think that might be?'

'I really have no idea.'

Grenville believed that. He believed she probably never had an idea. 'They are standing up because they can't sit down. They can't sit down because the clone of Albert Einstein who designed the seating decided to bolt the chairs too close to the tables for human beings to fit in them. The problem with the seating is, the seating cannot be sat upon.'

'I see. Yes. That *is* a problem, isn't it?' And she made the mistake of smiling.

'It is indeed a problem. And it's not a funny problem, young lady. It's a serious problem. I think it's a basic human right to be able to sit down to eat, don't you? Slaves on galley ships were allowed to sit down to eat. Serial killers on Death Row sit down to eat. What have we done to be denied this simple dignity? We are here voluntarily. We are not here to suffer unnecessary privations and humiliations because of the incompetence of the camp's administrators, are we?'

'Of course not. You should fill out a complaint form. I've got one h—'

'I've filled out a complaint form, thank you. To date, I have filled out ten complaint forms on this very subject. And, yesterday, I got rather cross that someone appeared to be using my complaint forms to wipe their arse with, because my complaints were not being acted upon. You can get some idea of quite how cross I did get by observing that a chair has been ripped from its bolts on that table there, and then by admiring the dent in yon wall over there, which was the ultimate destination of that liberated chair. And had the then duty Residential Consultant not ducked in the nick of time, he would no longer be in possession of his own teeth.'

'I see,' she said and looked back down at the old clipboard. Grenville would have loved to get his hands on one of those clipboards, to find out quite what was so fascinating about them.

'And at that time, I was fervently assured that the seating problem would be addressed forthwith and sorted in time for breakfast this very morn.'

'I see,' she said, and didn't look up.

'Which it has not been.'

'No.'

'And you don't even have a record of the problem on your magic clipboard, do you?'

'I don't, no.'

'Well, perhaps you could tell me exactly how much furniture I have to rip up to get someone's attention, and how far I must hurl it, and precisely at whom?'

'I'm sure it's being acted on as we speak.'

'I'm equally sure it isn't.'

'Why don't I go and get the Residential Manager?'

'Why don't you do that? He and I are very good friends. He'll be delighted to see me again.'

'It'll take a few minutes. Will you still be here?'

'I'll be right over there, my dear, standing at that table by the window, eating my breakfast. I need to be near the window in case the Residential Manager needs throwing through it.'

'Right.' She smiled uneasily. 'Back in a tic.' She turned to go, then turned back. 'What shall I tell him your name is?'

'You won't need to bother, love. He'll know.'

She scarpered, no doubt grateful to be still blessed with teeth. Grenville crossed to the buffet table and picked up a tray. As usual, the fresh fruit section was stocked with canned fruit, and the 'freshly pressed' juices were watered-down cordials.

Grenville smiled brightly at the serving assistant, who had the temerity to be wearing chef's attire. 'Good morning, young sir. And what superb epicurean delights has the swillmeister cajoled out of his satanic cauldron today?'

The server looked at him, puzzled, scratched his head like a monkey and said, 'It's all labelled.'

'It is indeed. It is all labelled. But the labels hardly do it justice, do they? This, for instance, is labelled as "Low-Fat Oatmeal", which doesn't even come close to conveying the true horror that lurks bubbling in the pot, posing as food.

You should, in fact, adjust the label to read "Shite", or "Watery Shite", if I may be so bold.'

'Would you like a complaint form?'

'No, no, no. I would simply like a steaming bowl of shite, please.'

'Have you got your card?'

'I have indeed.' Grenville handed his card over. 'I see you have still not managed to resolve your dispute with your fresh fruit supplier, more's the pity. While I once upon a time truly enjoyed a glass of orange-coloured water posing as fruit juice, that has not been the case since my fourth year on this planet.'

The youth handed Grenville his card back. 'I'm sorry, sir: I can't serve you.'

'And why would that be, my young friend? Are you too close to the chimpanzee in your evolutionary development? Are your thumbs not yet opposable?'

'You're out of food credits.'

'No, that's a mistake.'

The youth shrugged, apologised again and moved on to the next customer.

Grenville called him back. 'Just one second here, good fellow. Swipe the card again.'

Reluctantly, the kid took the card and swiped it through his reader again. And again, he returned it. 'Sorry. You're definitely out of credits.'

'That's not possible. I've got enough credits on there to buy a small Pacific island. I have sufficient credits to purchase an entire field of oats all to myself and spend the rest of my life seeking out the arcane alchemical secret of how to turn them into sloppy human excrement.'

'Would you like a complaint form?'

'No, I just want my breakfast.'

'I can't serve you, mate. Sorry.' And the youth moved on again.

Grenville stared at his card.

There was a young sous chef from Hitchin . . .

FIFTY-SIX

Jeremy stepped out through the hospital doors and breathed. There was something about hospital air that did not feel right. It was artificial, in some way. It was air from your childhood, preserved. There were daffodils lining the path. Normally, Jeremy thought daffs were a bit naff: cheap, or something; but the flash of colour filled his spirit. The whole Jason business was, in his opinion, ambiguous at best. Sending the stinking idiot cokehead in to see that kid might have been a good thing, but, on the other hand, it might just have finished the poor mite off. The moron had a vocabulary of what? Twenty-seven words? Twenty-nine, if you were being generous. And fully half of them were synonyms for cocaine. Why, then, was he feeling so good? Was it because, for the first time in his adult life, he had actually thought of somebody else? His mobile beeped. Jeremy had it set to just a single beep. The very notion of setting a ringtone was disgraceful, frankly, and ought to be punishable under law. He checked the display. It was Derrian.

'Hi, mate, it's Derrian.'

'Yeah. I guessed somehow. I have this modern thing, see, called "caller ID".'

'Yeah, you twat. Listen: did I see you on TV last night?'

'I dunno. Were you watching the Bravo Channel's excellent documentary *The World's Largest Cock*?'

'No, mate, I think it was that Living TV game show *My Arse Cheeks are Open and Anyone May Enter*.'

'That'll be it, then.'

'No, but seriously, were you standing next to the fucking Prime Minister and his unspeakably ugly wife?'

'She wanted me, big time.'

'Jesus. What kind of cock did you have to suck to get that gig?'

'Oh, lots of cock. Lots of big, ugly cock.'

'I bet. Listen: I'm having a birthday bash—'

'Shit. What are you? Twenty-nine now?'

'We're not talking about it. I've booked the chef's table at Gordon Ramsay's at Claridges. Next Friday. Can you make it?'

Now, Jeremy knew that Derrian must have bumped someone off the invitation list at this kind of notice, for that kind of gig. You have to book that particular table months in advance. On the chef's table, in the kitchen at Claridges, you don't even get to order, you just get what the chef thinks is special. He'd tried, once, to book it himself, but he'd been about two months too late. So he knew there were only a limited number of places available, and he thought he might try a ploy.

'The chef's table? What kind of cock did you have to suck to get that?'

'Lots of cock, mate. Lots of big, ugly, diseased cock.'

'Well, I'd love to come. Can I bring a friend?'

It was a test, really, of his current pulling power. Derrian would have to burn someone else off to accommodate his outrageous request, and by rights, he should have told Jeremy to sod right off, but he didn't.

After only the tiniest of pauses, Derrian said, 'Well, of course, mate.'

'You have got to stop calling people "mate", Derrian. You sound like a bloody barrow boy.'

'Oh, Christ. Am I doing that?'

'It must stop. Mate.'

'You know you're cockney rhyming slang, don't you?'

'Yeah. Jeremy Slank: money in the bank.'

'Right. Catch you later, you big fucking slanker.'

Well, well, well. Jeremy Slank *est arrivé*. He'd been walking down the path during the phone conversation, and he found himself, now, outside the hospital gates, standing by the flower stall. There were some nice red roses on display, and he thought about buying them.

He'd got a round-robin email from Jemma that very morning, with a change of address on it. It was impersonal, and she may not even have realised he was in her address book. Now, maybe she was moving to another love nest with the ancient Keith, or maybe, just maybe, she'd come to her senses and left him in the hope of finding someone to date who still had his own teeth and wasn't drawing a pension. Maybe, even, Keith had experienced a senile moment and kicked her out himself. It struck Jeremy that Jemma was the type of girl who would be rigorously honest in a relationship, and he'd lay down good money she'd made the ridiculous mistake of telling old Keith about the nearly blow job in his flat. However it had happened, all pictures of the doddery bastard had been expunged from Jemma's blog. It was a fairly safe bet she was suddenly single.

And her new address was only a couple of Tube stops from the hospital. The change of address had been dated from today, so it was a fair bet she'd be there, actually moving in.

Well, he'd already been a knight in shining armour once today, and here was another damsel in distress. Well, maybe not a damsel. She was a bit too feisty to qualify as a damsel. And distress was probably putting it a bit strongly. Still, he'd give it a try with his trusty lance. He could help her move in, then take her out to dinner somewhere nice. The Palais du Jardin in Longacre. Yes. Some pan-fried foie gras with Sauternes jelly and a couple of lobster thermidors should do the trick. He asked the flower seller how much the roses were, then changed his mind. Jemma was much too classy for an adolescent manoeuvre like that. She'd see right through that little ploy.

On the Tube, on the way to Jemma's, he actually gave up his seat for a large Jamaican woman who was struggling with her shopping. Dear me. How gallant. Sir Galahad or what?

He was actually nervous ringing the doorbell, like he was fourteen years old again. What if he'd read the whole thing wrong? What if Keith opened the door? Worse yet, what if Keith opened the door, recognised him as the would-be usurper, the nearly recipient of the almost blow job, and started beating him up with his Zimmer frame? But no, it was Jemma who answered. She was wearing sloppy clothes, and was flushed from exertion. There were cardboard boxes stacked all along the hall. She smiled when she saw him, and brushed an errant lock of fringe behind her ear.

'Bloody hell. What do *you* want?' And before he could answer, she went on, 'You know, I was just thinking about you. You could have called, couldn't you? I mean, I know I was way out of order, but it was an honest mistake. Not that anybody seems to believe me. I thought we were friends. And didn't you promise you'd keep in touch, about the project and all that? Honestly. Men. You're a law unto yourselves, you lot.'

'To answer your first question: what I want more than anything right now is for you to shut up for two seconds.'

Jemma shook her head, and looked quite cross. 'I won't be shut up, Jeremy. If you don't know that about me—'

'You're right. I don't want you to shut up. I *never* want you to shut up. How about, though, you hit the pause button for just a couple of seconds?'

'What f—?'

Jeremy cupped her lovely face gently in his hands and kissed her. That was more like it. Now *this* was a proper 'first kiss' kiss.

FIFTY-SEVEN

From *Private Eye*, Week Ending March 24th:

CELEBWATCH
TV CHEF IN WELL FARM RAMPAGE

Celebrity Chef Grenville Roberts was once again on the warpath this week. Allegedly. The object of his latest tantrum: the Government's widely publicised new Well Farm initiative in Norfolk. Apparently disgruntled with certain aspects of the regime there, Roberts, it is claimed, went postal in the cafeteria, wrenching furniture from its moorings and hurling a circular table through the huge panoramic window like a giant frisbee, before dousing several staff members with lukewarm porridge. Inside sources claim he then stole a staff member's tractor and carved several obscenities into the lawn with it, including, we are told, some very specific instructions on how the Prime Minister might spice up his sex life all on his own. He was then purportedly chased by the in-house security team, but they were unable to prevent him from reaching the institute's sports stadium and doing some similar damage to the pitch. The security team, without powers of arrest, and fearful both of personal injury and lawsuits, could only look on helpless as he etched a single, gigantic expletive from one goalpost to the other.

He was finally brought under control when the local constabulary arrived, and he spent the night in custody. Or should that be custardy? Under the terms of a legal deal between the Well Farm's lawyers and Mr Roberts' agent, prosecution will not be pursued, and Mr Roberts has agreed to refrain from public comment. The official statement from the Well Farm spokesman said: 'Mr Roberts felt he had genuine grievances, and whilst we disagree with his response to those grievances, there is no bad blood between the parties. The Well Farm initiative is set to be a rip-roaring success, but of course, these are early days, and in any enterprise of this magnitude, there are bound to be one or two annoying teething problems. We wish Mr Roberts well, and hope to have him back as our guest in the very near future, once all our little glitches have been ironed out.'

And the corpulent cook's punishment for spitting out the dummy in this petulant display of berserker rage? Humiliation? Ignominy? Banishment from our screens? Incredibly, quite the opposite. The very next day, Roberts' agent, Seth Meriden, announced plans for an upcoming BBC TV series entitled *Roberts' Rampages*, in which the furious foody will visit various catering establishments and 'sort them out' in his own inimitable style. A spokesman for the BBC commented: 'We like our chefs to have fire in their bellies. Grenville is certainly fiery. He is also a magnificent chef. We believe this show will put him firmly where he belongs: right at the top of the celebrity chef food chain.'

Heavens. I feel a tantrum coming on. Somebody pass me a wok.

FIFTY-EIGHT

Mum was helping Hayleigh redecorate her wall.

Jason's pictures were, most assuredly, coming down.

The decision had caused a certain amount of confusion in some quarters, but Hayleigh's mind had been made up, and there had been no point in discussing the matter further. The pictures were coming down, the advance order with Amazon for the upcoming Big Boys Cry album had been cancelled, and white surgical tape had been painstakingly wound around the cast on her leg to obliterate every last trace of purple from it.

'This is a nice one.' Mum held up a cheeky poster of Jesse McCartney.

Hayleigh smiled and nodded. 'Okay, that is, like, *moderately* cute,' she said, grudgingly. She wasn't a big fan, unlike Jade Kolinsky, who would happily have thrown herself under a racehorse just to get noticed by him. 'Over there, d'you reckon?' She nodded vaguely at the wall near the couch.

'Here?' Mum held it in place.

Hayleigh shrugged. 'Fine.' She wasn't too precious any more about who took what place in the poster rankings. She had made a permanent unbreakable sacred vow to herself never to give her whole heart to a single crush ever again. At least, not one she'd never actually met.

The meeting with Jason Black – he was no longer 'Jase', in her mind, anyway – had been a total, humiliating disaster. Well, he was gone in body, but his memory certainly lingered. Mum had scrubbed down the sofa several times, with increasingly powerful cleaning agents, but it was beginning to look like the damned thing would have to be thrown out, ideally in a nuclear waste dump, deep underground and, preferably, not on this planet. Not on a nearby planet, either. Pluto would just about do the trick. She'd brought plug-in air fresheners, lit fragrant candles and burned enough joss sticks to cause an addiction in the passive breather, but still the pungency loitered.

And here's the funny thing: neither of them had actually mentioned the smell, not out loud, anyway – Mum because she was probably afraid of upsetting Hayleigh, and Hayleigh because she felt vaguely responsible – but they did share funny looks and wrinkled noses, and once in a while, they had actually both burst out laughing with the horror of it all. She wasn't all that bad, the old cow detective, so long as she wasn't on your case.

'Oh, look at this, Hay.' Mum held up a picture from a Sunday supplement magazine. 'It's a picture of Jeremy.' She passed it over to Hayleigh.

Jeremy? Who was Jeremy? Hayleigh looked at the picture, and, yes, it was old Lush Mush himself, standing next to a bunch of politicians. He wasn't dead centre of the picture, because the photographer had been more interested in snapping the Prime Minister, the fool, but it was a pretty good photo. His hair looked nice, and he was wearing *the* most gorge smile. 'It's a bit small,' Hayleigh said.

'Well, we can get it blown up. Dad can scan it and blow it up in Photoshop. We'll give it to him when he visits tonight.'

'Can he get rid of the Prime Minister?'

'I'm sure he can. Only in the picture, though, unfortunately.'

Hayleigh looked at the wall. Currently occupying pride of place was a super duper poster of Old Faithful, Chad Michael Murray, stripped to the waist with his jeans well bopped, showing off his fab abs. She reached round and took a chicken nugget from her plate and chewed on it absently while she contemplated this weighty dilemma. Much better to have a piccie of someone she'd actually *met*, wouldn't you say, in pride of place? Someone who'd actually shown her some kindness. No. Apologies to Chad, the old darling, and all that, but he would have to step aside. She lifted him carefully off the wall and replaced the poster a foot to the right, then stuck the Jeremy picture slap in the middle of the wall, where it rightly belonged, but only as a marker, until he could be enlarged: it would have been disrespectful to have him dwarfed by the likes of Jesse McCartney et al.

She wheeled back and squinted, trying to imagine the effect. Mum made a funny sound. Hayleigh looked over at her, but she was facing away, towards the window. Spring was definitely in the air now. There was a shock of early-bird daffodils beginning their valiant assault on hoary old winter in the beds that lined the hospital path. In a couple of weeks, the trees would be sprouting cherry blossoms, which Hayleigh loved. They're only around for a week or two, and then the blossoms blow off and carpet the pavements with their beautiful pink petals. It was a magical time, really. Not like you were walking into school at all; more like you were walking into Camelot on Guinevere's wedding day. If you strained really hard, you could almost hear the trumpet fanfares. Maybe she would be back home by then. Maybe. She noticed Mum's shoulders were shaking. Was she crying?

'Are you all right, Mum?'

'I'm fine, baby,' she said, but her voice was cracking. 'I'm just being silly.' And a little sob escaped.

Poor thing. She was probably menopausal or something. She burst into tears at the drop of a hat these days. Best to let her get on with it and not make a fuss, in Hayleigh's experience. She looked back at the wall display. Yes, if you caught it unawares like that, you could definitely tell what the finished article would look like. Not bad. Not bad at all.

She reached around absently to pluck another nugget from her plate, and – look at that! Would you believe it? They were all gone.

ACKNOWLEGEMENTS

Without Jonny Geller, this book would never have happened. Whether that makes him loveable or loathsome is up to you. Simon Spanton, my unfeasibly skinny editor, also made invaluable contributions, *and* he bought me beer, and for that I can almost forgive his body mass index. I'm also indebted to my good pal, Charlie Moggach, for his dodgy insights into arrest procedure and his bloody annoying inspirational text messages.

This is, of course, a work of fiction. If you're interested in exploring further some of the issues raised, I recommend the following books:

The Cholesterol Myths by Uffe Ravnskov, New Trends Publishing, 2000.

The Epidemiologists by John Brignell, Brignell Associates, 2004.

The Obesity Myth by Paul Campos, Gotham Books, 2004.

The Obesity Epidemic by Jan Wright and Michael Gard, Routledge, 2005.

Panic Nation by Stanley Feldman and Vincent Marks, John Blake, 2005.

The Rise and Fall of Modern Medicine by James Le Fanu, Abacus, 2004.